TITLES BY PENELOPE DOUGLAS

The Fall Away Series

BULLY

UNTIL YOU

RIVAL

FALLING AWAY

THE NEXT FLAME
(includes novellas *Aflame* and *Next to Never*)

Stand-Alones

MISCONDUCT

BIRTHDAY GIRL

PUNK 57

CREDENCE

TRYST SIX VENOM

The Devil's Night Series

CORRUPT

HIDEAWAY

KILL SWITCH

CONCLAVE
(novella)

NIGHTFALL

FIRE NIGHT
(novella)

HIDEAWAY

DEVIL'S NIGHT 2

PENELOPE DOUGLAS

BERKLEY ROMANCE

New York

BERKLEY ROMANCE
Published by Berkley
An imprint of Penguin Random House LLC
penguinrandomhouse.com

Library of Congress Cataloging-in-Publication Data

Names: Douglas, Penelope, 1977– author.
Title: Hideaway / Penelope Douglas.
Description: First Berkley Romance Edition. |
New York: Berkley Romance, 2024. | Series: Devil's Night ; 2
Identifiers: LCCN 2023022546 | ISBN 9780593642016 (trade paperback)
Subjects: LCGFT: Novels.
Classification: LCC PS3604.O93236 H54 2024 | DDC 813/.6—dc23/eng/20230515
LC record available at https://lccn.loc.gov/2023022546

Hideaway was originally self-published, in different form, in 2017.

First Berkley Romance Edition: January 2024

Printed in the United States of America
3rd Printing

Book design by George Towne

For Z. King

A man cannot destroy the savage in him by denying its impulses.
The only way to get rid of a temptation is to yield to it.

—*Dr. Jekyll and Mr. Hyde*

DEAR READER,

While the romance in *Hideaway* is a stand-alone, the plot is a continuation of events that began in *Corrupt* (Devil's Night 1). It is strongly recommended that you read *Corrupt* prior to reading this novel. This book deals with emotionally difficult topics, including animal cruelty, dubious consent, reference to rape, pedophilia, homophobia, self-harm, incest, grooming, physical and emotional abuse, child abuse, and misogynistic behavior. Anyone who believes such content may upset them is encouraged to consider their well-being when choosing whether to continue reading.

PLAYLIST

"Black Honey" by Thrice

"Castle" by Halsey

"Control" by Puddle of Mudd

"Cry Little Sister" by Seasons After

"Emotionless" by Red Sun Rising

"Go to Hell" by KMFDM

"Heavy in Your Arms" by Florence + the Machine

"Jekyll and Hyde" by Five Finger Death Punch

"Like a Nightmare" by Never Say Die

"Lung (Bronchitis Mix)" by Sister Machine Gun

"Paint It, Black" by Ciara

"Remember We Die" by Gemini Syndrome

"Save Yourself" by Stabbing Westward

"Scumgrief (Deep Dub Trauma Mix)" by Fear Factory

"Smells Like Teen Spirit" by Think Up Anger

"Smokin' in the Boys Room" by Mötley Crüe

"Waiting Game" by Banks

HIDEAWAY

CHAPTER 1

KAI

Rain was like night. You could be different in the dark and under the clouds.

I'm not sure what it was. Maybe the lack of sunlight and how our other senses heightened or the subtle shroud hiding things from our sight, but only certain times were acceptable to do certain things. Shrug off your jacket and roll up your sleeves. Pour a drink and lean back. Laugh with your friends and scream at the basketball game on TV.

Follow a girl you've been eye-fucking for an hour into the pub bathroom and have your friends nod in approval when you come back out.

Try doing that during the day with the intern at the office.

Not that I'd want the freedom to indulge in anything at any time anyway. Things were more special when they were rare.

But every morning, when the sun rose, the coils in my stomach wound tighter in anticipation.

Nightfall was coming again.

Letting my mask dangle from my hand at my side, I stood at the top of the second-floor landing and watched Rika sitting in her car. She kept her head down, her face visible by the glow of her cell phone, despite the downpour of rain hitting her windshield as she typed.

I shook my head, my jaw flexing. *She doesn't listen.*

I watched as my best friend's fiancée finished up, the light from her phone disappearing, and then she opened the car door, stepped out, and broke into a jog, dashing through the pounding rain. I darted my eyes, taking inventory of her. *Head and eyes cast downward. Keys wrapped in her closed fist. Arms shielding her head from the rain and hindering her line of sight.*

Completely unaware of her surroundings. The perfect victim.

Grabbing the harness at the back of my mask, I stretched it out and slid the silver skull down over my head, the inside hugging every curve of my face for a tight fit. The world around me shrank to a tunnel, and all I could see was what was right in front of me.

Heat spread down my neck, seeping deep into my chest, and I drew in a long, cool breath, feeling my heart pounding, getting hungry.

All of a sudden, the rain, like a waterfall in the alley outside, filled the dojo, and the heavy metal door downstairs slammed shut.

"Hello?" she called out.

My heart dipped into my stomach, and I closed my eyes, savoring the feel. The sound of her voice echoed through the empty building, but I stayed planted on the dark landing, waiting for her to find me.

"Kai?" I heard her shout through the large space.

I reached back and pulled the hood of my black sweatshirt up, covering my head, and turned to look down over the railing.

"Hello?" she asked again, more urgent. "Kai, are you here?"

I saw her blond hair first. It's what you always noticed about Rika first. In her black penthouse, in this black dojo, in the black alley outside, in dark rooms and on black streets . . . she always stood out.

I rested my hands on the rusted steel railing, keeping my feet planted on the grates, and watched her step slowly into the main room below, flipping up the switches on the wall. But nothing happened. The lights didn't go on.

She jerked her head left and right, looking suddenly alert, and then darted out her hand, flipping them off and then on again.

Nothing.

Her chest moved up and down quicker, her awareness peaking as she clutched the strap of her bag tighter.

I fought not to smile and cocked my head, watching her. I should show myself. I should play fair, let her know I was here and that she was safe.

But the longer I waited, and the longer I stayed quiet and hidden, the more nervous she appeared. And as she walked farther into the room below, I couldn't help but want to feel this moment. She was confused. Scared. Timid. She didn't know I was here. Right above her. She didn't know that my eyes were on her right now. She didn't know that I could run at her, get her in a hold, and have her on the floor before she even knew what had happened.

I didn't want to scare her, but I did. Power and control were addictive. And I didn't want to like it, because it made me sick.

It made me Damon.

I started breathing harder and tightened my fists around the railing, growing scared myself. This wasn't normal.

"I know you're here," she said, looking around with her eyebrows pinched together.

But the stubborn set to her eyes was forced, and I lifted the corner of my mouth in a smile behind my mask.

Her long gray T-shirt fell off her shoulder, and rain glistened across her chest and neck. The downpour pummeled Meridian City outside, and at this time of night—and in this neighborhood—the streets were empty. No one would hear her. Probably no one even saw her enter the building.

And by the way she began backing slowly out of the dark room, it looked like she was just beginning to realize that.

I took a step.

The grate flooring creaked, and she snapped her head left, following the sound.

Her eyes locked on me. Keeping my gaze on her, I walked toward the stairs.

"Kai?" she asked.

Why isn't he answering me? she probably wondered. *Why is he wearing his mask? Why are the lights out? Because of the storm? What's going on?*

But I said nothing as I walked slowly toward her, her pretty, small form getting more defined the closer I got. Wet strands of hair I didn't notice before stuck to her chest, and the diamond studs Michael gave her last Christmas sparkled on her ears. The points of her breasts poked through her shirt.

Her blue eyes looked at me warily. "I know that's you."

I smirked behind my mask, her rigid body belying her confident words. *Do you?*

I circled her slowly, caging her in, while she remained stubbornly still. *Are you so sure it's me? I might not be Kai, right? I could've just taken his mask. Or bought one just like it.*

Stopping behind her, I tried to keep my breathing calm despite the way my heart was pounding. I could feel her. The energy between my chest and her back.

She should've turned around. She should've been preparing herself for danger like I taught her. Did she think this was a game?

"Knock it off," she barked, turning her head just enough so I could see her lips move. "This isn't funny."

No, it wasn't funny. Michael was gone—out of town for the night—and Will was probably out getting drunk somewhere. It was just us.

And with the way my goddamn stomach was flipping right

now, it wasn't funny or good or right how much I needed to constantly push myself over the edge to feel in control anymore. It wasn't good how much I didn't want to stop.

I grabbed her, wrapping my arms around her and burying my nose under her ear. Her perfume made my eyelids heavy, and I heard her gasp as I tightened my hold, keeping her body against mine. "It's just us, Little Monster," I growled. "Just how I want it to be, and we have all night."

"Kai!" she shouted, tugging against my arms.

"Who's Kai?"

She twisted, fighting my hold and struggling. "I know you by now. Your height, your form, your smell . . ."

"Do you?" I asked. "You know how I feel, huh?"

I buried my masked face in her neck and tightened my arms around her. Possessive. Threatening. I breathed out in a whisper, "I miss you as a little high school girl, Rika." I moaned, acting like I loved the feel of her squirming against me. "You didn't give any lip."

She stopped, every part of her body freezing except her breathing. Her chest caved and then began to shake under my arms.

I'd gotten to her.

Someone close to us said those words once, someone who scared her, and now she was doubting whether or not I just might not be him. *Damon had disappeared last year, and he could be anywhere, right, Rika?*

"I've waited a long time for this," I said, hearing the thunder crack outside. "Get this shit off." I yanked down her shirt, exposing her in her tank top, and she let out a scream. "I wanna fuckin' see you."

She gasped, pulling away and throwing her arms at me. She immediately stepped back—the first countermove I showed her when someone grabs her from behind—but I pushed off my back foot, knowing what she was going to do.

Come on, Rika!

And then, all of a sudden, she dropped, the full weight of her body slipping through my arms straight to the floor.

I nearly laughed. She was thinking quickly. *Good.*

But I kept up my assault. She scrambled to her hands and knees, getting ready to scurry away, and I lunged out, grabbing her by the ankle.

"Where do you think you're going?" I taunted.

She flipped over and kicked my mask, and I reared back, laughing. "Oh, God, you're going to be fun. I can't fucking wait."

A whimper escaped her as she crawled backward and pushed herself to her feet again. She twisted around, fear etched across her face, and broke into a run toward the locker rooms. Probably going to the exit at the rear of the building.

I raced after her, grabbing hold of her shirt, my whole body on fire.

Fuck. I felt a trickle of sweat glide down the back of my neck.

It's just a game. I won't hurt her. It was like tag or hide-and-seek as a kid. We knew nothing bad would happen when we got caught and we'd bring no harm when we chased, but the irrational fear excited us anyway. That was what I liked. That's all it was. This wasn't real.

Twisting her around, I wrapped one arm around her and lifted her knee up with my other hand, picking her up off the ground. She threw up the other knee, but I twisted my hips before her jab landed between my legs. Flipping her back, I threw both of us to the ground, coming down on top of her.

"No!" she cried. Her body thrashed under me, and I forced myself between her legs, bringing her wrists up over her head and pinning them there.

She fought against my hold, but the steel in her arms began to shake, and her strength started to weaken.

I stilled and stared down. Damon and I both had dark hair and eyes, although his were almost black. She wouldn't be able to tell the difference under the shroud of darkness around us. But she could feel me. Handling her, forcing her, threatening her . . . just like him.

I slowly dropped my head to her breast, hovering an inch above her skin, and she'd stopped fighting. Her chest heaved so hard it sounded like she was having an asthma attack.

Looking up at her, seeing her body mold easily to mine and her hands bound helplessly above her, I saw her tear up. She knew this was it. No one to stop me, no one to hear her scream, a madman in a mask who could hurt her, kill her, and take all night doing it.

Her face suddenly cracked, and she broke, crying out as her fight was swallowed in the horror of what was happening to her.

Goddammit. I yanked back my hood and threw off my mask, furious. "You're a fucking baby!" I bellowed, slamming my hand down on the floor at the side of her head. "Get me off you!" I got in her face. "Now! Come on!"

She growled, her face turning red, and she launched up and wrapped her arm over the back of my neck. Squeezing me into a headlock, she reached her other hand under her arm and dug her finger and thumb into my eyes.

It wasn't much, but it got me to loosen my hold long enough for her to slam me in the side of the face, and when I reared back, she scrambled upright and grabbed her bag, swinging it at my head.

"Ugh!" I grunted, yanking it out of her hands.

But quickly, she scurried to her feet and ran to the wall, grabbing one of the kendo swords and assuming her stance, bamboo *shinai* raised and ready.

I sat back on my heels and pulled my hand away from my face, checking for blood. Nothing. I let out a sigh and raised my eyes to her, my body growing cold as the fear left her eyes and was replaced with anger.

The adrenaline still coursed through my limbs, and I took a deep breath, all of a sudden my body ten times heavier as I pulled myself to my feet.

"I don't like being ambushed like that!" she gritted out. "This is supposed to be a safe space."

I blinked, fixing her with a scolding look. "Nowhere is safe."

I walked toward the stairs, pulling off my sweatshirt as I climbed. "You're not alert." I picked up the water bottle I'd left by the window earlier. "I watch you. Your face was in your phone out on the street. And you could barely budge me. You waste too much time panicking."

I gulped down the water, so thirsty from more than just the exertion. Too much thinking and worrying and plotting. I'd needed this.

I missed all those nights, years ago, when I had a release. When I had friends to get lost with.

Her footsteps fell on the stairs, and I stared out the window, the bright lights of Meridian City on the other side of the river glowing bright, a sharp contrast to the darkness of this side.

"I've absorbed everything you've taught me," she said. "I trusted you, and I wasn't taking it seriously. In the moment, if it ever happens again, I'll handle it."

"You should've handled it this time. What if it wasn't me? What would've happened to you?"

I glanced down at her, seeing her pained eyes staring off out the window, and regret curled its way through my stomach. I hated seeing that look. Rika had been through enough, and I'd just shaken her again.

"I think you liked that," she replied quietly, still staring out the window. "I think you enjoyed that."

My heart skipped a beat, and I turned away from her, following her gaze out the window.

"If I did, I wouldn't have stopped."

She looked up at me, and I heard a car passing by below, its tires sloshing through the rain.

"You know, I watch you, too," she told me. "You're quiet, no one gets to see where you eat or sleep . . ."

I twisted the cap to the water bottle, the plastic container crackling in my fist. I knew what she was talking about. I knew I was distant.

But I had to keep everything inside or risk the wrong things slipping out. It was better this way.

And it was worse lately. Everything was fucked. She and Michael were so consumed with each other, and Will was sober only a few hours a day anymore. I'd been on my own more than ever.

"You're like a machine." She drew in a long breath. "Not like Damon. You're unreadable." She paused. "Except just now. Except when you're wearing your mask. You liked it, didn't you? It's the only time I see you feel anything."

I turned my head, softening my eyes. "You're not with me all the time," I joked.

I held her eyes for a moment, both of us knowing exactly what I was talking about. She didn't see me with women, and a slight blush crossed her cheeks. She gave me a half smile, abandoning her line of questioning.

I cleared my throat, moving on. "You need to work on your counterattacks," I told her. "And your speed. If you stop, you give the attacker a chance to get a good hold on you."

"I knew I was safe with you."

"You aren't," I replied sternly. "Always assume danger. If anyone other than Michael grabs you, they get what they deserve anyway."

She crossed her arms over her chest, and I could feel her aggravation. I understood it. She didn't want to live her life always on guard. But she was barely taking basic safety precautions, and there was no limit to how sorry she was going to be taking the wrong chances. Michael wasn't always around.

But when he was, at least he was with her. It had been weeks since I'd really talked to him.

"How is he?" I asked her.

She rolled her eyes, and I could tell the mood was shifting to something lighter. "He wants to fly off to Rio or somewhere to get married."

"I thought you both decided to wait until after you were done with college."

She nodded, sighing. "Yeah, I thought so, too."

I narrowed my eyes on her. So, what was going on then?

Michael and Rika's parents expected a wedding in Thunder Bay, and as far as I knew, the couple was fine with that. In fact, Michael had been very adamant about making a big deal out of it. He wanted to see her in a dress, walking down the aisle toward him. He grew up thinking she would marry his brother, after all. He intended to show everyone she was his.

And then it hit me.

Damon.

"He's afraid a fanfare wedding will entice Damon to return," I guessed.

Rika nodded again solemnly, still staring out the window. "He thinks if we get married nothing bad will happen to me. The sooner, the better."

"He's right," I told her. "A wedding—hundreds of people and Will and me at his side—Damon's ego couldn't take it. He wouldn't stay away."

"No one's seen or heard from him in a year."

I flexed my jaw, anticipation curling its way through my gut. "Yeah, that's what scares me."

A year ago, Damon wanted Rika to suffer unimaginably. We all did, actually, but Damon went a little further, and when we didn't stick by him, we all became his enemies. He attacked us, hurt her, and helped Michael's brother, Trevor, try to kill her. Michael was smart to assume that Damon's anger probably hadn't dissipated. If we knew where he was, that would be one thing, but the detectives we hired to find him and keep tabs on his whereabouts hadn't been able to locate him.

Which explained why Michael wanted to take measures to keep Rika out of the limelight, where such a grand wedding in our affluent, seaside hometown would put her.

"You don't care about a large wedding," I reminded her. "You just want Michael. Why not go off and just do it like he wants?"

She was silent for a few moments and then spoke quietly, her eyes in a far-off place. "No." She shook her head. "Just behind St. Killian's, where the forest ends and the cliffs give way to the sea. Under the midnight sky . . ." She nodded, a beautiful, wistful smile touching her lips. "That's where I'll marry Michael."

I studied her, wondering about that far-off, dreamy look in her eyes. As if she'd always known she would marry Michael Crist and had been seeing it in her head all her life.

"What is that building?" Rika asked, jerking her chin, gesturing out the window.

I followed her gaze, but I didn't have to look to know which building she spoke of. I'd chosen this location for our dojo for a reason.

Gazing out of the glass, I stared at the building on the other side of the street, about thirty stories higher than ours, the gray stone darkened by the rain and the broken streetlights.

"The Pope," I answered. "It was quite a hotel back in its day. Still is, actually."

The Pope had been abandoned for several years and had been built when there was talk of a football stadium being constructed over here as a way to bring more tourism to Meridian City. And a way to revitalize Whitehall, the run-down urban district in which we now stood.

Unfortunately, the stadium never happened, and The Pope went under after struggling to stay in business.

I scanned the darkened windows, the shadows of drapes just barely visible inside a hundred rooms that now sat quiet and empty. It was hard to think of such a large place not having an ounce of life in it anymore. Impossible, in fact. My leery eyes watched each dark void, my sight taking me only a few inches into the room before darkness consumed the rest.

"It feels like someone's watching us."

"I know," I agreed, surveying each window, one after another.

I saw her shiver out of the corner of my eye and picked up my sweatshirt, handing it to her.

She took it, giving me a smile as she turned to go back down the stairs. "It's getting cold. I can't believe October is here already. Devil's Night will be here soon," she singsonged, sounding excited.

I nodded, following her.

But as I cast one more glance behind me, chills spread down my body thinking about the hundred haunting, vacant rooms at the abandoned hotel across the street.

And a Devil's Night, so long ago, when a boy who used to be me hunted a girl who might be like Rika in a place that just might be that very same dark hotel out the window right now.

But unlike tonight, he didn't stop.

He did something he shouldn't have done.

I walked down the stairs, inches behind Rika and matching her steps in perfect time as I gazed at the back of her hair.

She didn't realize just how close danger was to her.

CHAPTER 2

KAI

Six Years Ago

Devil's Night. This was it.

Our last one.

We were graduating next May, and once the four of us went off to college, we wouldn't be home unless it was for winter or summer breaks. And by then, we'd be too old for this. We wouldn't have the excuse of youth to explain why we chose to celebrate the night before Halloween, indulging in pranks and other childish shenanigans, for no other reason than to raise a little hell. We'd be men. It wouldn't fly, right?

So, tonight would be it. The finale.

I slammed my car door shut and walked through the parking lot, past Damon's BMW and toward the rear entrance of the cathedral. Opening the door, I walked into the lounge area, consisting of some tables, a kitchen, a few couches, and a coffee table littered with pamphlets on how to pray the rosary and *Fasting in a Healthy Way*.

I inhaled a deep breath, the ever-present odor of incense filling the quiet halls. I was Catholic by birth, as was my friend Damon, but in practice, we were Catholic in the same way Taco Bell was a Mexican restaurant. I played along for my mother, while Damon played along for amusement.

I headed down the hallway to the actual church, but a loud thud pierced the silence, and I stopped short, looking around for where it came from. It sounded like a book dropping onto a desktop.

It was a Friday morning. Not many people would be here, although there were probably a few stragglers kneeling in the pews and praying their penance, since confession had just ended.

"What did we discuss yesterday?" I heard Father Beir's burly voice from somewhere off to my left.

"I don't remember, Father."

I smiled to myself. *Damon.*

Taking a left, I stepped quietly down another marble hallway, dragging my fingertips over the shiny mahogany paneling on the walls and trying to withhold my laughter.

Stopping just before the open door to the priest's office, I hung back and listened. Damon's smooth, calm tone answered Beir as if following a script.

"You're unrepentant and irresponsible."

"Yes, Father."

My chest shook. Damon's words were always in complete contradiction to how they sounded coming out of his mouth. *Yes, Father,* as if in complete agreement that he'd misbehaved, while at the same time *Yes, Father, aren't you proud of me?*

Most of us reconciled in the confessionals out in the nave, but Damon—after many years of failed "redirection" on the part of his father and his priest—was forced to be schooled face-to-face for weekly counseling sessions.

He fucking enjoyed it. He took pleasure in being anyone's devil.

Twisting my head around, I peeked into the room, seeing the priest walk around the desk while Damon knelt on a single pew, Beir's big, black Bible on the stand in front of him.

"Do you want to be judged?" the father asked.

"We will all be judged."

"That's not what I taught you."

Damon's head was bowed enough for his black hair to hang just over his eyes, but I could see the hint of a smile that Beir probably couldn't. He wore our school uniform, khakis with his typical wrinkled white Oxford, cuffs unbuttoned, and a loose blue-and-green necktie hanging around his neck. We were on our way to school, but he looked like he'd been in his clothes all night.

He suddenly turned his head toward me, and I watched as he jutted out his tongue, moving it from side to side suggestively and grinning like an asshole.

I broke into silent laughter, smiling at him and shaking my head.

Douche.

Turning away, I walked back down the hallway, toward the church, and left Damon to finish his "lesson."

There were many things I loved about this place, but being lectured like that wasn't one of them. The masses bored me, the Sunday school was monotonous, many of the priests distant and cold, and so many of the parishioners vile to each other Monday thru Saturday who suddenly changed their tune between ten and eleven o'clock on Sunday mornings. It was all such a lie.

But I liked the church. It was quiet. And you could be quiet here without the expectation of forced interactions.

Heading down the aisle, toward the back, I scanned the four confessionals, making sure no lights were on that signaled a priest inside. Since they were all empty, I walked down to the far right, choosing the last one, partially hidden behind a column and the one closest to the stained-glass windows.

I pulled back the curtain and stepped inside the small, dark cubicle, pulling the curtain closed again. The scent of old wood surrounded me, but there was something else I faintly noticed. A hint of being outside. In the wind and water.

Sitting in the hardwood chair, I looked ahead at the darkened wicker screen in front of me, knowing the other side was empty. The priests had all moved on to their other daily duties. Exactly how I liked it. I always did this alone.

I leaned down, my elbows on my knees, and clasped my hands together. The muscles on my arms burned with an involuntary flex.

"Bless me, Father, for I have sinned," I said in a quiet voice. "It's been a month since my last confession."

I swallowed hard, always more aware that when a priest *wasn't* listening to me, I was. And believe it or not, that was sometimes harder. No one to offer me absolution but myself.

"I know you're not there," I told the empty air on the other side. "I know I've been doing this too long to keep making excuses, but . . ." I paused, searching for words. "But sometimes I can only talk when no one is listening."

I drew in a deep breath, my shell falling away.

"I just need to say things out loud, I guess." Even if I didn't get the cheap penance that did nothing to absorb the guilt.

I breathed in the smell of water and wind, not knowing where it was coming from, but it made me feel like I was in a cave. Safe from eyes and ears.

"I don't need you. I just need this place," I admitted. "What's wrong with me, that I like to hide? That I like my secrets?"

Damon, I couldn't imagine, had any secrets. He didn't brag about his dirty deeds, but he never hid them, either. Will, the other member of our pack, didn't do anything without backup, so someone was always aware of what he was up to.

And Michael—our team captain, and the one I was closest to—hid only from those around him what he hid from himself.

But me . . . I knew who I was. And I made a concerted effort never to let anyone see it.

"I like that I lie to my parents," I nearly whispered. "I like that they don't know what I did last night or last week or what I'm going to do tonight. I like that no one knows how I like being alone. How I like fighting, and I like the private rooms in the clubs . . ." I trailed off, lost in thought, remembering the past month since my last confession and all the nights I'd lost myself.

"I like that my friends are bad for me," I said, continuing. "And I like to watch."

I wrapped one fist inside another, forcing the words out.

"I like to watch people. Something new I just discovered about myself." I ran my hand through my hair, feeling the ends rough with gel. "Wanting to be in it, to feel what they're feeling, is almost hotter than actually being a part of it." I looked up at the dark screen, seeing just a sliver of it left open. "And I like hiding it. I don't want my friends to know me as well as they think they do. I don't know why." I shook my head, thinking. "There are just some things that are more exciting when they're a secret."

Dropping my eyes, I sighed. "But as much as I get off on not being seen, it's lonely, too. There's no connection."

Which wasn't entirely true if you saw it from the outside. Michael, Will, Damon . . . we were all cut from the same cloth in a way. We all loved the wild ride and craved the high that only came from doing anything we weren't supposed to do.

But me? I liked my privacy. More than they did.

And I liked it sordid. As much as they did.

I pushed the shame away, coming back. "So, anyway, I lie. All the time. Too many times to count." *To everyone.* "I also resent my father most of the time. I've taken the Lord's name in vain about five hundred times the past month, and I've had premarital sex to break up the monotony of every waking minute consumed with impure thoughts." I shook my head, laughing at myself. "Penance won't make me stop, and I have no intention of changing, so . . ."

So that was why confessing to a priest did me no good. Again, I liked doing everything I did wrong.

But it felt good to admit it. At least I confessed, right? At least I knew I was doing things I shouldn't, and that was something.

Closing my eyes, I leaned back against the wall and breathed in the silence.

Fuck me, I couldn't wait for tonight. Thinking about the catacombs or the cemetery or wherever we ended up filled me with need. My mask, the fear, the chase . . . I swallowed the lump in my throat, feeling my body heat rise.

The lull of the fountain at the back of the church dribbled softly, and I heard the echo of a cough in the distance. I didn't know what I'd be doing first, breaking something, screwing someone, or fighting, but I wanted whatever it was now, and it wasn't even dark yet. Tonight was the highlight of my year.

"There's a story . . ." a voice suddenly said, jolting me.

I popped my eyes open, and my heart dropped into my fucking stomach. *What the . . . ?*

"What the hell?" I burst out, sitting up. "Who is that?"

The voice—a woman's—came from somewhere close.

Like the other side of the fucking confessional.

I leapt up from my chair, the legs screeching against the marble floor.

"No, please, don't," she begged, probably knowing I was about to rip open the door to the priest's chamber on the other side. "I didn't mean to listen, but I was already here, and you started talking. I won't say anything."

She sounded young, maybe my age, and nervous. I stared down at the screen, her voice inches away.

"You've been in there this whole time?" I growled, my head a flurry of all the shit I'd just said. "What the hell? Who are you?"

I whipped open my curtain, but then I heard the shutter on her side of the screen slide open all the way, and her plea, "Please," she whispered. "I want to talk to you, and I can't if you see me. Just give me a minute. Just one minute."

I stopped, locking my jaws together. What the hell was she doing over there? Did she know who I was?

"You can see me," she said. "Just give me a minute."

Something about her voice was fragile. Like she was a vase teetering on the edge of a coffee table. I stood frozen for a minute, debating whether or not to let my curiosity pull her ass out of that room or indulge her.

Okay. Just a minute, then.

"There's a story," she started again when I didn't move farther, "about The Pope Hotel in Meridian City. Do you know the place?"

I eyed the screen, barely seeing her outline in the dark.

The Pope? That multimillion-dollar waste on the shitty side of the river?

I closed the curtain, taking my seat again. "Who are you?"

"There's a rumor about the twelfth floor," she went on, ignoring my question. "It exists, but no one can get to it. Have you heard that story?"

I leaned back just slightly, my body still rigid and on guard. "No."

"Rumor has it that the family that owns The Pope built a twelfth floor in every hotel they constructed. For the family's personal use," she told me. "The entire floor is their residence when they're in a particular city with one of their hotels. It's inaccessible to guests, though. The elevator doesn't stop on that floor, and when it was investigated, there's not even a possibility for the elevator to stop there. The floor is walled in." Her voice evened out, and I noticed a touch of excitement in her words. "And so is the stairwell access."

"So, how does the family get to their secret floor when they want in?"

"Well, that's the question, isn't it?" she asked. "That's the secret.

For the longest time, people assumed it was just some mystery promoted by the owners and staff to increase the allure of the hotel." She paused, and I could hear her draw in a breath. "But then guests started noticing *her*."

"Her?"

"A woman—dancing," she answered.

"Dancing," I repeated, suddenly a little more interested.

A secret floor? A secret entrance? A ghost girl?

I felt like she nodded, but I couldn't be sure. "After midnight, when nearly every guest is tucked into their rooms and the hotel is quiet and dark, they say you can see her"—she nearly whispered, and I could hear the smile in her voice—"dancing by herself—like a ballerina—down in the dark, moonlit ballroom. Dancing to a haunting lullaby."

I watched her lips, concealed mostly in shadow, but I could make out the outline.

"Another story tells of a ballerina dancing on the twelfth-floor balcony, too," she continued. "They could see her from the windows higher up. The light rain, shining as it reflects the city lights, dancing with her as she twirls and leaps in the air. Stories added up over the years, sightings and questions . . . A girl who never checked in and never checks out, hiding by day and dancing by night." And then her voice dropped to a whisper, making the hair on my arms stand up. "Always alone, always hiding."

It couldn't be true, but I kind of wanted to believe it was. It was like a treasure hunt, wasn't it? A girl, concealed from the world, hiding. Right under everyone's nose.

"Why are you telling me this story?"

"Because she's still there," she replied. "Hiding on the secret floor. Alone. At least that's what I like to believe. Secrets and mysteries make life fun, don't they?"

I smiled to myself, leaning forward and resting my elbows on my knees again. "Yeah."

Her fingers came up to the screen, and I finally saw a piece of her. Her slender hand, fingertips, and short nails.

"I like your secrets." She sounded breathless. "And who are you really hurting by keeping them? Right?"

The wind and water surrounded me, and I realized that's where the scent had come from. I'd smelled her as soon as I stepped into the confessional. She was already here.

"Do you listen to other people's confessions often?" I asked, somewhat amused.

"Sometimes."

Her reply was so quick, I couldn't help but admire her. I liked that she felt so at ease being honest, and I kind of hoped it was because of me.

"I lie, too," she offered.

"To whom?"

"To my family," she said. "I lie to them all the time."

"What do you lie to them about?"

"Anything I need to keep them happy. I tell them I'm fine when I'm not. I see my mother, and I'm not supposed to. I lie about my struggle to be loyal."

"Is it important to keep the truth from them?"

"As necessary as their desire to know my every step, yes." Her fingers drifted down the screen, her nails scraping it barely. "They still see me as a child. Incapable."

"You sound like you might be," I mused. "Young, I mean."

A scoff escaped her lips, challenging me. "I was ancient at six. Can you hear the sound of *that*?"

I narrowed my eyes, trying to figure her out. Her voice, everything she said, who she was . . . *Ancient at six.* She'd grown up too soon. That's what she'd meant.

Leaning back again, I watched her dark form shift on the other side of the screen. I wanted to see her, but I didn't want to stop talking, either. Not just yet.

She said she couldn't talk to me if I saw her. Did I know her, then?

"We're only ever good because there are consequences," I told her. "Take those away, and everyone shows their true self. Kind of like taking off a mask."

"Or putting one on," she replied. "After all, there's freedom in hiding, isn't there?"

Yeah, I guess—

"Do you like the feel of a mask?" she chirped, changing the subject.

It was kind of out of the blue, and my heart skipped a beat. "Why would you ask me that?"

She knew who I was, didn't she? She knew it was Devil's Night.

"I like the feel of one," she said. "Like this screen and the darkness. They're kind of like masks, aren't they?"

Kind of.

"I could be anyone." Her fragile voice smoothed over, turning playful. "I could be a girl you grew up with. A classmate. Someone's little sister. The kid you used to babysit when you were sixteen . . ."

The corner of my lips lifted, and I entertained the idea. Although I didn't recognize her voice, that didn't mean I didn't know her. She could be a girl I passed in the halls every day. Someone I never gave a second glance to. Or she could be a buddy's girlfriend or one of the gardener's kids. Who knew?

"And you could be anyone, too," she pondered. "A friend's boyfriend, a teacher I had a crush on, or one of my father's friends. You could say anything to me. I could say anything to you. And there's no embarrassment, because we never have to face each other. Not if we don't want to."

I leaned closer again, trying to breathe in more of her scent.

I wanted to see her. I definitely had to see her.

"I'll keep your secrets," I told her. "No matter who you are."

"You are one of my secrets," she shot back. "I'm trying to steal you, but I wish I didn't want to."

"What does that mean?" *Steal me?*

"So, what do you like to watch?" she asked.

"Huh?" She changed the subject again. She was moving a mile a minute, and I was having a hard time keeping up.

"In your confession, you said you like to watch. Watch what?"

I chewed the corner of my mouth, hesitant. "I think you know," I replied, cagey. "Figure it out, big girl."

She laughed for the first time. It was this perfect, innocent sound, and my hands hummed with the urge to touch her all of a sudden.

"And what if I like to watch, too?" she teased. "Show me with your words."

"I can't." I looked down, embarrassed despite myself.

"Please," she asked again, her voice dropping to a whisper, and I swore I could feel the heat of her breath on my face. "Talk to me. Tell me what you don't tell anyone else."

I shook my head, struggling. The way she talked . . . Sometimes it was like a woman, straddling my lap with her lips inches from mine.

But just now, it was like a little girl, desperate for a treat.

"When was your last confession, little one?" I prodded, inching further into her territory.

"I've never had one."

"Aren't you Catholic?"

"No."

Then why was she here?

But then again, why was she in the priest's chamber, too? "You're a little mystery yourself, aren't you?" I asked, not expecting an answer.

"Come on. What do you like to watch?" she repeated, pushing me.

I opened my mouth but just ended up letting out a sigh.

Jesus. *What do I like to watch?* I can't tell her that. *Fuck.*

I closed my eyes. I needed to leave. What if she knew me? What if I went to school with her? What if she was someone I'd like? She wouldn't want to know this shit.

But as if she knew my fear, she told me, "Don't be afraid. I'm already imagining the worst, and I'm still here, right?"

I shook my head, feeling stupid, but I laughed anyway. "I like . . ." I ran a hand up and down my face. "One of my friends had a girl in the media room this summer," I said, starting over. "It was late, we were all really lit, and the mood was getting heated. He started kissing her and feeling her up, nothing I haven't seen before, but she would look over at me, probably expecting that I would join in, but . . ."

I inhaled a deep breath. I didn't feel like I was safe right now. I didn't feel like I was hiding in this dark, fucking confessional with a screen between me and this girl I may or may not know. I should shut up.

But part of me didn't want to. Every word brought me closer to the edge. Closer to falling. I wanted to fall.

I continued. "Something kept me rooted in my seat this time. I couldn't take my eyes off her, but I couldn't move, either."

The girl on the other side remained quiet, but I knew she was still there.

"I didn't want to move," I confessed. "And she couldn't take her eyes off me, either. She straddled him, fucking him, but her eyes were on me the whole time."

I closed my eyes for a moment, remembering the sight of her grinding on him. But it was all for me. Everything she did was to keep me watching. I controlled her.

"I could see her chest moving faster with her breathing, the sweat on her neck, her nervous eyes . . . She didn't know what I was going to do. She didn't know if I liked what I was seeing or if I was going to pounce at any second. She was scared. And excited."

She had no idea what I was thinking. How I liked what she was doing for me without laying a hand on me. I wasn't communicating with my hands or my mouth, just my eyes all over her body, and it drove her crazy not knowing. God, she loved it.

"He fucked her," I said, "but I was the one who made her come."

I realized my pants felt tighter, and I reached down to adjust myself, grunting under my breath at the ache.

"Sordid, right?" I said. "Disgusting, sleazy, vile . . ."

"Yeah." But I heard a smile in her voice. "So, what did you do about it?"

"What do you mean?"

Her fingertips pressed against the screen again. "You must've been turned on after that. What did you do?"

I held in my nervous laugh. She didn't miss a beat, did she? "You're skinning me alive right now, kid."

A breathy laugh escaped her, and I could nearly make out her lips close to the screen.

"How old are you?" I asked.

"Old enough to have seen and heard worse," she replied. "Don't worry. Now, what did you do after that?"

"I can't . . ." I breathed out. "I didn't . . . I didn't do anything."

But she waited. She knew I was lying.

I licked my dry lips, dropping my voice so low, I didn't know if she could hear me. "I didn't wait for my friends to get up and leave in the car to go get food," I told her. "And I didn't wait for the girl to trail down the hallway to the bathroom or for her to step into the shower. I didn't follow her or turn off the lights, scaring her . . ."

The memory of her gasp rang in my ears, and the world tilted in front of me. The dark bathroom, the swaying shower curtain, the steam I could already smell . . .

"It's okay," Mystery Girl said when I remained quiet.

"I didn't like frightening her or making her scream." I clenched my teeth, dropping my head into my hand. "Or watching her invite me into the shower, where I took hold of her and felt her come apart in my hands . . ."

My fingers slid through my hair, shame burning my face but also a weight lifting off my shoulders. If this kid didn't run, then maybe I wasn't so bad, right?

Right?

"And I didn't love every second inside of her tight body—"

"No, don't," she urged, stopping me. "Don't say any more. Please."

I raised my head, my insides shrinking. "I'm scaring you."

"No."

"Liar."

"Yes," she finally said. "Yes, you scare me. But I like it. I'm just . . ."

"Just what?"

"I'm just . . ." She paused, breathing erratically. "Just jealous."

"Why?"

"Because you hunted her." Her pale forehead leaned into the screen, and I caught a few strands of rich, dark hair. "Maybe I shouldn't let you see me just yet. Maybe I should let you hunt me, too. Sounds like you're good at it."

I leaned back up, a smile tugging my lips. I was no longer embarrassed. Keeping my eyes on her, I pulled my keys out of my pocket and stuck the sharp one to my car into one of the holes of the wicker screen. Before she even had time to rear back, I tugged the key downward, ripped a slit in the screen, and pushed my hand through, catching her shirt in my fist just as she tried to escape. I pulled her forward and leaned in, smelling the wind on her skin and feeling how small and light she was. I barely flexed a muscle, holding her.

"What makes you think I haven't been doing that this whole time?" I teased. "Do you think that little story is as naughty as I can get? Should I tell you about last summer and running into my former babysitter one night who was home from med school? She liked how I'd grown up."

She breathed in hard, shallow breaths, and her hands came up, clasping mine. "Yes."

I narrowed my eyes, releasing her sweatshirt and, instead, raising my hand to her face. At my touch, she shivered, but she didn't back away.

The smooth skin felt like water as I grazed my fingertips over her sharp jaw and up her cheek. I drifted past her delicate ear lobe and into her hair, deciphering the softness and the length she hid. Fabric brushed against the back of my hand, and I realized she was wearing a hood.

Her hair was tucked behind her, and everything was chilled. Her face, her hands, her hair . . . even her ear felt like an icicle.

"You're so cold," I said.

But she turned her face into my hand, her hot breath falling into my palm. "I don't feel cold."

Her lips barely touched my hand, and I wanted to go the extra centimeter—reach closer and touch them, but I didn't. She wasn't getting away from me, and I wanted to drag this out. Sliding my hand around the back of her neck, I held her and grazed my thumb down the front of her throat, feeling her swallow.

She was so still, as if she was really afraid. A sound broke from somewhere in the church, and I briefly registered a basketball bouncing. After years on the court, I knew the sound like it was my mother's voice.

"It's Devil's Night, and the day is young," she finally spoke up. "Maybe you'll find someone else to scare tonight."

I tightened my grip. "And if I want to scare you?"

I felt her body shake with a laugh. "Then maybe I'll be around," she said playfully, pulling away. "Happy hunting."

And I heard a shuffle and saw light pour into her little room before the door slammed shut, making it dark again.

"Hey." I pulled my hand back in. "Hey!"

I stood up and threw open the curtain, walking out and looking around before opening the door. The priest's chamber was empty. I whipped around and scanned the church, noticing only a few people in the pews, none looking like a teenage girl. Walking over to the row of columns near the windows, I looked around them, not seeing anyone there, either.

"What the hell?" *Where did she go?*

The bouncing sound registered again, and I looked up, seeing Damon round the last row of pews and walk toward me. He must've just finished up with Beir.

"What's goin' on?" he asked through the unlit cigarette in his mouth.

I straightened and closed my mouth, trying to breathe slower. "Nothing."

I had no idea how to start explaining what had just happened. Plus, it wasn't wise to put a girl on his radar if you planned on keeping her to yourself. At least, at first.

Holding the ball at his side, he leaned down and lit his cigarette using one of the prayer candles.

"Come on, knock it off," I scolded, trying not to look around for the girl. I still felt her there.

Damon rose, the end of his cigarette burning orange and a puff of smoke drifting up into the air. "Like we give a shit." He took the cigarette out of his mouth and blew out.

"But it's insulting to people who do. No wonder you're in confession every fucking week." I walked around him, growing impatient and not knowing why.

Damon did everything he could to be an asshole, but that was him. He was always the same.

And suddenly, I didn't want the same old shit tonight for some reason. I didn't want him to be him or me to be me. I didn't want to hide anything tonight.

It's Devil's Night, she'd said. She knew what we got up to. She knew me. If she didn't find me, I'd find her.

CHAPTER 3

KAI

Present

I grabbed a couple water bottles from the ice bowl next to the towels and walked toward the steam room, the wet heat snaking up my nostrils as I opened the frosted glass door and walked in.

Hunter-Bailey Men's Club was quiet this time of the day. And no matter how busy my friends and I were—or how hungover—we usually found ourselves here most mornings.

I looked up, instantly spotting Michael sitting two steps up on the marble seating that snaked around the room, while Will sat hunched over to my right, one step down. He lifted his head, and I could see last night's indiscretions written all over his pale and weary face. Dark circles sat under his eyes, and he dropped his head again, grumbling, "Motherfucker."

I shook my head, holding out a bottle of water. "You need new vices."

The asshole was drunk every day. And to add insult to injury, he was blowing through every cent his asinine, indulgent parents gave him, paying for any one of three things to which he'd dedicated his life: drinking, women, and, as I was starting to suspect, pills and powder.

He pulled the water out of my hand and held the chilled bottle to his brow, his shallow breathing growing shaky.

Taking my bottle, I climbed the step and sat down next to Michael. His back and head rested against the wall, and his eyes were closed as steam billowed in the air around us. Dim lighting cast a soft blue glow throughout the room, and I felt a trickle of sweat already sliding down my chest toward my towel.

"How are the renovations going at St. Killian's?" I asked him.

But he shook his head. "Don't. Don't talk to me about fucking renovations right now."

I narrowed my gaze, seeing his eyes open and his jaw flex as he stared ahead. He was angry? With me?

And then suspicion hit me. The night before last and what happened at the dojo with Rika.

Great. Not that I was in the right by any means, but I trusted her to not tell Michael every damn thing.

I let out a breath. "Man, I'm sorry. I wasn't going to hurt her. I—"

"You know who I've been thinking about lately?" he interrupted me, asking but not waiting for a response. "Your mother, Vittoria."

I kept my eyes on him.

"She was a prized piece back in the day, huh?" he mused, a slight smirk on his face. "Still is, if you ask me. Great ass. Long legs."

I stilled, clenching my jaw. I knew what he was doing, but anger was rising anyway.

He continued, "I don't think I ever told you how hot she always got me, did I? Back in high school, coming over to your house and seeing her in her skintight workout clothes. That woman still doesn't look a day over thirty." He smiled, savoring the insults he ground in my fucking face.

"You know what I think I'll do?" he taunted. "I think I'll go to your parents' house tonight. Wait until your father is asleep and see if she wants to climb on top of me. Yeah." He nodded. "She'll love the feel of me, and if she doesn't, who cares? Who cares how much she fights and cries? I'm gonna put fear in her, so every time I'm around she's gonna know I can take whatever I want from her no matter what."

I tightened my fists at my sides and stared ahead, fury burning its way through my gut. *Too fucking far.*

I stood up and walked down the steps, turning to Michael, who still sat relaxing against the wall. But his eyes were locked on mine, all too ready for this confrontation.

"I would never have hurt her," I said again.

"Hurt who—"

But Michael cut off Will's question and glared at me, leaning forward. "When I wake up in the middle of the night, I expect to find Rika there," he gritted out. "Not crying as she pounds the shit out of a punching bag downstairs at three o'clock in the morning because you made her feel ashamed of herself."

He followed me down the steps, crowding my space and trying to intimidate me. "And when I ask her what's wrong," he went on, "I don't expect her to lie to me to protect you. What the hell is the matter with you? Why would you go so far?"

"She needs to be able to protect herself," I told him. "She needs to be ready. She's not your doll."

"Don't tell me what she is!"

"You said she was one of us!" I retorted. "She's no different, right? You don't coddle Will or me. 'She's an equal.' That's what you said. We're her friends, too, and we have a stake in seeing her be able to protect herself. I'm not holding her fucking hand like she's five years old."

Michael darted forward, getting in my face. "You don't get to make decisions about my woman."

"Are you sure you do?" I shot back.

The dents between his eyebrows deepened. He was still pissed. But I was the one who was right.

Michael fucking primed Rika for years. Since they were kids, he played with her and mind-fucked her. He never handled her gently and always expected her to take care of herself and her own shit.

But now that she was his, he'd changed. We all fought our own battles, including Rika's. What the hell was he thinking? He wasn't doing her any good.

I heard the bones in his body crack as something tightened. If I were anyone else, he'd have hit me already.

If I were anyone else, he wouldn't be scared to.

"Just try it," I taunted him. "I dare you."

He took a step closer, and so did I, neck to neck and eye to eye as we both stood our ground. I never stepped on Michael's toes, and he never trod too far on mine. He knew he wouldn't win, so to save his pride I was always the first one to back off. On the few occasions we were angry with each other, anyway.

But I found myself not willing to relent this time. I didn't mean to make Rika feel bad, but she shouldn't feel comfortable, either. Not with Damon running around. I was right.

Sweat ran down my back, and we stared at each other, neither one of us blinking.

"Are you guys gonna get it on right now?" Will asked.

I hooded my eyes. *For Christ's sake.*

Leave it to Will to crack a joke right now.

Heaving a sigh, I walked around Michael and looked between the two of them. "We have enemies. And the list grows every day. Rika should be just as alert as we are."

The four of us had formed a corporation—Graymor Cristane, a combination of our last names—and Rika insisted on being an equal partner in the business. And in the group. She needed to know how to handle any threat.

But Michael turned toward me, shaking his head. "Damon's gone."

"No, Damon's hiding," I corrected him. "Have you stopped to

ask yourself why?" I tossed a glance to Will before going back to Michael. "Why aren't there any pictures of him online? Why aren't the detectives able to find him to keep track of him like we asked them to? They're not finding any hits on his credit cards, and his passport hasn't shown any activity for the last year."

I mean, assuming he's not dead, why isn't he showing up on anyone's radar?

"Damon doesn't hide," I told them. "Why is he hiding now? He knows we're not coming after him. Why isn't he hitting clubs in Moscow or buying shit in Tokyo or being spotted in Hawaii or Fiji or LA?" My tone grew louder, more demanding. "Why is he invisible?"

Michael and Will were silent for a moment, their expressions pensive, before Will finally answered. "Because he doesn't want people to know where he is?"

"Exactly." And then I met Michael's eyes. "And why wouldn't he want people to know where he is?"

Michael's gaze fell, and his voice was subdued. "Because he's somewhere he's not supposed to be."

I nodded. Damon's ego was a hundred times the size of a ship. He wouldn't hide from us. Not unless he had a good reason not to be found.

"What if the passport we tracked to Russia last year was a cover?" I asked them, not expecting an answer. "What if he's closer than we thought?" And then I approached Michael, dropping my voice to a whisper. "What if he never left?"

Michael's hazel eyes narrowed again, and his jaw flexed as the wheels in his head started turning. After all this time and all the failed efforts to locate Damon, it finally hit me. He was deliberately staying under the radar. And it wasn't out of guilt or shame for what he'd done. He was hiding because he was right under our noses. I'd bet my life on it.

"Whoa, whoa, whoa," Will chimed in, and I saw him rise out of the corner of my eye. "There's no fucking way! He couldn't have been here a whole year and we not know it. And if he is, what the hell's he waiting for?"

I turned my head toward him. "Devil's Night." And then I looked back at Michael. "We need to go. Now."

It took less than an hour to get to Thunder Bay, our coastal home-town where we'd all grown up. Rika was still in class, a junior at Trinity College in Meridian City, so Michael shot her a text, let-ting her know we'd be back in a few hours. I was sure she would've liked making the short commute home to see her mother, but Mi-chael didn't even give her the option. Probably because he had no intention of ever bringing her anywhere near Damon's home or his father.

And as much as I talked a good talk in the steam room earlier, I couldn't say I blamed him. Gabriel Torrance was a piece of shit.

We sat in a parking space off to the side of his circular driveway, idling in Michael's new SUV.

"Let me go," I said, sitting up in the passenger seat, staring at the stone mansion. "I want to talk to him alone."

"We'll all go," Will spoke up from the back seat.

"No." I turned my head toward him, narrowing my eyes. "You stay here."

I turned forward again, briefly meeting Michael's eyes. Will had been misbehaving like it was his fucking job ever since Damon left, and I wasn't sure it was the best idea to bring him here, let alone subject him to this house. For all I knew, Damon could be hiding out somewhere inside.

Clearing my throat, I pushed the door open and hopped out of the car, looking back through the open windows as I shut the door.

"Tell my mother I died well," I said sarcastically to both of them and then shot a look to Will. "No, actually, you tell her. Michael's not allowed around my mom anymore."

I turned away, hearing Michael's chuckle behind me. *None of that shit better be true, either.*

Heading up to the front door, I briefly glanced up to the tower built into the front house. The Torrance home was a château-style structure of light stone, but there were three watchtowers giving it a castle-like quality. One of the towers adjoined Damon's bedroom, where a spiral staircase across from his bed led up to a small alcove at the top with a single small window. I'd only been up in his room once, and he didn't let me stay long. That was one place where he coveted his privacy.

I reached out to press the doorbell, but the door suddenly opened, and I dropped my hand.

"Mr. Mori," Hanson, a blond man in a plain black suit, greeted me. "Please, come in."

I hesitated only a moment before stepping forward. Since we had to announce ourselves at the gate, they knew I was coming, but I felt a knot tighten in my stomach anyway at the quick response. A few more moments of delay before having to deal with Gabriel would've been appreciated.

He closed the door, and without a word, I followed him through the house. Damon's father could almost always be found at home. It's where he was safest.

Although he put up the front of dealing in media, investing in networks, news, and entertainment, I knew that was merely a drop in the ocean of how he made his money. Men of honest means didn't change their Russian surnames to English ones to hide their past. And only men of dirty deeds employed a team of muscle to protect them around the clock.

The servant led me through the vast house and out to the terrace, where the entire area was paved in a mosaic of gray stone with sporadic rows of Italian cypresses. Several people loitered around, many young women dressed chicly and holding glasses of champagne. It didn't seem to matter that it was barely noon.

A buffet of food sat to my right, while a table full of well-dressed men talked and laughed nearby. Gabriel, dressed in black slacks and a black shirt, stood over a rottweiler, grasping its collar.

I stopped, watching him. He rotated his fist into the back of the dog's head, the lion-headed gold ring on his middle finger digging into its skull. The dog whined, inching down, but still tried to keep its legs under it. The fight was still there.

I locked my jaw and raised a hard look to Gabriel. *Son of a bitch.* A sickening smile curled his thin lips as he pushed farther down and twisted the chain around the dog's neck, choking it.

I took a step but stopped, seeing the two huskies, the beagle with bloody gashes in its side, and the pit bull whose ribs I could see through its skin.

Given all my resentment of Damon Torrance—how he'd tried to kill me last year, how he'd betrayed Will and Michael, and how he'd tried to hurt Rika—I'd never failed to remember what a *true* monster looked like.

The dog finally broke and fell to its stomach, shaking as it lay down.

Gabriel grabbed a small chunk of meat from the plate on the garden table and tossed it down to the dog. He then stood up straight and grabbed some more meat, tossing the larger chunks to the trained shepherd and husky standing behind him as the other dogs looked on hungrily.

"So, they sent me the boring one, huh?" he said, not looking at me as he stroked the husky's fur. "Isn't Michael the alpha dog anymore?"

I tipped my chin up, keeping my tone level despite his slur. "Moscow Rules, Mr. Torrance," I reminded him. "Number eight. 'Never harass the opposition.'"

"Number nine," he shot back, flashing me his dark eyes under a gray brow. "Pick the time and place for action."

And he held out his hands, gesturing to his men and their guns, which were never far away, and his house, meaning I was on his turf. He had the advantage.

"So, what's this about?" He wiped his hands off on a linen napkin, digging between his fingers and under his ring. "Are we coming to terms? Will you leave my son alone if he comes home?"

"That depends. Are you open for business?"

All of a sudden, the German shepherd snapped, both he and the pit bull barking at each other as the latter tried to snatch meat. Gabriel took a step, shouting, "No. Heel!" He whipped the cloth, snapping it at the pit bull's face.

One of his men rushed to grab the dog as Gabriel scowled at the fighting animal.

"That spotted one is pissing me off," he told the man and then barked at the dog again. "Down. Down!"

The poor animal was dragged away and Gabriel came back to the table, tossing the napkin down. He glanced at me, coming back to our conversation. "Don't play with me, boy," he gritted out. "You're only still alive because Damon will want to do the honors himself."

"No," I replied, my tone dead calm. "Your son has made enough of a mess for you, and you don't need another one right now. If we can do this amicably, I know we'd both prefer it, so don't try to intimidate me."

He laughed softly, taking a drink from his rocks glass. Michael, Will, and Rika had agreed that they would move on with their lives and let Damon move on with his if he stayed out of town and away from us.

But not me. I needed to find him, and I couldn't tell my friends why.

And I needed to find him now, before he returned home and to the protection of his family.

"Your hotel in the city," I continued. "The Pope. It's on my side of the river, and I'm interested in it. Quid pro quo. You give me something. I give you something. Is it for sale?"

"Everything's for sale." He set his glass down and took a seat, gesturing for me to do the same. "But I'll want my son back."

Of course you do. I took a seat in the black wrought-iron garden chair, trying to look relaxed despite the ache in my knotted stomach. I hated him and this house.

"And even if that is on the table," he went on, "it still won't be enough to make a deal. I don't like you."

"I do." A young blonde approached, and I turned my gaze on her. She wore a white silk robe just long enough to cover her ass as she leaned over to set another drink in front of Gabriel. "And I'm for sale," she teased.

I cast my gaze back at Gabriel, trying to ignore the interruption. Neither was it unusual to see women dressed like that in this house, nor was her flirtation out of the ordinary. Entertainment was always within reach here. Even when Damon's mother had lived here.

I dropped my eyes, feeling adrenaline flood my veins at the memory of her. I didn't like her any more than her husband.

The young woman moved to walk away, but Gabriel pulled her back and into his lap.

"You know what your problem is?" he asked me as he snaked a hand around her and squeezed her breast through her robe. "Why, out of the three of you, you were the one I hated hanging around my son in high school?"

I remained silent.

"Your loyalty has a limit," Gabriel said, answering his own question. "I could always see that. Grayson and Crist, they would protect you even if they found a dead hooker in your bed and blood on your hands. No questions. No hesitation. And so would Damon." He nodded at me. "But I don't think you'd do the same for them."

His arrogant eyes held mine as he slipped a hand inside her robe, absently fondling her breast.

I curled my hands into fists. But then I relaxed, not wanting to give him the satisfaction. He would never know how much I'd done for his son.

"Even your love for your friends," he continued, "could never overshadow your sense of right and wrong, right?"

"I went to prison for assaulting a police officer. For a friend," I reminded him.

"No. For assaulting a man you believed deserved it for abusing his sister," he argued. "Even as a criminal, you're noble."

He then turned his eyes on the girl. "You see, honey," he told her, pulling his hand out of her robe and brushing her hair behind her ear. "Kai Mori is a self-righteous little fucker, and I want you to go over there and suck him dry right now."

Anger instantly heated my body. The girl locked eyes with me, cocking her head playfully, and then she walked around the table toward me.

That motherfucker. He knew how to work people, didn't he? If I left now, the conversation was over. No deal. Which is probably exactly what he had in mind. He might want Damon back, but he didn't want to deal with me. He expected me to jump ship and run.

Now, if I let the girl blow me, that would surprise him, wouldn't it?

She stopped in front of me, and I held her eyes as she knelt down, her merlot-colored fingernails slowly scaling up my thighs. She grasped my belt, and I grabbed her hands, shoving her off.

No.

Gabriel wasn't pushing me down into the gutter with him.

I rose, straightening my belt and smoothing my hand down my jacket.

"Always predictable." Gabriel laughed.

The girl looked to him, probably scared she'd done something wrong, and he jerked his chin at her, speaking Russian. She immediately stood and headed back into the house.

"You should try her, though," he told me, picking up his drink. "A throat a mile deep on that one."

"Everything okay?"

I jerked my head, seeing Michael and Will standing in the doorway to the house, watching us. I let out a breath, not realizing I'd been holding it. I wasn't sure if they'd seen what had just happened, but I didn't really care.

"Hanson," Gabriel called his man over, setting his drink back down and putting his arm around the waist of a brunette who had come up. "Take these gentlemen into the dining room." He glanced at the three of us. "My assistant will meet you in there to discuss terms and The Pope. I'll be in touch."

And off he went, taking the young woman with him into the house.

The flat expression that I'd been forcing faltered, and I glared at his back as he left.

Damon's father was nearly identical to Michael's in personality. I hated them both. And I completely understood why my father had rarely spoken to either of them at parties or sporting events when I was growing up. It was the one area where Katsu Mori and I agreed.

"Gentlemen." Hanson stepped forward, holding out his arm and gesturing for us to follow him into the house.

Michael pinched his eyebrows together, questioning me with his eyes, but I shook my head, following the servant.

The dogs. The girl. The crowd of people he didn't give a shit about seeing his filthy deeds. He wanted me to know he was stronger.

But I was going to be smarter.

Hanson led us back through the house, hands locked behind his back until we came to a set of double doors, and he opened them, inviting us into a dining room. He stopped and turned, letting us enter.

"Please, sit wherever you like," he instructed. "Refreshments will be served shortly."

He backed out of the room, closing the black double doors, and as soon as I heard the gold knobs click shut, I released a breath and closed my eyes.

"What happened?" Michael asked, sounding concerned.

I just shook my head, turning away and staring off out the windows to the terrace we'd just left. "I almost forgot," I mumbled to myself. "I almost forgot there was a reason Damon was so fucked up."

I kicked the leg of a chair, seething. *Goddamn him.* He called me a fucking criminal. *Even as a criminal, you're noble*, Gabriel had said. He could go fuck himself. His cruelty, his diabolical nature, his pleasure in others' pain . . . every inch of that guy was filth. I wasn't the criminal. I was nothing like him.

Michael stepped up. "What's going on?"

I gripped the back of a chair, seeing Will standing on the other side of the table. "I don't know yet," I said through clenched teeth.

"Why did he mention The Pope?"

"It's—" But I stopped as Hanson opened the door again.

A young woman, this one fully clothed with her hair stuffed up into a newsboy cap, wheeled in a cart with water glasses and a tray of some kind of pastry.

I pulled out a chair, and Michael and Will followed my lead as she got to work getting the refreshments ready. Hanson said something in Russian to her and backed out of the room, drawing the doors closed again.

"It's across from the dojo," I told Michael. "I thought we'd check it out for Graymor Cristane."

"We didn't talk about that," he griped. "Where the hell is this coming from? I thought we came here to see if Gabriel knew where Damon was."

I shot him a level look across the table, trying to tell him with my eyes that this wasn't the best place to talk. Michael knew me well enough by now to know I didn't make fast decisions. I had a plan.

"I don't think he knows where he is," I told Michael as I relaxed into the chair. "Why not put the past behind us and make a deal? The hotel is still in great condition. We could make something out of it."

"What?" Michael looked at me like I had three heads.

I almost laughed.

I made a show of glancing to my right, where the girl was working, and then said, with a smile in my eyes, cagey, "Did you know The Pope is a Torrance property?" I rounded my eyes on Michael, hoping the knucklehead knew how to pick up a hint. "It's been abandoned *all* this time. But it must be pretty nice inside, because all the entrances are fortified with an alarm system, cameras cover every door and corner surrounding the hotel, and there's even a security guard that still cruises past the hotel at the top of every hour and does a walk around the perimeter every four hours. I noticed that from the dojo."

Michael studied me, the wheels in his head turning, while Will still looked confused.

Come on, Michael. Figure it out.

And finally I saw the light go on in his eyes, realization hitting. "Oh, yeah." He nodded. "Right."

I smiled to myself, glad he finally understood.

Why all the security for a place not being used? Why not just lock and board up the doors? Or tear it down and sell it off? Why was it sealed up and guarded like a prison?

Damon was there.

I had no intention of buying the hotel, but I wanted inside it. And if the rumors about a mysterious, hidden twelfth floor were true, I needed *full* access to the place and privacy to explore.

Damon had tried to kill us. He wasn't going to be allowed to come home ever. But there was a reason I needed to find him. We had a loose end to take care of.

Cloth napkins and water glasses were set in front of us, and I heard a shuffle of dishes behind me. Where was this assistant we were supposed to meet?

"Just trust me," I mumbled to Michael, still speaking in code. "It'll be a great hotel. And if it's not clean, we'll clean it up nice and quick."

He laughed under his breath and then opened his mouth to speak, but the servant came around and placed a plate in front of him.

"I'm not hungry," he said, swiping his hands in front of him to stop the kid. "Nyet."

She quietly picked up the plate again and set the one in her other hand down in front of Will, before circling the table to come over to me.

"Do I know you?" Will spoke up, staring over my head to the young woman, who was filling my water glass.

But before the girl had a chance to answer, Michael turned to him. "Come on, dickhead. Not now," he grumbled. "You don't need to get laid every time we stop the car. Damn."

Will's eyes turned angry, every muscle in his body looking tight. *Jesus.* He shoved his chair back and stood up, walking out one of the glass doors leading to the patio.

I sat up straight and let out a breath. I knew Michael meant it as a joke, but not really, either. And Will knew it. He knew his extracurricular activities were becoming a problem, but he didn't want his friends pointing it out.

Michael stared at the table, his hazel eyes hooded and a little regretful. I watched Will through the doors as he lit a cigarette, a habit he'd picked up last year.

"So, anyway," Michael continued, "we get inside the hotel, do an 'assessment,' and see if everything is . . . copacetic before we try to buy it, right?"

I nodded, taking a drink of my water.

"And if it's not?"

Meaning *And if Damon is there?*

Then we handle it. But before I had a chance to answer him, I saw Michael jerk back as water and ice cubes spilled onto the sleeve of his jacket. "Jesus Christ . . ."

The girl hurriedly lifted the pitcher back up, bowing her head in apology.

"*Izvinite*," she gasped out in a small, scared voice. I glanced up at her, unable to see her face hidden under the hat. She pulled the container away and set it down, grabbing a napkin and trying to wipe off his sleeve.

"Just . . ." He snatched the napkin away from her. "Leave it alone. And take this away." He handed her his glass and the wet linen, immediately turning away and dismissing her.

She bowed her head again, hurrying off to hide herself somewhere behind me where the serving table and her cart sat.

I stood up, walking toward the doors to the patio and looking out. "If everything isn't how it should be," I said, "then I'll handle it."

"Just you?" Michael stood up and made his way toward me.

"You take care of Rika," I told him. "And Will."

The business I had with Damon was private.

Michael leaned in, speaking low. "We all need to face him, especially Will. He's floundering without Damon."

"Damon tried to kill him," I bit out. He'd tied a cinder block to his ankle and threw him in the fucking ocean.

"Yeah." Michael nodded, meeting my eyes. "His *best friend* tried to kill him."

"We're his best friends."

"Damon and Will were always closer," he said. "Just like the two of us are closer. Will needs Damon. You know he's spiraling. He needs to face him. So, let us all find the son of a bitch and give him a warning he'll never forget."

"You want him in the same room as Rika, too?"

Michael ran his hand through his hair and exhaled. That was a no.

"You take care of everyone else, and I'll take care of The Pope," I instructed. "He's no less of a threat to Rika than Trevor was."

And we both knew how Michael had handled his brother. The idea of doing the same to Damon—someone who had been a friend—made my stomach roll, but I would do what I had to do. To keep my friends safe.

And to keep Damon's goddamn mouth shut.

I turned and walked back to the table, remaining standing. I spotted Will outside the doors making his way toward us again, hopefully having calmed down.

"Enough of the fucking waiting," I told Michael, picking up my glass and taking another drink. "Let's take care of loose ends."

"Yeah, speaking of waiting," Will chimed in, stepping through the door. "Where is this guy? This assistant we're supposed to meet?"

I watched as he opened the doors to the hallway and called out to someone. "Hey?" He backed up, letting the man, Hanson, come into the room.

"Yes, sir." He looked to Will in question.

"Where is this assistant we're supposed to be meeting?" Will asked. "We don't have all day."

Will probably just wanted this over with so he could get away from Michael.

The man stared at Will hesitantly, and I suddenly felt like a shoe was about to drop. I narrowed my gaze on him. *What was going on?*

Hanson then turned his head, speaking to the young woman. "Banks?" he asked. "Did you need anything more from the gentlemen?"

Banks? What? My heart pounded in my chest.

I slowly moved my gaze to the servant girl he was speaking to, the one who had stood so demurely next to the wall, quiet this whole time.

I watched as she raised her head, the timid and submissive demeanor now gone. Her gaze met mine, dark brows framing green eyes with a blue rim around the iris. Her chin lifted, a subtle defiance in the gesture.

Oh, my God. *Her?*

"No, I think I have all I need," she told him.

She then untied the white apron around her waist and tossed it on the cart of food.

I forced down the lump in my throat. *Fuck.*

That dark hair hidden under a cap, the slender shoulders and narrow jaw, the men's clothes she still wore . . . Only instead of the dirty jeans, broken shoes, and oversize sweatshirt I remembered, it was now a pair of black suit pants, a black shirt, and a striped necktie.

I dropped my eyes. Her fingernails were still dirty, though, visible in her fingerless leather gloves.

She turned on her heel and left the room, grabbing a suit jacket off the chair in the hall and donning it as she disappeared from sight. I followed her with my eyes, my breathing gone shallow.

"Gentlemen," Hanson said. "Mr. Torrance's assistant will update him, and one of them will be in touch. If you're finished, I'll see you out."

"Wait a minute," Michael barked. "*That* was his assistant?"

I let out a breath, turning my eyes on him. "That was Banks."

He pinched his eyebrows together, not remembering, but then the light dawned, and he looked back down the hall to where she'd disappeared and then back to me. And his jaw dropped open.

"What did she hear that she's going to update him on?" Will spoke up, looking worried. "Did we say anything bad?"

I laughed to myself, my blood suddenly running hot as memories of that night came flooding back.

"Do you think she remembers us?" Michael asked.

I took a step, all of us following Hanson out of the dining room and toward the front door as I mumbled under my breath, "Does she realize he's not around to get in my way this time?"

CHAPTER 4

KAI

Six Years Ago

I'd been on edge ever since confession earlier.

Looking over my shoulder, taking second glances at everyone as I walked down hallways and sat in classrooms.

The girl in the confessional, I had to know her, right? She certainly knew who I was.

And steal me? What the hell did that mean? I shot a glance to the girls sitting and chatting in the bleachers, ready and waiting to give the guys on the court some attention after practice. Any one of them could be her. Any girl in this school could be her. While I liked a little mystery, I preferred being on the inside track. The one doing the playing, not the one being played with.

Shooting the basketball over to Will, I jogged to the end of the court with everyone else, ten sets of sneakers skidding across the floor as the ball changed hands twice more and then came back to me. I caught it, breathing hard, with sweat cooling my back, as I pushed into the point guard at my back, dribbling, twisting, and then shooting. The ball soared through the air and skidded off the rim, and I clenched my jaw as it missed the basket and fell into Damon's waiting hands.

He grinned, running back down to the other end of the court, satisfied in my failure.

Anger sat like a brick in my stomach, but I kept quiet. I shouldn't have missed that. I was thinking about her, and I would until I figured out who she was. I should've barged in there and confronted her when I had the chance.

Damon passed the ball off to Michael, and he caught it, his T-shirt hanging out of the back of his shorts as he ran down the court. There was a flash of something off to my left, and I turned my head in time to see the branches and leaves of the forty-foot sycamore outside the gym blowing against the windows above the bleachers.

"That fucking wind is going crazy," Will said, rushing up next to me. He moved light and quick, keeping one eye on the ball as he cast me a glance, smiling. "It's gonna be a wild night tonight."

Yeah, wild. Compared to what?

My friends didn't need Devil's Night as an excuse to get crazy. But I did. It was the one night I let myself make really bad decisions. Decisions made out of desire and selfishness and a need to not think methodically over every detail of every movement I made every day. I wasn't raised to be perfect, but I was raised to do everything with perfection in mind. Slow, careful, focused . . . showing the same consideration in pouring a cup of coffee as I do taking a math test. Or working on my car.

Or screwing a girl.

And I was more than ready to let go of it all. My rough edges were itching to get out.

But now, instead of anticipating all the ways I was going to get my hands dirty tonight, I was obsessing over her and whether or not I would see her. How would I recognize her?

The best part about talking to her this morning was that I didn't think she intended to be mysterious or to get under my skin the way she did. She wasn't working me like other girls tried to do. What she didn't say was just as interesting as what she did. Her breathlessness, her small voice, the flirtation that slipped out in her careful words as if she wanted something but had no clue how to be bold. I liked her innocence, but I could feel her desire to shuck it. So perfect.

"Hey, man." Michael nudged my arm. I glanced at him, trying to look like I hadn't just spaced out again when he tipped his chin, gesturing to my right. "Your dad."

I turned my head, keeping my scowl but straightening nonetheless. My father stood on the edge of the court, staring at me with his arms crossed over his chest, his sharp black suit in severe contrast to the cream-colored walls and the warm wood of the court floor. What was he doing here? He knew I was going out after school.

His black hair, same color as mine, looked as perfect as it had this morning, and his dark eyes and pinched brows leveled on me, telling me he was either happy about the weather, satisfied with last night's workout, or completely put out about the state of affairs in Ukraine. I could never really tell.

Without asking for permission to leave practice, I walked toward him, pulling my shirt out of the back of my shorts and slipping it back on.

"Father," I said, grabbing my towel off the bottom bleacher and wiping my face.

He didn't say anything, waiting to have my full attention before speaking. This is where I was both lucky and cursed. While my friends' fathers were in their fifties, my father was only forty-three. And he took care of himself. He had no trouble keeping pace with me and had the patience of a saint.

Stuffing my towel into my duffel bag, I pulled out my water. "I won't be home for dinner. Mom told you, right?"

"She did," he said, his expression stoic again. "But I would prefer that you change your mind. You can spend time with your friends another night."

"Another night won't be Devil's Night." I popped the top of my water bottle, unable to meet his eyes. "It's once a year, and it's the last one before I go off to college. I'll stay out of trouble."

He remained still, not arguing or moving as I took a drink and continued to pack up the rest of my gear. The laughter and energy grew louder as everyone picked up their bags, and I heard the locker room door swing open and closed several times.

None of it made the feel of his eyes on me fade.

"You're disappointed in me," I stated. "I know."

I zipped up my bag and swung it over my head. My father never forbade me from doing anything, but he wasn't stupid. He knew exactly what we got up to on Devil's Night.

"I wish you made better choices," he clarified. "That's all."

I finally looked up at him. "Your choices, you mean."

"The right choices." His eyes turned stern. "This is why respecting your elders is important. We have a lot more experience making mistakes, Kai."

I couldn't help it. I smiled. "I never make mistakes," I replied. "I'm either right or I'm learning. *Jaku niku kyo shoku.*"

I recited one of the many Japanese sayings he'd spouted over the course of my life.

The weak are meat, the strong eat.

And as much as I knew he wanted to say more, he nodded, letting it go with a barely visible smile on his face. Finally.

"Don't forget Sunday," he said.

"I never do."

And I backed away, turning around and heading to the locker room. Every Sunday morning, I joined him in the dojo at our home for a workout. It was the one thing we did together, and he never failed to be there. And so, of course, neither did I.

"No offense." Will ran up next to me, sweat soaking through his T-shirt and covering his neck. "But your dad scares the shit out of me. Even I want his approval, and I know he hates me."

"He doesn't hate you," I assured him, smiling to myself. "He's waiting for the better you. That's all."

He simply grunted, and I followed as he pushed through the locker room door.

Frankly, I didn't care if my father liked my friends. Damon's father didn't like anyone, and I'd be surprised if Michael's father knew my name, even after all these years. My friends were simply mine. That was it. They were separate from what happened at home, in class, or even in my head sometimes. That's what I liked about them. When we were together, we were a planet.

After I undressed and showered, I walked down the row of lockers, the room suddenly so noisy I could barely think. Everyone was ready, and so was I. I wanted to see her tonight. She had to find me.

I opened my locker and started pulling out my clothes.

"All right," Will called out, fixing his hair in front of the mirror in his locker. "The chicks already set everything up, and the paintball equipment is loaded in the cars," he told us. "We'll head out and do our shit, kill a little time at the cemetery, and then head to the city."

"Wait. The city?" Damon spoke up. "We're not going to the warehouse?"

I grinned. "You're absolved, right?" I asked him, reminding him of his confession this morning. "You need new sins for next week. Don't worry. You'll like it."

"I better," he said, tightening the towel around his waist. "Because, holy shit, I need my dick sucked."

Locker doors immediately slammed shut, and I looked up, all of a sudden seeing three of our teammates vacate the area quickly. Will burst into laughter so hard, he hunched over, shaking uncontrollably.

Damon turned and shouted, "Hey, where y'all going? One hot, wet mouth is as good as another, as far as I'm concerned!"

Smiling, Will shook his head, and raising his hands in the air, he met Damon's palms in a high five.

Damon chuckled and stuck an unlit cigarette in his mouth, but then a bellow echoed through the locker room.

"Torrance!" Coach shouted. And Damon immediately spat out the cigarette.

"Goddammit," he growled in a low voice.

How Lerner always knew when Damon was about to smoke, I had no idea. His aggravation, though, didn't stop Will from breaking out in Mötley Crüe's "Smokin' in the Boys Room," teasing him.

"All right, let's do this," Michael called out, shutting them up. "It's time."

I pulled on my jeans, glancing at the clock behind me and seeing it was nearly two in the afternoon.

Time to round up the party.

We quickly finished dressing, pulled on our black hoodies, and grabbed our phones, wallets, and keys, leaving everything else behind. The bell rang, signaling the start of the final period of the day, and the four of us stepped out into the empty hallway, hearing the faint chatter of teachers carrying on with their final lessons on this Friday afternoon.

I wish you made better choices. That's all.

I looked from left to right, seeing the dim afternoon light barely igniting a glow on the blue and green lockers. The dark corners lurked beyond, and we all stood quiet for a rare moment, enjoying the calm before the storm.

"Let's do this," I said, still staring down the hallway and seeing the branches with red and orange leaves outside the front doors going wild in the wind.

I heard the shuffle of the bag and knew Will was pulling out our masks one by one. Damon pulled on his black skull, the teeth in the mouth looking like claws. Will handed Michael his red one with deep black gashes across the face that were just as vicious as the gnawed lips. Will tossed me my metallic silver mask with slits for the eyes that were small and dark, and the gouges in the skin mean and hard. Then he slipped on the white one with a red stripe down the side of the face. All of us looked like some postapocalyptic death squad, which suited the egos of a bunch of spoiled, rich boys who had never really known danger.

Will tossed the duffel back into the locker room, and I pulled my mask on like a helmet. I closed my eyes, savoring it. In here, I was invisible. I could be whomever I wanted.

In here, I wasn't hiding.

Pulling out my phone, I texted Kylie Halpern in the front office, cueing her to play the music. Within ten seconds, Sister Machine Gun started beating out of the speakers down the halls and all around, and I slipped my phone in my back pocket, taking a deep breath.

Michael stepped forward, looking left, then right. "Now," he said.

Go, go, go!" Max Cason shouted into the wind, his head sticking out my passenger-side window.

A half hour later, fourteen cars, trucks, and motorcycles were on their way, packed to the breaking point with every player on our team, some of their girlfriends, and a few just along for the fun. The school didn't stop us or anyone from leaving for what had quickly become a Devil's Night tradition to boost team camaraderie and morale.

Storming the school at two in the afternoon to kick it all off had turned into one of my favorite parts of the night. Barging into classrooms, grabbing my fellow basketball players—and whomever else we wanted—and dragging everyone out of school was like an amphetamine to the brain. We had everyone's attention, their awe, and sometimes, their fear. It was power, and for one night a year, we enjoyed a limitless supply of it. Teachers didn't stop us, cops stood aside, and for a while, I really loved being me.

Everyone wanted to be us.

Will's black Ford Raptor drove in front of me, and all the guys in the bed of his truck laughed and shouted out with beers in their hands already. Some of them had water bottles filled with a clear liquor, which was an interesting tactic to drink in class. As long as it looked like water, teachers never knew the difference.

With my mask tucked on the console beside me, I shifted into sixth, racing ahead and following Will. Damon led the motorcade, and I glanced to my left, seeing Gavin Ellison speed past on his motorcycle with his girlfriend sitting behind him, her arms wrapped around him.

Damon must've seen him coming in his rearview mirror, because just as Gavin sped up to overtake Damon's BMW, Damon swerved left, blocking his path. I laughed to myself, but then I spotted a kid on a bike, inches from Damon's car, swerve and fall to the side of the road, and my face fell.

"What the hell?" I barked, pressing my foot lightly on the brake to slow down.

The kid tumbled to the ground, spilling down the small incline, and his bike crashed into the grass.

And Damon and the motorcycle just fucking kept going.

Goddamn him.

I braked harder, slowing the Jeep to a stop and seeing Will's brake lights glow red ahead of me. I shifted into neutral and yanked up the parking brake, hopping out of the car.

I glared at the road ahead, seeing Damon and the motorcycle still racing in the distance. Did it even occur to him to fucking stop?

"Damon's such an asshole." Will looked back at me, jumping down from his cab and taking a bite of the beef jerky in his hand.

A few of the guys from the bed of his truck hopped out, too,

I squatted down once more, grabbing her shoe off the ground, and then pulled up her foot.

Her skin was freezing, and I jerked in surprise. Her jeans had holes everywhere and she had no socks. Why wasn't she dressed properly?

She pulled her foot away, grabbing for the shoe. "I can do it."

But I held firm, giving her a defiant look as I pulled up her foot.

"God, can't you take a hint?" she snipped.

"Your skin is freezing," I remarked, slipping the shoe on. "Maybe you should—"

"Hands off," someone ordered behind me.

I whipped my head around and saw that several men had arrived, their sport bikes parked in the middle of the road. Over Will's truck engine, I hadn't heard them pull up.

I stood up as they came around, and I watched as they placed themselves right in front of the girl, standing between us.

What the hell?

"Excuse me?" I looked around them, trying to see her.

"She's fine," said the one in the middle with the shaved head who was dressed in a white sleeveless T-shirt. "We'll take it from here."

I let out a little laugh, feeling Will inch closer at my side and seeing Michael approach.

"Who the hell are you?" I asked.

But he just ignored me, turning his head to her and whispering, "Pull your hood up."

She followed directions, quickly covering herself and keeping her chin down. Two guys flanked Shaved-Head, as Michael and Will did me, all of us walls.

"Leave," the one in the middle ordered me.

"Yeah, no way." I tilted my head, trying to make eye contact with the girl behind them. "Are you okay? Who are these guys?"

They could be her brothers, but they damn well didn't look anything like her.

She stole a few glances up, and then I noticed it. A small smile pulling at her lips and an amused look crossing her features, her shyness all of a sudden disappearing. "They're far more of a handful than you are, Horsemen."

Her new pals broke out in a laugh, looking smug.

I lifted my chin.

"Let's go," Shaved-Head told her.

They all glared at us as they walked past, and the young woman followed, brushing my arm as she slipped by. I inhaled her faint scent. The energy in the air was suddenly so thick you could take hold of it. There was something familiar about her.

She handed her books to the tall one with blond hair and a silver chain around his neck, while another one hooked her bike over his shoulder as he straddled his motorcycle.

She climbed on behind Shaved-Head, and I narrowed my eyes, watching her circle her arms around him.

I stepped forward as their bikes all roared to life.

She looked back over her shoulder one more time, and I finally saw her eyes. A beautiful green with touches of gold. "Thought you had some people you wanted to scare tonight," she said.

What?

She turned away but not quick enough to hide the smirk on her face, and off they went, all three sport bikes whirring down the road as they sped away.

What the hell did she say? How did . . . ?

I clenched my jaw, realization hitting.

The day is young. Maybe you'll find someone else to scare tonight.

The girl from the confessional today. *Fuck, that was her.*

I watched her and those pricks disappear from sight, everything I'd told her today playing in my head again. How did she know who I was? And why had I never seen her before?

She was playing with me.

How confident and bold as fucking brass she got when they arrived. She thought those guys—whoever the hell they were—could put us in our place. We were playing at being bad and they were the real thing. Was that what she thought?

"Do you know her?" Michael asked next to me.

I focused down the road, not sure how to answer that.

"If you want her, she's yours," Michael said.

I kept my smile to myself. Michael talked about women the same way he talked about cheeseburgers. It really was as easy as that.

"Want her?" Will cut in. "What the hell would he want with her when we have top-shelf chicks in our cars right now? Didn't you see how she was dressed? No makeup, guys' clothes . . . She's a *feminist.*"

I closed my eyes, laughing to myself. *Jesus.* "I thought you liked the hard-to-get ones," I joked, looking over at him.

But he just twisted up his lips, the secret object of *his* obsession no more primped up than the girl who'd just left. "Yeah, well . . . you want me to call Damon, or what?" he asked. "Someone said she worked at his house."

She did?

"No," I replied. "I don't want him telling me anything about her. I'll find out myself."

He was already gone anyway, probably at the cemetery by now.

"So, are we going to get her, then?" Michael probed.

But I just stared ahead, thinking.

She'd challenged me, hadn't she? She'd made it a point to let me know who she was before she made her little escape with those assholes. To let me know she got me today only when she thought she could get away from us.

I barely nodded, every muscle in my body tight as a rope. "I kind of want to scare the shit out of her first."

I heard Michael laugh softly and then saw him twist around, shouting, "Hey, Dayton!" He called to one of the cars, and I watched him throw his keys down the line. "Switch cars with me. And clean yours out! I need the trunk."

Will cooed excitedly and rubbed his hands together, suddenly very much on board with this plan.

We turned to hand off our keys for others to take our cars to the cemetery, so the three of us could go on this run together. This was more over-the-top than my usual taste in pranks, but I couldn't stop myself.

I didn't want to stop myself.

I wanted to slam through every wall in my head and race so fast I wouldn't have time to think. Right now, as far I was concerned, this night would never end.

She'd fucked with me today.

Now I was going to fuck with her.

CHAPTER 5

KAI

Present

I walked into Sensou, the strap of my duffel bag falling across my chest as I looked around, taking inventory of everything going on. Foils clanged off to my right, coming from the room where Rika led her fencing class three nights a week. Weights clanked together and hit the floor in the weight room to my left, and grunts filled the entire dojo, echoing in the rafters, as students worked on forms and sparred in the great room.

I hurried silently across the new floors, itching to work out some energy. The collar of my shirt chafed my neck, and a light sweat cooled my chest and back. I needed to get out of these clothes.

While I drove back to Thunder Bay every Sunday to work out with my father and eat breakfast with my family, per my mother's request, I didn't let half of what I had inside me out. My father was in great shape, but he was still nearly fifty. I couldn't hit him.

But at the dojo, I could hit as hard as I wanted, and after today, I needed it.

Following the meeting with the "assistant" earlier, I'd intended to come straight here, but instead of taking the exit off the bridge, I'd just kept going, getting lost in my car for nearly two hours.

Banks.

Jesus Christ. Six years ago, she'd more than piqued my interest. Today, she had been cold, eerily calm, and very collected. I remembered her far differently, though. She'd tried so hard to be tough that night, but those eyes and how they could level me, and those lips . . . Yeah, I remembered. She didn't stay controlled for long.

And then a couple years later, when Rika hung with us one night and Banks had become a memory, I'd been captivated by our Little Monster because she reminded me of Banks. The innocence, the fight, the way I wanted to look out for her . . .

But as quickly as she'd torn into my world, she'd run away, and all inside of a few hours, one night, six years ago.

Who was she? Where did she come from?

I pushed through the door to my office and slammed it behind me, dropping my bag and ripping off my jacket.

I quickly changed into some workout pants and running shoes, grabbing a towel and pulling on a T-shirt as I left the office. At the front desk I passed Caroline, one of the college-age part-timers we'd hired, who gave me a sweet smile as always. I held up my hand, and she tossed me a water bottle from the cooler behind her. Same drill every day. She knew what to do.

"Uh, Mr. Mori?" she spoke up as I kept walking.

I slowed to a stop and turned around. "What is it?"

Her blond ponytail sat high, and her black polo with the Graymor Cristane logo on the left breast was pristine and ironed, as always.

She looked behind me and gestured to something, and I turned my head, getting aggravated. Really, the girl acted like I was going to eat her if she spoke.

But, spotting the two visitors loitering in the lobby, I suddenly forgot about Caroline.

Banks stood next to the wall to my right, holding one of the bamboo poles from the rack hanging there. She looked up at me and then back down, absently examining the weapon as if she were window-shopping with no other purpose for being here.

Across the room, to her right, stood a man who seemed vaguely familiar. Clearly one of Gabriel's henchmen, judging by his shaved head, silver chain, tacky leather jacket, and black-and-blue marks around his eye.

I set the water bottle and the towel down. Their presence was either a very good sign or a very bad one. I didn't want trouble, not here.

Walking slowly toward the girl, I held her eyes as I reached out and gently took the stick from her hands.

"It's a *shinai*," I told her. "A Japanese sword."

She stared at me, expressionless, and the rise and fall of her chest was steady and slow. Controlled. Too controlled. I backed away with the weapon, trying not to take in her appearance or revel in how it amused me.

A simple black ski cap covered every single piece of what I knew was rich, dark brown hair underneath, and instead of the suit she'd worn today, she now hid nearly every inch of her shape in a pair of old jeans with rips on the knees, combat boots, and a short black jacket buttoned up to the neck, her hands disappearing into the pockets.

But before she hid them, I noticed she still wore the same fingerless leather gloves she was wearing earlier today. The only visible skin on her was a bit of her neck and her face.

I liked that. She was still a mystery.

I pulled my gaze reluctantly from her, turning my head to the other man. "Have you come with a message?" I asked. "Will Gabriel do business?"

The man, whom I judged to be in his mid-thirties by the wrinkles setting in around his eyes, cast a quick glance at the girl and then tipped his chin up at me.

"Why do you want the hotel, exactly?"

"I'm a businessman," I replied. "I'm acquiring property, like businessmen do."

His eyes shot to her again, and I narrowed my own, following his gaze. Banks stared back at him, and I swore I saw a slight smile on her face.

A silent dialogue passed between them, and I watched them both carefully.

The man finally drew in a deep breath and nodded. "Mr. Torrance is interested in opening up a dialogue with you."

But I just scoffed. "Opening up a dialogue . . ." I mocked under my breath. "Yes, I know Gabriel's dialogue very well. And I already agreed that his son could return, but I'm going to need assurances of my own."

He shot a quick glance at Banks—again—and then answered me, resolute. "Ms. Fane will be safe."

"You can't guarantee that," I argued, stepping forward. "We both know Damon doesn't let anyone speak for him."

"Damon will do what his father says."

I stood there, keeping quiet and thinking.

If Gabriel was willing to let me buy the hotel, that meant Damon might not be there after all. Or, quite possibly, Gabriel just didn't know where his son was. Prison had embarrassed our families immensely, and Gabriel Torrance was not interested in seeing his son screw up again.

If he knew where his son was, he'd bring him home. My intent, though, was to find him before his father did.

"I want inside the hotel first," I told him. "I need to dig around a bit and evaluate how much work it will take me."

His eyes darted over to her again, but it was so quick I missed her silent response.

"No problem," he finally answered.

Why did he keep looking at her? What the hell was going on?

I looked at them both, perplexed and forgetting I'd just agreed to buy a multimillion-dollar hotel.

Licking my lips, I twirled the staff in my hand in a circle, musing. "You know, when I was fourteen, Gabriel told Damon and me something I'll never forget. 'Women' he said, 'are either toys or tools. They're good for play or good for pay.'" I spun the staff slowly and watched them carefully. "In all the years I was friends with Damon, I noticed a striking difference between his home and mine. My mother has never been a docile woman, while any woman I encountered in the Torrance house was either for sex or a servant. Toy or tool."

"And?" the man asked.

"And I'm not sure which category she fits into," I said, pointing the staff at Banks. "Every time I ask you a question, you look to her for the answer. It's odd for a woman to have that kind of power, given what I know of Gabriel Torrance."

He glanced at her again, appearing to look for direction.

She was the one in charge.

Not him.

That's it.

How interesting.

I held the weapon at my side and approached her, staring down. "Let's cut through the shit and deal direct, huh?" I said, my patience now gone.

As I entered her space, the man approached quickly, probably on guard, and I shot out the pole, hitting him in the chest and stopping him. "And if I remember correctly," I said, looking over at him, "she knows how to do her own fighting, so go wait in the car."

His jaw flexed, his body stiffened, and he was ready for a fight. But he glanced at her, waiting for the order.

She hesitated a moment, finally giving him a nod and

dismissing him. He shot me a glare before turning on his heel and storming out of the dojo.

Banks fixed her eyes back on me, cocking her head.

"Are you scared of me now, kid?" I asked. "Can't do your own talking anymore?"

I wanted to make her uncomfortable as payback for playing with me today, but I didn't want her to lose her spine, either.

But instead of answering, she just turned her head away, seemingly bored.

I chuckled to myself, walking to the wall and placing the weapon back on the rack.

"So, what impression did you gather today to pass on to Damon's father?" I inquired. I wanted to know what we said in that room that gave her assurance when we thought it was only a servant eavesdropping.

"Whatever it was," she replied, "he liked what he heard, because he has a proposition for you. I'm here with his authority."

My hand shook, and I pulled it away from the wall. Her voice. She'd only said a few words earlier today, but now . . . That same smooth taunt I remembered showed itself, bringing me back. I walked around, facing her and folding my arms across my chest.

She was a good six inches shorter than me, but with the cocky glint in her eye, she might as well have been six inches taller.

"Kai, is everything okay?" Rika asked behind me.

"It's fine," I said, not looking at her.

Judging from all the chatter in the distance and the sound of locker room doors swinging open and closed down the hallway, Rika must've been done with her class.

"Rika?" I called over my shoulder, catching her before she walked off. "Would you get Will and Michael and meet us in the office, please?"

I didn't see her face but heard her hesitant "Sure."

She left, and I turned, waving my arm and gesturing to Banks. "Down the hall. Ladies first."

I expected some flash of aggravation to cross her face, but there was nothing. Her stare remained flat as she brushed past me, heading toward the hallway, and I followed close, my heart pumping a little harder as I gazed at the back of her.

The lace of one of her black boots dragged on the floor, and although I had no doubt she could look after herself, it was amusing how little she cared about her appearance. So different from the women I'd grown up around, at home and at school.

But my hands knew how beautiful she was. They remembered.

She stopped next to a door labeled OFFICE and waited for me to open it. I reached around and turned the knob, and she entered, walking in and immediately heading toward the far corner at the back of the office. She turned to face me.

I almost laughed. Unlike Rika, Banks immediately went into survival mode in an unsure situation. While in enemy territory, take the vantage point with the fewest variables. Positioned in the corner, she needed to see only what was coming at her, not what was coming from behind. I'd been trying to turn that lesson into instinct with Rika for months.

Closing the door, I moved around the room, taking chairs and placing them at the round table toward the back. One that could hold all five of us.

"I imagine dealing with some of Torrance's associates can be difficult for a woman," I broached. "Is that why you speak through that mouth-breather out there?"

Her eyes drifted to me briefly before turning back to the framed charcoal drawing on the wall, an art piece Rika admired and had put in here, since this office was used by all of us. She said it looked like me. Not sure how. It was a figure without a face, various strokes going outside the lines. Abstract art was a love of my father's I hadn't inherited, sadly.

"Did you forget you were the one who told me about The Pope?" I went on, changing the subject.

"I don't forget anything."

I stopped, leaning on the back of the chair I'd just moved, studying her. After so many years, not only was that shell still there, but it was a lot thicker now. She'd grown up.

"Do you still think there's a hidden twelfth floor?"

"I think you're far too concerned with the secrets you know exist rather than the ones you don't."

And then she focused her attention back on the pictures and weapons lining the walls, dismissing *me*.

What did that mean? What the hell didn't I know?

"Hey, what's going on?" Michael walked in, looking sweaty and tossing a towel over a chair. Will and Rika followed him and shut the door behind them. Will was shirtless and breathing hard, probably having just been amping it up in the weight room.

"Gabriel's *assistant*," I said, "has come with a proposition."

"Hi." Rika approached her with an outstretched hand. "I'm Erika Fane."

Banks simply looked at her. Her eyes fell to Rika's, a hint of disdain on her face before she turned away again, ignoring her.

Rika glanced at me with a question in her eyes, and then she pulled her hand away, taking a seat at the table.

We all followed suit, sitting down.

Banks took something out from inside her jacket and set it on the table, face up. It was a photo. She pushed it slowly across the wooden table toward me, and I studied the small headshot of a young woman I didn't recognize. Dark blond hair, blue eyes, angelic face, pretty enough . . . Definitely Michael's type. Her high cheekbones were tinted pink, and her mouth looked like a candy apple. Young and beautiful.

"Who's this?" I asked as everyone silently inched closer to get a better look at the picture.

"Vanessa Nikova," Banks replied. "Mr. Torrance's niece."

"And?" I sat back in my chair, trying to appear relaxed.

"And this is far more than just trading a hotel for a prodigal son, don't you think?" She eyed me, a condescending look on her face. "Mr. Torrance wants undoubted assurance that you and your friends will bring no harm to his son or his family. It's going to require more of an investment than just money."

She looked down at the picture again. "She's very beautiful."

I narrowed my eyes on her. Beautiful? What?

They thought I wanted to buy the hotel, but what did this have to do with the arrangement?

"What are you getting at?" I pressed.

She cocked her head, a coy smile in her eyes. "Something a little more concrete," she said. "A future. Alliances are still made this way."

Alliances? I looked at my friends, trying to gauge any understanding of what the fuck she was talking about in their eyes, but they seemed just as lost as me.

But as I dropped my gaze to the picture again, it slowly started to hit me. My heart pumped harder, and my fists under my crossed arms clenched.

She wasn't serious.

"You're talking about a marriage?" Rika blurted out, glaring at her.

But Banks spoke to me. "She currently lives in London," she informed me. "She speaks fluent English, French, Spanish, and Russian. She's well educated—"

"Get the fuck out." Michael laughed bitterly.

"And she's . . . untouched," Banks finished, as if Michael wasn't about to explode three feet from her.

I leaned forward, staring at her. *Untouched. A virgin.*

"You're joking," I charged. What century was Gabriel living in? A marriage? This was fucking ludicrous.

Hell, no!

But she just cocked her head at me. "The only way we can see that you won't be tempted to hurt the Torrance family is if you're invested with the Torrance family," she explained. "We want an alliance that's binding."

I could barely breathe. I mean, I couldn't say she was wrong, I guess. Marriages in certain families could be much more about keeping wealth and alliances secure rather than anything else, but there was no way I was doing something like that.

"For this, you will have complete autonomy over her inheritance," she told me, "including the properties which her parents left her when they passed away several years ago." She paused, drawing out the last bit. "And you'll have The Pope. Free of charge. As a wedding present."

Will sat with his arms folded over his chest, watching the scene with mild amusement, while Rika looked at me, troubled. Her entire body was stiff, and she cast a hard look at Banks out of the corner of her eye.

"He's not marrying Damon's cousin, okay?" Michael stood up, looking like he was done talking. "This is fucking bullshit. We don't need the hotel. We'll . . . find what we need on our own." He gave me a knowing look, indicating our search for Damon.

Will grabbed the picture off the table and joked, "Well, I'll marry her."

But Michael ignored him, prodding me. "Kai? Tell her to fuck off and leave."

But I held her dark gaze, seeing the corner of her mouth turn up just slightly, unable to hide her enjoyment at this.

"Kai?" Rika prompted when I didn't answer Michael.

I took a deep breath and sat back in my chair, clearing my throat. "Guys, leave us alone for a minute, okay?"

"Kai?" Michael said again.

I looked up at him, trying to appear at ease. "A few minutes, okay?"

My friends all hesitated, looking between the girl and me and clearly not wanting to leave me alone with her. It was a credit to her, I suppose. That they thought she was that dangerous.

They left the room and closed the door behind them, and I picked up the photograph, holding it up. "You think you can show me a picture and that alone is supposed to tell me that's the woman who should have my children?"

She shrugged. "She's young, healthy . . . What more do you need to know? She'll please you."

I laughed quietly. Jesus Christ. "It takes a lot to please me," I taunted. "Remember?"

Her small smirk fell, and she straightened in her chair.

I flicked the picture back at her, sending it flying across the table. "Tell him to go fuck himself. It's the most absurd thing I've ever heard of."

And this time, she did smile as she picked up the photo in front of her and slid it back inside her jacket.

"What are you smiling at?"

"I told him you wouldn't agree."

"You think I should?" I countered. "You think this isn't just some horrific way for Gabriel to bring me under his control? It's ridiculous." I licked my dry lips. "And I'm surprised he'd want a half-Jap polluting the family blood anyway. Seems unlike him."

Actually, it was exactly like him. Binding my family to his. Forever in my face.

She exhaled slowly as if calculating her next words as she folded her hands on the table. "I know what you really want," she said. "You want to know where Damon is. You don't want to be surprised. And right now, you're a rat in a maze. You don't know which way to turn, and you won't see that you've gone the wrong way until you've gone too far."

"Meaning what?"

"Meaning you're the prey right now," she shot back. "And once . . . you were the hunter."

I leaned forward, resting my forearms on the table again. "You *want* me to find him?"

"I couldn't care less if you tore apart this entire city looking for him," she retorted. "I'm here to deliver a message. Nothing more."

"But you must've known I'd refuse."

She nodded once. "Yes."

"So, why come?"

Now she was the one to hesitate. She reached out and grabbed a piece of notepaper and a pen from the middle of the table, looking down as she began writing and speaking at the same time.

"Because after you refuse," she started, "I'm going to leave." She scrawled on the paper, taunting me with her smooth words. "You'll then go upstairs and out to the open terrace to work on your forms in the evening air. You're liking it out there more now, I can tell."

My eyes burned as I glared at her. What?

"The weather is cooling off, so it's more comfortable to practice outside, isn't it?" she went on, still not looking at me as she wrote. "And resist as you may, your mind will eventually drift to our discussion tonight. You'll think about how so very little is in your control anymore. You'll think, 'What do I do now?' and how your life is in a stalemate, and how the small itch under your skin called anger is growing stronger."

I stopped breathing, and she looked up and met my eyes, complete fucking pleasure pouring out of her gaze and cutting into me.

"It's building and building and building every day," she said, slicing even deeper as I sat frozen. "Because your life embarrasses you. It hasn't even become close to what it was before you were arrested."

She dropped her eyes and began writing again. "All of your high school friends—well, nearly all of them—moved on to college, prestigious law schools and medical schools, bringing their families pride," she continued, "and at night, they get to go to clubs and pick up hot young undergrads who blow them in the car rides back to their penthouse apartments. They're on top of the world, without a care."

The slow strokes of her pen scratched across the paper, sounding like a blade carving into wood.

"But not you," she jeered. "You think you're a joke to them. How far the golden boy did fall. A disgrace to his family. The infamous story they'll tell at the high school reunion in five years, which, unfortunately, you won't be attending, because deep down you know they're right."

She recapped the pen and placed it back in the holder at the center of the table.

"Then you'll come inside after your workout, and you'll go take another shower. Your third one today. It washes off the self-hate for a little while, doesn't it?" She folded the paper in half, sharpening the crease as her eyes held me like an anchor. "Then you'll drive and go to a club and find someone—anyone—to take all that rage out on, so you can at least sleep for a few hours tonight."

I tightened my fists, pressing them into the table as I rose from my seat. It took everything I had not to grab her by the fucking neck. Walking over, I leaned down, pushing her chair to recline. Her proud eyes stared up, daring me. Where the fuck did she get all that? *She's been watching me?*

I didn't hate my life. I wasn't angry. I'd served my time. Deed was done, and I wasn't wallowing in self-pity. I knew how to pick myself up and get on with it.

Or at least I was trying.

"And when you wake up," she said low, nearly whispering up at me. "You'll realize how much everything around you sucks and how it's time to get in the goddamn game, Kai Mori, and take some chances."

Goddamn her.

She held up the folded piece of paper between us. "Her inheritance," she said, handing it to me. "It will make you a very powerful man. More powerful than your friends will ever be."

She rose from the chair, forcing me back, and my body filled with a sudden unease. She'd gotten under my skin, and she knew it. But I hadn't affected her in the least.

"I'll wait until tomorrow to tell Mr. Torrance your answer," she told me. "Just in case I hear from you tonight."

I reached out and grabbed her arm, stopping her. "I've made a lot of bad decisions in my life," I said, standing at her side. "I won't be making any more."

She looked up at me and pulled her arm out of my grip. "I hope not. You've made too many."

She moved to leave, but I blocked her again. Slipping the paper she gave me into her jacket without looking at it, I retrieved the picture instead. I made a show of looking at it.

I needed Damon.

And I needed in that hotel.

But if he wasn't there . . .

I looked down into her piercing eyes, remembering the smell of her hair, the sight of her smile, and the feel of her fear and excitement. She was the one thing I'd ever seen him possessive of.

If he wasn't in the hotel, then she was leverage.

"Tell him we've got a deal," I told her.

She blinked up at me for a split moment, and I knew she hadn't been expecting that.

But when she reached for the knob, I put my hand on the door, keeping it shut. "But I'll pay for The Pope," I clarified. "Instead, my wedding present . . . will be you."

She whipped around, and I finally saw some emotion on her face as she glared at me. "I'm not on the table."

And I couldn't help but smile down at her, my dirty mind finding the double meaning.

"You work for me until the wedding. That's the deal. Go and tell him my terms." I backed away, suddenly very confident. "And you'll find out that you're exactly what I said you were. Toy or tool. Nothing more."

I left her side and walked back around behind my desk. While her position with Gabriel perplexed me, I knew that man would sell his soul to make a buck. There was no chance one little girl was of that much value that he wouldn't sacrifice her to see me agree to his terms.

"And, Banks," I said, seeing her yank open the door, a small ember of the fire I remembered in her all those years ago finally showing itself again. "Once he agrees, gather the keys, codes, and blueprints for the hotel and bring them to me. I want in tomorrow."

She didn't turn or acknowledge my order, but I saw the little snarl on the side of her face before she left the office, slamming the door behind her.

My chest shook as I let out a quiet laugh. Following her out, I watched her stuff her hands back into her jacket pockets and ignore my friends, who stood in the lobby. I stopped next to the front desk, seeing her disappear out the doors, and moments later a black SUV charged off.

"What did you do?" Michael walked over.

But I just kept staring out the doors after her, mumbling, "She said 'tear apart the city, looking for him.'"

"What?"

"She said that she didn't care if I tore apart the entire city, looking for him," I said again, louder. "I never told her I thought he was in the city." And I nodded, now more sure than ever. "He's here."

I turned to head back to the office.

"You're not getting married," Michael called out after me.

I glanced back. "I'm not getting fucking married."

CHAPTER 6

BANKS

Six Years Ago

Maybe I'll be around?

I'd said that. Why had I said that to him in the confessional? And why had I taunted him on the road earlier? There was no way I'd be around or allowed to go anywhere tonight. Not on Devil's Night.

But finally being able to engage with him, I couldn't stop myself. He was like a puzzle, giving the impression that there were so many things he wanted to say, but he struggled to get his words out. And then . . . every once in a while in that confessional, he showed himself. His real self. The monster my brother said everyone had inside of them.

I coasted back down the long driveway, testing out my bike after the repairs I'd made. I unclenched my fingers from the handlebars, and spreading out my hand, I studied my dirty nails.

He wouldn't like me, right? I wasn't his type.

He was used to girls who looked like models, with magazine hair, hundred-dollar eye shadow, and heels for days. I glanced down at my brother's old Vans on my feet—the ones he'd grown out of six years ago—permanently stained from oil that he'd spilled on them so many summers ago and the fabric shredding along the rubber sole. I didn't look like a girl, much less a woman.

And at seventeen years old, I was so far behind other girls my age. Kai couldn't be seen with me even if he wanted to. I'd embarrass him.

And I'd never be able to afford to look like I could even try to fit in with him and his crowd.

I breathed in the evergreens on both sides of the blacktop as the wind blew back my dark hoodie and caressed my hair.

In all the times I'd spotted Kai around Thunder Bay, around my house, at a basketball game . . . he was cool and calm, touched by nothing.

But not today. I'd made him nervous.

I smiled, pedaling faster as I clicked the little black remote secured to my handlebars. "Smells Like Teen Spirit" droned in my ears, and I swerved left, zooming right through the iron gates just as they parted for me. I held on tight as the road dipped, and raced down the steep, paved hill of my driveway. Holding the handlebars straight, I closed my eyes, instantly feeling my heart jump up into my throat at the rush of wind and the sensation washing over me.

I made him nervous. My skin still tingled where he chafed it when he grabbed my sweatshirt. What would he have done without that wall between us?

A horn honked, and I popped my eyes open, seeing one of my father's cars racing toward me.

Shit. I swerved out of the way, turning right, and flew past the Bentley, avoiding eye contact. The driveway evened out, and I continued down the length, feeling eyes on my back as I disappeared around the back of the house, out of sight of the car.

Last night's rain still chilled the air, but the ground was dry as I hopped off my bike and walked it behind the hedges between the two garages, one loaded with cars that were never driven and one with blacked-out windows and a keypad code that almost no one knew.

I hid the bike out of sight and jogged up to the back of the house. Entering the kitchen, I immediately smelled all the food and nearly groaned as I closed my eyes for a moment.

Marina, one of the household's cooks, was making bread today, and I closed the door, feeling warm all over.

"Where ya been?" I heard David's voice and I glanced over at the long wooden table in the middle of the room where he sat with two others of my father's security, Ilia and Lev.

I looked away, walking to the stove. "Fixing my bike."

Marina wiped her hands on a towel and winked at me, lifting the lid off the pot on the stove. I leaned over, breathing in and smiling at the chestnut and mushroom soup.

"When your brother calls me," David barked, "and I don't know where you are, I feel like he's going to reach through the phone and rip out my throat. You're getting me into trouble, Nik. And if you're going to confession, let us know and one of us will give you a ride."

I kept my eye roll to myself, taking the bowl that Marina loaded up and handed to me. Walking over to the table, I climbed over the bench seat and plopped down next to David, tearing some bread off the loaf already sitting in front of me.

"Leave the kid alone," Marina scolded, coming up behind me and pulling my hair out of the back of my sweatshirt, combing her fingers through it. "She needs some freedom."

He scowled up at her. "You try explaining that to him."

I remained silent, knowing he was right. He had a right to be mad. No one wanted to deal with my brother. Standing up, I walked over to the sink to retrieve a clean spoon.

I heard Ilia speak up. "Yeah, I can't even tell him you stole some of my beers last night." He grabbed me and yanked me down into a headlock. "He'll just blame me for leading you into temptation."

I twisted, trying to free myself. "Cut it out!" I shouted, the odor of cigarettes and sweat assaulting my nostrils and making me gag.

"I didn't steal any of your beers!" I growled. "You were probably too drunk to remember you drank them all!"

I finally whipped my spoon on the back of his head, and he released me, laughing.

I stood upright again and slammed down into my seat, scowling. *Asshole.*

Dipping some bread into the soup, I stared down, eating and trying to keep my damn mouth shut. The warmth spread through my mouth and down my throat, filtering through my body as I tried to ignore everyone's eyes on me.

"So, how much penance did you get? Huh?" Ilia nudged my shoulder, not letting up. "Stealing my beer, not doing as you're told like a good girl . . ." He listed my sins. "You having any impure thoughts yet?"

"Ask your girlfriend," I retorted, my mouth full of food. "She eyeballs me more than she does you."

Lev snorted.

"You little shit," Ilia gritted out, jabbing his fingers into my stomach.

I jerked away, but he circled his arms around my body and tickled me. I squirmed, hitting him in the chest. "Leave me alone!"

But he just laughed, moving his hands under my arms and then back to my stomach.

"Leave her alone," I heard David say.

"Mmm." Ilia's hand "accidentally" found itself close to my ass. "Getting kind of perky back there, aren't you?" He pinched me through my jeans. I wiggled away and swung my hand at him, slapping him on the neck.

"All right, enough," Marina barked. "Out of my kitchen. Go. All of you. Now!"

Ilia and Lev chuckled, jostling the benches as they rose and left the room, Ilia flicking me on the side of the head as he left. David stood up, emptying his coffee and setting down the mug before leaving the room without another word.

I downed a few more spoonfuls of soup and stood up, ripping a hunk of bread off the loaf on the table to take with me.

Climbing off the bench, I walked toward the back stairs, leading up to my room.

But a voice from behind stopped me. "Nik."

I halted, squaring my shoulders to brace myself. I had hoped to escape, but I was too late.

Marina wasn't my mother, but she assumed the job. We had an agreement. I came and went as I pleased, and she reserved the right to tell me what she did or didn't like about that.

My real mother could barely take care of herself, much less me.

Turning around, I took a quick bite out of the loaf in my hand, hoping that would signal I didn't want to talk.

But she approached anyway, her blue eyes leveled on me and a sympathetic tilt to her smile. "Try as he might," she said, "your brother can't stop time. No matter how you cover up or how big you wear your clothes, you can't hide forever. Your body is changing."

Heat immediately rose to my cheeks, and I wanted to look away but didn't. "So?"

"So, men are starting to notice you," she pointed out, more urgent. "You're a pretty girl, and I don't think it's a good idea to . . ." She paused as if looking for the right words. "I don't think they should be handling you like that anymore. They'll start to get ideas."

She raised her hands and rubbed them up and down my arms, adding, "If they haven't already, that is. You're a woman now, and your body is yours."

This time I did look away, inhaling a heavy breath.

A woman. I wasn't growing up. My body could change all it wanted, but I'd never be a woman. I'd never be anything other than what I was right now.

"It's okay to grow up," Marina nearly whispered as if reading my mind. "It's okay to dress and wear makeup like other women do, if that's what you want."

I held in my bitter laugh. "I don't see how that makes any sense. I don't want those guys to notice me"—I jerked my head to the hallway where Ilia, Lev, and David had just walked—"so why draw further attention to myself?"

Why dress up and even try to look pretty?

"Because." Marina smiled gently, taking a tube out of the pocket on her apron. I watched as she uncapped it and twisted the base, making the cherry-red lipstick rise.

She raised it to my lips, and I jerked back out of reflex, but stilled as she started to dab it on my mouth.

Smiling, she pulled her hand away and turned me to the mirror she had hung on the wall next to the pantry.

I blinked, taken aback. I rarely looked in mirrors anymore, refusing to face what I knew was happening to my appearance, but I couldn't stop staring all of a sudden. Rolling my lips together, I felt something I hadn't felt in a long time. A rush.

The red seemed to make my olive skin glow in a way I never noticed before, and my green eyes pierced me as they stared back through the mirror. Even my hair seemed a richer brown.

"Because eventually," Marina continued, "there will be someone whose attention you do want."

And an image of Kai popped in my head. What did he think of me today?

Marina turned around, getting back to work, and I glanced in the mirror once more before heading up the back stairwell.

Things were changing. My brother kept me all to himself, and while he was my world, I was starting to feel like I could fit in more. I wanted more. A bigger life.

I was seventeen. I had no friends and no formal education. What would I do next year when my brother left for college? I could ignore how my body was changing all I wanted, but time was passing anyway, making sure our lives evolved. I'd have to be an adult, eventually.

Reaching the second floor, I jetted down the hallway, heading for my brother's room, but a scraping sound caught my attention, and I stopped. I looked toward the window at the end of the hall, seeing the tree outside whipping like a flag in the high wind. I stepped up, gazing outside.

What was Kai doing now? Pulling some prank, partying, or maybe doing one of the things he confessed today? On his way to a private room in a private club or something equally painful for me to think about?

Looking down, I noticed a red Charger facing me—fairly new—with a black stripe running down the side. I pinched my eyebrows together. Whose car was that? I didn't recognize it.

But then a pop went off in the distance, and I jerked my head back, staring into the air above me as I listened to the whir and whistle that followed. Was that . . . a firework?

All of a sudden, a second, third, and fourth pop went off, sounding like they were coming from the forest nearby, burning and fizzing overhead, and I heard a ruckus downstairs as what sounded like more fireworks began exploding in the sky near the house. Doors slammed shut, and I peered over the railing, seeing servants run to the rear of the house, probably to head outside.

What the hell was going on?

I turned to head back down to investigate, but just then something was shoved over my head, turning my world black, and I whipped around, gasping.

"What?" I cried, my heart jumping into my throat.

Hands gripped my arms, the cloth over my head tightened around my neck, and my feet were swept off the floor as I was carried down the stairs.

"Let go of me!" I thrashed and kicked. What the fuck was happening? Who were they?

A hand came down over the cloth, covering my mouth, and I continued to writhe and twist against their hold as their hard footfalls trampled down the stairs. How many were there?

"Help!" I screamed through the hand. The muscles in my stomach burned as I resisted them with everything I had inside me.

Oh, God. Cool air hit my back where my sweatshirt rose up in the struggle, and I felt their footsteps quicken.

"Get her in!" one of them barked. "Hurry!"

The fireworks went crazy, whizzing in the distance, and I continued to thrash, twisting my head back and forth to get my mouth free.

"Help!" my muffled cry broke out.

That's what the fireworks were for. A diversion.

I faintly heard something click, and a male's voice jeered, "Hope you don't mind tight spaces, little one."

Someone else laughed, and all of a sudden I was falling, hitting a hard surface too high to be the ground. And then any light coming through the hood disappeared completely and something was slammed shut over me, all noise faint and dull now.

Tight spaces. I shot out my hands and legs, every one of them hitting a barrier, like I was in a coffin. The floor under me rumbled to life, I heard car doors slam, and I moved my hands in front of me, finding a feltlike upholstery above.

I was encased. The engine roared, and realization hit me. I was in a trunk. I immediately began pounding and kicking. "No!" I bellowed, the hand covering my mouth now gone. "Please! Let me out!"

Ripping at the tie around my neck, I pulled it off and yanked the bag off my head, sucking in a lungful of air.

And then I beat the roof above me. I screamed as loud as I could and made as much noise as possible in the hope anyone would hear me.

"Let me out!" I yelled, my throat burning raw as I howled until every last ounce of breath left my lungs. "Ilia! Lev! David! Help!"

Fuck! The car under me moved, and I rolled a little as it took off. "Help!" I pounded my fists harder and faster, going crazy. The farther away they took me, the greater the chance I'd never be found.

Music started blaring dully from the inside of the car, and my metal coffin vibrated under me, the noise drowning out the sound of my screams.

"Oh, God," I cried, my eyes welling with tears. "Please."

I started whimpering uncontrollably, sucking in short, shallow breaths as I patted my hands around the trunk floor, trying to find anything I could use as a weapon. A tool, a tire iron, anything.

But the trunk was completely empty, and I shook my head. My father would never come for me.

Fuck it. I slammed my fists, beating the lid above me again and again, not even stopping when they began to ache. They were going to do what they were going to do. I wasn't going to lie here and wait for it. There might be a chance, any chance, a passing car or even a kid on a bike might hear me.

"Help!" I screamed, trying to make my voice carry. "Heeeeeelp!"

The car jostled, and I rocked back and forth in the trunk. I thought we turned, and suddenly the road underneath turned gravelly, and we slowed.

But I kept belting and pounding, kicking and shouting. I turned to my side and began kicking against the wall behind the back seat, hoping there might be some kind of escape, since I knew some cars' rear seats folded down, opening into the trunk. But since I hadn't seen what kind of car I was tossed into, I couldn't be sure. So I tried anyway.

The car continued to slow, and then it finally stopped. I breathed hard and listened. Shifting my eyes around the darkness, I heard the music die off, the car going silent, and doors started to slam shut. How many of them were there? At least two had carried me out of the house.

Fear coursed through my body, and a small gasp escaped. I covered my mouth with my shaking hand as a tear spilled across my temple.

Three knocks hit the trunk lid, and my eyes rounded.

"Go ahead and scream," a male's cocky voice—the same one from before—said. "There's no one around to hear you now."

I heard muffled laughter, and I didn't know what to do. I wanted out of here, but I also didn't. What were they going to do?

But another voice spoke up, this one smoother and darker, sounding an inch away from me. "You said you wanted to be hunted. Right?"

My breath caught in my throat.

Kai?

I pinched my eyebrows together as the dots started to connect. Fear morphed into anger, and my gaze tried to burn a hole through the trunk lid.

"You see that little green glow-in-the-dark lever in there?" he asked. "Pull it."

Lever? What? I darted my gaze around, finally seeing something green glowing in the corner on my right. It was small but readily visible, and I didn't know how I'd missed it. It had a picture of a car on it, and I reached out and pulled it, the trunk immediately clicking open and a sliver of daylight suddenly pouring in.

I exhaled, my nerves relaxing.

Pushing the lid open, I looked up, seeing three of them standing over me, their eyes barely visible through their masks. A chuckle came from the slightly shorter one to the left, in the white and red mask—Will—and I quickly wiped my tears away and scrambled out of the trunk.

"Assholes!" I growled, shoving the one in the silver mask I knew to be Kai with both hands, and then darting out and slamming Michael in the solid red mask with a hand in the chest. They might not know much about me, but I knew exactly who they were and the bullshit they liked to pull simply because they could. I couldn't believe they did this! Rich boys playing at being bad.

But the joke was on them. You're not really bad when you only do shit under the security of never having to suffer consequences.

And where was Damon? I looked around for their fourth, but aside from all the cars in the lot, it was empty.

"That wasn't funny," I barked.

The one in the middle simply looked at me, while the other two chuckled softly, walking away and leaving us. I followed them with my eyes, seeing them head off into the brush and disappear into the trees. More than two dozen cars were parked around us in the makeshift gravel lot, but there were no buildings, no houses, just forest and cars.

Where the hell were we? It looked like just a clearing in the woods.

I turned back, seeing Kai approach me, his mask still on. He placed one hand on the lid and pointed at the lever I'd pulled inside.

"Every car made since 2002 has one," he told me. "If that ever happens to you again, you know what to do."

I scowled up at him. "If that ever happens again, my crew won't be as polite as they were earlier."

David might get on my case a lot, but he'd cut out their tongues if he knew what they'd done.

But then, suddenly, Kai pressed into me, making me fall back into the trunk and land on my ass. My legs dangled over the side, and I looked up him, his long body blocking my escape.

"Is that supposed to be a threat?"

And then he leaned down, his vicious mask an inch from my face, making my stomach flip. "I was raised to be a gentleman," he said, "but if you send other men after me, catching my interest will be the worst mistake you ever made."

I forced a sneer, but a shiver ran down my spine anyway.

He straightened and lifted the mask off his head, revealing the face I knew was underneath. His dark eyes, underneath even darker eyebrows, stared down at me like a dare, and a sense of foreboding nipped at my insides. But I didn't look away.

A light layer of sweat matted the edges of his hair, making it messy and sexy. So rare for him to have anything out of place.

Without saying a word, he walked away from me, toward the front of the car and out of sight.

I heard the crunch of gravel slowly getting fainter and fainter, and then it was gone, and I twisted my head, confused.

What? I hopped out of the trunk and slammed it shut, looking over the hood. Where did he go?

Where did they *all* go?

A sea of cars spread out before me, a forest of trees in every direction, and I looked up, seeing the first stars peeking out of the sapphire sky. The sun had set a while ago, and it would be dark soon.

Chills covered my arms. *Shit.*

Twisting my head, I saw the narrow, unpaved road behind me that we came down. The emptiness of it as it wound around a turn and disappeared creeped me out. I should go that way. It had to lead to the highway.

But music made my ears perk up, and I turned back to the way Kai went. A girl's cheer rang out in the night, and I studied the darkness of the dense forest ahead as the beat of subwoofers vibrated off my body.

All these cars, all these people . . . they were in the woods somewhere. This was a party.

I glanced behind me again. I should take the road. Walk home, catch a ride . . . whatever.

But he'd brought me here, hadn't he? Maybe I was a little curious. He was daring me.

Walking around the car, I headed straight for the woods. Someone at this party would have a phone, and I'd call David. He'd blame this on me, but he'd keep his mouth shut. Neither one of us wanted to suffer the consequences of my being here.

I jogged, looking around as gold and orange leaves shuffled under my shoes. The scent of burning wood drifted into my nostrils, but I didn't see a fire or any people yet. Where were they? I could still hear the music in the distance, so I continued straight into the darkening woods.

I shot a glance back to the parking lot, the light from the clearing getting smaller and smaller.

Maybe this wasn't a good idea after all. I searched the brush again. "Hello?" I called.

Where was I exactly? I'd taken walks in the woods, but I didn't think I'd ever been out this far. I was pretty sure the sea cliffs sat half a mile to my left, Loch Lairn Cave was behind Stuart Hill to my right, and the Bell Tower should be . . .

Right there. I looked up, off to my right, and squinted my eyes ahead, making out the stone tower about two stories high and the tall, green shrubbery around it.

The Bell Tower was a ruin, part of an old village that died out over a hundred years ago when a bad storm drove everyone inland a few miles for safety.

"Hello?" I called again. Maybe someone was over there. "Hello?"

My heart raced. It was getting dark.

"Kai!" I shouted.

My foot caught on a log, and I stumbled forward, hearing a creaking branch to my right. I jerked my head, looking for where it came from.

Nothing.

Then a swoosh of leaves sounded behind me, and I spun around, panting.

"Who's there?"

I caught sight of something black and turned my eyes just a hair to the left.

Kai stood there, leaning his shoulder into a tree and watching me.

I immediately took a step backward. "Wha— What are you doing?"

How long had he been there? He had been behind me, which meant I passed him on my trek. A chill ran down my spine.

He took a step, his mask dangling from his hand.

I glanced around. "Where is everyone? Why'd you bring me here?"

He didn't answer, his eyes locked on mine as he moved closer. What the fuck?

I moved one step back for his every step forward.

"It was stupid of you to eavesdrop on me today," he stated calmly. "And an even bigger mistake to reveal yourself earlier. I might never have known it was you."

I swallowed the lump in my throat, still retreating. The music in the distance felt like a lifeline all of a sudden, and he probably knew what I was thinking.

"You *should* run," he said, his warning cool and quiet.

Should I? But this was Kai. I didn't know him, but I'd watched him. He was the good one. The quiet one.

He was playing with me.

"You . . ." I stammered. "You won't do anything."

"Like I didn't do anything to that girl in the shower?" he challenged me. "You think I'd go to all this trouble to get you here just to let you go?"

Maybe. Yes. Okay, no, but . . .

"You see, I don't like being teased," he continued, one of his eyebrows arched. "Respect and reverence are important to me, and you have neither. You need to learn a lesson."

"That's not true." I did respect him. I didn't know he was going to be in that confessional today. I didn't mean to listen.

"I'm not afraid of you," I told him, but my feet betrayed me, still backing up.

"That's because you think you know what's happening right now."

And suddenly, I hit a wall.

"But you don't," he finished.

I froze, feeling something behind me. Slowly, I twisted around to see Michael standing there, towering over me.

What? I shot my eyes back to Kai, seeing one corner of his mouth lift in a small smile.

Oh, shit.

My breath caught in my throat as Michael's red skull stared down at me, and I understood the feeling of walls closing in from before. I looked around. We were out here alone. Them and me.

And what about Will? Was he still out here somewhere, too?

I changed direction, moving left and backing away from both of them now. They stepped slowly toward me, Michael pulling off his mask and then his hoodie and T-shirt and dropping them to the ground.

My mouth fell open, and heat rushed to my cheeks. His long torso, tan from playing ball out in the sun, stood right in front of me, and I dropped my eyes. I'd seen David and the guys without their shirts plenty of times, but they didn't look like that.

"She's pretty," he told Kai, the two of them walking side by side toward me as I kept backing up. "And she looks easy for us to handle. Together."

I heard Kai's quiet laugh, and I took another step back, suddenly hitting a tree. I dug my nails into the bark behind me.

"Don't be afraid," Michael told me, and I glanced up just

enough to see his boxer briefs sticking out of the top of his jeans. "We're good. We're really good."

We're good? They weren't serious.

I fucking bolted. Without turning back, I ran through the forest and toward the music. Get to a phone, get a ride, and get home. For once, the hiding I always had to do sounded pretty damn good right now. My brother was right. Guys were assholes.

I panted, digging in my heels harder and harder to get away. Kai would've let that happen? For me to be used like entertainment? There was an air of danger about him at the church today, but he was also gentle.

All of a sudden, Kai was in front of me, cutting me off and bringing me to a halt. "Wait," he said.

But I didn't care what he had to say. I shoved him in the chest, pushing past him and running away. I dug in my heels, racing as fast as I could without even watching where I was going.

Arms wrapped around my waist, and I was lifted off the ground as a husky whisper breathed in my ear, "It's not what you think," he told me. "It was a joke."

Oh, even better. Something for them to get a laugh out of.

"Why did you bring me here?" I cried, trying to wriggle free.

"Shhh."

He tried to soothe me, but I just shook my head. I just wanted to go home. If I wasn't seen, I couldn't be humiliated.

"Get off me!" I thrashed, feeling him stumble as we both fell to the ground.

I landed on him and heard him grunt, but when I tried to sit up and scurry away, he hauled me back to the ground and climbed on top of me. His body nestled between my legs, and he squeezed my wrists, pinning them above my head.

"Let me go," I said firmly. "Now."

But he just held himself up, staring down at me. His groin rested on mine, and I tried to ignore the nerves coming to life.

"Say it," he whispered.

"Say what?"

"That you only want me."

"I'd rather lick an ice cream cone of razor blades," I gritted out.

He smirked. "You let me touch you in the confessional booth today. You liked me touching you."

I slowed my breathing, evening out my expression. "Really? I barely remember."

He then shifted between my legs, rising to the challenge, and a small moan escaped me.

Jesus.

Leaning down, he tickled my lips with his. "Stay?" he asked, heat filling his eyes. "I'd like you to."

God, he was on top of me. I'd never felt someone's weight on me like this. Unless I counted wrestling with the guys growing up, and even then, it wasn't like this.

"What's going on?" someone asked. I darted my eyes up to see some girl come up to Michael, who stood behind Kai. How long had he been there?

She probably came from the party. We had to be close, then.

Kai twisted his head, talking to Michael. "Go on to the cemetery. I got this one."

Michael didn't say anything, but I saw his shoes walk over to our side and then a condom dropped to the ground right by my arm.

My chest caved. What?

Michael left, taking the girl with him, and Kai looked back at me. He released my arms, planting his hands on the ground instead.

"Pick it up," he ordered me. "Or run."

I picked it up and flung it away from us, somewhere behind him.

"*We* don't need it," I told him, calling his bluff. "You're just trying to scare me."

But then he moved his body, nudging his groin into me, and I felt the rock-hard ridge inside his jeans.

"Ah," I moaned and then clamped my mouth shut. What the hell?

"We *might* need it," he said, a cocky smirk on his face.

My clit throbbed, and I shifted under him, wanting more.

"Who are you?" he asked.

But I couldn't tell him. The confessional was an accident, and I didn't have any intention of running into him again. I didn't think I'd ever have to face him.

I stared up into his dark eyes, wanting to talk to him again like we did today. Wanting him to know me. But I wasn't allowed.

Instead, I uttered in a small voice, "I'm cold."

It was all I could think to say.

Kai rose to his feet and took my hands, pulling me up. But he didn't release me. Instead, he led me in the opposite direction from where we'd come.

Into the Bell Tower.

I looked around, still hearing the music in the distance, and I could make out shouts and laughter, too. We were close to the party. What was he doing?

I stumbled along anyway, though, not resisting. My insides were twisting and knotting in the most exciting way. This was what I wanted, right? A chance to be close to him?

The gray stone structure was about half as tall as a lighthouse, with a bell chamber at the top. I wasn't sure if the bell was still there, though. The clock had long since stopped working, and an archway welcomed us with a gated door.

I stepped inside, looking around and taking in my surroundings.

The walls were lined with a few windows, and a couple of stone benches were built into the room. There used to be some kind of house or meeting place attached to the tower, but it was long gone now.

Black vases hung from the walls with decaying roses the color of ash sitting inside. Who knew how old they were?

A little light streamed in, making the red, blue, and gold of the stained-glass windows dance off the walls, and wooden stairs wound around a wall and spiraled up, disappearing from my sight.

Kai released my hand and pulled out a book of matches, lighting the small stub of a candle sitting on the windowsill. The small room glowed a little warmer, and I suddenly became very aware of how quiet it was, the music nearly inaudible in here.

His presence—the anticipation—was a weight on my chest. God, he was beautiful.

His skin was a little darker than mine—warm, tanned, and glowing—and I bit the corner of my lip, gazing at his neck. I could see the ridge of the vein coming through the skin, and I wondered what it would feel like to touch it.

I'd seen his mother once. He had her lips and smile and lashes.

But Kai definitely took after his father, too. Angular jaw, lean body, straight nose, and while his hair was thick like his mom's, it was coal black like his dad's. He had also inherited his father's sharp gaze . . . so sharp and stern it intimidated me.

Kai turned, the candlelight flickering in his eyes, and I heard the wind howling in the trees through the open gate.

"How do you know me?" he asked, walking toward me.

"Everyone knows you."

"Do you go to our school?"

I shook my head. "I'm . . . homeschooled."

Which was, I guess, the best way to describe it. I'd only made it through the sixth grade, missing more school than I attended, when my brother moved me in with him and made me start doing all of his homework, while I stayed home all day. And that's how I learned algebra and Spanish and how Shakespeare used corruption, betrayal, and deception as themes to portray guilt, sin, and retribution. He attended the classes, absorbing just enough to pass tests, while I did the written work, absorbing just enough to not be completely ignorant. There were gaps, of course, but I'd done a really good job of disciplining myself to do the work and his assigned readings. I had always been less than everyone around me, and it made me want to be more. I'd try to get my diploma, at some point.

"I see you around, though," I explained. "My bro . . . my mom cooks for the Torrances."

I swallowed, my throat like a desert. That was a lie. Marina wasn't my mother, but it was the explanation we decided to give people, since my father didn't want anyone outside the house to know who I really was.

Neither did my brother.

I finally looked up, seeing Kai just watching me with probably a thousand more questions in his head that I hoped he wouldn't ask.

"I should go," I told him.

I moved to head around him for the door, but he blocked my escape, stepping in front of me again.

"No." He placed his hands on both sides of me, on the wall, locking me in. "The thing is, you heard all my shit today, and I like my privacy. How do I know you won't talk? How do I know you didn't Instagram yourself in that confessional, bragging that you were punking me?"

I shot my eyes up. "I wouldn't . . . I . . ." I rushed out, stammering. "I would never do something like that."

"Why should I believe that?"

Because it wouldn't have even occurred to me! I wasn't devious. I'd been elated when he started talking in that confessional.

"Because I . . ." I trailed off, searching my brain. "I don't even have Instagram."

He cocked his head, his eyes scolding me for such a stupid response.

"I don't even have a cell phone!" I blurted out. I didn't even have the capability to record his confession, dammit.

"You don't have a phone?" He didn't look like he believed me. "Everyone has a phone."

Apparently not.

But before I got a chance to retort, he reached out and put his hands on my hips, squatting down and trailing his hands down my thighs.

I sucked in a breath, jerking. His hands drifted around to my ass, sliding over my back pockets and his fingers digging just a little.

"Are you kidding me?" I complained. He was searching me?

But an electric current shot through me, and the room in front of me started to spin anyway. He was touching me.

Holding my eyes, his gaze hardened as his hands ran up my back and then over my stomach, searching for the hidden cell phone he apparently assumed I was lying about not having.

Then he stood up, leaning in close as one of his hands cruised slowly up the inside of my thigh, and a throb hit me between my legs. I sucked in a breath.

"Stop it," I gasped, knocking his hands away.

A cocky little grin crossed his face. "Your knees are shaking," he said. "If I'd known you were this innocent, I wouldn't have let Michael and myself tease you before."

I breathed shallow and licked my dry lips.

"Have you ever even been kissed?"

I kept my mouth shut, but I knew that was answer enough for him.

"Turn around," he instructed.

I looked at him skeptically.

He laughed under his breath and turned me around, leaning into me and hugging my back. I could feel him over almost every inch of me: my spine, my legs, and my arms. He dipped his head next to mine, his cheek on my ear, and he grazed my fingers with his.

"Do you feel that?" he whispered.

"What?"

His long arms blanketed mine, my hands resting inside his. "You fit me like a shirt. It's a perfect mold."

I smiled to myself, feeling a blush heat my face. "For now," I said. "I'm done growing, but you're probably not."

Men typically kept growing a little longer than women.

His breath hit my ear. "Then we're on borrowed time, aren't we?"

I closed my eyes, goose bumps spreading down my arms as he ran his lips over my lobe.

Oh, God. It suddenly felt like my body was a thousand matchsticks, every one sparking to life, one after the other.

Taking my hands, he placed them on my thighs and scaled them up my body.

"Is this okay?" he asked.

My body trembled, and I nodded. *Yes.*

"You'll have to go to confession again tomorrow," I joked.

"Why?"

"Kidnapping."

His chuckle hit my neck as he ran his lips over my skin there. "Hate to break it to you, kid, but I got that place rigged. No penance for me. Unless you want to go with me," he added. "Purge some of your own sins, maybe?"

"Not Catholic, remember? I wouldn't even know what to do in there."

"Well," he began, sounding suddenly mischievous.

He took my hand and led me to the wall with one of the benches. He sat down and then grabbed me, pulling me in. I yelped in surprise as I fell into his lap.

"First, you go in and sit down," he instructed, squeezing my hips. "Are you sitting?"

I turned my head to look at him, and he pinched his eyebrows together, looking serious like a teacher.

I rolled my eyes. "I am now."

"Then you make the sign of the cross." He took my right hand in his and touched my fingertips to my forehead. "And you say, 'Bless me, Father, for I have sinned.'"

I let him guide me, my own touch to my chest sending tingles through me as he showed me how to make the sign of the cross.

Our lips hovered an inch from each other, and I tried to talk, but only a whisper came out. "Bless me, Father, for I have sinned."

"'This is my first confession,'" he said, telling me what to say next.

I inched in, our lips nearly meeting as I stared at his mouth. "This is my first time."

He sucked in a breath. His eyes dropped to my mouth, and he placed my hands on my thighs, threading his long fingers through mine.

"Jesus," he growled under his breath.

A smile pulled at my lips.

"Then he'll say, 'And what would you like to confess?'" And then he cleared his throat, his stern priest voice sending a flutter through my stomach. "What would you like to confess?"

I folded my lips between my teeth. "I don't know if I can. I . . ." I sucked in a deep breath. "I'm nervous."

"Relax, my child. You're in God's hands now."

I laughed softly. I liked this foreplay. I knew I shouldn't care, but I didn't want to say something stupid to ruin the game. I didn't want to bore him. Every girl eventually lost my brother's interest. I hated the thought that Kai would get tired of me and just want to leave.

"A boy got ahold of me, Father," I told him, looking into his eyes.

"Did he?"

I nodded. "Inside the dark Bell Tower, by the cemetery. I know I shouldn't have let him, but he grabbed me and . . ."

"Did he steal you away from everyone else?" Kai taunted. "Get you alone?"

"Yes, Father."

His fingers dug into the tops of my thighs and his eyes thinned, turning heated on me. "What did you let him do to you?" he accused. "Hmm? What did you let happen?"

"He kissed me on the neck first," I confessed.

And Kai threaded his hand into my hair, taking the hint as he gently pulled my head back and out, his lips on my neck, slowly nibbling.

I released a breath, closing my eyes. "I liked it when he did that."

"You know those boys . . ." he scolded, kissing and biting me up and down. "They like the sweets too much. You have to be stronger and resist."

"And if I like the sweets, too?" I moaned, feeling my skin tingle.

"Was he the first man to touch you?" Father Kai asked.

"Yeah."

He groaned.

I bit my lip, scared, but I pushed further.

"And then he put his hand under my shirt," I said, my chest caving at my own words. "I was so scared, but I knew he'd feel good. I craved it so bad."

I wanted more. I wanted him to touch me places my brother would want to kill him over.

He pulled his head up and looked at me. His teeth were slightly bared, and I noticed a bulge underneath me.

Reaching around me, he slowly lifted my brother's old sweatshirt over my head, dropping it to the ground, and then he slipped his hand under my T-shirt, keeping his eyes on mine the whole time.

"I'll bet you wanted it," he said, his fingers grazing my stomach.

"I'll bet you even rubbed yourself on him to show him how much you liked what he was doing."

I groaned, noticing the wetness between my legs. "Yeah."

I leaned my head back on his shoulder and rolled my hips, grinding my ass on him just a little. The hard ridge underneath felt so good, the ache of the emptiness inside me grew.

I reached back with my hand and took his face, wondering if he was going to kiss me. He still hadn't kissed me on the mouth.

But instead of that, I felt his hand trail higher under my shirt, and I snapped my eyes open wide, remembering. Oh, God, the wrap. The ACE bandage I wrapped around my chest to flatten myself.

Shit! I shot up, pulling my shirt down and covering myself. He hadn't seen, had he? Tears sprang to my eyes, embarrassment heating my skin.

Other women wore bras. He'd be confused and definitely turned off if he saw what I wore. He'd think I was weird.

"It's okay," he said, his hands suddenly gone. "It's okay. You don't have to do anything you don't want to. This place, these games, they're not for you anyway. I shouldn't have brought you here."

Yes, I know. It was a laugh for him and a fantasy for me. What was I thinking? I couldn't do this with him anyway. It could never happen.

He took my chin and turned my face toward him. "I didn't mean to push you, okay? I'm an asshole," he said. "I don't want to seduce you in here. You're different."

"Different how?"

"I talk to you," he replied. "And I like talking to you. That's rare for me."

My shoulders relaxed just a little, and he nuzzled my ear again, making me tremble.

"And I want it to be special," he continued. "I want to take you to movies and hang out and go for drives and sit you on my lap like this whenever I want. And when we're ready, we'll take a long drive down to the inlet and to my family's boathouse, and I'll go slow with you." His whisper caressed my ear, sending chills down my body. "Taking my time where no one can interrupt us. Taking all night."

God, I wanted that. I wanted to believe it could ever happen.

But—I looked down at my brother's old shoes and my chewed fingernails—I was deluding myself. Trying to escape my life and dreaming that I could ever look like I belonged at his side.

"Well, well, I'm shocked," a deep voice spoke up somewhere behind us. "Saint Kai, about to get his dick wet this early in the night, huh?"

My eyes went wide, and we both stilled.

No.

A dark laugh I knew all too well followed, and I hurriedly fixed my shirt, knocking Kai's hands away.

No, no, no . . .

"I knew you'd come around," Damon said, his voice getting closer. "Who do you have there?"

I shrunk in on myself, trying to hide in front of Kai.

"Get out," Kai ordered over his shoulder. "This one's off-limits."

I closed my eyes, praying silently and willing myself to be invisible. *Please, go away. Please.*

Kai must've felt me shaking, because he squeezed my arms, giving me reassurance.

But then I felt *him*.

He was there.

The heat of his glare fell on the side of my face, and I slowly opened my eyes and cast a glance out of the corner, seeing the black shoes on the ground to my right. Looking up, I saw Damon at Kai's side, his stare meeting mine.

A wave of nausea hit me.

He looked calm, but I knew better. His slightly open mouth closed, and his jaw flexed. It was a subtle gesture, but I knew the signs.

My brother was never calm. If he wasn't having it out with me now, he would eventually, and I wouldn't see it coming.

He let out a scoff, continuing the charade of not recognizing me. "Like I would bother," he bit out at Kai. "She's a fucking mess. Are you kidding me?"

His eyes fell down on me in a show. He wasn't taking in my appearance. He knew what I wore every day. They were his old clothes, after all.

He was keeping up pretenses. Outside of the house, I wasn't supposed to know him. I was a ghost. He didn't want me to have friends, and he didn't want his friends to notice me. If anyone knew I was his sister, they'd question why I didn't go to school with him, dress as nicely as him, or go to parties with him. And if anyone knew Gabriel Torrance was my father, they'd question why I wasn't treated like a daughter. Too much of a story for people who didn't need to know.

"There's beautiful girls out there, man, and you choose the one who looks like a boy?" He pulled out a cigarette and packed the tip on the top of his hand. "Who is she, anyway?"

"None of your business," Kai snapped, "and don't be a prick."

"Relax." He popped the cigarette in his mouth, lighting it as he spoke. "I wouldn't touch the dirty little rat if you paid me. Clean yourself up, honey." He took the cigarette out of his mouth and blew out a stream of smoke. "Women are good for one thing, and you're failing at even that."

I shrank, wanting to disappear.

But Kai jerked in front of me, his body going rigid as he yelled. "Knock it off."

"Oh, fuck you. I'm leaving anyway."

I heard Damon's footsteps retreat across the dirt floor, and I didn't look, but I guessed he'd left the tower.

I swallowed the lump in my throat. It was one thing for my brother to catch me somewhere I wasn't supposed to be, but finding me here with Kai? There would be no mistake in Damon's head about what he'd walked in on just now.

I stood up, combing my hands through my hair and righting my clothes.

"Hey, fuck him," Kai told me, trying to ease what had just happened. "He's an asshole."

"He's your friend."

"And he is for a reason." He approached me. "He's just got a lot of ugly inside of him, and he takes it out on people. Just ignore him."

I swiped my sweatshirt off the floor. "I have to go."

I had to get out of here. I hated it when he was mad at me. I'd go home and stay in my room, and when Damon got there later or in the morning, he'd find me sleeping right where I was supposed to be. Waiting for him.

"Hey." Kai took my arm.

But I jerked away from him.

"Don't leave."

I didn't want to, but I had to. I pushed away the longing still raging through my body and brushed past him, bolting from the room.

"Hey!" Kai shouted after me.

But I just ran, hurriedly pulling the sweatshirt over my head. The tears pooled as I raced back into the woods, diving into the dark shadows of the trees.

"I don't even know your name!" I heard his shout behind me.

The muscles in my legs felt like they were on fire as I dashed toward the parking lot and the road we came in on.

But then a hand grabbed my sweatshirt and yanked me back,

the scent of my brother's cigarettes flooding me as my body slammed into his.

I sucked in a breath and watched as Damon towered over me, his carefully constructed calm now gone.

"Oh, you're off-limits, all right," he growled Kai's words back to me. "I should rip off every single piece of clothing on your body right now. Everything I've given you. I told you all women were selfish, lying cunts. He doesn't get to have you, and you don't get to have him." He bore down on me, the liquor on his breath wafting through my nostrils.

"Damon, please?" I begged softly, laying one hand on his chest. "I didn't—"

"Don't touch me." He slapped my hand away. "I told you not to get dirty."

"I'm not," I assured him, shaking my head.

But he just looked down on me, fury in his eyes and pain he tried to conceal in his voice.

He grabbed my jaw, and I whimpered as he pressed my back to a tree. "Why did you do this?" he gritted out. "I told you to never let a man touch you."

"I didn't mean to let it happen," I breathed out. "But he didn't touch me anywhere, I promise."

"Oh, yes, he did." His eyes narrowed on me. "And you liked it. All you sluts like it. You're going to let him take you away from me. You're going to screw me over, and if you do, I will kill you. Do you hear me? I will fucking kill you."

My stomach rolled as I looked up at his dark eyes staring at me like I was dirt. Like I was his mother.

I'd lost his respect. He thought I was nothing. He hated me. The last time I did something he didn't like I was thirteen, and he wouldn't look at me for a week. I'd trod very carefully since then.

Until now, that is.

"Please. Damon." I'd never seen him this angry. "I love you. You're all I have. Please. I made a mistake."

I wanted so many other things, but not if it meant losing him. I couldn't lose him.

I pushed his hand away and dived in, wrapping my arms around him and burying my head in his chest. I hung on tight with every muscle I could muster.

Forgive me.

"I've always been good," I pleaded. "I won't do anything wrong again. I promise." I squeezed him tighter. "I'm yours. I love you."

He reached up and gripped my arms, like he was ready to push me off, but then he stilled, and I kept my eyes shut, hoping. *Please, love me again.*

No one else in the world loved me except him. He protected me, took me away from my mother, kept my father away from me, and if anyone ever tried to hurt me, he hurt them worse.

I still felt unsafe sometimes, but at least I never felt alone anymore.

Damon's breathing calmed, his chest moving up and down, slower and slower. His fingers around my arms loosened.

"You can't take him away from me," he said in a low voice. "And he can't take *you* away from me, either. You understand?"

I nodded quickly, an ounce of relief starting to settle in. "I know. I'll be good."

Raising my head, I looked up at him, the tears drying on my face as I kept my arms around him.

"I don't want him. I just got bored," I said. "When you're not home, I don't want to be there."

When he wasn't home, I stuck to our room as much as possible, so I didn't run into our father. But the older I'd gotten, the more restless I'd become.

His face softened, and I saw a small smile appear. "I know." He caressed my hair. "Someday we'll have our own house, and you can be free. I'll surround you with a hundred fucking acres, and you can go wild. No one will ever look at you wrong or treat you badly."

I forced a small smile at that dream of ours. The one where he'd go to college and come back for me and we'd disappear to some house, far away, in the middle of a forest or at the edge of the world, and I wouldn't have to hide from anyone.

But I knew it wasn't real. It never would be.

"What's wrong?"

I dropped my eyes. "Someone's going to take *you* away from me, though, aren't they?" I asked. "Eventually, anyway. She won't want me in your house."

Forgetting the fact that the older I got the more I wanted things that Damon didn't want me to have, *he* was growing up, too. We weren't thirteen and twelve anymore. We were eighteen and seventeen, and Marina was right. We couldn't stop time. Wouldn't he eventually want a family? I couldn't tag along and crash the party forever.

But he just laughed at me. "You're such a dumb shit." He pinched my chin, nudging my head and forcing me to meet his eyes. "What'd I tell you? There's pawns and rooks and knights and bishops, but only one queen." He smiled playfully. "We're a pair, Nik. Everyone else comes and goes, but you never escape blood. Blood is forever."

The corner of my mouth lifted in a smile. And I let out a breath, feeling relief that he had forgiven me.

He dug his phone out of his jeans and started dialing. Probably for David, Lev, or Ilia to come and pick me up.

"I can walk home," I explained, trying to stop him. "It's okay."

But he just raised the phone to his ear, staring at the air over my head as I heard the other line ring.

They answered after the first ring. "Damon."

I recognized David's voice.

"You'll never guess who I wrangled five miles from the house, in the dark, without protection. You're fucking fired."

"Damon, I can't watch her every second!" David barked. "You want me to tie her up?"

"Fuck you." My brother's cool voice was like the slow slice of a knife. "You and the guys get down here to the Bell Tower and get her now."

I couldn't help but drop my shoulders a bit. I knew I had to go home. I just still didn't want to.

"And bring her to the cemetery," Damon finished.

I popped my head up, my stomach somersaulting. Really?

Damon gave me a small smirk as he spoke. "She can come to the bonfire, but keep her quiet and keep guys away from her."

"All right. We'll be there in fifteen."

"Five," my brother ordered and hung up.

I bit my bottom lip, but he still saw my smile trying to escape.

He tipped up my chin again, warning me with his glare. "They're going to surround you like a fucking wall, you understand? Don't piss me off, and don't let Kai see you."

I nodded, trying hard not to look too excited.

"That way you get to see what he doesn't want you to see." His smirk disappeared. "Who he *really* is."

CHAPTER 7

BANKS

Present

I'm not part of the deal." I stared at Gabriel sitting on the other side of his desk. "You can send Lev or David or anyone else to work for him."

"Yes . . ." My father laughed under his breath, puffs of his cigar smoke escaping before he blew the rest out. "Because that's exactly what he wants you for, isn't it? To clean toilets in his dojo and to chauffeur his ass around."

I tipped my chin up at his sarcasm. "He doesn't want me for . . ." I breathed out, hesitating. "For *that*. And if he does, he's not getting it."

Kai might very well want me to wait on him hand and foot, but my father had other ideas. In his head, if Kai was demanding me in particular, then he wanted me for nothing less than a little fun.

And he wasn't fucking getting it.

Gabriel didn't know that I'd met Kai before. Gabriel didn't know that I'd already played Kai's version of fun. I refused to be his tool. Or his toy.

"You'll do what you have to do," he told me.

"I won't—"

"You'll do exactly as you're told!"

Every muscle tensed, and I locked my jaws together, shutting up. A sudden light sweat covered my forehead where my hat sat.

Damon.

This was all for Damon. He was the only reason I stayed in this house. Remember the end game. *Find him, get him home, and keep Kai and the rest of those pricks away from him.*

My father's dead eyes stared off, barely paying me any mind now. Kai was right about one thing. I was only as valuable as what I was good for to Gabriel Torrance. I knew it the moment I'd left Kai's office tonight at the dojo. I knew it when I stepped into this office an hour later. I always knew my value here.

A woman wasn't good for much in this house, so I did everything I could to make my father and brother forget that I was one.

Gabriel rose from his seat and slowly walked around his desk, the night wind howling outside his office windows. Coming to stand in front of me, he leaned back on his desk, slightly more relaxed as he offered me a patronizing look. "You've been useful," he said, blowing out smoke and turning to set the cigar down in the ashtray. "You're smart, and it took a long time for you to earn my trust, but you did. I know I can count on you. Your entire world is Damon."

Even though it was true, it wasn't flattering to hear. My brother was my world. But while I loved him more than I loved anything else in my entire life, I hated the way my father said it.

Like I was Damon's pet dog.

"But now," Gabriel continued, "you have an opportunity to prove yourself invaluable. Irreplaceable."

Important.

Despite my hatred of my father, my loathing of Kai Mori, Michael Crist, Will Grayson, and Erika Fane, I couldn't help the shred of pride that seeped in.

I *was* irreplaceable. If my father didn't see that yet, he would. *Even if it's the last thing he ever sees.*

Gabriel inhaled a deep breath and stood up, his expression turning somewhat pleasant.

"This is actually perfect," he said as he walked back around his desk, sounding almost chipper. "You'll be able to keep an eye on him. You'll get his house ready for Vanessa when she arrives. You'll spend time at the dojo, working for him, training, whatever . . . You'll be where he is and let me know if there's anything I should worry about. With him or the rest of those little cunts." He picked up his cigar and took a few puffs. "And if your brother comes out of hiding and provokes them again, you'll protect him. Right?"

I averted my gaze. Of course I would. I always did. But I didn't want to do this. I couldn't be around Kai every day.

Anger boiled under my skin.

I could argue. I could even leave. I didn't love my father, and I was probably better off for it.

But I could best protect Damon with a seat at the table, and if I left I had nothing, goddammit. He needed me. Whether or not my father ever admitted it, he knew that.

When Damon got arrested in college and was sent to prison, I was on top of the situation before Gabriel. I bought all the muscle I could on the inside to make sure no one touched my brother, and when he got out last year, I cleaned up all of his messes. And whenever our father tried to rein him in and he couldn't be controlled, I did what I always did. I exhausted my older brother and broke him until he collapsed and all the anger was gone. For a while anyway. It always came back.

Damon, Gabriel's only son and sole heir, was only at his best when he had me taking care of him. Only when my brother had his keeper.

Gabriel stood there, looking at me with a rare interest all of a sudden. "How many men have you been with?" he asked.

I remained silent and steady, but my patience was getting harder to muster. How many men have I been with . . . Jesus.

My father came back around the desk to me, crowding my space and forcing me to look at him. I raised my stare, not bothering to hide the distaste in it.

"Do you know how to fuck?" he demanded plainly, getting to the point. "Do you know how to please him?"

Him.

Kai.

My insides shrank, and I jerked out of his grasp, looking away again.

But he didn't relent. He slowly pulled my hat off, letting it fall to the ground, and began unbuttoning my jacket. A jolt of fear hit me, but I didn't fight, and I didn't resist. I watched him through the long, dark strands now hanging over my face.

My father had never touched me, but I knew the reason most likely had nothing to do with the fact that I was his daughter and more to do with the fact that Damon didn't want *anyone* touching me.

He pulled the jacket down my arms, and I sucked in a quick breath as he pushed my hair out of my eyes, the smell of diesel in the strands from working on one of the trucks earlier today drifting into my nose.

His fingers ran down my skin, and he sat back, studying me, tipping up my chin to take in my face like he hadn't seen me nearly every day for the last eleven years.

He circled me, his hand drifting around my waist, and I ground my teeth as he lifted Damon's old T-shirt to look at my stomach. He let it fall back down and his eyes came to rest on my chest, nodding in approval.

"You're not still a virgin, are you?" he asked, probably suspicious when I didn't answer. "I mean, Damon took care of that a long time ago, right?"

Bile rose, swelling my throat, and I pushed his hands away. "You're disgusting," I gritted out, my eyes burning with tears.

How could he be so vile?

But he just laughed me off and walked back around his desk. "That boy would fuck a brick if it was wet enough. Don't think we all didn't know what was going on up in that tower."

I could feel the tears springing up, but I just snarled and snatched my jacket and hat off the ground and charged from the room.

My stomach churned with the prospect of what he expected from me. I could shoot, I could fight, I could convince every man in town to spend a thousand dollars on a twenty-dollar whore if I wanted to . . . But I would not be turned over from one man to another like I was chattel to be gifted at will. I was more. I was invaluable. This was my home.

I didn't want to be around Kai Mori or his friends.

Swinging around the corner, I bolted up the stairs, hearing David's voice coming from below. "Banks, I need to talk to you."

"Later."

I ran up to the second level, skipping stairs, and dug in my heels as I turned a corner and headed for the dark wooden door to my right. Taking my key out of my pocket, I unlocked the dead bolt and opened it.

I walked in, the soft glow of the wall sconces lighting another set of stairs as I closed the door and turned the lock again. Jogging up the second flight, I came right into a circular-shaped bedroom, the only room on the third floor.

Walking across the shiny hardwood floors, I unlocked the window and softly pushed open both panes of glass. The unusually warm October evening was made just a little crisper by the sudden winds, and I closed my eyes, inhaling the smell of earth and burning leaves carried on the breeze.

My skin started to buzz, and I already felt better. This room was another world. Our world. Damon's and mine.

Leaving the window open, I walked across the room and opened the laptop, clicking on a playlist. "Like a Nightmare" began playing, and then I leaned over the bed, picking up a pillow.

Raising it to my nose, I inhaled, the faintest hint of fabric softener making my nostrils tingle. I knew I wouldn't smell my brother's scent on it, but I was disappointed anyway. I'd gone without him long enough. I was tired of being alone.

The bedding was new—I'd replaced it several months ago, and I cleaned the room regularly, just to make sure it was spotless if he ever showed up. But even though he hadn't slept here in over a year, I still hoped every time I stepped foot in here that I would find some evidence he'd been home.

I placed the pillow back in its spot, the blacks, whites, and grays of the bedding crisp and perfect as I pulled the corners of the pillow, taking out the wrinkles.

Everything had to be perfect.

Gazing around the room, I took in the pristine floors, the dark walls and gold sconces, the black-and-white photos he'd hung up in high school . . . Women and legs and glowing skin, not distasteful, really, but sex nonetheless.

I didn't like looking at them.

And then, raising my eyes, I looked toward another small set of stairs in the corner of the room. Shrouded in shadow, the flight led to the "tower," as we called it, a small alcove with an even smaller landing at the top. It was surrounded by windows, almost like a lighthouse up there, where you could see over the trees outside for miles. That was my space. When I lived here.

It still housed my mattress, a lamp, and a few clothes, just in case I ever needed it again. Not that I ever used it much anyway, even when I lived here. Damon kept me close.

I walked toward the window again and planted myself against the wall next to the window, sliding down it until I rested on the floor. Taking my hair, I wound it around and around like a rope and twisted it up on top of my head before pulling out my hat and covering my hair again.

I let my shoulders finally fall, and I closed my eyes, safe in the knowledge that no one could see me right now.

Not that I was seen much, anyway.

But I did like to watch other people. Kind of like Kai did.

A long time ago, I watched him from a distance, part of me wanting him so much. I thought he was good.

Loyal. Beautiful.

But he could be scarier than Damon.

And my brother, Damon Torrance, had been a nightmare since the first time I met him. An exquisite nightmare.

*P*ull up your sock," my mom orders as she slams the passenger-side door. I bend over and pull up my dingy knee-high, both of us standing next to our car parked outside a big black gate. It's open, and cars have been streaming in steadily. Mom said there was a party going on today. It was a good time to see him.

"Remember what I told you." She pulls me up, buttoning the top button of my cardigan and straightening my blouse underneath. I look away, impatient. I'm twelve, and she has me dressed like a five-year-old.

"If he starts being mean," she continues, her voice shaking as much as her hands, "you need to help me, okay? Tell him we need money. If we don't get help, Nik, you're going to have to leave the apartment, your bedroom, and all your stuff. You'll be sleeping in strangers' houses. And they could take you away from me." She grasps my shoulders, breathing hard. "You want to go home tonight, right?"

I nod.

"Then smile pretty," Jake, her boyfriend, yells out at me from the driver's seat through the open window.

Yeah, smile pretty. Be nice to someone who's never been nice to me. Who's never wanted to meet me. My stomach keeps churning, and I can't fist my fingers. I feel weak.

"Hurry up, Luce," *he says to my mom.*

I know why he wants us to hurry up and what he wants money for. Both of them. Of course, if we're lucky enough to get anything, I'll get fed and maybe some used clothes and shoes. My socks are so old they don't fit right, and I've been washing my hair with bar soap for a month now.

But they'll just party with the rest. Every time we have any money, it's gone before we've had a chance to exhale.

My mother takes my hand, and I follow her through the gates and down the long driveway. As I look around, my heart instantly aches. It's so beautiful here. Acres of green on both sides of the black drive, trees and bushes and the smell of flowers . . . God, what would it be like to just go out there and run? To do cartwheels and climb the red oaks and have picnics in the rain?

Looking ahead, I spot the house, the white stone stunning against the blue sky. Cars circle the driveway, and around the house lie splashes of red, which I guess must be rosebushes, though I'm not yet close enough to see.

But the closer we get, the more unnerved I become. I want to dig in my heels and stop. I want to turn around and say, "I'll rip off food from the Shop-and-Go down the street from our apartment if I have to." *I've done it before. We needed milk and cereal, and my mom asked me to get it. If I get caught shoplifting, as a minor I won't get in as much trouble as she would.*

We head up to the house, and she stops me just before we get to the door. She squats down, her long coat the only nice thing she has to cover up her cheap clothes.

She holds my shoulders and looks up at me, her eyes sad. "I'm sorry," *she says.* "These are things kids shouldn't have to go through. I know that." *She looks around, tearing up and looking desperate.* "I wish you *knew how much I want you to have everything. You deserve everything, you know that, right?"*

I just stare at her, my eyes starting to water. My mom is a mess, she doesn't always put me first, and I hate the positions I'm put in sometimes, but . . . I know she loves me. Not that it always feels like enough, but I know she tries.

"I wish I could take you away and buy us a house like this," she says wistfully, "and all you would ever do is smile." She stands up, brushing the wrinkles out of her coat. "It kills me that his little shit of a son gets everything he wants and you get nothing."

Damon. My father's son. The only child he claimed.

She's only mentioned him a few times, not that she's ever met him. He had just been born when my mom got pregnant with me, but we've heard enough over time. He's supposed to be kind of trouble.

She takes my hand again and leads me to the front door, where a servant is holding it open, greeting guests as they enter.

A woman in a sparkly dress looks down at me, narrowing her eyes and taking in my clothes. I quickly look away.

People enter the house, and we follow, but the man at the door puts his hand on my mother's shoulder. "Excuse me. Who are you?"

"I need to see Gabriel."

The man, who's wearing a white waistcoat, moves in front of her, blocking her way.

I peek around him, seeing all the fancy people in suits and dresses walking through a door to the back of the house.

"Mr. Torrance is entertaining guests right now," he tells her.

My mother puts her arm around me, replying flatly, "This is his kid, and if I don't see him now, I'm going to run through your quaint little village here in Thunder Bay and shout it to the world."

The man purses his lips, and I notice a few people around us turn to look. I cringe on the inside. Would Gabriel even care if she did that?

The servant nods to the man standing next to the wall, and he walks over. My heart races as I watch him pat my mother down.

But then the burly guard finishes with her and steps over to me, running his hands down my arms. I jerk, and my mother pulls me away.

"Keep your hands off her," she demands.

I shake and move into her, hiding as much as possible.

"Follow me," the servant who opened the door says. He leads my mother and me through the house, and I look around, noticing a library, a den, and some kind of sitting room. Everything is dark, and nearly everything is made of wood: the stairs, the furniture, some of the walls . . . We pass by the staircase, and my eye catches a figure standing at the top. I look up.

A boy stands there, leaning on the wall, with his arms crossed over his chest. He stares at us, his eyes following me as I pass by. He has dark hair like mine, but his eyes are darker, narrow and calm. But something in his look makes me shrink. Is that him?

"Wait here," the man says.

My mother and I stop outside a door, while the older man rounds a corner.

My mom takes my hand and holds it with both hands. She did the same thing a couple years ago when CPS came to our house and also on the rare occasion I had a pushy teacher who went the extra mile to convince her to come to parent-teacher conferences. She's nervous.

I hear hard footsteps hit the floor. My heart starts beating in my throat, and I stop breathing for a moment.

A shadow falls on the ground, and I look up, seeing a tall, well-dressed man charge around the corner.

Graying black hair, beautiful black suit and shirt, shiny shoes . . . I stare up at him wide-eyed, my breath caught in my throat at his strong scent, a mixture of cologne and tobacco.

He gets in my mom's face, his voice sounding so mean that my hands start to shake.

"You know what's more tragic than a poor junkie whore?" he bites out at her. "A dead poor junkie whore."

And then he looks down at me. "Sit," he orders. "Now."

I take a shallow breath—it's all I can force in—and drop to the bench, fidgeting with my hands. He pushes my mother through the door, and I see a desk and some books before he closes it.

Oh, God. What the hell? He's so mean. Why? I know my mom can be trouble, and she's embarrassing, even to me sometimes, but I haven't done anything.

I blink away the tears that spring up all of a sudden. I don't want to be here. These people are awful. My mom said my dad owns a media company and sits on the boards of others—whatever that means—but there's also other things he does. She worked for him, but she won't tell me what she did.

I just want to leave. I don't want anything to do with him, and I don't want to know anything more.

Movement catches my eye, and I look up to see the dark-eyed boy coming down the hallway. He looks relaxed, holding a green bottle by the neck and stopping at the entryway, leaning on the wall as he stares at me.

I lick my lips, feeling every hair on my arms stand up. I avert my eyes, embarrassed, but they keep coming back to him.

His black pants and leather shoes look like someone tried to dress him up, but his white shirt is partially untucked, and his sleeves are rolled up. His hair is combed, though, and I notice how thin his gaze is on me, as well as the striking arch of his dark eyebrows. I have the same arches, and my mom says they make the green of my eyes so piercing, but it does the same for his dark ones, too.

He takes a swig from the bottle—some kind of beer, I think, but he doesn't look much older than me.

I hear a muffled argument from behind the door and look over at him again. My father seemed to know who I am. Does this boy?

"Are you my brother?" I ask.

His lips lift in slight amusement, and he doesn't look the least bit shocked at my question.

Walking over to me, he stops, his legs hitting mine as he tips the bottle back, downing the rest of the drink. I watch the lump go up and down in his throat before he turns the bottle over, stabbing the neck into the soil of the potted plant on the table.

He leans down, one hand planted on the wall above my head and the other one caressing my face. I rear back, but I have nowhere to go.

The beer on his breath hits my nose as he gets closer, and I feel a cool sweat break out on my neck. Is he going to kiss me?

His mouth hovers inches from mine, and he looks into my eyes. "Do you like snakes?"

Snakes? What?

I shake my head.

A spark of something flashes in his eyes, and he suddenly stands up, taking my hand. "Come on."

He pulls me off the bench, and I stumble after him.

"No, wait," I say. "I think I'm supposed to wait for my mom. I don't want her to be mad."

But he just keeps going, dragging me up the stairs, and I don't fight. If I do, he might be mad, too. And if I make him mad, it could make my father madder.

He pulls me after him, his hold on my wrist making the skin burn a little as he rushes us around the banister at the top of the stairs. Heading toward the end of the hall, he opens a door and pulls me through. I'm suddenly in darkness with only a small glow above. My heart is beating so hard I feel nauseous. Where are we?

The boy pulls me, and I follow, but my foot catches on something, and I stumble. I grab the back of his shirt to keep myself from falling, and I realize I'm on stairs. He continues up, and I grab the wall, trying to steady myself as I scale the steep incline. There's a third floor to the house?

We come up to the top, and he opens another door, shoving me through. Chills spread down my skin, and I whimper under my breath, suddenly scared. What if my mom can't find me? What if my father makes her leave, even without me? Why am I up here?

Will he let me leave?

I pull my sleeves down over my hands, fidgeting again, and glance around quickly. The messy room has a large, unmade bed, posters all over the walls, and some heavy metal song about wanting to "go to hell" playing on speakers I can't see.

I inhale through my nose and catch the subtle odor of cigarettes.

As he heads over to his computer and turns down the music, I'm unable to stop the fear, but I also feel a sliver of admiration. Damon's only supposed to be thirteen, and he's drinking and smoking? He can do whatever he wants. Like an adult.

He turns around and crooks his finger at me, and despite how worried I am, I don't dare refuse.

He takes my hand and leads me over to a long wooden dresser, and I notice two fish tanks on top. One has sand with a large branch and a water pool, and in the other one there's mulch with leaves and more branches. In the left one, I see a red, black, and yellow striped snake.

My heart skips a beat. That's why he brought me up here.

"This is Volos," he says. "And this is Kore." He points out the white snake in the other tank, hidden inside a burrowed log. I look hesitantly, seeing the red splotches on its skin.

I glance at him out of the corner of my eye, worried that he's going to remove them from their cages.

"Do they . . . bite?" I ask.

He looks down at me. "All animals bite when they're provoked."

I lean down, looking through the glass. Hopefully, if I show interest, he won't want to try to scare me by taking them out.

Their tanks are large, lots of room to move, and they look clean. The snakes lie still.

"Wouldn't they like to be together?"

"They're not puppies," he retorts. "They're wild animals. They don't play well with others, and they don't like company. They don't make friends."

He removes the top of the cage on the left, and I immediately take a step back. No.

"If one of them gets aggravated or stressed," he says, reaching in and picking up the red, black, and yellow one, "it'll eat the other one."

Damon pulls out both hands, the snake coiled through his fingers, and he turns to me, the snake inches from my body.

I scurry back, and he walks toward me, laughing. "How could you think I'm your brother? Look how scared you are."

He shoves the snake in my face, and I scream, my back hitting the wall.

"No, I don't like—"

"Shut your mouth," he growls, grabbing for my hands with his free one.

I struggle, trying to get away from him, but his body pins me to the wall as he holds the snake with one hand and gets my wrists in a lock with the other. Pushing them over my head, he pins my hands to the wall, and I start tearing up, my chest filling with dread.

"No, no, please . . ."

"Shut up."

I twist my head back and forth, squeezing my eyes shut as he holds me there.

"Do you know who I am?" he asks.

My breathing shakes, and I don't want to open my eyes. Then, something touches my cheek, and I jerk.

"Stay still or he'll bite."

I pant, instantly stilling every muscle.

"Please," I whisper, begging.

But I don't move. The touch comes back, and it's smooth, like water. Oh, God. Please.

"Look at me," he says.

My lungs empty, and I hesitate. But slowly, I peel my eyes open.

I see a red, black, and yellow blur in front of me, and I shake with a cry. He's holding it to my face. I feel its tongue flit over my skin, and I start breathing fast, my chest racing up and down faster than my heart.

"Shhh . . ." Damon says soothingly.

I force myself to raise my eyes to him, and all of a sudden . . . my breathing starts to slow. He's piercing me with his eyes—which I see now are more black than brown—and I'm locked in.

"Look at them out there," *he tells me, turning his head toward the window to my left.*

I follow his gaze, slowly turning my head away from the snake to see men in black skulking on the lawn, two valets in white waistcoats, and a man and woman exiting a shiny black car.

"When I come on the scene, they all fucking look away," *he whispers, staring outside.* "When I speak to them, their voices shake. They don't even let their wives, girlfriends, or daughters come around if they know I'm home."

I pinch my eyebrows together in confusion. Who's he talking about? The servants? Or the guests?

"I know everything, everyone does what I want, and everyone is afraid of me," *he continues, and then turns his eyes on me,* "and money doesn't buy that. Money and power don't go hand in hand. Power comes from having the guts to do what others won't."

He drags the snake's body over my mouth, and I gasp, jerking away again.

"You're nothing like me," *he snarls in a low voice.* "A dirty little nothing. A mistake."

He releases me and steps back, and I quickly wipe away the tears that spilled over my lids.

He turns around and sits down in a deep, cushioned chair, petting his snake. "Don't let your mom come back here again, you understand?" *he orders, pinning me with a look.* "Or I'll lock you in a closet with Volos."

I run for the door and grab the handle, but my hand shakes so hard I can't turn it. "It's not my fault," *I blurt out, turning my head toward him.* "That my mom had me. Why would you want to hurt me?"

"You're not special." *He raises Volos and looks at him, acting like I'm not even here.* "There are lots of people I want to hurt. And maybe I will someday . . . when I figure out the best way to get rid of a body."

He gives a half grin, acting like he's joking, but I'm not sure he is.

"I am special," I say. "My teacher says I'm the smartest in my class."

"Doesn't matter." *He shrugs.* "In five years, you'll be riding dicks in the back seat for twenty dollars just like your mom."

My stomach retches, and I nearly choke on a cough. What? How could he say something like that?

"Damon?" *A voice rings out.*

It's coming from the speaker system on the wall, next to the door.

"Damon, your mother wants you," *the woman's voice says, not waiting for him to answer.* "She's in her room."

I turn my head and look at him, pinching my eyebrows together when I notice blood trailing down his finger. The snake suddenly strikes him again, and I suck in a little breath. He's squeezing it too hard. Why's he doing that?

But he just stares ahead, his eyes heavy like he's lost in thought. Did he even hear the woman on the intercom?

"Damon?" *I say. That snake isn't dangerous, right? He wouldn't keep a venomous animal here.*

What's wrong with him?

He finally raises his eyes. "Get out."

Jesus. What a jerk. I whip open the door and take a step. But then I stop and spin around once more.

"A cemetery," *I say.* "That's how I'd get rid of a dead body."

He looks up at me again, his eyes narrow, and I lift my chin, shrugging. "I'd find a freshly covered grave. That way they wouldn't be able to tell it was re-dug. Put another body in there and cover it back up. That's what I'd do."

And I pulled the door closed, slamming it shut on his dark stare.

I exhaled, breathing hard but standing a little bit taller.

God, he was a mess. And horrible and mean, and why did he lose it like that when whoever-that-was came on the intercom? For a moment, he looked so alone.

He's got everything. Why's he so angry? I'm the one who should be angry. I'm the one who's alone. A father who doesn't care about me and a mother who hurts and makes me do things I don't want to do.

He doesn't know what it's like to suffer. To have something to be angry about.

Minutes later, as my mother and I are shown the door—empty-handed, of course—I walk down the driveway, glancing behind me one last time. Damon stands at his bedroom window, watching us leave.

The orange end of a cigarette burns brightly as he takes a drag, and I hold his stare for as long as I can, unable to look away.

Not until a tree passes through my line of sight, and I lose him.

I go home with the last image of him on that lonely third floor, the dark boy in that dark room, and I grow uneasy.

He's not okay.

I dream about him that night.

And eight days later, he shows up on my mother's doorstep. He hands her nine thousand four hundred sixty-two dollars, a Rolex, and some emerald earrings.

And he takes me home with him.

I rested my arms on my bent-up knees, running my lips over my interlocked fingers as the memory leaves me. I was twelve then, and here we were, eleven years later, and here was where I'd stayed ever since. My father let me stay because he rarely denied his son anything, but legal guardianship had been relinquished to Marina. Just so my father wouldn't have the tedious task of taking me to the doctor when I was sick or answering to the police if I ever got into trouble.

But I belonged to Damon Torrance.

I didn't know why he wanted me. Not at first. And I was scared bad things were going to happen to me.

And they did.

But he always took care of me. He scrounged up what he could get his hands on around the house to buy me from my mother, who, in a perfect world, would've loved to not do what she had done, but the money and the small prospect that I might actually have a better life here in Thunder Bay won out.

Mostly, it was the money, though. Which was spent as easily as it was earned, in no time at all. She tried to get me back several times over the years, maybe because she hated what she'd done, or maybe she just wanted to renegotiate for more cash, but Damon had what he wanted, and he wouldn't even hear her out. Not when he was fifteen or seventeen or nineteen.

Not that I wanted him to, anyway. It could be so strange how things happened. How the people you never suspect become your only lifeline, and you hold on to them as hard as you can, because you have no choice. There was nothing else to keep you from falling. Falling into loneliness or despair or fear. He reached for me, and I reached back.

Within days of arriving, moving into my cubby in the tower, and spending hours upon hours being his shadow, I was captivated by him. I idolized him and wanted to be like him.

We were our family.

I looked over at the tanks, seeing Volos and Kore II basking under their heat lamps. Standing up, I walked over and removed the lid, gingerly picking up Volos and helping him curl around my hand. He should be dead already. Kore passed years ago, but Volos was hanging on. Perhaps for his master.

He rested peacefully, not moving, and I ran my fingers down his scaly skin.

After the first meeting with Damon, I'd researched his snakes on the Internet at the library and found out Volos was a milk snake and Kore was a corn snake. Both completely harmless, neither venomous.

Although what Damon said was true.

Every animal bites when it's provoked.

CHAPTER 8

BANKS

Six Years Ago

You stay with us," David ordered, opening his car door. "You piss me off, and I'm dragging you home no matter what Damon says."

Yes, I know. You told me twice.

We all left the SUV, Ilia and me climbing out of the back doors while David and Lev jumped out the front. The locks clicked behind us, and we headed down the hill, into the secluded section of the cemetery where the glow of the party was like a firefly in a pitch-black sky.

After David and the guys had arrived at the Bell Tower earlier, they'd put me in the car, and we'd driven around the cemetery, through the main entrance.

Puddle of Mudd filled the air, and I looked down at the party, slowing my steps, in awe of the sight. A sea of flames lay before us, hundreds of candles sitting on top of headstones, surrounding graves, and lining the perimeters of various tombs. The beautiful green lawn—black in the dark—appeared to be alive with shadows of the flames dancing across the grass.

And farther off, in the distance, blazed the bonfire, so bold and bright I could hear it crackling from here.

Someone took my hand.

I looked to see Lev standing next to me, squeezing my limp fingers in his.

I tried to pull away. "I'm not a baby," I told him.

I needed my hand held? Really?

"Well, you're getting into trouble like one," he shot back. "Now, if you wanna get into trouble, I'm coming with you."

I couldn't help but laugh a little. He really was my favorite. Probably because he wasn't much older than me. Only a few years.

Circling around him, I jumped up on his back, forcing him to release me as I wrapped my arms and legs around him. "Please . . ." I replied in his ear. "If I want to get into trouble, I only have to follow *you*."

He grunted, readjusting his stance with my added weight. "Get off me, wench."

"You don't want to make me cry, do you?"

He scoffed, grabbing me under the knees and hefting me up for a more secure hold. "I wouldn't dream of it."

"Let's get some drinks," David called, leading us down to the party.

Ilia lit a cigarette. "Yeah, let's see what these rich little shits think is the 'hard stuff.'"

"Pull up your hood," Lev told me.

I followed directions, covering myself as we descended into the noise.

Anticipation was making me giddy, but I didn't know if I was excited to be "out" at a party, anxious that I would see Kai here, or nervous about Damon's last words to me. What did he mean? What could possibly shock me after everything I'd seen growing up? I didn't want anything to ruin Kai in my head.

Yep, definitely nervous.

Groups of people surrounded us, some of the girls turning their heads and following the guys with their eyes. Not a shocker. Not only did we look like we didn't belong here in our less-than-fifty-dollar T-shirts and no-name shoes, but the guys were clearly thugs.

David stood a little less than six feet with a stockier build, but it was the shaved head and full sleeves of tattoos that made him stand out.

Ilia was the model. Or could've been, probably. Blond hair, bedroom eyes, sharp nose, narrow jaw—all of which made him look like a Russian James Bond.

And Lev. Still very much a kid at twenty-one years old. Infectious smile, longer black hair, shaved on the sides, looking more like he belonged in a band than buried in Thunder Bay under mundane tasks a third grader could do.

But they were attractive, I guess. Just not to me. I grew up hearing how they talked when they didn't have to filter what they said and smelled their vomit after long nights of debauchery. Super hot.

Yeah, no. They were like Damon. Like brothers.

The guys stepped up to the bed of a truck with its tailgate down and a makeshift bar on display. I jumped down from Lev's back as David and Ilia grabbed cups and walked over to the keg, filling up. Lev took a bottle of Patrón and poured a shot in a red cup.

I thought about asking for one, but he'd just say no. It wasn't like I was a virgin to alcohol or anything. Damon liked having someone to run with when his friends weren't around, so I'd had beer, wine coolers, mixed drinks . . .

But never in public. They probably knew my brother wouldn't like it.

Looking behind Lev, I noticed David and Ilia still hanging around the keg, but another guy had come over and started up a conversation. They were smiling easily, looking relaxed. For once.

"Walk me around?" I asked Lev.

He raised his eyes, only briefly hesitating before he nodded. Shooting a look over his shoulder at David, he said, "We're going to make the rounds. Be back."

David's eyebrows dug in with a warning. "Don't. Lose. Her."

I caught Lev's eye roll as he nudged me along, getting us both out of there.

Veering right, around the truck, I took us in the direction of the bonfire, where I noticed a fight going on nearby. It looked playful, though, as people sat around watching. I cast glances left and right, looking for my brother.

And Kai.

But I didn't see them. I knew they pulled pranks on Devil's Night, so they could be off somewhere still. I kept my head down, though. At Damon's request. I was to observe. Not interact.

"You're gonna be eighteen next summer," Lev pointed out. "You getting out of here?"

I shook my head, watching some kid shoot marshmallows with a hockey stick, hitting a group of guys. "I wouldn't know where to go."

"But you can, you know?" he told me. "You can do whatever you want. You don't have to stay with him."

I turned my eyes on him, narrowing my gaze. It was unusually gutsy of him to say something like that. Since when did he care what I did?

And I didn't know how to respond.

It wasn't as if I hadn't thought about it. I knew things would change soon, but I didn't think they were changing for good. I'd tread water until Damon got out of college, and then . . . like he said, we'd be on our own. The idea of leaving forever—of living by myself, working by myself, making my own friends, coming and going without consequence—it seemed too far-fetched to consider. Even if I wanted to—which I didn't—Damon wouldn't allow it.

I averted my eyes, dropping my voice. "He's all I have."

"And who told you that?" he tossed back. "Him?"

I shot him a look. *Asshole.*

I changed the subject. "Toward the fight?" I gestured toward the group of guys in the distance, and he nodded.

We walked through more headstones, and I could hear the chanting from the fight ahead. I was used to seeing tussles, the guys around the house constantly starting shit with each other when they were bored. I'd even picked up a few moves.

"Who's she?" I heard a woman ask.

Stopping with Lev, I looked up to see a young redhead, her arms crossed over her chest and looking at him like she was two seconds away from spitting battery acid.

But without waiting for him to respond, she spun on her heel and started to walk away.

"Come here," he said, grabbing her arm.

But she yanked it away. "Go screw yourself."

"Until when?" he shot back, getting in her face. "The next time your boyfriend can't get you off, princess, and you come begging me for it?"

My eyes widened. He was screwing around with a Thunder Bay girl? What was he thinking?

To her, this was slumming and getting her kicks. He had to know that.

The girl jutted her chin over at me, scowling. "Who is she?"

"It doesn't matter."

She whipped around and stalked away from him, her red hair flying.

He looked at me. "Stay there. I mean it."

I watched as he spun around and caught up to her, forcing her behind a tomb, the edges of their bodies just visible.

"Where is he?" Lev asked, and I watched her thigh hike up around his waist at the same time I heard the sound of fabric tearing.

He? Her boyfriend?

Heavy breathing, fingers up her skirt, and . . . yeah, that's all I needed to see. I didn't know what was happening there, and I didn't care. I turned around, leaving them to it.

Pulling my hood lower and covering my eyes, I headed toward the fight, hearing cheers break out and seeing a body hit the ground. I peered through the gaps in the crowd, watching as a dark-haired fighter straddled the guy on the ground, and he raised his head just enough for me to see his face.

My heart leapt into my throat. *Kai*.

His hair was wet with sweat, and I noticed a trickle of blood spilling out of his nose. They continued the bout, rolling, punching, and wrestling, and I stopped behind a tall grave marker, hiding myself and peeking around the edge.

Kai rolled onto his back, holding the kid's neck above him, his arms flexed and every muscle defined as he kept the other guy at arm's length. Abs tight and jeans having settled low on his waist in the struggle, he made my cheeks go warm.

My brother's friend was hot. Why did I have to want him?

Damon might eventually resign himself to me falling in love someday, but he wouldn't tolerate it being with his best friend.

I smiled to myself, watching how he looked so happy right now. Not that I'd seen him a lot, but I didn't think I'd ever seen such an easy expression on his face before. Like he was finally alive.

I could watch him all night.

Until I smelled the all-too-familiar scent of my brother's cigarettes. Turning my head, I watched him blow out a stream of smoke, drop the butt to the ground, and stomp it out. He walked up and stood behind me, leaning his arm on the tombstone.

"So, this is what you wanted me to see?" I asked him, both of us watching Kai pummel his opponent. "It takes a lot to shock us, remember?"

"Not this." He shook his head. "Just wait."

I turned my gaze back, waiting for the big mystery about Kai

Mori to reveal itself. I couldn't imagine what Damon thought would be so shocking. I was hard to impress.

He let out a sigh at my side, looking around. "They left you alone again. I'm really going to kill someone one of these days."

I smiled, even though I felt sorry for the guys who were supposed to watch me. It was a shit job, and they were built for more.

"You're not that merciful." I glanced at him, my gaze immediately dropping to the corner of his mouth. "And you have mustard on your lip. And your breath stinks."

He opened his mouth and huffed right in my face, the stench of cigarettes and hot dogs—or whatever he'd just eaten—assaulting my nostrils.

I winced and turned away.

"Last girl didn't care," he taunted playfully. "Of course, I wasn't kissing her lips. Not the ones on her face anyway."

And he proceeded to hook an arm around my neck and lick my cheek like a sloppy dog.

"Gross!" I snarled, pushing him away and wiping off my face. "Jesus."

He just shook with laughter.

"Yeah, that's all I need, some girl's 'juice' all over me. Thanks."

He ruffled my hair through my hoodie, still laughing. Of course, his damn delight in life came from fucking with everyone around him, and I wasn't excluded from that. Ever.

I calmed down and turned back to the fight, watching as Kai took a hit across the left side of his jaw. He returned with a right hook and shoved his opponent in the chest. Wet strands of the kid's brown hair hung in his eyes, but he must've seen Kai coming for him, because he shot out his hands, waving for Kai to stop as he hunched over, trying to catch his breath.

Kai turned around, facing us, and I saw the smile on his face. My blood warmed.

Everyone cheered as the other guy tapped out, ending the fight with Kai as the winner. I kept my smile small, but I couldn't hold it in entirely. He was good. Better than good. He probably could've ended the fight a lot earlier.

I watched him grab his shirt off the ground and wipe his face and body with it as he breathed hard.

And then I watched as he tucked the end of it into his back pocket, while a blonde grabbed hold of his belt and pulled him to her. My smile fell.

She looked at him with a coy smile while his expression softened as he went to her, placing his hands on her waist and looking down at her.

What—

"That's Chloe," my brother said, his tone expressionless. "His girlfriend."

My chest started to rise and fall heavier and heavier, and a burn hit my eyes. He didn't have a girlfriend. I mean, he *did*. I'd seen him with girls, but . . .

No. He wouldn't have cornered me in the Bell Tower, he wouldn't have confessed all those things he'd done, if he had a girlfriend. Kai wasn't like that. He wasn't . . . Damon.

Kai's hands drifted around to her ass as she ran her lips along his jaw. She looked like she was whispering things, because he responded with a laugh or a grin.

I dropped my eyes, knowing I had no right to be mad. He wasn't mine.

I just thought he was different.

And yes, I was a little jealous.

"He's always in the mood after he's gotten excited," Damon explained. "A fight, a car race, watching . . ."

Or a chase, I finished in my head, remembering all that had happened today and how what my brother said made complete sense. Kai liked foreplay.

"And she's always there for him," Damon continued at my side, watching the couple in the distance. "Besides us, she's one of his best friends. State champion in tennis, captain of the math team, works on the school paper, and competes with the chess club . . . everything Kai's father wants for him. A girlfriend to be proud of." He placed a hand on my arm, gently squeezing it as I watched Kai and his girlfriend.

My brother went on. "Someone with opportunities, ambition, and drive. And speaking as someone who spotted them on a picnic table last summer when we all went camping up the coast, she looks like a good little fuck, too."

I closed my eyes at the picture in my head. Tears welled.

"Yeah, she likes it, all right. Especially from him," Damon told me.

I kept my head down, but I glanced up through the tears in my eyes, seeing her hands all over him, her body plastered to his.

A perfect fit.

"I told you," Damon said in a low voice in my ear. "Guys will say anything. And we don't even have to lie that well. Girls want to believe it." I felt his arm circle me as he leaned his cheek into my temple. "But your eyes will tell you the only truth you need. You know that. Just look at her."

I quickly wiped away a tear on the rim of my lid.

"That's who goes out with him—looks how a girlfriend's supposed to look in his lap," my brother continued. "That's who will be in a pretty little prom dress at his side next May. That's who meets his parents and has dinners with them. That's who texts him late at night and makes him hard. That's what his normal is, Nik. You have a place, and that's not it. It would never work."

My chin trembled, and I nodded. Her plaid miniskirt or my hand-me-down jeans? Her tight shirt or my oversize sweatshirt? Her money, education, and whole fucking future in front of her or my . . . nothing?

I shook my head. Fuck him. I didn't need all that stuff, and if that's what interested Kai—appearances—then I was better off. I'd be more than all of them.

Twisting around, I pulled out of my brother's grasp and took off, heading in the opposite direction. Damon wouldn't follow me. He knew I was out of danger now, no doubt pleased with himself that he'd gotten me away from Kai.

I could be angry with my brother for never protecting my feelings or understanding some of the things I wanted, but he always told me the truth and fed it to me straight. Dancing around my poor little heart wouldn't help me.

He was my best teacher.

I looked around for David, taking off my sweatshirt and tying it around my waist. I was suddenly so hot, an irritating nip biting at my skin.

Traipsing across the graveyard, I checked near the keg where I'd last seen him, and then headed up the hill, scanning small groups of people for the guys. A brick settled in my stomach, anger solidifying. I needed to get home. I didn't want to look at these people anymore. Or hear their music. Or run into drama. I wanted to get out of here before Kai saw me. He would think I followed him.

"How about this one?" someone spoke up.

I looked up, coming out of my head.

Four guys loitered around an open grave, two of them sitting on nearby headstones. I'd wandered outside of the party area, all of the noise and light behind me.

Shit. Was that grave empty?

"Looks like she scares easily," another one said, getting up from the stone and blowing out smoke. "Works for me."

What?

I started to back away and turn around, but then one of them stepped in front of me, making me jump.

"Want to play a game?" he asked, mischief in his brown eyes.

"No."

"It's called Seven Minutes in Heaven." He took my hand, handing me a penny. "Toss this into the air. Whichever one of us catches it gets to take you there."

"There"? Heaven?

"No, thanks." I turned in a circle, looking for anyone. Lev's black Mohawk, David's shaved head, Damon's cigarette smoke billowing in the air . . .

"Toss it," another guy demanded.

"Bite me!" I threw the fucking penny at him, and all of a sudden, every single one of them dived for the coin.

Shit! They scrambled, falling over each other and laughing, but before I thought to spin around and get my ass out of there, the brown-eyed one with the black leather jacket stood upright, raising his fist triumphantly, no doubt with the penny inside of it.

"Get her!" he shouted.

"What?" I blurted out.

They all rushed right for me, and I reared back as they grabbed my arms, the skin of my wrists burning as they hauled me forward.

"No, no!"

But they didn't listen. They swung me over the hole, and I squirmed and struggled, but they quickly dropped me the shallow distance to the bottom of the black grave.

I landed, stumbling to stay on my feet, and slammed into the wall of the grave, my wrist suddenly aching. I sucked in breath after breath, instantly spinning in a circle to make sure the grave was empty.

Dirt all around, dirt under my shoes . . . I didn't know if this was a fresh grave dug for a service this weekend or an old grave just not dug deep enough to reach the casket underneath.

"Oh, God." I jumped up, trying to grab hold of the land at the top, but I only got dirt, my fingers sliding right through it.

"Get me out of here!" I barked.

I tried the other side of the hole, jumping again and again, trying to get a grip.

But then a figure landed to my right, and I turned around, facing the brown-eyed one again.

"It's only seven minutes," he said in a cocky tone. "How much damage can I really do?"

"Let's find out!" one of his buddies crowed.

Brown-eyes smirked and moved for me. "Come on, baby."

"Stop!" I shoved him, twisting around and jumping up, pushing myself as high as I could and finally catching some grass.

But my fingers tore right through it, and I fell back down, crashing into the other side of the grave. My bare arm ground against the wet earth, the roots spilling out and scratching my skin.

And he was on me again. He pushed me into a corner, gripping my waist. "What's your name?"

"What's your name?" I retorted, gritting through my teeth.

"Flynn."

"Good." I pushed his hands down, trying to get out from the corner. "I hope you like snakes, Flynn."

"Huh?" Confusion etched across his face, but I didn't bother to explain my brother's favorite method of torturing anyone who messed with me.

Every muscle in my body tightened so hard they burned, and I raised my fist, knocking him on the side of the head. Off target and sloppy, but he stumbled back and winced. I pushed him in the chest again, knocking him on his ass.

"Help!" Jumping up, I slapped my palm against the dirt wall. "Let me out of here!"

"Ow, fuck!" I heard the growl from up top, but I couldn't see anyone all of a sudden.

I breathed hard, glancing nervously between the asshole crawling to his feet next to me and the top of the grave, now vacant. Where the hell were his friends?

And then someone stepped up to the edge of the grave, looking out of breath as he gazed down.

Kai? Why wasn't he off with his blond prom queen?

He took a step, falling into the grave and landing on both feet. I ignored the skip in my heartbeat as he looked at me, his eyes scanning worriedly down my body.

"Kai, Jesus, what the hell?" the other guy said, still holding the side of his head. "We were just playing around."

But Kai just turned toward him, walking into his space. "Five . . . four . . . three," he gritted out, and the guy's expression fell.

"Two," Kai continued, "O—"

And Leather Jacket bolted before he finished counting, running up the wall and climbing with his hands and his feet until he was over the edge.

Gone.

Kai turned to me, reaching out for my face. "You okay?"

But I slapped his hands down, backing up. What the hell was the matter with all of them? Sick, sadistic . . . I should've stomped right on his dick when he was on the fucking ground.

"Hey," Kai said, snapping his fingers in my face. "They're gone. It's okay. Are you hurt?"

I blinked, trying to process what he asked me through my anger.

No. No, I wasn't hurt. But my nerves were shot.

I brushed past him, jumping up and grunting as I tried to grab anything to get myself out of here. How did that asshole do that so easily?

"That's not going to work," Kai told me.

I stopped, fisting my hands and seething. "Then get me out of here."

"All right, just hold on."

He backed up to a short side of the grave, looking like he was making room to get a running start so he could scale the wall.

But then he reached over and grabbed my arm. "Wait, what happened?"

I twisted my arm around, seeing blood trickle down from my elbow.

Huh. I hadn't even felt that happen. Must've been during the struggle.

Kai took his shirt out of his back pocket and wiped off the blood.

"Banks!"

I sucked in a breath and shot my eyes up at the call of my name. "Shit," I mumbled under my breath.

"Banks! Where are you?"

I lowered my eyes to see Kai looking at me, his brows narrowed. "Is that your name?"

Dammit. They wouldn't walk away if they found me with him, even though this wasn't my fault. They'd tell Damon, and I'd never get out of the house again.

Kai dropped my arm and ran, leaping up to the ledge and peeking over. After a moment checking it out, he fell back to his feet.

"Who are those guys?" he asked. "They're the same ones who picked you up on the road earlier today."

"Just let me out."

"Who are they?"

"Brothers," I replied sarcastically. "They share me, okay? Sometimes they loan me out for parties. You want a piece?"

"Banks!" I heard David bellow, the patience in his voice now gone. I glanced worriedly to the top of the grave, shrinking back into the corner.

Dammit.

But Kai just rolled his eyes, amusement crossing his face.

"She's here!" he called out.

What the—? I lunged for him, putting my hand over his mouth

while holding the back of his neck with my other hand. "Shut up!" I whisper-yelled.

I pulled him back with me, shrouding us in the darkness of the corner.

"Shhh," I pleaded in a whisper. "If they find me with you, I'll be on lockdown until I'm old and gray."

I felt his mouth spread into a smile behind my hand, and he planted his palms against the dirt wall behind me, his dark gaze making my stomach somersault.

He twisted his head, nudging my hand away. "You're a lot of trouble."

"So, stop taking an interest."

We stared at each other, locked in a challenge. His body was pressed to mine, and I could feel it move as he breathed. *Inhale, exhale. Inhale, exhale.*

I dropped my eyes to his lips, wetting my own.

He leaned in, the caress of his breath falling on my face, and I knew he was going to kiss me.

But someone called out, stopping us. "Kai!" A woman's voice pierced the night air.

And I saw his eyes close as he mouthed "Fuck."

Reality came crashing back down.

"Would that be Chloe?" I teased.

His eyes popped open, studying me. "Do you know her?"

"I know you're hers."

"Who told you that?"

I remained silent, noticing the deep etch of confusion across his face.

"No." He laughed, shaking his head. "Okay? No. We were off again and on again for a long time, but . . ."

"But . . . ?"

"But we're off," he maintained. "Have been for a long time."

"But you still screw around with each other, right?"

He averted his eyes, looking uncomfortable as an embarrassed smile peeked out.

"Kai?" I pressed.

And he shrugged, looking apologetic. "The devil I know is better than the devil I don't, okay?"

Whatever. She couldn't be all bad if he still liked sleeping with her. It was just more convenient to bank on a sure thing than to do the work to seduce someone new.

Typical.

"Look." He took my chin, forcing me to look at him. "I would never have tried anything with you in the Bell Tower if I had a girlfriend. She's seeing other guys. We are *not* together."

"Doesn't matter."

I darted around him to try to climb my way up the wall, but he grabbed the back of my jeans and yanked me back into his body, searing my ear with his hot breath. "I like you more."

My lids felt heavy all of a sudden, and tingles spread over my body. But I forced myself to stay angry. "Like I care," I said. "If I weren't here, you'd be 'liking' her a lot in the back seat of your car right now."

He laughed in my ear. "You're so mean." And then he quieted, his voice turning soft and sincere as he twisted me around to face him. "I really like you, though."

I didn't know what to say. What could I say? For some reason, though, it was really nice to hear. Kai was nice.

"Let me touch you," he whispered, holding my eyes and pulling me in.

I saw him come in, and I slowly dropped my head back to give him access to my neck. His lips touched my skin, and my eyelids fluttered. He was the best feeling in the world.

"I don't want to go on dates," I told him, laying it down straight. "I don't like a lot of people."

I felt him smile against my skin as he continued his path. "Me neither. How about you, me, and Netflix?"

Hell, yeah. "And no one can know I'm messing around with a rich boy, okay? I'd lose my street cred."

He snorted, shaking with laughter. "Hey, it's not the label on the jeans but what's inside that matters." And he hefted me up, gripping my ass and pressing me to him.

I moaned, feeling the heat between us. *Yeah, okay, smart-ass.*

Leaning in, I parted my lips, and he dived in, capturing them. I groaned into his mouth. *Oh, my God.* The warmth, the taste . . . He was slow but strong and deep, and I melted into him, following his lead and sucking and nibbling.

My entire body was alive, an electric current spreading from my lips down the rest of me, and I wanted him to kiss me everywhere.

"Where do you come from, Banks?" he whispered, biting my lip. "Why do you live with the Torrances?"

I held the side of his face, pulling my lips away but touching my forehead to his. "It doesn't matter. I don't want to be me tonight, okay?" I pulled back, giving him a small smile and challenging him. "We're in the confessional, and no one can see us. Let's just run and not look back tonight."

His eyes lightened up, and he caressed my face.

"Hell, yes," he answered. "On one condition."

He put me back on my feet and reached into his jeans, and I looked down between our bodies, watching as he pulled out some kind of card.

He held it up, the words "The Pope of Meridian City" written across the black piece of plastic.

A key card?

I darted my eyes up to his, seeing the thrill there that was also coursing through me.

He got a room? At The Pope?

"I want to find that twelfth floor," he said. "Want to go on an adventure with me?"

I broke out in a smile and couldn't help it—I dived in and wrapped my arms around him. I was going to fall hard if he wasn't careful.

That would *totally* destroy my street cred.

How had he gotten a room? It had to have been earlier today after confession, I guessed.

I leaned back and nodded, climbing off him and standing up.

"Let's go—"

But then, all of a sudden, something grabbed my shirt and hauled me up off my feet. Hands squeezed my arms, and I was plucked up and out of the grave.

"Hey!" I screamed, my heart lurching into my throat.

"What the hell?" I heard Kai's bellow from below.

I landed on the cold grass above, the wind knocked out of me. I flipped over, seeing several pairs of black boots.

Who . . .

But I instantly found their faces. David, Lev, Ilia, and . . . Damon all stood over me, staring down. My brother's black eyes were on fire.

Oh, no.

I slowly rose to my feet, keeping my eyes down.

But I kept my chin up. Cowering wouldn't do me any good this time.

Kai hopped out of the grave, pushing himself to his feet and coming to stand in front of me. "Damon?" he said, breathing hard as he looked at my brother. "What the hell, man?"

I opened my mouth to say something—I didn't know what—but Damon grabbed my wrist and hauled me over to his side, behind him.

"Stay fucking still," he growled at me.

Kai advanced on him. "What the hell are you doing?"

My brother turned to him. "You're not messing with what's mine, are you? I thought we were brothers and all."

I closed my eyes. *Oh, God.* I could feel Kai's eyes on me. His confusion.

"Yours?" he shot back. "I didn't know she was yours. You acted like you didn't know her in the Bell Tower!"

I glanced quickly between him and my brother, tears springing up. People were starting to gather around, and I saw Michael and Will step up to the scene, as well.

Kai's eyes narrowed on me; he was still holding the hotel key in his fist.

"And I'm sorry to say," he continued, "but it doesn't really look like she wants to be yours." He said to me, "You want me to take you home?"

No.

Take me anywhere else.

"You want him to take you home?" My brother looked down at me, daring me with his icy voice.

It wasn't a choice, though.

I would love to be someone else, somewhere else, but this was it. Damon needed me. Kai didn't. What would happen to my brother if I broke his heart?

I reached over and took his hand, shaking my head.

And I could feel Kai's silence like a knife slicing through my gut.

"Well, this is fucking fun," Will chimed in. "Come on, man, leave her alone." He nudged Kai. "Damon's got dibs. What does it matter?"

"Since when does Damon give a shit about dibs?" Kai barked at Will. "If one's not available, he moves on to the next. No one woman is worth the trouble, right?" He challenged my brother. "You've never put a girl before us. What if I want her, too?"

"Well, you can't have her," Damon shot back. "It's kind of nice having one piece of pure, clean pussy all to myself."

Vomit rose from my stomach as laughter went off around the circle.

Damon turned to me. "Who do you belong to? Who do you love?"

I shook my head, anger shredding every bit of happiness I'd just felt down in that grave. Goddamn him.

But blood was forever.

"I love *you*," I said, looking up at him.

And I caught the glint of relief in his eyes before they turned hard again. Did he actually have any doubt?

He kissed my forehead. "Go to my room and wait there," he instructed, slapping me on the ass and looking back to his friends. "I may want a piece when I get home. Whenever that'll be."

Chuckles surrounded me again, and David put his hand on my back, leading me away.

The four of us walked toward the SUV, leaving my brother and his friends, but I caught his warning to Kai as I pulled my hood back up.

"No one else touches her," he told him. "Not ever."

No. Not ever.

CHAPTER 9

BANKS

Present

K*ai Genato Mori*, I read to myself. *Born: September 28, Thunder Bay . . . no siblings.*

Page after page detailed his life, his impeccable grades, and his basketball and swimming stats.

And his arrest and activity since he'd gotten out more than a year ago.

Aside from what got him arrested—assaulting a child abuser who just happened to also be a cop—he had always been a model kid. He knew how to party but never went over the limit like Will.

He enjoyed women, but they never seemed to hate him for it like they did Damon.

And he could be tough and hard and scary, but it never came off as mean like it did with Michael.

Kai was the best of their whole little crew.

Until he got out of prison. Now he was different.

No women, at least not publicly. Never more than one drink, at least not publicly. And not only was he mean, he seemed almost cruel at times.

I stopped on the photo of him taken as he was walking to Hunter-Bailey one day. The PI caught him on the sidewalk, his black suit coat whipping in the wind, his white shirt collar open, a duffel bag hanging on his shoulder, and his black hair making his eyes stand out, looking stern. I stared at his crisp shirt, remembering the feel of the man underneath when it was a T-shirt and hoodie.

Warm. That's what I remembered.

Really warm.

I shut the folder, inhaling a deep breath and shoving it under the seat with the others. I'd seen my brother play with countless girls, treating them like insignificant toys and then throwing them to the side like trash. I knew how horrible men could be to women they were fucking. And not only did the women take it, but they came back for more. Begged for it, in fact.

That would never be me.

"Where the fuck is he?" David grumbled from the driver's seat, flicking the ash off his cigarette through the crack in his window.

I turned my gaze out the rear passenger side, looking through the streams of rain pouring down the window, up to the black brick house. We'd arrived fifteen minutes ago, and I'd texted him to let him know we were here. He hadn't texted back, but I knew he was home. His RS 7 was in the driveway, under a tree, getting shit on by all the thistles above coming loose in the rain.

Checking my phone, I saw it was now eight fifteen. If he didn't get out here, I was going to leave. I had other things to do besides wait on him.

Lev yawned to my left, and I glanced over, seeing his seat reclined and his eyes closed. He still wore the same black jeans and sleeveless white T-shirt from last night, and he smelled like a bar bathroom.

"When is Vanessa due to arrive?" David asked me.

I stared back out the window, my heart pumping hard despite itself. "A week or so."

"How did she take the news?"

"Does it matter?"

I could feel his eyes through the rearview mirror but ignored him. Gabriel had made the call to London late last night and sent me instructions to handle her when she arrived. She wasn't happy, but she knew this day was coming. Eventually she would've been sold off to someone, and as long as that someone kept her in the lifestyle to which she'd become accustomed, she'd do what she was told.

She was, Gabriel divulged, happy that Kai was at least young and good-looking.

I let my eyes drift closed for a moment. *Kai won't go through with it.* That was one thing that I was confident hadn't changed. His integrity. The Nikova princess, who pouted if she had to suffer a sneeze, would annoy him to no end.

I smiled to myself. There was no way he'd endure her.

"You know, if you need me," David said, and I opened my eyes, meeting his in the mirror, "anytime—I'll be there."

I wanted to give him a nod. I'd worked hard to get the notice and respect I now had in Gabriel's house. I hated being sent off like I was expendable. But my shoulders relaxed a little, knowing I wasn't really doing this alone. They were still there for me.

He blew out smoke, shaking his head as if thinking out loud. "I don't like this guy."

I kept my smirk to myself. "What kind of guys do you like?"

Lev started laughing under his breath, his eyes still closed, and I glanced up, seeing David shoot me a bemused middle finger in the rearview mirror.

I looked back up at the house. The shades on the windows were so cheap. I could tell from here. The outside paint was worn away, and the bricks were chipped in so many places. I hoped the inside was better. It would take a shit ton of guys to get this place in shape in two weeks.

"Damon was fucked up," David went on, "but he never hid it, either. This guy . . ." He looked over through the passenger-side window to the house. "I don't know."

He laid his head back on the headrest, and while my heart warmed that he was actually worried about me being left with Kai, I didn't want him to be. I wanted to keep the power I had and earn more. It didn't help if the guys I worked with tried to help me traverse every damn puddle just so my petticoats didn't get muddy. I could handle Kai Mori.

"He's too controlled," David said. "People who are wound that tight are unpredictable."

I tucked my phone inside my ski vest and pulled down the sleeves of my sweatshirt.

"Don't worry about her," Lev said, eyes still closed. "In two weeks, he'll have his pretty little bride to play with."

And I couldn't help it. My lips twisted in a little snarl before I quickly hid it away again.

Yeah, he'll have her, won't he? And an image of them came to me, alone in that house, looking at each other, bumping into each other, connecting and shit . . . I sat up and threw off my seat belt.

"If Gabriel wanted you guys to think, he would've put you in charge," I mumbled. "I'll be back."

Fat raindrops pummeled the cap on my head, and I squinted through the downpour, stuffing my gloved fingers in my pockets and running up the cement-slab stairs.

I rang the doorbell.

This place was a dump. Dingy-looking, overgrown and neglected landscaping, and a filthy porch strewn with newspapers, empty flowerpots, and dead leaves. Why did he live here? I was sure he could've moved into Delcour—Michael Crist's high-rise luxury apartment building on the other side of the river—for free. Erika Fane and Will Grayson lived there, so why did Kai choose to stay so far away, here, and without his friends?

Of course, I knew where he lived when he'd bought this place a year ago, but it didn't occur to me to be bothered by it then.

Now, since I had to ready this pit for a wife, I was starting to realize how much work needed to be done.

I hit the doorbell again, growing aggravated. Where the hell was he?

I pounded on the screen door, the old wood hitting the frame with each knock. "Hello," I called out, more like a demand than a question.

Peering through the window to my right, I could make out a dusty floor and a small overturned table, the rest hidden from view by the yellowing plastic shade hanging by one corner over the window.

Suspicion crept in as I stood up straight again.

This didn't feel right. No one lived here.

I never got the impression Kai Mori needed a palace to be content, but he was definitely the sort of man who took pride in himself and anything that belonged to him. He took care of his shit, and this place was *not* taken care of.

I glanced up to the top of the hill, to my right, seeing a big gray stone house. A little small to be considered a mansion, but it was damn close. It was surrounded by a tall black gate, and it was Kai's only neighbor. I should've researched who lived there. Made sure they weren't nosy.

Casting a quick glance back at the car, I couldn't see Lev through the tinted windows in the back, but I could see David in the front, watching me.

Fuck it. Turning back around, I swung open the screen door and twisted the knob, finding it unlocked. I pushed the door open and hesitantly took a step inside, my gaze shifting from left to right as I took in the inside of Kai Mori's house.

Gray light hit the floors, streaming through filthy windows, while shadows of raindrops danced across the dingy wood.

Dust-covered sheets lay over objects that looked like chairs and tables and one couch.

Leaving the door open, I walked slowly into the living room, taking in the fireplace with its soot-stained brick and a pile of charcoaled kindling, before heading to the kitchen and taking in the fifties refrigerator and stove, as well as the ancient linoleum and retro-pink countertops.

I choked out a laugh. Jesus. Who was he kidding? This wasn't his house. No fucking way.

Charging back through the foyer, I climbed the stairs, taking two at a time, and walked into two bedrooms and a bathroom, none of which looked lived-in. There was no food, no used dishes, no toothbrushes, no laundry, no TV, no lamps . . .

Until I walked down the hall, entering the last room, and looked around. I stopped, instantly seeing a bed. The only room with one.

There were sheets on the bed, and it was perfectly made. Was I supposed to believe he just slept here, then?

"Hello!" I called out again.

I heard nothing but the sound of rain outside.

Walking out of the room, I entered the hallway and threw open some closet doors, checking every nook and cranny. The shelves were empty, not even containing bath towels.

What's with the mystery here, Kai? "Hello!" I bellowed.

I closed the last door and turned, suddenly seeing him standing right in front of me.

I gasped, my heart stopping so hard it hurt. "Shit!" I burst out, breathing fast as he just stood there. "Where the hell did you come from?"

He stood in the hallway, wearing jeans and an expensive-looking black pullover, partially unzipped to reveal the white T-shirt underneath.

He jerked his head behind him, his perfectly styled hair not moving. "The bedroom."

I narrowed my eyes on him. "I was just in there," I told him. "And you weren't."

There was a bed and candles and a dresser and nothing else. Where was he? Hiding in the closet?

I realized I was breathing hard, so I forced myself to calm down.

"I rang the doorbell and called out. It was like no one was here," I said.

But he ignored me, looking bored as he asked, "Did you bring the blueprints, keys, and codes like I asked?"

His stern expression looked impatient. *Okay, fine.* I'd have to get in here and dig around soon, anyway, so I could wait to be nosy.

"In the car," I answered curtly.

He nodded and walked for the stairs, taking them down and knowing I would follow.

We stepped out onto the porch, and his gaze instantly found David and Lev sitting in the SUV, waiting.

Kai turned his dark eyes on me. "You're with me now. Tell them to beat it."

I hooded my eyes in aggravation. But I turned around and headed down the steps, toward the car, while he walked to the side of the house toward his.

David rolled down the passenger-side window.

"Go back to Thunder Bay," I told him, reaching in and gathering the files for The Pope and the roll of blueprints off the seat. "I'll see you tonight."

He thinned his eyes, looking uneasy.

"It's fine," I assured him, starting to walk away. "Finish the collections, don't forget the inventories for Weisz's and Brother's, and make sure Ilia got the kennels done." I glanced at the time on the dash. "And remember, De Soto's coming in at three. Make sure a car picks him up."

I turned around before he had a chance to respond and walked toward Kai's Audi. He backed down the driveway, the heavy rain slowly washing away the thistles all over it, but he stopped when he saw me heading toward him.

Rounding the car, I climbed in the passenger seat, tossing everything in the back and wiping away the rain on my face. I could feel the water seeping through the fabric of my hat, and I wanted to take it off, but I'd have to wait until I was alone.

Without speaking, Kai let off the brake and backed the rest of the way out of the driveway, and I cast my eyes anywhere but to him. He shifted the car into first, and my breath caught, feeling him move next to me as the smooth whir of the engine vibrated under my feet.

He hit the gas and raced down the avenue, pulling down into second and up into third as the car propelled us faster and faster.

"You don't live in that house," I said in a low, even voice.

He held the wheel, the top arm locked steel-rod straight as he stared ahead.

"You think I can't rough it?" he joked, reaching over and turning up "Emotionless" playing on the radio.

"Rough it?" I hid my smirk. "I think Howard Hughes was less anal than you. You would never live in that dump."

"I lived in one for two and a half years," he replied, his voice turning hard. "Things change."

I looked at him out of the corner of my eye, seeing his eyes drift off faraway, impassive. I swallowed through the sudden dryness in my throat, shutting up for the moment.

It was easy to forget, given his clean fingernails and expensive clothes. But not long ago he was in a three-dollar T-shirt and locked in a cage with people telling him what he would do with every minute of his day.

Still, though, he deserved it. He did the crime.

"You're not staying at the Torrances' anymore," he told me, shifting into fourth and laying on the gas. "You work for me now. I want you in Meridian City."

"I live in Meridian City." I turned my eyes out the passenger-side window. "And even if I didn't, you don't get to dictate where I sleep."

When they got out of prison last year, I moved to the city to be close to Damon. My father started paying me—barely enough to keep a rat—but it was enough to find a place to sleep.

"And where do you sleep?" he asked.

"Not far."

He adjusted his rearview mirror, giving it a lengthy glance. "With one of them?"

I slowly turned my eyes on him and then looked behind us, seeing the Escalade following. I couldn't help but smile a little.

I should be angry they disobeyed an order, but . . .

If Gabriel had told them to go home, they would've. He only had their loyalty as long as he paid them. I didn't pay them anything.

I let my head fall back on the headrest, the rare peace of contentment washing over. "It's all I'm good for, right?"

His lips twisted up. "Damon must really have done a number on you to keep you so loyal," he spat out. "I've seen him with women. Do you really like what he does to you?"

What he does to me . . . I fixed my eyes on the rain-covered windshield, zoning out. I belonged to Damon, and whether or not Kai ever learned the real reason why, it didn't change that I would always stand at his side.

"That night—"

"Don't," I said, interrupting him.

He stopped, and I could hear his heavy breathing pouring out of his nose.

"I love that he saw us that night," he went on, his voice almost a growl. "Loved that furious look on his fucking face when he saw you all over me."

I tightened the muscles in my legs, wincing at the memory. I was so awful that night. And the feeling of every inch of him on me was still so clear.

"There's something about you, kid," he said, still watching the road ahead. "I don't know what it is, but most of the time, teaching those classes, meeting with contractors, talking to my friends, shit . . ." He shook his head. "I can barely stand it. I even have trouble chewing my goddamn food most of the time." And then he looked over at me, shifting into fifth. "But not around you. Around you, I get hungry. Like I'm starving."

I kept my gaze forward, the instinct to shrink into myself and try to be invisible nearly taking over.

"You're wearing his belt." His deep voice sounded dangerous and made the hair on my skin stand up.

Damon's belt. I shifted in my seat, suddenly very aware of the tight leather band around my hips.

He gestured down to the belt before turning his eyes back on the road. "I recognize the tally marks carved into the leather for every slam dunk he got in high school. On and off the court."

On and *off* the court? *Jesus, Damon.* I held back my sigh.

I'd taken the belt when he went to prison, and he never asked for it back.

"Wear it every day, Banks," Kai ordered. "Every damn day."

"Oh, I do," I whispered, but I knew he heard me.

I bet he wondered if there was a tally mark for me on the belt. Damon was right. It was strategically advantageous for no one to know who I was to him. If Kai thought I was a Torrance toy and tool, he wouldn't know exactly what he had or what cards he could really play.

God help me if he ever found out, though.

Kai kept driving, descending into the Whitehall district, and I could see a cargo ship and a few tugboats drifting down the river in the rain. The city loomed in the distance, skyscrapers partially shrouded in cloud cover, and I could just make out the black and gold of Delcour, sitting in the center of the best shopping and the finest restaurants.

Kai slowed as we pulled up to The Pope, and I noticed Michael Crist's new Rover parked along the curb. What was he doing here?

We turned, driving into the small alleyway on the side of the hotel, toward the back, and the car was suddenly steeped in darkness. The overhang blocked out any light, and I ran my hands slowly down my thighs, feeling a buzz all over my skin. The car seemed so much smaller now.

The darkness.

The confessional. The trunk. The Bell Tower. The grave. Small spaces with him. Always small, dark spaces.

Without giving me a glance or a word, Kai parked the car and opened his door, stepping out into the rain. I quickly followed and watched him reach in the back and grab the blueprints I'd brought.

He broke out in a jog, heading for one of the rear doors, and I noticed two dumpsters, some wooden pallets, and an overflow of cardboard boxes getting soaked nearby.

"What are you doing out here?" I heard Kai ask. I looked up to see him talking to Michael Crist and Will Grayson, who were waiting under an awning.

Will wore only a pair of jeans and a white T-shirt, while Michael was dressed for the weather, looking eerily similar to what he looked like in high school in his hoodie. Splotches of water covered his jeans.

"Why aren't you guys waiting in the car?" Kai asked them.

Michael's eyes veered to me, narrowing, as Will pushed off the wall and took his gum out, tossing it into the rain. "Didn't want to miss you," he said.

Kai held out his hand to me, and I handed him the hotel keys.

"Where's Rika?" he asked the guys.

Michael turned as he approached, ready to follow him through the door. "Class." And then he looked to me again. "It's just us."

A sense of foreboding swirled in my stomach, and I stood behind, letting them all enter before me.

We walked through a dark tunnel, and I couldn't see clearly from behind the more-than-six-foot-tall men in front of me, but after a few moments, I saw some white. Bright walls came into view, and I noticed several freezers, refrigerators, and stoves. We'd entered through the kitchen. It was only visible, though, due to the poor light streaming in from the windows.

Each of the guys turned on their flashlights, and Will handed me one.

I took it, switching it on.

"So, Kai?" Will called out as all of us walked through the kitchen. "You wouldn't need me to break in your virgin bride for you, would you?"

He started laughing and turned his head to me before Kai could answer. "Kai doesn't like virgins. He likes women who know what they're doing."

And then he let his gaze move up and down my body.

I arched a brow. Yeah, I didn't believe that. I was a virgin that night years ago, and it didn't deter him from wanting quite a lot from me.

"But me?" Will went on. "I like 'em from scratch. I can teach them exactly what I like and how to do it the way I want."

"You mean you like that they don't have anyone to compare you to," I said, "so they can't tell how bad you are at it."

Michael's snort was small, but I caught it, and I could see the back of Kai's shoulders shaking with silent laughter.

Will turned back around, leaving me alone.

We all followed Kai, and I waited outside the control room as they flipped switches, trying to get the electricity on. After a few minutes, though, nothing.

"Good thing we brought flashlights," Michael mumbled as he walked out of the control room.

Kai followed and stopped, all of us standing together.

"Well, at least the rooms will all be unlocked," he told us. "Bad news is, we're taking the stairs."

Up twelve flights. *Excellent.*

"Let's split up," he told us, starting to walk for the kitchen doors, which probably led into a dining room. "Take pictures of any rooms you go into and close-ups of any potential problems. Rodents, plumbing, leaks, any kind of damage . . . I'll have contractors come in and get better estimates, but I want an idea of repairs and what we have to chalk up to losses."

Michael and Will walked off, leaving the kitchen, and Kai turned to me. "See if you can find the generator," he told me. "We can at least get a few lights working."

Yeah, okay. I kept my vitriol to myself and headed for the stairwell access, turning on my flashlight as I descended to the basement. There were no windows down here in the stairwell, and my pulse started to race, remembering the stupid fucking horror flicks Damon watched when we were younger. I'd shine my flashlight, and all of a sudden a girl in a white dress and a mouthful of bloody fangs would jump out at me.

Opening the door at the bottom, I entered the basement and instantly let out a breath. It was a huge open boiler room with windows lining the wall at the top. I could just spot the feet of a few pedestrians walking by. A little natural light poured in, but I kept my flashlight on since it was still pretty dim.

I strolled slowly down the aisle, shining my light on pipes and tanks, furnaces, and other machinery I didn't recognize. Really, the hotel hadn't been closed down that long. Most of this stuff probably worked fine still.

I spotted a generator near the wall and headed for it. I had no idea how these things worked, but I'd seen them, and I knew how to Google if I needed to.

Leaning down, I blew the dust off the switches, rubbing away the dirt. This thing wasn't big enough to power much, and it definitely wouldn't power the elevators, but maybe it would get the hallway lighting going. I flipped the *Power* button.

But nothing happened. Did it plug into something? Well, it wouldn't plug into a wall, of course. If we had electricity, we wouldn't need a generator.

Maybe it connected to a battery of some sort. I quickly took off my jacket, dropping it on the ground, and got on my hands and knees, shooting the flashlight underneath and around, searching for any wires or cords.

Something took hold of my ankles, though, and I yelped as they pulled them, my knees sliding out from under me and my body being dragged across the floor.

"What the hell?" I barked, flipping around to see who had grabbed me. My heart pounded. Michael and Will stood in front of me, and I kicked at them. "Get off me!"

Michael reached over, grabbing me by the shirt and hauling me up.

Asshole. I looked around, but Kai wasn't here.

Michael gripped my collar and planted me against the wall, releasing me.

I glared at him. I expected to get into it with them soon enough—I knew what they did to Rika last year, so I knew how they liked to throw their weight around—but for some reason, I kept still. He was going to have a huge problem with me soon, but I'd make my move when I was ready.

"I have no idea what Kai is thinking right now," he said with a bite to his tone, "but I will give you one warning and one warning only."

I lifted my chin slowly, bracing myself for his threat.

"If you fuck with us, we will make you disappear," he growled. "The moment I start to feel the slightest bit concerned that you might have something up your sleeve, I won't hesitate. Do you understand?" He thinned his eyes. "You work for him, and you take care of him, and you do whatever it is he wants you to do, and you do it good, honey. Just don't give me a reason to sink you to the bottom of the fucking river, because that is just how fast you can end. You got me?"

Oh, yeah. I got you.

I started breathing hard. I brought my fingers demurely to my lips and faked a look of fright. *What did I do? Oh, no, please don't hurt me. Please?* I let out a little whimper and pinched my eyebrows together in confusion.

And then I stopped my fake sobbing and broke out in a smile, looking at him with a quiet laugh.

That shit may have worked on Erika Fane, but he had another thing coming.

"I will do my job," I told him, "and you don't scare me."

His glower grew deeper.

"What can you do?" I asked. "You're an athlete, in the public eye, about to get married to the girl you've loved forever, with so much to lose. And this one"—I gestured to Will behind him—"is only sober from the time he drags his ass out of bed in the morning until the time he can make it to the beer cooler he keeps in his kitchen."

Will scowled at me.

"The Horsemen are weak and dying," I continued, feigning a concerned look. "Perfect time for enemies to strike." I reached over and picked up my jacket, sliding my arms in. "Damon's father would love to undo you, your father is trying to hinder a couple of your real estate deals, Damon is who-knows-where, Rika walks around every day, armed with only her little kung fu tricks." I looked at Will. "And hasn't that cop you went to prison for attacking been sniffing around you lately, itching for some payback?"

Michael's eyes narrowed, and he shifted his gaze, looking taken aback. *Yeah, you didn't know about that, did you?*

"You have so much going on, Michael, really," I taunted him like he was five years old, putting my hands in my pockets. "And all the while you're watching me, you're not watching them."

I pulled out both hands, and Michael caught the flash of silver in my right hand and grabbed my wrist, stopping me.

I laughed as he held the small blade away from his face and fixed me with a snarl.

But I let out my smirk and twisted the point of the blade in my *other* hand, the one he didn't see, poking just above his groin.

He jerked back, a little snarl on his face.

"Not only are your ducks not in a row, Michael, but they're shitting all over the place." I stuck the blades back in my pockets. "You boys need a role model."

Slipping to the side, I walked around them and headed out of the basement, hearing Michael's angry whisper behind me. "What the fuck?"

"I was gonna tell you!" Will whisper-yelled back.

I shook my head.

What a waste of time.

After all the years of grunt work—cleaning, inventorying, drop-offs and pickups—I finally had a little respect. Now I was tasked with shadowing Kai and his little crew, watching them fumble to take five steps when they could get what they needed in one.

I pulled the front of my hat down farther, trying to resist the yawn that was pushing its way out.

My phone vibrated in my pocket, and I pulled it out as I headed up the stairs.

Meet me on thirteen.

Kai. How did he get my number? And then I remembered I'd texted him that morning. *Great.* Thirteen, and I was in the basement. Shoving my phone back into my pocket, I grabbed the railing and started vaulting up the stairs, jogging and skipping steps as I flew. Reaching each landing, I looked up and took note of the floor number, but on nine I stopped, my lungs now feeling tight and small. Looking upward, I saw the dim flights above me, lit only by the emergency lights.

Taking a deep breath, I jogged a little slower up the remaining flights, coming to thirteen and opening the stairwell door.

A stitch cramped my side, and I swallowed through the dryness in my throat. I thought I was in good shape, dammit.

I stepped into a dim hallway and looked left and right, the gray carpeting with a white filigree design slowly fading into the black voids down each dark hallway.

"Hello?" I called out.

I turned right, switching on my flashlight, but a draft hit my back, and I looked behind me. A subtle wind cooled my lips.

Turning left instead, I walked down the hallway, inspecting each door as I passed and finally noticing one that was wide open. I peered inside, seeing white sheer curtains on the other side of the room whipping in the wind.

The balcony doors must be open.

I walked into the room, looking both ways as I crossed, and finally noticed Kai's form out on the balcony. Peeling back the curtain, I stepped outside.

"The twelfth-floor balcony," he said, leaning over the railing and turning his head to look at me.

I followed his lead, peering over the railing and looking down. Every floor had a balcony on it, and the one directly below us was no different. Intricate carvings in the stone, a thick banister, everything wet from the rain . . .

I straightened, cocking my head at him. *The twelfth floor.*

Suspicion started to creep in.

"Did you really think I'd help you search The Pope if I thought Damon was hiding here?" I asked. "You're not buying this hotel because of some story I told you when I was seventeen, are you?"

I saw the corner of his mouth lift in a smile. "A, yes," he stated. "I think you'd help me search it, if for no other reason than to point me in the wrong direction." He pulled himself back up and looked at me. "And B, I'm not sure Damon told you where he was hiding."

"And why's that?"

"Because I remember him being particularly possessive of you," he said. "I think you know he's in the city, but I think he might be watching you as much as he is us."

I laughed to myself.

I'd heard about the twelfth floor after I moved in with Damon and my father. Gabriel fiercely protected his privacy and had built four hotels back in the day: one each in Meridian City, San Francisco, St. Petersburg, and Bahrain—the places he traveled most. Privacy, security, and invisibility were sometimes a necessity to someone who made at least some of his money outside the law.

But my brother wasn't here. At least not the last time I checked. Kai was wasting his time.

"We already explored this place once, remember?" I told him.

He flashed his amused eyes to me, sounding cocky. "We didn't get very far, *remember*?"

A blush instantly heated my cheeks, and I turned away.

Kai peered over the railing again, and I did the same, taking in the vast drop to the ground below. I looked back at him, studying the curiosity written all over his face. The way his dark eyebrows pinched together as if he was calculating his next move, and the way his neck stretched as far as it would take him for a better look.

He seemed so young. Like a kid trying to find the courage to follow his friends off a cliff.

What was he doing?

Straightening, I unwound the scarf around my neck and pulled it off, out of the jacket. Kai watched me as I held it over the banister.

Gauging the light wind, I lowered it as much as possible, finally letting it drift out of my fingers and float down to the twelfth-floor balcony. The fabric billowed as it sank and finally caught on the banister spokes, the wind plastering it to the inside of the balcony.

Without looking at him, I headed back into the room. He had no choice but to follow.

Seriously, if he wanted to climb over the railing and kill himself, it was no skin off my nose, but . . .

He could be right. Damon wasn't here when I looked for him, but that didn't mean he wasn't changing hideouts, either. He could be here, and I needed to buy some time.

Walking into the corridor, I turned right, heading toward the stairwell exit I'd come through.

Both of us quickly descended the stairs, but after taking two flights, we came to the next landing, where a door should've been, marking the twelfth floor. The wall was bare, though. No door. No markings indicating what floor it was, nothing. Just a white wall.

I spared him a glance, an unspoken understanding passing between us. We continued down, both of us reaching for the knob of the eleventh-floor entrance at the same time. His hand brushed mine, and I quickly pulled away, an electric current flowing up my arm. He pulled the door open, and both of us raced through, heading straight for 1122, the room directly below 1322.

I twisted the knob and charged in, making my way for the balcony doors, which I swung open, a gust of wind instantly hitting my face. Kai and I stepped over the threshold, looking around for the scarf.

It took only a quick survey, but there was nothing, as I knew there would be. Nothing except a dead potted plant, a rusted wrought-iron table, and a leaf.

The scarf wasn't here, of course, but . . .

I walked over to the right side of the balcony, hung my head over, and peered up.

And there it was. The black scarf whipped happily, a few inches hanging off the side of the balcony right above us.

"There." I nodded upward.

Kai pinched his eyebrows together and stepped, leaning over the side and turning his head up. He stared, either confused or annoyed, but I smiled a little all the same.

"What the hell?" he grumbled. "We need to get up there," he told me.

And how do you plan on doing that? The elevators weren't working at the moment, and it wasn't like we had rope.

I watched as he started to climb up on the railing, but I immediately reached out and pulled him down.

"It's fine," I said curtly. "It's not valuable. Forget it."

His eyebrows shot up. "You're worried about me?"

"Yeah. Like the price of tea in China."

He shook his head, smiling to himself. But again, he made a move to climb up.

I pulled him back. "I can't spot you. You're too big. You can spot me, so let me do it."

Stepping around him, I hopped up on the railing, and he darted out, grabbing my arm to steady me. I knew if I looked right, I'd see the drop below that was only one mistake away, so I didn't look.

My legs shook, but I curled my toes, gripping the thick banister. Dammit. I didn't need the fucking scarf back, but I didn't want to find out if he was able to scale his way up there. Not yet.

Squeezing his arm with one hand, I held out the other arm for balance and slowly rose to stand. My belly flipped.

"I've got you," Kai told me. I glanced down, seeing his dark eyes holding mine as he wrapped his other arm around my legs. My hands went weak, and for some reason, that didn't make me feel better.

I reached up with both hands and swiped for the frayed fabric, Kai's embrace tightening. Unfortunately, though, I was still at least six to eight inches shy of touching it.

Placing my hand on Kai's shoulder to keep steady, I slowly arched up on my tiptoes to raise myself higher. I extended my other arm, stretching my muscles and joints centimeter by centimeter until finally, I went as far as I could go. I winced, trying to catch the small thread that dangled. Shifting my body just slightly, I continued trying, but it was no use.

I let out a sigh. "I can't reach it."

Falling back to my feet, I looked down at Kai.

And stopped breathing.

He was just staring at me. Right there, looking up, with his arms wrapped around my thighs and his face damn near between them. I opened my mouth, but no words came out.

An amused smile hit his eyes, and my heart started pumping wildly. I didn't want to know what the hell was running through his head right now.

"You okay?" he asked. I could tell the fucker was holding a smirk back.

I jumped down, forcing him away, and straightened my clothes, pulling down my T-shirt and jacket. "I'm fine."

He would only use you. I had to remember that his goal was Damon. Revenge. And he knew Damon cared about me, so that made me valuable.

I ignored the beat in my chest and shook off the look in his eyes.

Don't make the same mistakes. Don't let him touch you. Don't want him. You can't have him.

I forgot that six years ago, but I wouldn't this time.

The silence crawled over my skin, and the sound of the light rain droned on around us.

"Why do you wear that stuff?" Kai's voice was quiet and soft.

Stuff. My clothes?

I averted my gaze, my armor thickening. I'd taken more than enough crap about my appearance over the years.

What, you don't like my secondhand combat boots with broken laces and scuffed toes? Do they offend you? Was there some rule that my jeans were supposed to be tight, so men I didn't know could take pleasure at looking at my ass like I was a car on the street?

"I wear what I want," I snipped. "I don't dress to please anyone else."

"On the contrary . . ." I felt him approach, and I looked down, seeing his shoes stop a foot away from me. "I'm wondering if you do dress like this to, indeed, please someone else."

I met his gaze, the long, exhausting practice of showing no emotion coming easier than it did when I was a kid.

Okay. Point taken. Maybe I did start dressing like this to please Damon. I was never allotted money for clothes, and even now my pay was too minuscule to afford much. But I was happy with what my brother gave me and would've gladly worn anything if it meant I could stay with him.

And growing up, these clothes kept me safe. There were too many men around, and I looked younger when I was wearing this *stuff.* It hid my shape and helped keep me invisible.

"Those are men's clothes," he pointed out, his voice growing hard. "Used men's clothes. Whose are they? Are they all Damon's?"

"What do you care?" I shot back. "I'll do my job. Drive you around, fix your shithole of a house, clean your dojo, and I don't need to wear a ball gown to do it."

He broke out in a smile. "You're a complete mystery, and I'm curious about you. That's all. So, let's start simple. What's your name?"

"Banks."

"What's your name, Banks?"

I almost snorted.

Almost.

He was a little faster on the pickup than his friends, wasn't he?

Banks was my last name. I liked it because I thought I'd get more respect sounding less like a woman, and my father preferred it because he hated my first name.

And none of that was Kai Mori's business.

Kai went on. "And where are you from? Where are your parents? Were you really homeschooled?" He began walking into me, and I tripped backward, stumbling. "Where do you live? Do you have any friends? How can you work for that disgusting piece of shit, huh? How do you sleep?"

I hit the glass door, and he closed the distance between us, hovering and dropping his voice to a whisper, "Or how about an even easier question?" His heat filtered through my jacket, and every inch of me hummed. "I'm going to confession today. Want to come . . . *Banks*?"

His eyes locked on my lips, and my breathing turned shallow. Oh, Christ. The wind carried his smell, and I inhaled, the world in front of me starting to spin.

I blinked, turning away. The memory of our first encounter—the story he fed me that got under my skin that day in the confessional— God, I'd liked the way that felt. Talking like that with him.

I balled my fists and met his eyes again, forcing my tone to stay even. "Oh, Mr. Mori, have you forgotten?" I replied, faking innocence. "You always go to confession at the end of the month."

I fixed him with a knowing smile, watching his amused expression fall and turn dark.

Yeah. Never forget I know all about you.

His eyes remained calm, but I could hear the acceptance of my challenge in his taunting words, "See you at work."

And stepping around me without another word, he walked out of the room, leaving me by myself.

I stayed for a moment, staring up at the dangling threads of my scarf on the balcony above me.

I prided myself on always staying one step ahead. Information was power. It was more valuable than money.

But apprehension quietly crept in, anyway.

Kai wasn't stupid.

Eventually, he'd catch up.

CHAPTER 10

BANKS

Present

Delcour sat on the other side of the river from the Whitehall district. I remembered seeing the building from a distance from our apartment downtown when I was a kid and lived with my mother. Tall, black, with gold trim, it reminded me of something out of an old movie. Gangsters in pinstripe suits, cars with white-wall tires, ladies in fancy gowns . . . A tad of the art deco look, a bit of old Hollywood, and entirely too ostentatious, but it always filled me with awe when I caught a glimpse of it. I didn't know how anything could be glamorous and haunting at the same time, but Delcour proved that there was such a thing. It sat in the middle of the city like an ornate jewel on someone wearing a potato sack.

I didn't fit in places like this, and my nerves were acting of their own accord.

There'd probably be young people like me, but unlike me, they'd be hyper on a completely different set of priorities: designer shoes and triple venti no-foam soy lattes.

The elevator stopped and the doors opened, the vibrations from the music under my feet hitting my ears now.

My mouth dry, I forced a step and entered Michael Crist's penthouse.

"Hello," a man in black pants and a black shirt greeted me. "May I take your coat?"

"No."

I passed the racks of coats in the entryway, ignoring his taken-aback expression, and rounded the corner into the rest of the residence. Music played loudly, but I could still hear the chatter of the couples I walked by. Men moved about, dressed casually, some in suits with open collars, others in jeans and T-shirts, while the women were dressed to the nines. As usual.

The dim lights shone over the black marble floors, and I walked into the living room, the hair on my arms rising at the sight of all the people.

But I forced myself to relax. Crowds made me nervous, but I could deal. A few pairs of eyes drifted over me, trailing up and down my appearance, but I just continued my scan of the room.

Where the fuck was he?

I walked, slowly surveying the party for his sharply styled black hair and usual bored stare, but it appeared to be impossible. Many of the guests looked like they were Storm players—Michael's teammates—because even Kai's impressive six foot two was going to get lost in the midst of some of the six-and-a-half- and seven-foot guys here.

"Cry Little Sister" droned out of the speakers, and I caught sight of Erika, walking back inside through the terrace entrance. Candlelight flickered across her skin, and our eyes met. She made her way over to me.

"Hi," she said calmly, her smile small but warm. Even though she must know I didn't want to have anything to do with her, she didn't show it.

"Is Kai still here?" I asked, gesturing to the envelope in my hand. "He wanted this tonight."

She didn't say anything for a moment but just looked into my eyes.

"This way," she finally answered.

Falling in behind her, I followed her past the kitchen and down a hallway, looking to my left and seeing a sunken basketball court, right here, in the apartment.

Because of course there was.

Several guys in suits sans jackets raced up and down the court. I quickly searched the players' faces but didn't see Kai there, either.

Erika trailed farther down a dimly lit hallway, and my gaze fell on her back, kind of admiring the sleek and flowing black jumpsuit she wore with crisscrossed straps over her shoulder blades. Beautiful, simple, and the Horsemen's center.

Everything I would never be to anyone.

Still, I couldn't see why Damon was so obsessed with her.

She veered right and opened a door, deep voices and laughter immediately drifting into the hallway. Rika turned with her back to the open door, making room for me to enter.

I stepped in and looked around. A card table with half a dozen men, including Michael and Will, sat in the center of the room, and Kai occupied a chair, his back to me. Several more men loitered at various tables around the room, and a woman leaned on the wall in the corner, a drink in her hand.

A few, including Michael and Will, cast me a glance, pausing a moment, but most didn't pay me any mind.

I marched to Kai's side, not looking back to see if Rika stayed or left.

"I could've brought this to your house later," I said, annoyed as I shoved the envelope at his chest. "Or to the dojo in the morning."

He'd had me working and running errands nonstop for the past two days, after all. It was late, and I needed sleep.

Ignoring my complaints, he took the envelope and opened it.

I turned to leave.

"Stay," I heard him say.

I stopped, turning back.

Kai pulled out the papers Gabriel had given me while my gaze flashed to Michael, who was watching me. I almost smiled. Tenderfoot was still probably pissed about yesterday at the hotel.

I watched Kai flip through the contract but then stop to pull out a pen from his inside breast pocket. That was to be expected. Gabriel knew he'd fight certain stipulations.

"Aren't you going to introduce your friend, Kai?" a man on the other side of the table asked.

But Kai just cocked the pen, his eyes narrowing as he read.

And then I saw him shift in his seat and look up, eyeing me. "Is he kidding?" He pointed the tip of his pen to a bullet point on the contract, something about making sure Vanessa had children in a timely manner.

One of his eyebrows damn near touched his hairline as he looked at me like it was my fault.

I shrugged. "If you can't get it done, we can give her to a better man. Just say the word."

He just looked at me, not even the faintest scowl marring his impassive features. He turned back to the document. Slicing his pen across the page, he crossed out the provision and moved to the next page, also X-ing out several others.

"So, it's that easy in your world, huh?" he asked, keeping his voice just between us. "Just give one person to another person?"

"You should know," I shot back.

I was given to *him* until the wedding, wasn't I?

"This is Banks," he spoke up again, louder, so everyone at the table could hear. "She works for Gabriel Torrance. How long have you worked for him now?" He glanced up at me but didn't wait for me to answer. "Kind of odd how such a young girl got taken into a millionaire scumbag's mansion like that, don't you think?" His pen moved swiftly across the pages, circling and jotting notes. "Does he know your family? Do they have connections to him?" A wisp of a smile softened his stern face as he looked over the rest of the contract. "It would be interesting to find out how that happened. What use a woman could be to a house full of men, I wonder."

A few people around the table chuckled under their breath at his insinuation.

"And how much does he pay you or . . ." He paused, drawing out his last words. "What did he pay *for* you?"

He looked up at me, flipping the pages back into place and slipping the document back into its envelope. He might've been thinking out loud, or he might've been hinting at finding out the answers himself. It wouldn't be hard. A PI would only have to talk to my mother.

"Gotta be less than what I pay for a woman," I heard Will toss out, followed by more quiet laughter from around the room. He shot me a look, letting his distaste scale up and down my appearance.

"Oh, please," the woman in the corner interrupted. "Like I even charge you anymore. All you want to do is cuddle half the time anyway."

One of the men at the table snorted, barely able to contain his laughter, while others didn't bother trying to hide it.

Will turned to her with a scowl, whining, "Fuuuuuck."

She smiled and winked at him.

That must be Alex. College student and overpriced escort from the sixteenth floor. Friends with Rika, and has Will Grayson as a regular customer.

Damon liked her energy. Didn't like that she wouldn't do everything he wanted, though.

"So many questions . . ." Kai held up the envelope, offering it to me. "Almost makes you wanna hire someone to find out the answers."

I blinked slowly, trying to look bored, but my heart sped up just a hair. I'd expected this. Kai negotiated learning curves faster than most. I'd been researching him and his pals. He'd start doing the same with me, of course.

I'd have to pay my mother a visit.

Tomorrow.

"Have him agree to these changes, and I'll sign it," he said.

I grabbed hold of the envelope, but he didn't release it. Instead, he pulled it down, bringing me with it.

"And by all means," he whispered, his breath falling across my cheek. "Keep underestimating me."

We both clutched the envelope, and I turned my eyes on him, momentarily frozen.

So close. I wanted to pull away but couldn't. Something swelled in my chest, and his dark eyes turned black as he held me, locked.

You said you wanted to be hunted. God, why had I thought of that after all this time? I almost closed my eyes at the memory.

His smell, his mouth, his body pressing into mine . . . He was as cold as ice all the time.

Until he wanted it. I knew just how greedy he could get then.

The pulse between my legs began throbbing, and I yanked the envelope out of his hand and stood up straight.

"Can I do anything else for you, Mr. Mori?"

He dropped his hand to the armrest and appeared to focus back on the card game. "Go restock towels for the guests in the pool."

I arched an eyebrow. "I'm not here to wait on your friends."

"You're here for me and whatever I tell you to do." He pinned me with a warning look. "Unless you want to go back to Thunder Bay and tell Gabriel you broke the contract."

Yeah, you might just love that, huh? You've got the keys and codes to the hotel, haven't signed the contract yet, and the blame would fall on me for breaking the deal.

Holding Kai's glare, I stalked out of the room, hearing Michael's voice behind me. "They're in the hallway closet upstairs!"

I gritted my teeth, seething as chuckles drifted out of the room behind me. *Fuckers.*

Rounding the corner, I slipped in between people and grabbed hold of the railing, climbing the stairs quickly. I wasn't in any hurry to be of service, but I wanted out of here, and as soon as they got their damn towels, I was leaving with or without his permission.

The music downstairs faded, and I reached the top, a large open area full of TVs and couches, and a few people greeted me.

I continued down the hallway, in the dark, opening a few doors to find a couple bedrooms, a bathroom, and an office, before opening another and finally finding shelves of bedding and towels neatly stacked. I started plucking out as many towels as I could carry.

"Hi."

I jumped, my breath catching in my throat. The young woman from the poker game earlier peeked around the open door, her hand on her hip.

"I'm Alex," she told me.

"I know who you are."

I grabbed one more towel and added it to the stack in my arm.

"I'll take that as a good thing."

Take it however you like.

"I can't believe Rika tolerates your presence," I said, closing the closet door. "How many of her guests are you making clients tonight?"

But to my surprise, she laughed. "Not working tonight, actually."

A twinkle lit up her eyes, and I had to hand it to her. I'd been purposefully rude, but she rolled with it like a champ.

"And Rika likes having me everywhere," she taunted, leaning in. "She thinks I'm a good kisser."

Yeah, okay.

"Women are typically better kissers in my experience, anyway," she continued, giving me a look up and down that suddenly made me hyperaware. "I mean, men have no idea what to do with their tongues." She laughed. "I charge them extra for the kissing."

My mind drifted back to when I'd kissed Kai, and the nerves under my skin sparked to life. Kai definitely knew what to do with his tongue.

Alex went on, rolling her eyes. "It's either, *I'm an ice cream cone*"—she closed her eyes and licked the air, grunting and making exaggerated movements with her tongue—"or it's like tornado fucking alley with that thing." And again, she closed her eyes, making circles in the air with her tongue and demonstrating a cyclone. "It's like, I'm sorry. Am I supposed to need a bib when I kiss you?"

She winced, and I couldn't help but breathe out a little laugh. Thank goodness I hadn't had the same misfortune. I'd probably be tempted to bite anything stuck in my mouth that wasn't pleasant to be there.

She drifted across the hall, peering through the crack in the door there.

"But Will?" she whispered, the light from inside the room making her eyes sparkle. "He's really good. He knows how to use just the right amount that you can feel it like his tongue is right between your legs instead. He touches every nerve."

I followed her, spying Will inside the room with a girl pinned to the wall. His mouth covered hers, her lids fluttering as his hand trailed all over the dark skin of her thigh before lifting it up and pressing himself deeper between her legs, their clothes the only thing between them now.

I caught her little moan.

"Gentle at first," Alex went on, watching him as though she was narrating. "He savors and teases, and then goes in stronger and harder, and you've never been fucked so good and his dick's not even inside you yet."

I could see his tongue moving in her mouth, not too deep, but then he licked her upper lip before quickly snatching up her bottom one between his teeth. Then he dived back in, capturing her lips again.

My teeth tingled, and I clenched them, closing my eyes for a moment.

"He does the work, you know?" Alex said, and I could hear her breathlessness. "No part of a woman's body should be left unkissed. Will truly makes the most of what he's good at."

The beat of the music downstairs vibrated up through my legs, but I couldn't hear it. All I could hear was her. The girl in the room, her gasps and moans, and not really wondering what he was doing, because I could already see it in my head.

Part of me knew everything my brain told me was true. Men would hurt me, use me, and throw me away, blah, blah, blah.

But no matter what my head said, I still couldn't help the longing that always seeped in, more and more lately.

I wanted to grow up.

"I'd really like to do that to you right now," a voice said in my ear, and I popped my eyes open, noticing Alex had come to stand at my back. "I'd like to strip you down and bury my tongue between your legs."

My eyes rounded, and I dropped the towels. *Shit!*

"Alex." A deep voice suddenly pierced the silence, and I froze.

Alex stopped, too, and I felt her shift behind me.

"Not that one," Kai told her.

"You took the threesome I wanted with Michael and Rika, and now her?" she retorted. "I'm beginning to think you're my competition, Kai."

Threesome. I swallowed the lump in my throat. I'd known about it, but I didn't need reminders of it.

There was a silence, and then I finally saw Alex leave out of the corner of my eye, walking back down the hallway. I clenched my thighs, feeling the wetness between my legs as I turned around.

Kai leaned against the opposite wall, staring at me with his arms crossed over his chest. But there was nothing cold in his eyes. They had me rooted.

The sounds from the room where Will and the girl were started to get louder, and an unbidden image of Kai on top of me six years ago popped in my head.

My breathing shook as my stomach flipped, and I felt dizzy. "I'm . . . I'm going to be sick."

"You're not sick." He remained on the wall, looking me up and down. "You're turned on."

Heat rose to my cheeks, and I shook my head, trying to control my breathing.

"Spread your thighs," I heard Will order through the cracked door. "Open 'em up for me, baby."

Amusement touched Kai's eyes as we both stayed rooted, our gazes locked.

"Yeah," the girl panted. "Hurry. I'm about to come."

"Oh, that's so hot," Will told her, adding, "Keep rubbing that pussy. Make it nice and wet."

My chest caved, and I immediately pictured her on the bed in there and what she was doing for him.

"Mm-hmm," she moaned, begging, "Come on, let's do it."

"Turn over."

A cool sweat broke out all over my body, and I stared at Kai, letting my eyes fall down his body. Even under his clothes, I could tell how beautiful he was. I closed my eyes for a split second, trying to push away the need building between my legs. I wanted to be touched. I wanted these clothes off. I wanted his full attention on a bed somewhere. I didn't care where. He felt so good, and I remembered. Everything was still so clear.

The headboard in the room started hitting the wall and grunts and small cries drifted into the hallway.

I trailed my eyes down Kai's narrow waist and long legs, wishing for a moment that it was me in that room.

Entertaining for a moment that I would ever let it happen.

"Keep looking at me like that," Kai spoke up, "and we're going to have problems."

I turned my eyes away. I needed to get out of here.

"Can I leave now?" I shot out.

But he didn't answer. Instead, he moved, dropping his arms and walking straight for me.

"You know what I've thought about so many times over the years? More times than I care to admit?" he asked, planting a hand on the wall behind my head. "You and me in that tower, my hands on you, just feeling you. Remember that?"

I said nothing, and he leaned in. "I liked having control of you," he continued, his words coming out softly. Thoughtful. "It was different than it was with other girls. Control is an illusion. It usually only lasts a few minutes." He raised his eyes, meeting mine. "But with you, I felt like I'd have control of you for good. It felt like I could hold everything you are in the palm of my hand. You had to do and say so little to make me want you."

I inched back, hitting the wall. What did he want from me? Did he get off on slumming or something? Not that I thought I was disgusting or ugly, but Jesus. I purposely dressed in clothes too big in order to deter attention, and Kai acted like he didn't even see the clothes, the tangled hair, and the dirty fingernails.

He acted like he did six years ago. Like I was just a girl.

But not average, either. I was special. Wanted. Desired.

He leaned into my ear, sending a flutter through my stomach as he whispered, "Take off your jacket and open your shirt for me."

The urge to push him away hit me, but I remained still, because I really wanted to do what he asked me. I wanted his hands again.

I just shook my head instead.

He reached up, pulling the hat off my head, and my hair came free, spilling out around me. He took a tendril of my hair, curling it around his fingers. The small sensation made my eyelids flutter.

But then he shot up, grabbing a fistful of my hair at the back of my head, and I gasped, wincing at the pain.

"Fair's fair," he growled low, forcing me to hold his eyes. "You watched me. You followed me. Counted how many times a day I showered. Did you watch that, too? Huh?"

I clenched my teeth, the heat of his breath hitting my lips.

"Did you watch me fuck?" His eyes fell to my mouth. "Open your shirt for me, little one. Let's see if I like what I'm getting for my trouble."

His lips hovered over mine, and the longing in my body raged.

"No," I whispered, and planted my hands on his chest. "You take off your shirt."

He paused, staring at me curiously as he held my head an inch from his. My skin was burning, and my clothes chafed. It was almost painful. I wanted them off. I wanted to feel him against my body.

Reaching up, I touched his face, running my hand across his jaw and down behind his neck. Warm and smooth, but I wanted more.

He watched me warily, his eyes briefly dropping to my mouth again as his own lips parted. But he didn't stop me. His hold relaxed.

I dragged my fingers down to his shirt and held his eyes as I started undoing the buttons, but my fingers were shaking so badly I grabbed the shirt in both hands and ripped it open, the buttons flying in both directions.

He let out a heavy breath, sounding almost like a growl, as he tightened his hold and lowered his forehead to mine.

But I pushed him away, sending him stumbling back. "Don't touch me." And I advanced on him, pushing him again until he slammed back into the opposite wall.

A mix of shock and anger crossed his face, but I didn't give him a chance to respond. I rushed up to him, taking his wrists in both of my hands and planting them against the wall at his sides as I shot up to my tiptoes and buried my face in his neck.

And I ran my lips over his skin.

Slowly up and then down, over the bump of the vein in his neck and down the hot curve toward his collarbone.

He shuddered.

God, he was so smooth and warm, and a tingle hit my lips, spreading across my face and down my whole body. I opened my mouth, dragging my lips everywhere. Dipping under his chin to the other side, I explored him with my mouth, so tempted to kiss him. Just once. To sink my lips into his skin and taste what smelled so good. I ran my nose under his ear, inhaling his scent and then breathing out my warm breath. He melted into the wall, tipping his head back and closing his eyes, inviting me in further.

He started to push against my grasp, wanting his hands free, but I squeezed as hard as I could, sending him a warning.

Coming back to stand flat on my feet, I released his wrists. "Keep them there."

Pulling his shirt and jacket open wide, I moved my hands and mouth to his chest. My fingers scaled down his skin, humming at the feel of the ridges and dips, and my mouth followed the path set by my hands. I circled his nipple with my middle finger and then followed it with my lips, my thighs clenching at the skin there and the hard nub.

I closed my eyes. I didn't want this to end. I wanted him to wrap his arms around me, locking me into his heat and intoxicating scent.

But if I let him, that would be my first mistake.

I raised my head, watching him watch me as his chest rose and fell with heavy breaths.

"I'm not your little one." I dropped my hands, backing up. "But you're right about control. It's an illusion. Look at yourself. You never had it."

I let a smirk slip and dipped down to pick up my hat.

But the next thing I knew, Kai grabbed me and pulled me back into him. "And neither did you," he whispered in my ear. "You only have as much control as I allow you to have."

"Oh, yeah, you win. Brawn over brains every time, right? But you forget one thing." I turned my head, speaking to him. "I can say no whenever I want, and it ends. Unless you want to go to prison again."

He stilled, not saying anything.

He knew I was right. Of course, he could say no, too, but it wasn't likely.

His breath fell on my hair, and he released my arms, lowering his head next to mine.

"You're right," he said quietly. "You can say no anytime." And he began running his lips across my neck just like I'd done to him. "Anytime you want."

My eyelids fluttered, and his hand took the side of my face, turning my head toward him. Our noses nudged, our lips a hair away from each other, so close I could taste him, and we weren't kissing.

I was throbbing between my legs, and I thought about that piece-of-crap house and that lone bed in the room upstairs, and how there was nowhere else I wanted to be right now.

Who was really in control of whom? We were both fucked.

His hand grazed over my stomach, going lower, and I grabbed hold of it just as he took hold of me between my thighs. I whimpered. "Oh, God." I meant to pull him away, but it felt so good.

Fuck. I couldn't get air, and I gasped. These goddamn bindings. I couldn't breathe.

"Stop," I cried, shoving his hands away. "Stop, stop, stop. I can't breathe. I can't breathe."

I sucked in air, resting my palm on the wall to support myself. *Jesus. What the hell?* My ribs and lungs ached, and I winced, desperate to get this shit off.

I needed to get out of here.

"Hey, Kai," I heard a woman say.

I turned my head to see two girls walking down the hallway, neither of whom I recognized. Not that I should know them.

They glanced at me, their eyes dropping down my body and taking in my appearance. They turned their eyes away again, but I didn't miss the look they shot each other as they passed me, barely waiting to make it into the bathroom before breaking out in quiet laughs.

I looked down at the floor. "Can I get the hell out of here now?"

Kai stared at me, his jacket and shirt partially open, revealing the olive skin of his chest. "Don't worry about them. They're just drunk."

I pulled my hat on, not bothering to stuff my hair back up into it. I couldn't muster the patience. "Like you give a shit," I spat out. "You wanted me to be uncomfortable. That's why you had me come here, around these people, so you could remind me of my place."

"I didn't—"

"I don't care about your bullshit." I glared at him, familiar anger heating my blood now. "You think I'm not used to the way people like that look at me? Men thinking if they prettied me up they'd be doing me some kind of favor, and women laughing behind their hands. It's been that way my whole life. I don't give a shit what they see when they look at me. Your world is empty, and it can teach me nothing."

I'd let myself down. I'd gotten carried away with him. Again. But thankfully, it hadn't gone too far. Blame it on stress or the attraction toward him I always felt, but I'd stopped it. I could at least feel good about that.

I tilted my chin up. "I have Damon. He's all I want."

Kai's eyes thinned on me, and I could hear his slow but hard breathing from here. Yeah, think what you want, but it was true. My brother was the only man who wanted me strong. The only man who would never hurt me.

I turned on my heel and walked back down the hallway, toward the stairs.

Rounding the banister, I quickly descended the steps, seeing Kai following me out of the corner of my eye. He trailed slowly, though, so I knew he wasn't trying to catch me.

In two minutes I'd be outside and away from here. *Just go.*

But reaching the bottom, I looked up, seeing a scuffle starting in the middle of the living room. What the—?

Lev stood with his hands locked behind his head, grinning at David and Michael standing toe to toe. Ilia stood back with his arms crossed over his black suit coat, while Rika and several by-standers stood near, watching what was boiling.

"What's happening?" Kai called behind me, brushing past me.

The desk clerk from downstairs, still in his three-piece suit, turned and spoke up. "I'm sorry, sir," he said, looking rattled. "Mr. Crist said anyone could come up, but they looked out of the ordinary, and when I called to check in, they just took the elevator. I'm sorry."

He looked between Michael and Kai, his eyes worried. I wasn't sure why he was apologizing to Kai. It wasn't his apartment.

"It's fine," Michael assured him and then looked to my guys. "Who are you?"

"They work for Gabriel," I called out, pushing through the people. "David, what are you guys doing here?"

I saw them in Thunder Bay a couple hours ago when I was picking up the contract, but they were supposed to be in for the night. I wasn't expecting them in the city this late.

David turned his head, looking down at me. "Do you want to go home?"

"I was just leaving."

But Kai stepped in, glancing at me. "Sit," he told me.

I steeled my jaw, glaring up at him. What?

Hell, no. Screw him and this power trip. I'd had enough for one night.

"You're not prepared to start something with these guys," I said, getting cocky.

Real easy to do when I had backup. Yeah, I was a little shit.

But Kai spoke to David instead. "Gabriel agreed to this. She works for me now. Leave."

"Gabriel didn't send us." He stepped forward, approaching Kai. "And we leave on *her* command. Not yours."

Kai turned to me, bowing his head to stare me down. "Go with him. I dare you."

My heart skipped a beat. How much he reminded me of Damon now.

But the contract still wasn't signed. Once it was, I could bolt, and it would be up to him if he wanted to chase me down. If I broke the agreement now, though, Gabriel would blame me.

Kai lowered his voice, everyone around us hushed, but the music and partygoers in the rest of the place still went hard. "Who do you belong to?"

"Kai," someone scolded.

"Quiet, Rika," he bit out, still looking at me. "Who do you belong to?"

I could feel eyes on me coming from everywhere, and I wanted to take out my pocketknife and sink it into his fucking gut. *Goddamn him.* Years and years of climbing over shit bags like him to just get a peek over the fence, and here he was, grabbing my ankles and yanking me back down into the pit. Everyone was going to know. Everyone was going to see me powerless here.

I held his eyes, my own burning with hatred. I clenched my teeth so hard they started aching.

Taking a step, I moved to his side and turned around, facing David, Lev, and Ilia.

"To you," I said barely above a whisper.

And I'm going to kill you for this. A lump lodged in my throat, and I felt nauseous.

"Now . . ." Kai said, sitting down in the black cushioned chair behind him. "You can take her home."

I didn't wait for the guys to do anything. I shot off, pushing through all the people, the guys turning and following me as I passed. I felt a hand rest lightly on my back.

"She knows how to walk," Kai barked behind us. "Don't touch her."

The hand, probably David's, immediately left me.

Swinging around the corner, we all charged into the elevator, and Ilia pushed the button. Once the doors closed, I was fucking done. I threw my fist into the wall over and over again, swinging my leg back and kicking it, growling at the top of my lungs. "Fuck!"

I swung around, throwing my elbow back, everything in my right arm, from my knuckles to my shoulder, screaming with pain. I slammed the wall again and again, punching and kicking. "Ugh!" I threw another punch.

Thankfully, the guys knew to shut up and stay on their side of the elevator.

I paced back and forth, breathing hard. He'd humiliated me in there. I slammed the wall with my palm again, pain shooting up my arm. *Humiliated me . . .*

"What do you want us to do?" David asked.

But I didn't look at them. Or answer.

I knew what needed to happen. I needed Kai to sign that damn contract. Once he did that, he was all I had to contend with. My brother would be allowed to return and be safe, and my father would be out of the picture, having gotten what he wanted. I could do things my way then.

But I suspected Kai never had any intention of signing it. That was the problem. He was going to drag this out and drag me with him.

I should never have let him touch me.

Guys just wanna fuck, I remembered my brother telling me once. *We'll fuck anything we can get our hands on. No one's going to love you. Not really. He'll just lead you on, get what he can take, and eventually, he'll move on to someone newer and hotter. Promise you'll never let anyone use you like that. Don't be a slut. Be strong.*

My brother taught me that men would only use me and hurt me, and from what I'd seen so far in this life, he was damn right.

Kai could get horny just like anyone else, but lust could never overshadow how cruel I knew he could be. How cruel he was to Erika last year and how cruel he'd just proven himself to be.

He was in complete control of me. He knew it, and he'd just proved it.

I needed to stop responding to him. Whether it was lust or anger or fear, I needed to shut down. I needed to bore him.

If I didn't, we'd both let loose.

And then . . . it would be war.

CHAPTER II

KAI

Present

Slamming the locker door closed, I stuffed my clothes into my duffel bag and zipped it shut. It was late, the gym was empty, and I walked out of the locker room not feeling as exhausted as I'd hoped.

After another workout and another shower, I was still far too awake at ten thirty at night.

Leaving the locker room, I walked down the hall to the office, grabbed my phone off the desk, and locked the door. Everyone was gone by now, the rest of the place quiet and dark.

My phone rang.

Looking down, I saw my mother's number.

My shoulders fell a little, but I knew she'd be calling. I'd canceled on showing up for dinner tonight.

I loved my parents, but I really envied Michael's parents' hands-off approach sometimes.

I brought the phone to my ear. "You're up late."

"I'm trying to not sleep," she chirped. "It seems to work well for my son."

I laughed to myself, walking around the lobby and making sure the computers were shut down.

"Are you calling to bust my chops?" I asked her.

"Maybe."

"I'm sorry, okay?" I walked toward the front door. "I should've been there tonight."

I made it home on Sundays for breakfast and to train with my father, so it wasn't like I never saw them. I just found it hard to force myself to be there any more than that when I could still feel his disappointment from across the table.

"Is Dad angry?"

"No," she replied. "He's just . . ."

I nodded. "Disappointed. I know."

My mother was silent, because even she knew it was true. We'd gone round and round, and while my father rarely yelled at me, his silence was harder to take.

"I marinated a couple extra steaks," she singsonged. "They're waiting for you if you want to come home tomorrow."

"Maybe."

Which meant I would see her Sunday, as usual.

"You're doing well," she told me. "And he sees it. He loves you, Kai."

"Yeah, I know." In theory.

If I died, he'd mourn me. I knew that. I doubted anything else would bring us out of this stalemate we'd found ourselves in since I got arrested all those years ago, though.

"I'll see you soon, okay?" I punched the code into the keypad and opened the front door, walking through and locking it.

"I love you," she said quietly, but those three words held so many more things she wasn't saying. I hated that I'd ever made my mother cry.

"Love you, too," I replied, and hung up the phone.

Sliding it into my pocket, I turned around and glanced up at The Pope. If I didn't find Damon, the shit was going to hit the fan again, and I'd probably never be able to look my father in the eye.

Walking toward the alley around the corner, I spotted Banks leaned up against the brick wall with her hands in her pockets.

"What are you doing?" I'd let her leave an hour ago.

"Waiting for my ride."

"You don't have a car?" I asked.

"Have you ever seen me with a car?"

I faltered. *Well, no.* She was always chauffeured around by those idiots.

And speak of the devil . . .

I looked up, seeing the same black SUV charge up to the curb, pulling to a quick stop. David and that kid—I forgot his name—sat in the front seats, shooting their eyes between Banks and me.

Whenever she called, they sure came running, didn't they?

I walked around her and into the alley. "I'll take you home. Get in."

"Like I said, it's covered," she bit out.

I stopped, turning and meeting her eyes.

"Besides, I'm going to Thunder Bay," she added. "I need to take care of a couple things."

"Awesome. I'm heading there, as well." And I turned, walking for my car and unlocking it.

I wasn't planning on going to Thunder Bay, but I guess now I was.

And I wasn't jealous. I just didn't like how these guys always showed up, acting like she was still theirs.

She wasn't, and everyone needed reminding.

I opened my car door, staring at her over the hood. "Banks."

She stood there a moment, shooting a sideways glance at the guys and looking embarrassed. She probably wanted to argue, but she did what she was told. Walking over and opening the door, she climbed in, slammed the door, and didn't bother putting her seat belt on.

I shot the guys a look, seeing them scowl back at me. I almost laughed.

Backing out of my parking space, I swung the car around and sped past them, out of the alley and into the quiet street.

She didn't say anything, and I let her be silent as I drove. I was pushing her around a lot lately, and I didn't want that to be every interaction we had. I liked talking to her.

After Michael's party a couple days ago, I'd stayed out of her way and let her stay out of mine, more because I was confused rather than angry.

I was supposed to be searching for Damon. I was supposed to be cleaning up what he had on me.

But the other night, in that dark hallway at Delcour, everything came flooding back. How easy it was to engage with her, talk to her, and how much I loved those rare moments of vulnerability when she almost needed me. And wanted me.

She was such a mystery, but right now, the only truth I kept wanting was what I would get with her underneath me, between the sheets. What would her eyes look like? What words would she whisper? Where would she put her hands on me?

But she was loyal to the Torrances. How could I do what I needed to do and keep her?

The car cut through the night, racing across the bridge and down the dark highway toward Thunder Bay with the headlights shining ahead. I drew in a thick breath, everything suddenly feeling so heavy inside the car.

My skin buzzed with the feel of her next to me.

I glanced over, seeing her staring out the window, her back straight and her hands in her lap. Slowly, though, she started to run them up and down her thighs, and I noticed how deep her breaths were growing.

She turned her head to the front again, and I noticed the quick glance out of the corner of her eye. She folded her lips between her teeth.

I turned my eyes back on the road, holding back my smile. "You're real good at self-control, aren't you, kid?" I kept my tone calm. "Do you want to say something to me? I can feel the weight of it. You may as well go ahead."

But she remained quiet, as I knew she would. I put my elbow on the door and ran my fingers over my lips. How do you play with someone who doesn't engage?

And then I got an idea.

"So, what is she like?" I asked.

Her eyebrows pinched together. "Who?"

"Vanessa."

She turned her eyes back out the passenger-side window, sighing impatiently. "Like she's going to look real good bouncing up and down on top of you on your wedding night."

I squeezed the steering wheel, grinding it in my fist. Such a fucking brat.

"So, you've never talked to her, then?" I pressed.

I wanted her to be jealous.

"A couple times," she answered. "And she once paid a boy to grab my breasts at a party when we were fifteen. Damon tied him to a tree for that and stuffed his snake, Volos, down his underwear. The kid screamed like a bitch."

I snorted.

And then my face fell, hating that, for a moment, I missed Damon. I didn't like hearing someone attacked Banks, but for some reason, I was appeased, knowing he avenged her. That was unlike him.

Why was he so attached to her?

But then again, I was fast becoming attached myself. For reasons I couldn't even try to understand right now.

"I talked to Michael today," I told her, changing the subject as I stared out the front windshield. "He said you threatened him at

The Pope. After he grabbed you and pinned you to a wall to threaten *you*."

I couldn't resist feeling amused at the picture in my head.

"You told him that we are vulnerable and unfocused?" I smiled at her, rounding a soft turn. "He actually seemed concerned, like you had a point."

Her eyebrows dug in deeper, as she clearly tried to ignore my attempts at conversation.

"You know, the last time I saw you, six years ago, you were timid and innocent. The type of girl who would flinch at a light breeze." I let out a long breath, wondering if that girl was still inside her somewhere. "Now it's like even a sip of water is calculated. And the next nineteen moves after it."

I could feel her tensing next to me.

"A couple years after that Devil's Night, Rika tagged along with us on one," I told her, but I suspected she already knew all about that. "She reminded me so much of you that night. Just learning about what it was that excited her. Just starting to put that first step over the line that she craved to cross so much. You're both so much alike."

Rika had reminded me of Banks that night. Someone I could be drawn to. Someone who would go down the rabbit hole with me. I had my friends, but it wasn't the same.

"Except for the control. Rika reacts from the gut," I added, licking my lips. "She wants what she wants, and she takes it."

Banks turned her eyes back out the window, acting like I wasn't here.

"But growing up, she, too, was very different." I steered the car around a right-hand turn. "When we're young, we are who we are out of necessity—we are who we're taught to be. With freedom, though, comes the liberty to broaden our horizons. When we only have ourselves to answer to," I said, and glanced at her again. "You haven't gotten that freedom yet, have you? Why? Do people hurt you if you step out of line? Does Gabriel hurt you when you misbehave or speak out of turn? Did Damon hurt you?" I kept prodding, hoping I'd exhaust her.

She drew in a hard breath and faced the front again, clearing her throat. "You and Michael can start by curbing Will's destructive habits. They've gotten worse since Damon left," she said, ignoring all my questions. "He's depressed. You need to give him something to do. Lots of things, actually, so he has no time to think. Give him a purpose."

I raised my eyebrows. I wasn't annoyed she'd changed the subject back to her discussion with Michael. She was talking, after all.

I thought about what she said. Will was hardly ever sober and that made him weak and an easy target. Maybe she was right. After all, I was functioning better than Will, and maybe it was just due to the fact that I kept really busy, so I didn't dwell on the past.

The car grew quiet again, and I caught sight of her hands, running up and down her thighs once more. I reached up and turned on the heat—low level—just in case she was cold.

The glow from the dash cast just enough light to make out her jaw, her nose, and a strip of the skin on her neck. I squeezed the wheel again, my body charged with new energy. Too much pent-up energy.

It had been a while since I'd been with anyone.

Maybe I should let you hunt me, too.

I blinked, trying to derail the heat coursing through me. She had too much of my interest, and I didn't need the distraction. There were other women to play with. Hell, Alex had given me her card like fifteen times. She was ready to go if I ever decided I wanted her.

A small sound broke the silence, and I realized it was Banks. Her stomach had growled. I glanced at the clock on the dash, seeing it was after eleven.

"When was the last time you ate?" I asked her.

But she didn't answer.

"I've never seen you eat, actually." I kept glancing at the road but back to her, too.

"I think everyone could say the same for you."

True. I kept strange hours, so I did things at my own pace.

But I couldn't ignore the dull ache in my own stomach, either. After meetings earlier, I'd been busy with payroll and making calls. I'd forgotten to eat.

"You're right," I said, swerving to catch the fork in the road. "And I'm starved. What do you like to eat?"

"I'd like to go home."

Yeah. I'm sure you would.

"No problem," I replied.

I meant *my* home," she bit out a half hour later, annoyed.

I laughed under my breath, walking past her as she stayed rooted next to a wall in my parents' dining room.

Instead of taking her back to Gabriel's, I'd brought her to my house. Or my parents' house, anyway. My mom and dad—both upstairs sleeping and oblivious that we were down here—still lived in Thunder Bay, as did Michael's and Will's parents, and of course, Damon's father.

I carried plates to the long wooden table, shining with the soft light of the wrought-iron chandelier hanging above. Despite my father's love of the traditional Japanese style of decorating, my mother won and furnished our house with lots of dark wood, carpets, paintings, and colors.

But she also aimed to please him. There were wonderful views of our property and plenty of natural light entering the house.

I set down two plates and napkin rolls with silverware.

"This is the best restaurant in town," I told her, tossing a bottle of water to her that I'd carried under my arm. "Sit."

But she just crossed her arms over her chest, water bottle tucked underneath, and looked away, ignoring me. "Can I leave now?"

I yanked out my chair. "I know you're hungry."

Her eyes drifted to the plate but quickly looked away again.

Unrolling my napkin, I sat down and grabbed the fork and knife inside, starting to cut one of the filet mignons my mom said would be waiting in the refrigerator.

She remained on the wall, and I dropped my elbows, losing my patience. "Sit."

She waited about three seconds, just to piss me off probably, but she finally yanked out the chair and dropped her ass in it.

After setting the bottle of water down, she promptly crossed her arms again. "I don't like steak."

Yeah, okay. Whatever.

I decided not to fight her on it.

Even though I knew she was lying. It was an excuse so she wouldn't have to be cordial for a meal with me.

I mean, who the hell didn't like steak? Unless she was a vegetarian, and no offense, but I got the impression she grew up eating whatever she was given. And more often than not, that was probably McDonald's and other people's leftovers rather than organic broccoli and fucking almond milk.

I dropped my eyes, looking at the plate holding the food. Baby potatoes, green beans, and a thick chunk of steak that I knew would cut like butter.

I was suddenly lost in thought. We were probably more alike than she thought.

I set my knife and fork down, my stomach groaning at the smell of the charred edges I loved on my meat.

"When I was little," I told her, leaning back in my chair, "we lived in this crappy two-bedroom apartment in the city." I drifted back there in my mind, trying to remember every detail. "The holes in my bedroom walls were so deep, you could smell the weed our neighbors were smoking and the curry the lady upstairs was cooking."

I stared off at the tablecloth, remembering the flights of stairs we climbed every day, my poor mom with me in tow.

"My mom did her best to make it nice, though," I said, remembering my scratchy drawings she decorated the walls with. "She was really good with money and making a little go a long way."

Banks remained quiet.

"My dad was finishing school and working all the time, so he was barely ever home," I explained. "I ate mac and cheese so much, I never asked what was for dinner. Not that I cared. Mac and cheese is awesome." I gave a half smile. "But my mom would do her best to make it all gourmet and shit. Pile it over some bread and add a sprig of parsley."

I didn't think I'd had mac and cheese since we left that apartment, now that I thought about it.

"I remember one night—I was, like, five—my dad came home," I continued, my voice quiet like I was talking to myself. "And I'd already eaten. Mac and cheese, of course. I was sitting, watching TV, and she put a steak in front of him at the kitchen table. I still remember hearing it sizzle on the plate. The way the butter it had sautéed in smelled. He was livid."

I remember him looking up at her from his chair, this mix of anger and confusion. My father had been used to doing without. He grew up poor. But my mother hadn't. She came from a wealthy family and left a rich fiancé forced on her in order to marry my father. She was disowned. My grandparents had still never met me.

"'How could you waste the money?'" I repeated my father's words to her in his stern voice. "'If my family doesn't eat steak, then I don't eat steak.' But my mother said that important men eat steak, and she didn't want my father to forget that he was an important man."

I raised my eyes, forcing a smile as I looked into her eyes.

"Instead, he became a great man, and now we can have steak anytime we want." I dropped my gaze, mumbling under my breath as I absently nudged the plate away. "I don't even need to be important."

I wasn't important.

Not yet.

My father worked his ass off to give my mother back everything she sacrificed in choosing him, and how did I repay him? I fucked around, driving cars he paid for and eating anything I wanted, no matter the cost. I didn't earn a damn thing.

I was nothing in the shadow of what he'd accomplished.

I took my trust fund after I got out last year, invested a lot of it, and tried to make something of myself, but the black cloud of being labeled a criminal still hung over me. I could always see it in his eyes. I'd never be able to erase the shame.

My eyes stung, and I blinked, looking away. I didn't deserve to be at this table, let alone eating his fucking meat.

But then I saw her move. I looked up just enough to see her unroll her napkin, taking out her silverware. Slowly, I watched as she cut into the meat, slicing off a piece and timidly putting it into her mouth.

She chewed softly and then suddenly squeezed her eyes shut, putting her hand to her mouth.

My body warmed. "Is it good?" I asked quietly.

She opened her eyes again and nodded, letting out a small whimper.

My shoulders relaxed, and I watched her take another bite, this one faster. I smiled.

My mother's homemade marinade was fantastic, but I was pretty good at cooking it just right, too.

I looked at my own plate and pulled it forward again, picking back up my knife and fork.

"Well, I'm glad I could change your mind about steak," I said, cutting back into my own.

She swallowed. "I've *actually* never eaten steak."

I took a bite of the tender meat, the juices sending my taste buds on a high. "Ever?"

She shrugged one shoulder, looking away as she chewed another bite.

"What do you usually like to eat?"

She sliced into the steak again, making short work of it. She must be hungry. "Eggs, toast . . ." she told me. "That kind of thing."

"Can't be that filling."

But she just looked away again, ignoring my prompt for more info. I let my gaze drop to her hands. A thin line of black smudge lay under her nails, and the black jacket she wore was frayed at the cuffs. Eggs and toast, huh? I got the sneaking suspicion that was all she could afford, goddammit. What did Gabriel pay her?

Well, I guess that was on me now, wasn't it? I'd sort something out tomorrow, then.

"You never used to wear those gloves," I pointed out, gesturing to the fingerless leather gloves she wore. "Is there a reason now?"

"So I don't tear my knuckles when I hit you." She stuffed another bite of food into her mouth.

My chest rumbled with a laugh I held in. Hey, I might let her get in a punch. She wouldn't win, though.

She downed the steak, green beans, and most of the potatoes, finally opening her bottle of water and taking a long drink.

She looked . . . satisfied, oddly enough.

I didn't know why, but it felt good to feed her. She wasn't the kind of person to let others do things for her, so this was going to be a rarity. I might as well enjoy it.

She took another long gulp and capped the bottle, wiping her mouth on her sleeve.

I finished a few more bites while she sat quietly, fiddling with the napkin on the table.

And then she finally spoke up, breaking the silence. "I don't know where he is." She raised her resolute eyes, meeting mine. "And if I did, I wouldn't tell you."

She wasn't trying to be difficult. Just honest and straight with me, and I turned her words over in my head, finally nodding.

I brought the napkin up and wiped off my mouth, setting it back down and holding her gaze. "I understand. I'm still not letting you go, though."

CHAPTER 12

BANKS

Present

A shrill ringing pierced the air the next morning, and I jolted awake, pawing the nightstand above my head for my phone. It dangled over the side, and I grabbed it, ripping out the charger as I blinked away the exhaustion. Gabriel's name appeared on the screen. I answered it immediately.

"Banks," I said, quickly clearing my throat as I sat up and swung my legs over the bed.

"A messenger will bring the contract to his dojo this morning," he informed me. "Make sure he signs it."

I rubbed my face, trying to wake up. Fuck, I shouldn't have eaten that meal last night. I had more energy when I ate less. "I told you, I don't think he has any intention of signing it. He wanted access to The Pope because he thinks Damon is there. He's screwing with us."

"What do I care what his plan is?" my father snapped. "He saddled this pony. Now he gets to ride it."

Kai wasn't signing the damn contract. I wasn't sure what he wanted with me—I wasn't even sure he knew—but I definitely understood Kai didn't like doing things the wrong way. After what I heard last night, he would never marry someone he didn't know and explain to his father that he'd just bound himself to Gabriel

Torrance. My father and Kai's didn't cross paths often, and despite the fact that their sons were good friends once, Katsu and Gabriel fucking hated each other.

"Damon isn't at The Pope, correct?" Gabriel asked.

I stood up and walked over to the window, peeling back the tattered shade to see that it was raining.

"Like I told you, I think he was at some point," I said. "But he appears to be gone now."

My brother, I was sure, had several hiding spots in the city. If he was at The Pope, he would've seen us coming in time to scram.

"You would tell me if he was calling you? Or if you'd seen him?" he pressed, a threat in his tone. I could tell he was nervous. Damon was a time bomb, and Gabriel was losing his grip on how to handle him. "I realize he has your loyalty, but I'm the one who pays you. You are only protected by my good graces, little girl. Remember that."

I released the shade, my ire rising. "And your only hold on him is me. Remember that."

I immediately closed my eyes, regretting my lip. *Shit.*

My father fell silent. I'd gotten mouthy with him once. And once was all it took for me to learn my place.

I took a deep breath, calming my tone. "I'm on board with you," I assured him. "Don't worry, and trust that I can determine the best way to do my job. I know Damon better than anyone. I will get him home."

He didn't say anything for a while, but I could hear voices in the background. Thank goodness I wasn't standing in front of him right now. If I were, his options about how to handle my impudence wouldn't be so limited.

But to my surprise, he simply released a sigh and said, "Fine." And then he added, "You should've been born a boy. You're the son Damon should've been."

I just stood there, the weight on my shoulders so heavy. Part of me liked hearing that. That he wished my brother was more like me and not the other way around. It filled my heart with pride.

But I still wasn't a boy. And I *never* would be. That's all it boiled down to. What was between my legs.

And no matter what I did or how hard I worked, there would always be that.

"Still, females aren't completely useless," he went on. "Kai likes you, so use what God gave you and get him to sign the contract. Don't bother coming back until you do."

And then he hung up.

I hit the *Off* button on my phone and tossed it onto the sheets on the bed. Crossing my arms over my chest, I ground my teeth together, trying to find my fucking focus again.

I was so tired.

I should've just come home last night. I shouldn't have gotten into his car or eaten his food or let him tell me stupid fucking stories that made my stomach knot with things I shouldn't feel.

What do I care that he likes mac and cheese, for Christ's sake?

I ran my hand over the top of my head, pushing back the hairs that had come loose from my two French braids.

Dammit. I squeezed my eyes shut, groaning as I dug my nails into my scalp. The hair was suddenly so tight I just wanted to tear out the rubber bands and rip apart the braids. My head hurt. My skin burned. And my stomach ached with hunger, craving to be full again like it was last night.

I forced breaths in and out.

Where are you, Damon? We don't have to live like this. Why did you leave me behind?

But I knew the answer. He left because he knew I would wait. I always did.

The more Kai was in my days, though, the more confused I was becoming. He'd been so candid last night, reminiscing about his old childhood apartment, but then his expression turned sad as he recalled how his father had succeeded in becoming such a great man. He left so much unsaid. So much he didn't really need to say, I guessed.

He thought he was a disappointment.

I looked around my small one-room apartment, the cracked floorboards vibrating under my feet every time someone walked down the hallway outside my door.

The dirty window was covered by a yellowed shade. The sink sat empty, my one dish, one bowl, one cup, and one set of silverware sitting in the dish rack next to it. There was a futon I'd bought at a secondhand store and some cinder blocks with a board on top functioning as the coffee table.

Kai Mori didn't know how lucky he was. At least he had people to count on, an education, opportunities, and chances.

I didn't even have a high school diploma.

No money, either, and I could never leave the one person I gave a shit about.

Kai could always rise higher, and I was getting tired of being around him and being reminded that I couldn't.

I would always live like this.

Jogging up the narrow stairwell, I swung around the railing and continued up to the second floor. Cigarette butts lay squashed into the chipped wooden floors, and I breathed through my mouth to keep the stench of everything else going on in this building from making me gag. It was no picnic growing up with Damon and Gabriel, but I was so thankful my brother had taken me away from here eleven years ago.

I pounded on my mother's apartment door, the 3 missing from the 232 above the peephole. Now just the dark mark of the glue shaped like a three remained.

"Mom!" I called out, pounding with the side of my fist again. "Mom, it's me!"

We both lived in the same broken-down neighborhood in Meridian City, so walking here took less than ten minutes.

When I moved to town after Damon went off to prison, I could've just moved back in with her, I suppose—to combine resources and all—but I didn't want to, and thankfully, she didn't ask. She still had a lifestyle that kids could cramp, so . . .

I needed to talk to her, though. We needed a straight story in case anyone—like Kai—came by to ask about me. Gabriel wasn't on my birth certificate, and the only other people who knew I was his daughter all worked for him, so my mother was the only weak link. I had to make sure she kept her mouth shut. Kai didn't need to find out exactly how much leverage he had at his fingertips.

After a minute of no response and no sounds coming from inside, I dug out my stolen key, unlocking the door. Opening it, I took a step in and immediately looked around, taking in the living room in shambles.

"What the hell?" I breathed out, wincing at the smell.

I spotted a man passed out on the couch, one leg hanging off, and closed the door behind me, not worrying about being quiet. He obviously hadn't heard me banging it down a moment ago anyway.

Sticking my keys back in my pocket, I took in the dark, dingy room, the only light coming from whatever was breaching the shades and the tacky blue velvet curtains. I walked over to the coffee table, sifting through day-old Chinese food containers, cigarettes, and tipped-over beer bottles. I picked up a pipe, the glass clouded from the residue of what had burned inside it. Every muscle tightened as I glared at it, and I shook my head.

Tossing it back down to the table, I glanced at the biker sprawled on the couch with his jeans and belt unfastened. Then, raising my eyes a hair, I glared at the camera sitting on the arm of the sofa. The nice, high-tech kind with an attached microphone.

Fuck her.

Spinning around, I charged for the kitchen table, tipped over one of the chairs, and stomped on one of the legs, breaking it off. Picking it up, I charged down the hallway toward her bedroom and whipped it open.

The knob slammed into the wall, and I found her with another fucking guy, this one younger and passed out on the bed next to her. Sheets curled around their legs, a lamp lay overturned on the floor, and the rain splattered on the sill where the window was cracked open. Clothes were scattered everywhere, and the stench of cigarettes hit me like a wave. I fought not to cough.

Turning my eyes right, I spotted the tripod for the camera.

Son of a bitch. I whipped the chair leg to my right, slamming it into her dresser.

"Get out!" I shouted. "Get the fuck out!"

I pounded the wooden stick again, sending the perfume bottles on her dresser tipping over.

"What the hell?" The man suddenly woke, trying to sit up and rubbing his eyes.

"Get up, asshole!" I raised my foot, stomping it down on the bed. "Get out of here now!"

My mom, her dark hair hanging over one eye, pulled the sheet up and sat up. "What? What's happening?"

"Shut up," I growled, raising the stick.

The young guy, probably only a few years older than me, looked at me like he was part terrified and part confused.

Okay, let me be clearer, then.

I got in his face. "Get. Out!" I bellowed, my face hot with fire as I slammed the wooden leg against the wall above his head over and over again. "Get the fuck out! Go! Go! Go!"

"What the fuck?" he barked, scrambling off the bed and scurrying for his clothes. "What the fuck is your problem?"

"Nik, what are you doing?" I heard my mother ask me, but I ignored her.

I breathed hard. The camera, the men, drugs . . . fucking slut. I swallowed the bile rising in my throat.

The guy scrambled back into his jeans, grabbing his shoes and swiping his shirt off the chair, and shot me a scowl as he bolted from the room.

My mother quickly slipped into her nightgown and robe, but I followed the guy out, making sure he took his friend.

I saw him hopping on one leg, trying to get his shoes on. "Man, get up!" he whisper-yelled to his buddy.

The other one started to peel himself off the sofa, but I bolted over and grabbed the camera.

"Hey, that's ours!" the young one shouted. "We paid her! What's on that is ours!"

But I just stood there, my fist squeezing the chair leg as I dared them. "Gabriel," I said slowly. "Torrance."

They quickly exchanged a look, and I watched as their faces fell. Yeah, that's right. That name was useful when I needed it to be.

They didn't know my father couldn't give a shit less about what my mother did.

"Get out," I repeated one last time.

They moved slowly, but they moved. They picked up their coats, grabbed their drugs, and walked out the door, the young one shooting me another displeased little scowl before he walked out. "She wasn't any good anyway," he spat, his eyes flashing behind me.

They walked out, and I charged over, kicking the door shut right behind them.

Hearing a shuffle behind me, I whipped around, tossing the stick onto the couch.

My mother stood in the living room, having just come out of the hallway, her red silk robe falling mid-thigh, partially covering her pink nightie. She chewed her thumbnail, chin trembling.

"What's the video camera for?" I asked.

"I needed money."

"I give you money!"

"That doesn't even cover rent!"

Her eyes pooled with tears, and I charged over to the couch, tossing off the new pillows she'd bought.

"What about this shit?" I charged, continuing to walk around the living room, sending a wall hanging swinging on its nail and a crystal bowl on the end table wobbling.

I turned around, taking in her fake nails with the French manicure and the spray tan. Gabriel paid me shit, a "woman's wage" compared to what David, Lev, and Ilia made, and after I paid my rent and the few utilities I had, she got the rest. I somehow managed to live on less! Why couldn't she? I felt a sob well up in my throat, and I just wanted to fucking strangle her.

"There's millions of other people in the world and they make it work somehow!" I shouted, charging up and getting in her face.

Everything was fucked, and the walls were closing in. I hated my life. I hated Damon and my father and Kai and everyone. I just wanted to go to sleep for a year. When were things going to be different?

"He was right," I gritted out, staring at her but seeing only myself. "You're just a sloppy, junkie whore! What are ya gonna do when no one wants to pay for your tired old pussy anymore? Your tits are already sagging down to your knees!"

Her hand whipped across my face, and my head slammed right.

I sucked in a breath, my whole body going still.

The burn in my face spread like a snakebite getting deeper and deeper, and I closed my eyes.

Christ. My mother had never hit me before.

I might've gotten a few spankings as a kid—I didn't remember—but she'd never hit me on the face.

Slowly, I turned my head forward again, seeing her staring at me, a world of hurt in her red eyes. She brought her hand up to her mouth, and I didn't know if she was shocked by what she'd done or sad that this was where we were at.

I dug in my pocket, feeling a tear spill over as I stared at the ground. I took the sixty-four dollars I had on my clip and walked over, dumping it on the coffee table.

"That's everything," I said.

Today it was all I was ever going to give her again, I promised myself.

But tomorrow it would be "enough to live on for a few days."

And next week I'd be back with more.

I always came back. What was I going to do? I didn't want my mother living on the streets. I still loved her.

Ignoring her soft crying and her head buried in her hands, I opened the front door to leave.

"Do you have money to eat?" she spoke up.

But I just laughed under my breath. "Give yourself a couple hits," I told her, gesturing to the pipe. "You won't care anymore."

Slamming the door, I let out a breath, my chest shaking as I squeezed my eyes shut.

"I am important," I whispered to myself.

Silent tears streamed down as I forced away all the doubt. Forced away the suspicions that I was being used. *No.* No, my father needed me more every day. And Damon wasn't using me, either. He wanted me to be happy. I know he did. And I would be, eventually.

And if I didn't take care of my mom, who would?

I was needed. I was valuable.

I wouldn't be thrown away like her. They wouldn't do that to me. Who was going to do what I did for them?

The camera cracked in my fist, and every muscle in my face ached with a sob, because even I could no longer believe my own words.

Oh, God. I broke into a run as the world in front of me blurred and all the tears started to spill over. I was going to be like her. Months turn into years, and people like me don't make it out.

She was going to die in that apartment. And I was going to die in this city, just as dumb and uneducated and poor as I was right now.

I raced down the stairs, swinging around the banister, and bolted out the door.

The cold rain pierced my face like an icicle, a welcome relief from the shit coursing like lava under my skin right now.

I breathed in and out, practically gasping as I bolted down the sidewalk, weaving between pedestrians already on their way to work for the day. I didn't know where I was going. I just needed to get away.

As far away and as fast as I could. Just go and go and go.

So, I ran. I ran, the rain pounding the pavement around me, seeing nothing but feet and legs as I whipped past others and raced across the streets. Horns honked, but I didn't look up to see if it was because of me.

The rain soaked through my combat boots, not hard since they weren't tied again, and soon my hat was plastered to my head, heavy with water.

I splashed through puddles, slowly feeling every piece of clothing on me start to stick to my skin. I wiped rain off my face, but the downpour was so thick, I could barely see twenty feet in front of me.

But I didn't stop. I raced, not giving a shit if there was a cliff or a car about to come through the mist and right for me at any second.

This was all their fault. Michael's brother got Damon arrested in the first place, and thank God he was dead, or I would've done it myself. If it wasn't for that, Damon would've finished college, and we'd be gone.

And then the rest of them . . . My brother would've taken a bullet for them, and they chose Erika Fane without hesitation. Years of him always having their backs, and they threw him away like it was nothing. They didn't even fight for him.

I heard a high-pitched sound ring through the air, and I looked up, seeing that I was on the sidewalk crossing the bridge. I turned my weary eyes out onto the water, seeing a tugboat pushing a barge downstream, its foghorn echoing through the storm.

Looking down at the camera in my hand, I raised my fist and launched it out into the river, seeing it disappear into the black water.

I dropped my eyes, shaking my head. That wasn't true, though, was it? I could see Damon's side because I knew how much he was hurting. I knew how he thought.

No one at home loved him. Our father was a tyrant, and his mother . . . He was terrorized by her. I groaned at the sickness rising from my stomach, remembering all the things he never meant for me to see in that tower.

All the things she didn't know I was there to see.

Because of all that, Damon became very possessive of the few good people in his life.

Me, his friends . . .

Anything that threatened us was immediately an enemy.

That's why he hated Erika—or Rika, as everyone seemed to call her. He wasn't right, but I knew where he was coming from, so I could understand it.

But he got himself arrested by fucking around with Winter, a girl he knew was off-limits. In more ways than one.

And it was he who went too far last year and had to go into hiding.

If he really wanted us to be on our own, he would've taken me with him. Forget his friends. Forget Rika. Just go and both of us get out of here, and we could finally be free.

But that didn't happen, and I now realized it would never happen.

I bit my bottom lip, trying not to cry anymore. We weren't ever going to leave, were we? He was using me, too.

Crossing my arms over my chest, I started walking again, trying to hold everything back, but I just couldn't. I walked and walked and walked, over the bridge, past the old farmer's market on State Street, and down the dilapidated, empty lanes of Whitehall, and I didn't cry, but the tears kept spilling anyway as I clenched my teeth together, shivering.

The rain had soaked my clothes, my head was weighted with the drenched hat, and icy coldness covered my skin. I could feel every hair trying to stand up as chills spread across my body.

I finally stopped, my arms hugging myself as my teeth chattered, and looked up.

"Sensou" shone in red, an emblem with a maze within a maze next to it and Japanese script in the center. I guess my feet knew where I was supposed to be.

Like a machine. That was me.

With shaking hands, I peeled back my cuff and looked at my watch, seeing that it was eight in the morning. Kai told me last night to be here by nine.

I needed to call David and tell him I didn't need a ride this morning.

Heading to the front of the dojo, I yanked on the door, but it didn't give. Locked.

Walking around the side of the building, I entered the dark alley, all the brick buildings around me painted black, even the fire escapes.

Jogging up to the side door, I huddled under the awning and pulled at the door.

But it also didn't give.

I wrapped my arms around myself again, leaning back against the building.

The cold was seeping down to my bones, and I hung my head, my eyelids falling closed.

My mother was either smoking away what I gave her or buying a new outfit right now. Whatever it took to make herself feel better.

Wouldn't she just love to see me doing whatever it took to bring in more money? Of course she'd feel sorry about it, but really, what did she think was going to happen to me when Damon bought me all those years ago? She had asked him what he wanted me for. He simply answered, "Does it matter?"

It didn't. In a perfect world she wanted to be able to afford to care, but when it came down to it, she had no idea what he could've done to me, and the unknown wasn't enough to stop her from giving me away.

I was what Kai said I was. A tool. Something others used.

My eyes welled up again, and I wiped my cheek with my sleeve.

"Morning."

I shot my eyes to the right for a quick glance.

Kai's black pants were covered in raindrops, and he approached, a duffel bag over his shoulder and a folded newspaper over his head. I turned my face away; I knew it must be red and splotchy. I didn't want him seeing me like this . . . my street cred and all.

"What . . ." He stopped at my side, under the awning. "You're soaking wet. What hap—"

"Don't ask me any questions, please," I begged in a quiet voice. "I just got caught in the rain, and I . . . I'll be fine."

I squeezed my fists, trying to warm my hands, but I failed to hold back the shivers.

I hadn't looked at his face, but I didn't hear him move for a moment, so I didn't know what he was doing.

Finally, I heard the door unlock and open.

"Get in here. Come on," he told me.

He held the door open for me, and I ducked in under his arm, entering the dojo's kitchen. I could call David and ask him to come, after all, to bring me some clothes. Or maybe there were some extras of those polos the employees wore. I could stick it out in my wet jeans for now.

I bit my lip, shaking, as Kai came in, dropped his bag, and turned on the lights. I glanced up, seeing he was in a white button-down, his chest visible through the wet drops. I just stared at him for a moment. His hair wet and sticking up, looking incredible and beautiful and taking my mind off the cold for a moment.

He came over, handing me a towel, but then he took my other hand, trying to take me somewhere.

I jerked out of his hold.

I didn't need to be taken care of.

But he turned around, fixing me with a glare. "You don't want to fight with me right now," he warned. "Just do as you're told. You're good at that."

And he took my hand again and pulled me after him. I stumbled a step, following him through the kitchen, into the lobby, and down the hall. The whole place was empty and dark, except for the small glow of the lights lining the trim on the bottom of the walls.

He pushed through the door to the women's locker room and led me past the lockers, toward the showers.

Opening a stall door, he reached in and turned on the water, the rainfall showerhead high overhead coming to life. Water started to pour and steam instantly billowed.

God, that looked good.

"You're freezing," he said, turning back to me. "Get these clothes off."

He reached for the buttons on my jacket, and I knocked his hands away. "No."

I crossed my arms in front of me, embarrassment swelling up inside me. "Don't touch me."

"I wasn't going to touch you," he said, his voice suddenly softer. "I just want to take off your jacket, okay?"

I shook my head.

"Look, you don't have to take off your clothes," he explained, his tone growing more urgent again, "but you have to get warm."

I stared down at my white knuckles still clenched into fists. "My clothes will dry."

He let out a sigh, sounding like a hushed growl, and before I realized what was happening, he wrapped his arms around me and lifted me off the ground, carrying me into the shower.

I pushed against his chest as he closed the shower door and put us both under the hot rainfall.

"No!" I argued.

But, his lips tight, he gave me an angry, "Shhh . . ." and dropped me to my feet, his arms locking around my body and holding me to him.

Asshole!

I planted my hands on his chest, snarling up at him, but soon, the heat from the water started to seep into my clothes, and then the water was coursing down my skin.

Oh . . .

My skin erupted in a wave of delightful pinpricks, making my blood come alive as everything tingled with the heat.

I wanted to smile, it felt so good.

My eyelids started to feel heavy, the hot water blanketing my back, running down my legs, and spreading over my head and neck.

Warm. I was so warm. I just wanted to . . .

I groaned, starting to waver.

My body was so tired. Kai strengthened his hold, letting me relax into him, and I did. I didn't fight it.

I laid my head on his chest, and after a moment, I felt him carefully brush my knit cap off my head, the water hitting my scalp and drowning out the rest of the world.

I closed my eyes and savored the feeling.

Just for a minute, I told myself.

Tucking my arms in, I huddled into his chest, letting myself give up for a minute. His arms circled all the way around me, one resting on my waist and the other one on my arm, while the heat of the water mixed with the heat of his skin through his wet shirt lulled me into a feeling of peace I couldn't remember ever having before. Not even with Damon.

I couldn't remember the last time I was this close to somebody.

The shower pounded around us, drowning out the sound of the storm outside, our breathing, even my thoughts . . . I didn't want to think. For five fucking minutes, I didn't want to talk or worry or fight or be scared or angry or hate everything. I didn't even want to stand.

"This means nothing," I mumbled, still snuggling into his body.

His chest shook under my head. "Absolutely nothing. I promise."

Something brushed my forehead, and I felt his fingers wipe away the hair on my cheek. His hand smoothed the strands back over the top of my head, and another small wave of pleasure hit me right down to my toes. I was suddenly aware of my wet thighs molded to his and the rest of my body pressing into him.

This was heaven.

His hand smoothed my hair a few more times, slower and gentler, and then he wrapped his arms around me again, holding me tight.

"I like your braids." His deep voice suddenly sounded raspy. "Your hair is a beautiful color. Like mahogany. Why do you hide it?"

I opened my mouth to hit him with a nasty remark but closed

it. I didn't want this to end quite yet, and I guessed it was normal for him to wonder.

But it was still none of his business.

"You cover your hair, you wear men's clothes," he went on. "Who are you, kid?"

It almost sounded like a rhetorical question, like he was just thinking out loud. And part of me wanted to come clean.

I gave a half smile he didn't see. "I'm nobody."

"That's not true," he argued, and I heard his voice closer to my ear. "I've never seen Damon possessive over a woman, but he was over you that night." He tipped my chin up, forcing me to look at him. "Who are you to him?"

I opened my mouth, but again, I didn't know what to say. I shook my head.

"Did he hurt you?" Kai's onyx eyes pleaded with me for more as he dropped his voice to a whisper. "No one's here but you and me. Did he hurt you? Why are you loyal to them?"

I stared into his gaze, my eyes starting to burn again as I struggled with my love for my brother and the pathetic desire building inside me to latch on to someone.

The rain shower spilled down his black hair, streams coursing down his neck and over the vein there. The water disappeared under his collar, and I let my eyes drift back up over his angular jaw to his mouth. Full lips, his bottom one with a unique little flat spot like someone had pressed their finger there and the dent remained. I stared at it, and my teeth suddenly ached. I could feel the meat he fed me last night in my mouth again and the sensation of biting into it.

Confusion wracked my brain. He wasn't really my enemy. Not really.

He wanted answers. I wanted my brother back.

"What was it like for you in prison?" I asked him. "We paid off people to keep Damon safe, but what about you and Will? Was it bad?"

Pain suddenly crossed his eyes, and he stared at me, lost for a moment.

"Michael did the same," he told me. "Paid people to keep all of us safe, but . . ."

He trailed off, and I waited. Like in the confessional all those years ago, he had to work up the courage to talk.

He swallowed. "I told Rika once that I was never going back there. That I never knew people could be so ugly." He met my eyes. "But I was talking about me."

He caressed my hair, looking troubled.

"It wasn't as simple as Michael thought it would be. Paying people off, I mean. We were rich, young, privileged, and we were doing half the sentence that others were doing for the same crimes. The threats, the looks, the nighttime taunts carrying down the cells toward us," he told me. "I just wanted to go home."

A lump stretched my throat painfully; I was sad for both him and my brother.

"My father taught me to fight," he went on. "He taught me how to kill if I ever had to. But he also taught me to make the world better." He paused, thinking, and then spoke again. "A trick of survival in prison is, on your first day, walk in there with your head high, look around into everyone's eyes, and find someone to hit. Establish your strength and make sure everyone sees it."

I listened, remembering I'd heard the same thing somewhere.

"I waited until day three," he said. "I picked the biggest guy I could find, someone I'd seen throwing his weight around, someone who'd threatened Will on our first day, and I went over, and I hit him."

I could almost see it in my head.

"To my surprise, though, he didn't go down right away," Kai continued, a half smile on his face. "I ended up with a broken nose, three cracked ribs, and a fat lip."

I laughed a little. A Horseman didn't fall often, so he got his comeuppance, I'd say.

But his expression turned solemn. "He ended up with a fractured spine."

Oh, Christ.

"I was the trained one," he said, looking like he was still angry with himself. "I should've known where I was kicking."

"Did he heal?"

He nodded. "Yeah, but it took a couple months, and he has some nerve damage. He has no feeling in three of his fingers on his right hand anymore."

Well, it could've been worse. A lot worse.

"The next day," he continued, "my lunch table was the fullest in the cell block."

"So, you got respect, then."

"Yeah, by acting like an animal," he pointed out. "That scared me, because it wasn't the first time I'd chosen to react with violence when I shouldn't have. Was it going to be a habit? I was losing grasp of the life I wanted to have and the person I wanted to be, because I kept being stupid." He dropped his eyes, breathing so hard and looking vulnerable. "I don't want to ruin my life."

I stared at him, unable to take my eyes off him. He wouldn't look at me, and I realized he felt just as useless and inadequate as I always had.

An urge pulled at me to make him feel good.

"Hey." I brought up my hand, nudging his chin.

He raised his eyes.

I gave him a small smile. "Sometimes when everything and everyone around me is hard to face, I look up."

He pinched his eyebrows together, looking like he didn't understand, and I tilted my head back, looking up at the ceiling.

Slowly, he did the same, following my gaze.

The steam billowed in the air above us, parting here and there to show the white granite ceiling of the shower. Particles of crystal in the rock glittered in the dim light, and for a moment, my brain was floating amid the mist. Light as a feather, soaring on the clouds.

"Changing your view . . ." I trailed off. "It helps. Right?"

He smiled, his shoulders relaxing. "We'll have to try that outside at night sometime."

We?

Suddenly, he cleared his throat and straightened up, releasing me. "I'm going to get you some clothes, okay?" he told me. "Why don't you sit down? Warm up some more under the water."

I nodded, reluctantly backing away as he stepped aside. Was he embarrassed? I didn't want him to leave, but he looked like he was in a hurry to get out of here. Maybe he regretted telling me all that, but I was glad he did.

He pointed at the shower floor. "Stay here, okay?"

He walked to the door, opening it, and stepped out. "Alex," I heard him call, but before I had a chance to look, he'd closed the shower door again.

I remained there, all the chill now gone. Legs growing weary, I fell softly into the wall to help support my weight.

He didn't touch me. He'd just put his arms around me and held me, not getting greedy or trying to get more out of me or anything. Even Damon had never been as patient and comforting with me.

On the rare occasion my brother felt compelled to show any affection, no embrace ever lasted more than a few seconds. My mother was probably the last person to hold me like that.

I slid down the wall, my ass planted on the tiles and my knees drawn up. I closed my eyes, feeling my blood flowing warm under my skin, my breathing slow and steady.

My mind tilted sideways, and every limb was a ten-ton weight. I didn't know how long I drifted off for.

"Banks?" I heard a soft voice say.

Could've been an hour later or a minute. I wasn't sure.

I shifted, letting out a little moan.

"Banks?" the voice said, closer this time, and I slowly peeled my eyes open.

Alex, the girl from the party, was crouching down next to me, dressed in some hot pink workout shorts and a white sports bra. She stayed back from the spray of the shower.

"Kai wanted me to get you some clothes," she explained. "I've been waiting outside. I just want to let you know I have something for you to wear. You can stay in here however long you want, though."

I sniffled, opening my eyes and sitting all the way up. "I'm fine."

I got to my feet and stood up, Alex rising with me.

"Okay," she said, backing up and pointing to the hook on the wall. "Towels are here, and there's a bag for your wet clothes, too. I've got some dry ones sitting on the bench right outside."

I nodded, reluctantly appreciating how she'd thought of everything. I hadn't called any of the guys, so I didn't have clothes, and I'd need to wear something while my own dried. I knew they had washers and dryers available for the gym towel service.

She quickly left, and I reached over, shutting off the water. Taking one of the towels off the hook, I patted my still-braided hair dry and hung it back up, hurriedly taking off my clothes. I peeled off my soaked jacket and dropped it to the floor, following quickly with my flannel shirt, shoes, socks, jeans, and underthings. Every unraveling of the bindings around my chest felt more glorious than the last, until finally my breasts were freed, hitting the air.

I closed my eyes, letting out a small moan. I wrapped myself in the same towel and quickly stuffed the wet clothes in one of the white tote bags Sensou sold at the front desk that Alex had apparently brought me. Undoing the braids in my hair, I shook the locks free, massaging my scalp with the other towel.

Reaching outside the door, I grabbed the small stack of clothes, hearing several other women in the locker room talking. The gym must be open for business by now.

Closing the door, I peeked through the stack, looking for the rest of the clothes.

"What?" I blurted out.

Black stretch pants that looked like a second skin and a gray sports bra with a Nike symbol in the middle. I groaned. Where was the fucking rest of it? I couldn't wear this shit.

"Ugh," I growled, holding on to the bra and slipping the pants on. She had to have something else out there. Or at least a sweatshirt.

I pulled up the pants, the soft fabric wrapping around my thighs and behind, and I groaned at the discomfort. It was weird to have something matted to my skin like this. But when I pulled the towel off and reached over to hang it up, I paused, noticing how good the formfitting pants felt to move in. A ton lighter.

Slipping my arms through the openings in the bra, I squeezed my head through the middle and pulled the bra down, quickly adjusting my breasts to fit inside.

I blinked long and hard. *Oh, God.* I felt naked. I pulled my hair over one shoulder, trying to cover my breasts, which were damn near popping out of her top, and folded my hands over my bare stomach.

I opened the door a crack, peeking out. I didn't want to walk out there like this.

Oh, who was I kidding? Practically every woman here was dressed like this. I wouldn't stand out. Damon had made me so self-conscious, like if I showed an ankle, men would pounce like wolves.

Patting my feet dry again, I stepped out, picking up the bag of clothes and tossing the towels in the basket right outside the shower.

I walked into the locker room, seeing a few women scurrying about to get to their workouts.

"You look good," a voice said.

I looked up, seeing Alex standing with her hands on her hips and nodding at me as her eyes scaled me up and down.

I tensed.

"We're about the same size," she mused, coming over and taking my hand. "Wouldn't know it by the way you drown in your usual clothes."

She grabbed the bag from me, and I watched as she tossed it to an attendant—a young woman in a black Sensou polo—who carried it off somewhere, hopefully to the dryers.

"My clothes aren't that big," I mumbled.

She led me over to the vanities and pushed my shoulders down, my tired legs giving out under me and my ass slamming into the seat. She immediately started brushing my hair.

"I can do it," I snapped, reaching for the brush.

But she pulled away. "You can't," she told me, plucking a foil-wrapped object off the counter and dropping it in my lap. "You have to eat."

I picked up the soft, warm roll. "What's this?"

"Kai had some breakfast burritos delivered."

I dropped it back to my lap. "I'm fine."

"He said you'd say that." She held a fistful of my hair, working intently on brushing the ends. "He also said you're smart enough to pick your battles, and someone as practical as you wouldn't split hairs over a stupid burrito."

A smile escaped me. Okay. Point.

The floury scent of the tortilla hit my nose, and my stomach suddenly rumbled. I hadn't eaten this morning.

She finished brushing out my tangles as I unwrapped the burrito and bit into it. Soft egg, spicy sausage, some onions, peppers, and jalapenos with a little cheese, and I couldn't help myself. I bit into it again, not waiting to swallow the first bite.

"Good girl." Alex winked at me and turned on the hair dryer.

My hair blew around me, the whirring noise drowning out everything but me and this fucking burrito. Most of the time, I rarely stopped moving long enough to notice if I was hungry or not, so I'd often go all day on an egg and a piece of toast. Marina always had something cooking, too, so I might grab a few pieces of leftovers or a bowl of soup from the pot she kept on the stove, but usually, it was grab-and-go or eat nothing.

Alex smoothed the brush through my hair as she dried it, the long strands tickling the bare skin of my arms and back. I felt chills spread across my skin and found myself dropping my head back to give her better access with the brush. I breathed out, closing my eyes as I ate. The prongs of her brush dragged over my scalp.

Soon I'd finished the burrito and sat, savoring the feel of the brush combing through my hair when I realized the hair dryer was no longer running. I opened my eyes, seeing Alex staring at me in the mirror, her cute ponytail sitting high with hair around her face.

My own hair, all foot and a half of it, cascaded down my back, and she'd put a part in the side. I hadn't had it down, clean, and blown out all at the same time in ages.

"When's the last time you've been touched?" she asked, studying me. "Like really touched?"

I dropped my head forward again, avoiding her eyes. I suppose I'd enjoyed getting my hair combed a little too much?

She sat down next to me, straddling the bench and facing me.

"We all need it, you know?" she said quietly. "We need contact. It's only human. But if you're not getting it from someone else, there's nothing wrong with a little self-love, either. Just pointing that out. You strike me as uptight, and it'll help. I self-love at least twice a day."

I shot her a scowl. I didn't like people who overshared.

She laughed, and I noticed her bright, wide smile that gave her a child-like, girl-next-door sweetness. Very much in contrast to her un-child-like body that I knew half the men at that party the other night had probably taken to bed. Had Kai slept with her?

"I'm serious, though." She nudged me, bringing me back. "Being touched is a need. Close your eyes for me."

Huh?

"It's an experiment," she explained, probably seeing my confused look. "I won't touch you anywhere personal."

No. I inched away.

But she just followed me. "Close your eyes, and imagine I'm *him*."

"Him?"

"Your fantasy."

My fantasy? Wha—

"Indulge me for two minutes," she leaned in, whispering, "and I'll give you my sweatshirt."

I let out a scoff.

But still . . . I'd like a sweatshirt.

Fine. Fuck it. I closed my eyes.

Without my sight balancing me, my brain seemed to start floating, but I still felt her shift next to me, and then a hand touched my stomach, making me jump.

"Do you see him in your head?" she whispered, her breath falling across my jaw. "Your fantasy. Picture him—or her—what they're wearing, the room, how they're coming for you."

My eyelids fluttered, the images popping into my head on instinct.

"No," I muttered, the word accidentally slipping out.

Her fingertips grazed my abdomen, sending delightful chills up my arms. "Yes," she breathed in my ear. "You see him, don't you? He's touching you right now. This is his hand on your stomach. His body next to you. His voice in your ear. Do you see him?"

I shivered, my breathing turning shallow. I was suddenly back in the grave.

Kai's bare chest was in front of me, and I wanted to sink my fingers into his waist and bury my nose in his neck. The faint scent of his soap and the wet earth under our shoes surrounded me, and another scent that was just Kai. It was in his hair, his mouth, his skin . . .

"I want you," he gasped out, his hot breath in my ear. "I want you in my mouth."

His hand slid up the back of my neck, threading into my hair and gripping it lightly. I whimpered, feeling my nipples harden.

He sank his mouth into my neck, and I sucked in a breath through my teeth, his lips kissing and sucking my skin. Oh, God. I leaned my head to the side, letting him in.

"I'm going to eat you so fucking deep," he said, his possessive hand on my stomach trailing down the inside of my thigh.

I could see us on a bed, his head buried between my legs, and even though I felt the heat of a blush on my face, I wanted him there.

"You feel me?" he asked. "You feel how much I want you? I'm going to stick my tongue up inside you and lick until you're screaming for me to let you come. You're mine."

My chest shook, and I moaned, feeling him nibble my ear, his hands growing more demanding, making me sweat.

"Take my hands, baby," he whispered. "Put my hands on you."

I licked my dry lips, not even hesitating. I grabbed his hand on my thigh, but stopped, feeling a soft, slender hand that didn't feel like a man's.

I popped my eyes open, seeing Alex at my side.

"Oh, my God." I put my hand over my mouth, embarrassment wracking through me. That was all her. Holy shit. I released her hand, watching her reluctantly pull away and let out a sigh.

"He's a lucky guy. Whoever he is."

I shook my head, baffled at what had just happened. And the somersaults still going on in my stomach.

She leaned in. "Tonight, you should remember that fantasy and finish it, even if it's just you, by yourself, in your bed."

No wonder Will kept her on payroll.

"Or if you want," she said, teasing, with a smirk in her voice, "call me, and I'll finish you off."

The pulse between my legs throbbed harder.

Fucking amazing, I thought to myself. I could take on a two-hundred-fifty-pound guy, but a twenty-year-old escort got me shy.

I was about to stand up when a shout rang out through the locker room. "Is Banks done in there yet?!"

It was Kai.

Alex hopped off the bench, grabbing her brush and pushing my hair behind my shoulders. "Yeah, she's dry and dressed!"

"Get her out here, then."

I quickly stood up and scurried over to Alex's locker, snatching the gray zip-up on the bench in front of it. It was long, hopefully long enough to cover the curvy parts.

I walked for the door, seeing it partly open and Kai's form through the frosted glass. I slipped into the sweatshirt.

"I'm here," I said, opening the door. "What do you need?"

He immediately turned and started walking, without looking at me, clearly expecting me to follow him.

"I need you to handle the front desk for an hour. The first shifter is caught in traffic."

I made to zip up the jacket, but all of a sudden it was ripped off me from behind, and I jerked around, seeing a smiling Alex snatching it back and shoving me in the chest, out the door.

What the fuck?

She slammed the locker room door closed, and I rushed back, jiggling the knob, but she was planted against it, not letting me in.

I opened my mouth to yell but just fisted my hands, growling low.

Damn her.

"Everything slows to a goddamn halt, like people have never seen rain before," Kai went on, still walking down the hallway. "Just scan cards, hand out towels if they ask, and answer the phones. It shouldn't be too long."

I tucked one side of my hair behind my ear and followed him reluctantly, fidgeting my hands and trying to cover my stomach, and then my cleavage, with my arms.

"I'll show you how to use the intercom to page me if you need me," he instructed.

I stopped at the desk as he reached over it, grabbing a set of keys and a walkie-talkie.

But then something dropped in the middle of the lobby, and Kai and I both looked over, seeing Michael standing frozen with his fucking eyebrows up at his hairline. He was staring at me.

I shifted my eyes around, grinding my teeth together. *Yeah, laugh it up, asshole.*

Kai held out his hands, annoyed, as he looked at Michael and Rika standing still in the middle of the lobby with a Gatorade spilling out on the floor.

"What's the matter with you?" he burst out.

And then he followed their gaze, finally turning around and looking at me.

His eyebrows nose-dived, his back straightened, and he looked at me like I had just kicked a puppy.

His gaze dropped to my bare feet, slowly scaling up Alex's tight workout pants, my bare stomach, the sports bra, and my hair hanging long and free.

My fists clenched at my sides.

Kai's eyes finally met mine, and my stomach dropped. I knew that look. It was the same one he had in his eyes on that Devil's Night, right before he chased me.

He cocked an eyebrow and turned his head toward his friends.

"What are you looking at?" he growled to Michael. "Locker room's that way."

Michael had a grin he was trying to hold back, and Rika scowled at him.

"Breathe, asshole," she said, and then she stomped off down the hallway.

He followed her, a choked laugh in his voice. "Babe, I was just a little shocked. It's a huge change!"

"Shut up."

"Rika, come on . . ."

And their argument disappeared down the hall.

I stood there, my head level but my gaze on the floor as I chewed the inside of my cheek. "I'll change as soon as my clothes are dry," I told him, looking up. "Where can I get one of those polos the other desk clerks wear?"

He didn't answer for a moment, his gaze hesitantly glancing down and back up again.

Hooding his eyes, he walked around me, toward the hallway. "We're all out."

CHAPTER 13

BANKS

Six Years Ago

Tossing my keys on the desk, I closed the door and walked across the room, pulling the curtains closed. I peeled off my sweatshirt, kicked off my shoes, and dug in the top drawer of Damon's chest of drawers, pulling out some boxers and a T-shirt. Yawning, I walked into the bathroom, the white marble floors feeling cool and smooth under my feet.

My brother wouldn't be home until at least dawn. Was Kai still planning to go to The Pope tonight? He must've gotten that key after our conversation this morning, before he knew that he'd run into me again.

I hated the idea of him going without me.

After tossing my clothes into the hamper, I changed into a T-shirt and boxers, washed my face, brushed my teeth and hair, and walked out of the bathroom, hitting the light on the way out.

I crawled onto the bed, grabbing the pillow and hugging it as I reached up and pulled the chain on the lamp. The room went dark, the subtle hum of the air-conditioning flowing through the house soothing me. My breathing slowed and my heartbeat calmed.

Kai was probably really angry with me. He had no reason not to believe Damon. He probably felt betrayed, lied to, and pissed off.

Pissed off enough to think he damn well should've stayed with the devil he knew rather than the devil he didn't. Maybe he'd be sharing that hotel room with Chloe tonight.

And for some reason, I liked the ache that caused in my chest. Anger was easier, and I almost wanted him to go running to her. It would make him the same as every other man I knew. Self-serving, insincere, and greedy.

If he failed me, I could go back to not minding not having him, right?

I had Damon, after all, and here, I was queen, at least. He never brought girls to his room. He never made me leave so he could have privacy. This was our space, and no woman was above me in his life at home.

I just had to find contentment in everything I already had.

I yawned again, my eyelids growing heavier and closing.

But then I heard the door behind me open and the floor creak.

I turned my head over my shoulder, tensing when I saw a tall black figure moving toward the bed. I could just make him out, removing his shirt as he stood over me.

"You're home already?" I said, remaining still.

But he just replied, "Shhh," and I didn't press further as I turned my head back around, staring off into the dark.

He didn't turn on the light, so I guessed that was a good sign he didn't want to yell at me.

I felt the bed dip behind me, and he lay down, making it creak with his weight.

I didn't know why he wanted me here. I mean, I slept next to him more than I didn't, but I knew he was mad, so it was better just to give him his space tonight.

But then I felt him at my back as he rolled toward me and snaked an arm around my waist.

My lungs got smaller as I tried to take in more air, and I could feel the vein in my neck pulsing.

What was he doing?

His breath hit my neck, and before I knew what was happening, he was kissing my skin and reached under my shirt, taking my breast possessively in his hand.

A cry caught in my throat. "What are you—"

His hand moved to between my legs, and he gripped me, holding me tight as he thrust his hips against my ass.

"Damon, no!" I cried, scrambling to push his hands away and get off the bed.

But he held me tight. Pushing me onto my back, he climbed on top of me, pinning my hands above my head and slamming his mouth down on mine, rough and possessive.

I tried to scream through his attack as tears spilled from my eyes. *No, no, no, please! Don't do this.* I squeezed my eyes shut, trying to twist my head away. Nausea rolled through my stomach like an avalanche. No, no, no . . .

Until he forced his tongue in my mouth, and I paused, realizing something was off. I froze, inhaling deeply through my nose.

No Davidoffs. Not even a hint of any cigarettes on his skin, his breath, his hair . . .

I fought, screaming into his mouth as I ripped my arms out of his grasp and slapped him across the face.

"You're not Damon," I barked.

He grabbed my wrists, securing them above my head once again. His hot breath fell on my face, and I breathed fast and shallow, his weight on me too heavy.

"And you're not fucking him like he said, are you?"

Michael? What the hell was he doing here?

"Who are you?" he asked.

"Get off me," I growled, squirming. "What are you doing?"

It would be just my luck for one of the guys—or worse, my brother—to walk in right now and look for some way to make this my fault.

He released one of my wrists, leaning to my left, and the next thing I knew, the light was on, and Michael Crist was staring down at me.

Releasing my other arm, he propped himself up, letting his eyes drift down my body. I quickly pulled my shirt back down.

He smirked. "No wonder he keeps you under wraps."

He rolled off me, onto his back, and lay at my side, sliding an arm underneath his head.

"I sometimes feel possessive of Rika Fane like that, too," he said, turning his gaze on me. "Although *she's* not my sister."

I dug in my eyebrows, suddenly on alert. How did . . .

He knew?

Or maybe he just suspected, and I'd confirmed it when I freaked out during his little gamble.

He half smiled, probably amused by the confusion on my face. "You look just like him. I don't know how Kai doesn't see it."

"I'm not his sister, and—"

"Damon's business is Damon's business." He sat up, swinging his legs off the bed and standing up. "But you're ruining Kai's night, kid."

I rolled my eyes, sitting up as well. "Well, I'm out of the way now," I pointed out. "You and your bestie can go have a ball."

He laughed, holding my gaze. "I have a better idea," he said, giving my thigh a slap. "Let's go into the city."

And then he reached down, grabbing my ankles and yanking me to the end of the bed.

"What?" I slid over the sheets, falling to my back. "No!"

But my protest fell on deaf ears. He hauled me up, and my heart caught in my throat as he threw me over his shoulder and my whole world turned upside down as I dangled more than six feet off the ground.

"You can't!" I thrashed, making him stumble. "I'm not even dressed!"

"Jesus Christ!" he barked, falling into the nightstand. I shot my hands out to the wall to keep us from falling.

"You know, I'm getting tired of telling assholes to let me go," I told him.

"So, don't. You know you want to go."

Something fell on my back, and I grabbed at it, seeing the sleeve of his hoodie he must've picked up from somewhere.

He started walking, and I got farther away from the bed, the nightstands, and the bedroom.

"Come on, man," I whined, his shoulder digging into my stomach. "Damon won't like it."

"He won't know."

Yes, he will! My brother would be where they were. How would he not see me?

He wrapped his arms tightly around my thighs, and I stopped fighting as soon as he began descending the stairs. I didn't want him to drop me.

He stopped, and I felt a draft on my legs as he opened the door at the bottom.

"Seriously," I begged. "I don't want to go. Damon would kill me if he found me with Kai again."

But he just ignored me.

"Come on!" I yelled, kicking and hitting his back. "Don't be an asshole! I don't want to see him anyway. The dickhead barely put up a fight when I left, not man enough to come for me himself, huh?"

A smack hit my ass, and I yelped. The burn spread out, making me wince.

He walked for the stairs, and I caught sight of my father's bedroom door opening, light pouring into the dark hallway.

"What the hell is going on?" He stepped out, immediately meeting my eyes as I hung upside down and twisted my head to see him.

"Gabriel," I panted as Michael halted. "He just came into Damon's room. I don't want to go with him."

My father just arched a brow, but I lost sight of him as Michael turned around to face him.

There was silence, and I stayed frozen, waiting for Michael to put me down.

But he didn't.

Instead, my father spoke up. "Gates are locking for the night," he informed Michael. "You take her out of this house, you can't bring her back until dawn."

I squeezed my eyes shut, frustration boiling my blood. I wasn't surprised. What did I expect him to say when a half-naked guy sneaks into his house to kidnap his daughter?

Absolutely nothing.

I heard the door close again, and Michael spun around, descending the stairs as his body shook with laughter.

"Model father, that one." He squeezed the backs of my thighs. "I think you'll actually be safer with me."

We made it down the stairs, and he opened the front door, walking out.

"Listen," I said, seeing the driveway as my hair blocked the rest of my view. "I can't go with you. He's already angry enough."

"I told you, he won't know you're there."

And then I was swinging back upright, my feet finding the ground.

My head swam with dizziness, but I saw him open the back door of his G-Class, and all of a sudden, music and laughter poured out. I looked in, seeing the car packed with people. No one I recognized.

"Make room," Michael told someone.

He then turned and pushed me into the seat. "Ty, do her face," he said to someone, and the door slammed behind me.

I looked around, finding people piled in the back seat, girls on laps, while the front had two bodies sharing the passenger seat. Michael moved around the front of the car, heading for the driver's side. People glanced at me, but they were smiling and still carrying on their conversations.

Drunk already, I would assume.

Michael climbed in the car, tossing his shirt and hoodie on the people to his right, and started the car.

And then a girl was on me.

I sucked in a breath, looking up as she straddled me. She was in short shorts, but she also wore a brown leather jacket, boots, and a scarf. Her face was painted like a sugar skull. Black rimmed her eyes, and she had beautiful designs of flowers across her temple.

What was she doing?

Raising some kind of spongy wedge, she dabbed it in some white makeup and came at me.

I reared back. "What are you doing?" I yelled over the radio blaring "Save Yourself" in the background.

"She's disguising you," Michael said as he put his car in drive and pulled around the driveway, heading down toward the gate. "Cooperate."

She smiled, her burgundy lips spreading to reveal pearly white teeth. Leaning in, she started dabbing makeup on me again.

"It's almost midnight," she whispered excitedly. "Día de los Muertos."

Day of the Dead? It lasted from Halloween until after All Saints on November first, I knew, but why . . .

Oh, the makeup. It hit me why she was wearing face paint and what she was doing to me.

And the candles in the cemetery, too.

I didn't know much about the holiday other than a parade I'd seen as a child in Meridian City.

"Are you cold?" Michael asked, and the next thing I knew, a sweatshirt came flying into the back.

I snatched it up. *Awesome.* All I had on was the thin boxers and a T-shirt.

And then my Vans came tumbling back at me, too. He grabbed my shoes? I hurriedly pulled everything on, immediately feeling warmer.

"Where are we going?" I tucked my hair behind my ears, making it easier for Ty to work.

Her eyes gleamed. "Hide-and-seek."

Bellows and cheers instantly hit my ears as Michael swung open the double doors to The Pope.

It took less than forty-five minutes to get into Meridian City; the streets all the way from our seaside village to the bustling metropolis were now dark and quiet for the evening.

At least thirty people loitered in the lobby as I looked around and instinctively pulled up my hood—or Michael's hood—worried that the face paint wasn't enough to disguise me. Groups of teenagers were scattered among black columns that stretched up to the dark, high ceiling with ornate woodwork and crystal chandeliers. A few sat on sofas and cushioned chairs or stood near the large windows boasting beautiful white drapes and tall potted plants and baby trees nearby.

I'd never been here before. Our father rarely found a reason to bring us—or Damon, anyway—to the city. I knew it was in danger of closing, though. The stadium that was supposed to have been built years ago never happened and business was suffering. It really was a shame it was so empty and unappreciated for its grandeur.

An arm hooked around my neck, and I saw Michael standing next to me. He still had his shirt off.

"You got nice legs," he said, staring around the lobby. "You might be safe from Damon at the moment, but don't think you're safe from the rest of us."

He then looked down at me with a challenge in his eyes.

"And don't think I don't know how to take care of myself," I retorted. "I don't mind hitting a girl."

His lips spread wide, and he laughed under his breath. Michael didn't seem like a guy who ever gave much away, but I felt a tug of pride that he seemed to find me amusing, at least.

Everyone fanned out, the girl who'd done my makeup taking my hand and dragging me toward the elevators. Michael and a few others followed.

"The game is," the girl stated, "a cross between hide-and-seek and seven minutes in heaven."

Seven minutes in heaven? I groaned inwardly. I'd already played that tonight.

"You hide, and if you're found," she continued, "you and him get to have a few minutes alone."

"And if I don't want to play?"

"Why wouldn't you?" Michael pushed the button for the thirteenth floor and the doors started to close. "It's fun."

Yeah, fun. You're telling me my brother plays this with only the hope of copping a feel in a dark closet? They were either lying or extremely sugarcoating this game for my sake. I had no interest in this.

"How many 'seekers' are there?" I looked back to the girl, ignoring Michael.

She shrugged. "One for each of us. Sometimes more."

More?

The elevator ascended, but my stomach was sinking. Chills spread up my legs, and my mouth went dry.

Then Michael leaned into my ear, whispering, "You don't want Kai to find someone else, do you?"

My lips quivered with a little snarl. "There's no guarantee he'll find *me*."

"Then make sure he does."

I licked my lips, immediately tasting the black cherry lipstick the girl had painted on. She released my hand as the doors opened, and I watched as everyone brushed past me, shooting out of the elevator.

But I took my steps slowly.

The hallway was dark and loud, an abrasive Fear Factory song growling over the chatter, and I clenched my fists, suddenly feeling nervous. I didn't want to get into a situation I couldn't get myself out of. I'd actually feel a little more comfortable with David here.

I laughed to myself at the irony.

I followed everyone as they trailed down the hallway, which was littered with more people and room doors wide open like this was one big, communal space.

The wall sconces glowed with dim light, but the overhead chandeliers were off, so it gave the floor a haunting, cave-like feel. We drifted down past open doors, music coming from every room, and it seemed more like a dormitory than a hotel. They must've bought out the entire floor.

Masked teenagers filtered in and out of dark rooms lit only by candlelight, and I looked in one room, seeing several dancing slow and heated. Two girls were making out, hands everywhere, and another girl straddled some guy on a chair.

If my brother saw me, I'd blame this on Michael. It was his fault I was here.

"All right!" someone shouted, and I looked up. Will stood on top of a cooler outside a room, looking back and forth down the hallway.

A dozen or so people started to gather, and I kept my hood up and my head down. I hadn't seen Kai yet, but Michael was still next to me, so I felt less unsafe. I smelled the room service drifting out of the room to my right and a hunger pang hit me. I hadn't eaten since . . . the bread and soup this afternoon?

"To keep this workable, we're going to limit it to rooms 1312 through 1322," Will instructed. "Ladies, you know the drill. Find a hiding place in any of those rooms, and make it a good one. You can change hiding spots, but if you're caught in transit, you're caught." His face was adorned with a knowing smile as he looked around to the guys, warning them. "And if you're told to back off, you back off."

A few chuckles went off around the area, and I immediately took a step back. Where was Kai? If he wasn't playing, then I didn't want to. And for Christ's sake, what if my brother was the one to find me.

So, what do I do? Find somewhere safe to loiter until this shit was over or go now and find the best hiding spot?

And then I saw a dark figure step out from one of the rooms behind Will and slowly approach. As the glow of the sconce fell across his mask, I wanted it to be silver.

But it was black, and the vein in my throat started throbbing. It was my brother's. I cast my eyes down again.

"You have one minute to hide," Will said, and then he looked at the guys. "And then you get fifteen minutes to lock yourself in a closet with your buddy's girlfriend if you beat him to her." Laughter exploded, followed by some catcalling. "When everyone hears this horn," he held up a foghorn, "time's up and you come out."

He tossed the horn to a nearby kid, probably a lowerclassman whom they pegged to do their shit work, while Will jumped off the cooler and pulled his mask over his face. I guessed he was playing, too.

I started walking backward, taking step after step. I wasn't going to just hang here and let Damon see me, but I had no intention of being found, either. I knew the perfect hiding spot.

"Ready?" Will called out. "Set?"

I looked right, counting down the room numbers. *A little farther.*

"Annnnnnd . . . go!" Will shouted.

I didn't wait to see what anyone else was doing. Spinning around, I ran down the dark hallway, hearing laughter and squeals behind me as I raced to 1312, pushed open the door, and quickly whipped my head from left to right to see if anyone was in here.

But it was empty. *Yes.*

Feeling the vibrations of the other girls running down the hall, I ran to the bed and gently climbed on top, stepping behind the three rows of soft, cool pillows propped up against the headboard. Holding the pillows up and keeping them in place with one hand, I slid behind them, lying down across the top of the bed with my back to the headboard. I sank behind the pillows, quickly reaching out and feeling them to make sure they still stood propped up, not giving me away.

My heart raced, and my lungs seemed like they were getting smaller. I could barely breathe out of fear. I wasn't so sure I was scared, though. It was just the chase.

But I knew I had a good hiding spot. It was in plain sight.

One morning when I was younger I woke up to Damon in a fit. Somehow, during the night, I'd gotten burrowed back in the pillows, and I was still pretty little at thirteen. Skinny. He'd woken up that morning and didn't see me in the bed, big as it was. He thought I'd gotten up already. However, when he went downstairs and couldn't find me, he'd searched the house and the grounds, calling for me.

By the time I woke up to all the commotion and crawled out of where I'd been sleeping the whole time right under his nose, he wasn't happy.

I think he was a little scared that day. I also realized he might actually care about me.

I heard the door swing open all of a sudden and bang into the wall, followed by giggles. I tensed, stopping my breathing.

"Behind the drapes!" a girl whisper-yelled. "I'll see if I can fit in the cabinet."

Another squeal followed, and I heard shuffles, the squeak of a hinge, and a thud. The music still drifted through the walls like a subterranean echo, and I clenched the pillow at my side, trying to stop my shaking.

And then I heard it. Howls from somewhere distant.

And then there was thunder. Like the heavy footfalls of a dozen guys charging down the hallway.

I closed my eyes. *Ten rooms.* Unless they ripped this place apart, they wouldn't find me.

Doors slammed against walls, sounding like they were being kicked open, and deep voices called out, but I couldn't make out their taunts. More doors opened, each one sounding closer than the last, until finally . . .

The door to my room was thrown open, the doorknob hitting the wall again, and I jerked in fright. My blood raced, and I froze.

"Come out, come out, wherever you are," a smooth voice teased.

And I heard a giggle from somewhere in the room.

That's it. Lead him to you. I just had to stay here until they found the others and got busy doing whatever they wanted to do.

Various sounds drifted in from the hallway, as well as a yelp from some girl in another room. Someone had been found.

"Check in the closet," someone else said.

There were two in here.

I kept as still as possible, but then I heard a shuffle, and I trained my ears, listening.

"No!" One of the girls laughed. The rings on the curtain slid down the rod, and I knew one of the guys had found the girl in the drapes.

"Piss off," she snapped. "I don't mess around with juniors."

"Well, lucky for you," he replied, "I like older women."

I heard a scoff from her and a chuckle from him.

"There's a girl in the cabinet. Go for her," she told him.

Just then, wood hit wood, and it sounded like the metal handle of a cabinet jiggling. "Bitch!" I think the other girl hiding in the cabinet exclaimed.

"Hey, thanks," the other dude said. I heard some more shuffling and protesting, a door slamming shut (the bathroom?), and then footsteps.

Silence followed, and then the voice of the girl who'd been hiding in the drapes spoke up. "Don't tell anyone about this." The bed dipped under me, and I jostled from side to side, my eyes going wide with alarm.

"Don't worry," he told her. "You'll want to tell everyone about this."

And I felt them both moving and shifting on the bed.

I held on to the pillows, trying to make sure they stayed covering me, as they started going at it. Heavy breathing, constant rolling, kissing, and a few moans from her, and then suddenly the headboard hit the wall.

Jesus! For a girl who didn't mess around with underclassmen, she was certainly giving this her all.

My body rocked back and forth, and I shook my head. I couldn't stay here while they had sex.

Turning onto my stomach, I dug my elbows into the bed and pulled myself off the side, sliding onto the floor. I crouched down on the carpet, still for a moment and listening for their moaning and kissing.

It was still going.

They didn't notice me.

Crawling around the bed, I headed for the door to see if the hallway was clear. Everyone had to have been discovered by now.

But just then the hotel room door swung open again, and a young guy, his mask pushed up on top of his head, immediately spotted me.

"Well, well."

Oh, hell, no.

I pushed myself to my feet and barreled past him, running into the hallway.

And right into someone else's arms.

I screamed, drew back my hand, balled my fist, and popped the guy right in the face of his mask.

He stumbled back. "Shit!"

Pulling off his mask, he let it drop to the floor and grabbed his nose with both hands.

Will Grayson.

I backed away, maintaining my distance. But I kind of wanted to laugh. These people had been grabbing me all night. It was only a matter of time.

A few hoots of laughter filled the hall, and Will pulled his hands away to check for blood.

"Can't you take her, man?" someone shouted.

People laughed, but I kept my eyes on him, ready. I wasn't getting caught.

"Well, what do you want me to do?" He held out his hands, arguing with his buddies. "I can't hit her back!"

"No, you can't, can you?" I egged him on.

And the crowd went wild.

He shook his head at me. "You little shit."

And I smiled even though my hands were shaking. This was more comfortable for me. I was used to roughhousing with guys.

But he inched forward, threatening, "I'm going to get you in a closet for that."

"Not if you can't catch me." Then I sucked in a breath and stepped forward, launching my fist toward his face, but he knocked it away. I quickly shot my left palm up under his jaw, sending his head jerking backward.

Oh, shit, it worked!

He stumbled and growled, grabbing me by the sweatshirt, yanking me in, throwing me over his shoulder. Not again!

"Is that the only way you can win, huh?" I barked, squirming as the bystanders reeled with enjoyment. "You pick up the guys you fight, too? Or do you like your men bent over, is that it?"

Laughter filled the hallway, but then I was flying again, and I squealed, my ass crashing into the ground. What the hell?

The wind was knocked out of me, and I coughed, trying to get in a breath.

Will came down on top of me, pushing me onto my back and grabbing my wrists. I fought, my burning muscles struggling against his hold, but he eventually forced my hands above my head, holding them there. I wasn't strong enough. *Son of a bitch.*

I shifted under his weight, the crowd howling around us as he pinned me to the floor.

Will grunted, the stench of beer all over his breath as he struggled to keep hold of me. "This is what you really want, isn't it, runt?"

"Eat shit!"

I thrashed under him, but he just busted up laughing.

They were all laughing. My brother was right. This was what it always turned into with women. I was reduced to being on my back, no doubt where Easy Cheese here thought I belonged.

I belted out a growl, throwing all my weight up into him, and flipped him over. I landed one punch, knocking him in the nose, before he threw me off. I landed on the ground, and we both scrambled to our feet, him holding his nose and wincing.

I launched for him again.

But someone caught my sweatshirt from behind and an arm wrapped around my waist, lifting me up off my feet.

"Whoa, there, tiger." The broad chest at my back shook as the man behind me laughed.

I breathed hard, jerking my head to get a look.

I came face to face with a silver mask. The hood of his black hoodie was down, but I met his eyes as they gazed down at me and saw his dark hair.

Kai.

He looked ahead, jerking the chin of his mask. "What the hell are you doing?"

I looked to Will, his head tilted back, his finger under his nose, and blood trailing down to his top lip. "Getting the shit kicked out of me," he grumbled as the crowd's amused chatter surrounded us. "She's a scrapper."

"I only got hits in because you let me," I spouted off. "Let's finish it. For real this time."

Will rolled his eyes, and Kai tightened his hold, but I heard his breathy laugh behind me.

"No one wants to see you hurt, babe," Kai said, lowering my feet to the ground and coming to stand at my side, looking down at me. "You okay?"

I pushed my hair behind my ear, pausing when I realized my hood had come down. I glanced from left to right. *Please, let Damon not have spotted me here.*

I pulled up the hood, covering myself as much as possible.

"Are you from another school?" Kai asked. "This is a Thunder Bay party. Are you supposed to be here?"

He didn't recognize me.

The makeup. I'd forgotten about the makeup I was wearing.

Plus, I was in my pajamas and a sweatshirt, different clothes than at the cemetery.

I started to back away.

The longer I stayed, the bigger chance I'd be discovered. It was time to leave.

"Wait a minute," he said, stepping toward me. "This is a private party. Who are you?"

My gaze flashed to the people around the hallway, seeing them watching us.

"I can call you a ride," Kai offered, slowly advancing as I backed away. "Do you have a car? How old are you?"

"Kai, let her go. Come on!" Will called, heading into another room.

I took a step, holding Kai's eyes, my heart pounding. "Old enough to have seen and heard worse," I told him.

And he stopped mid-step.

A shot of thrill swelled in my throat, and my legs burned with the urge to run.

He stared at me, his chest rising and falling faster. He remembered. I was scared he wouldn't. Maybe I'd dreamed the confessional this morning, and it never really happened.

But he cocked his head, and it felt like he was zoning in.

Shit.

I took another step back, past the crowd, and kept going.

"Michael brought me here." I swallowed, my mouth so dry. "It has nothing to do with you. I don't even want to be here."

I stumbled over something on the floor, looking away to find my footing and quickly looking back at him. But he just stayed rooted in his spot, watching me.

Wasn't he going to say anything?

I continued backing away, afraid to turn my back on him.

And then he took a step.

I sucked in a short breath. "What are you doing?"

He took another step. "Giving you a head start."

My stomach leapt. "But I don't . . . I didn't want to play!"

"Oh, you've been playing with me all night," he said, a growl lacing his voice. "Run. Because I turn into a very different person when no one's looking."

I lost my breath and whipped around, taking off. The lobby. There would be people in the lobby. And desk clerks. I raced to the end of the hall, past the elevator, without looking back, and bolted through the exit door leading to the stairwell.

Bright light blinded me, and I grabbed the railing as I ran down the stairs, swung around the banister, and leapt down the next flight. I heard the door above slam shut, but then a loud *gong* echoed in the stairwell, and I knew it was the sound of it swinging open again.

I choked on a breath and swooped down another flight, jumping stairs as I did. But I couldn't not look back. Twisting my head over my shoulder, I searched for his shoes or any movement, but nothing. Not even the sound of steps being taken.

But then, all of a sudden, he landed with a loud thud on the landing one short flight up, having leapt over the railings and two flights.

He straightened his bent knees, standing tall again, and his dark eyes pierced me through the horrid mask. My heart lodged in my throat, and I squealed, racing faster down the stairs and feeling him on me like the clothes on my back.

The muscles in my legs burned, and sweat covered my brow, but God, I was excited.

I wanted him to catch me.

Launching myself down, down, down the stairs, I could hear his jumps getting closer and closer. But I didn't look back. I didn't want to see him coming. I just wanted to feel it. Feel his arms wrap around me and danger take hold, forcing me to face it.

I sucked in short, shallow breaths, every inch of my skin desperate to be grabbed, squeezed, kissed, bit, and sucked. God, what was he doing to me?

Reaching the lobby, I swung open the door, catching sight of black out of the corner of my eye and smiling, almost delirious, because I was so fucking scared he was damn near right behind me.

I ran through the door, into the lobby, and looked around, seeing a few stragglers still sitting around the dimly lit hotel. No clerk stood behind the desk, and I swung around, not seeing any security guards or janitors or anyone. Not that I was planning to run for help, but I assumed what Kai would or wouldn't do depended on who was watching.

Whipping around, I stumbled backward, watching the door and the white wall of the stairwell visible through the small rectangular window suddenly turning black as his form covered it.

A raging heat burned low in my belly, and I stopped breathing as he swung the door open and stepped through, locking eyes with me.

He seemed so much bigger now. He was already tall, but I was scared, and the fear had me gauging his size to mine. He could probably wrap his arms around me nearly twice.

Do it, I dared him with my eyes. It had been a fucking long day, and I was so tired, but fire coursed through my veins, never making me feel more alive. I wanted to see everything he was made of. Quiet, pondering, stoic, and reserved Kai Mori. *Come on. Fuck with me.*

I dipped my tongue out, licking my lip and tasting the sweat on my skin.

And he shot off, rushing me.

I gasped, spinning round and darting for the first doors I saw. I ignored the attention we'd attracted from the people sitting in the lobby and ripped open the door, rushing through.

It slammed behind me, and I dashed across the ballroom and scrambled behind a set of black drapes, just as the door swung open again.

I clamped my hand over my mouth, desperate for air, but I couldn't stop gasping. It was too loud. The door shut again, and I couldn't hear anything else, my heart was pounding in my ears so hard. Was he in the room?

Did he give up?

I wanted him to find me, adrenaline from the chase heating my blood, but I was so scared, too.

"You feel it, don't you?" he called out.

I closed my eyes, shaking uncontrollably.

"I'm already inside you."

My clit throbbed, aching, and I reached down, holding myself between my legs. *Oh, God.*

"I know you're in here," he continued. "I see the drapes moving."

My hands fell away, landing on the window seat behind me as I fell back and stared at the black cloth in front of me.

"I want something that's not mine," he growled, and I knew he was right there. "But we're not here, are we?"

What?

"We don't exist, and this isn't happening," he told me.

I bit my lip to keep from smiling. Damon would never know, and what he didn't know wouldn't hurt me.

"We're not here," I whispered back, following his lead.

And then the drapes swiped open, and he came at me, mask off, and grabbed the back of my neck and pulled me in.

I whimpered, my mouth crashing to his, and suddenly he was everywhere. Squeezing my neck, a hand gripping my ass, my arms around his neck, and his narrow waist pressing achingly hard between my thighs, I struggled to get closer. I wanted him all over. His mouth covered mine, and we kissed, going hard and fast, eating each other alive. He tasted like everything I'd ever need.

I bit his lip, dragging it out between my teeth as I fumbled with his belt buckle.

"I only want you," I breathed over his mouth, our soft lips taunting each other. "It's not like that with him. I only talk to you."

He pushed me back, shoved up my sweatshirt and shirt, and started sucking on my breast as he nestled himself between my legs, grinding forcibly.

I closed my eyes, groaning. Fire blossomed on my nipple and spread over my skin. *Oh, God.*

"We're not talking right now," he gritted out, moving to the other one. His tongue was so hot; it lit a bonfire between my legs.

Jeans open, he ground on me, and I rolled my hips to meet him again and again. The thick ridge under his briefs teased my clit as it rubbed over it again and again.

I cried out, and he planted a hand over my mouth, dry-fucking me as he leaned in close and bit my ear.

"I can feel it," he whispered, his other hand gripping my hip. "You want me, don't you? You want this?"

I nodded, grunting, sweating, and rubbing harder, trying to chase my orgasm, which was cresting.

"I'm gonna sneak these legs open and fuck you in every corner I can get you in."

Groaning again, I turned my head and snatched up his mouth, so fucking hungry. His words. God, his words. "Fuck me," I breathed out. "Chase me, steal me, and fuck me. Hide me, I don't care."

He grabbed the back of my head, pulled me into his chest, and dry-fucked me harder, both of us panting and grunting and finally kissing as we both came. An electric current jolted and spread down my legs, my pussy so warm as I got wetter.

"Mine," he groaned.

I slipped my hands under his hoodie, feeling his wet back, and buried my face in his chest as the orgasm faded away and my heart pulsed in my ears.

We stayed there, still and hot, but unable to move. I hooked my legs around the back of his and just breathed in as seconds turned into a minute and a minute turned into two.

His fingers threaded through my hair, and he forced my head back and my eyes up as he leaned down and kissed me softly. Deep, long, and slow. I could kiss him forever.

"Meet me at the Bell Tower tomorrow," he told me.

But I shook my head. "I can't so soon. I'll be on lockdown."

"I'm not waiting." He leaned down to kiss a trail to my ear as he reached between my legs to rub me. "You either find a way out, or I'll find a way in. I don't mind doing this behind another set of drapes if we have to." And then he slipped his hand down the front of my sleep shorts and the tips of his fingers inside me.

"Ah," I squirmed back. It hurt.

But I quivered, too. There was still so much to feel.

"I like chasing you," he said, a hint of a smile on his lips. "I like our foreplay."

I nodded. "I like it, too."

"Hide with me, then?"

Hide from my brother? Hide from David, Lev, and Ilia and sneak around with Kai?

I nodded again. "Okay."

He kissed me, and while I knew we weren't being realistic—hiding each other wouldn't last—I couldn't help but be excited for the promise of more stolen moments. I just wanted to be with him. I wanted to feel him.

Lost in his lips, I didn't notice the music at first. A sprinkle of raindrops all around, and I almost looked out the window to see if it was raining, but then I heard the tune quickly follow. The tinkling high notes of a xylophone or some such instrument that sounded like a haunted lullaby hung in the silence of the ballroom.

We both stopped and looked up and then around.

And I couldn't believe what I was seeing. Suddenly, a beautiful woman came twirling out from around the stage, onto the dance floor, her black ballet slippers laced up her ghostly white, but strong, legs, while her midnight hair danced around her. She stepped and spun like a dream to the eerie melody, her tattered but fancy black costume like a swan around her, adorned with feathers and sparkles. She was dreamlike.

"Do you see what I'm seeing?" Kai whispered.

"Yeah," I replied, unable to tear my eyes away. "It's the dancing woman."

CHAPTER 14

KAI

Present

H ey, kid." I called Banks as she walked past the office door. "Come here for a minute."

She stopped, hesitating before she entered. I took in her clothes, all dry and back on her body, covering every possible inch of skin again. She just couldn't wait to get Alex's stuff off, could she?

I stood behind the desk and picked up a set of keys on a ring, tossing them across the room to her.

She caught them, studying them. "What are these?"

"Keys to the dojo. In case I need you to pick something up, drop something off . . . There's also the showers, cots upstairs, laundry, food in the staff kitchen . . ." I drifted off, stuffing the month's receipts in a folder in the drawer. "Come and go as you please."

"I have a shower, a bed, and somewhere to do laundry."

I looked up, meeting her stubborn eyes and not the least bit surprised at how clever she was. Yeah, okay. Maybe I was leaving a not-so-subtle hint.

But I blew it off. "I'm not saying you don't. You need keys as part of your job. It's not complicated."

"How do you know I won't rip you off?"

I closed the drawer, a smile pulling at my mouth as I stood up straight. "Because I'm a great judge of character and petty thievery doesn't strike me as your style," I told her.

She might need the keys on the off chance she had to get in here while it was closed, but her initial suspicions were also correct. Gabriel let her live like a rat—that was apparent in her attire—and I still wasn't sure what her living situation was like. She said she lived in the city, but I couldn't imagine her residence was the least bit safe or nice. I wanted to make sure she had another option should she want it. The dojo was secure and clean, and she would have everything she needed here.

Except a car. I should make sure she had one, so she didn't get caught in the rain like she did this morning.

She shoved the keys in her pocket and turned to leave.

"Clothes are dry, I see." I let my eyes fall down the backs of her legs—legs I'd only ever seen the skin of once.

"I have some more provisions for the contract you can take to Gabriel," I told her, clearing my throat. "It's on the table."

She walked over and grabbed the envelope, holding it at her side. "Anything else?"

No, not really.

But I didn't want her to go yet, either.

"Yes." I stuck my pen in the holder and raised my eyes to her. "No matter how you cover yourself, it's never enough. You're beautiful."

She frowned and then turned on her heel and headed out the office door as quickly as she could.

I shook my head, smiling to myself. The most stubborn woman I'd ever met in my life.

Alex crossed the open doorway, heading down the hall.

"Alex?" I called.

She entered the room, a white towel over her shoulder and sweat glistening across her chest.

I dug in my wallet and pulled out a black card. "Take Banks

shopping in the next couple of days," I told her, handing over the credit card. "Will's party is coming up, and she'll need something to wear."

Her impatient expression turned delighted as she snatched up the credit card.

"I'm a personal shopper?" she asked playfully. "Hoo-yah."

"Bill me for your time."

"Eh." She shrugged. "Treat me to an outfit, as well, and we'll call it even."

She spun around and headed for the door.

"Alex?" I called. "Get her some clothes, too. Just everyday, average clothes."

"And if she puts up a fight?"

I turned off the desk lamp and made my way toward the door. "Then buy whatever you want for her to wear. She'll have some options if she ever decides to remove the stick in her ass."

I opened the door wider, both of us walking out.

"How much can I spend?" she asked.

"I'll call you when the text alerts start scaring me."

I wrapped a rubber band around all the envelopes and grabbed my duffel bag. It was after six, and while we still had a steady flow of people coming in and out, I was done.

Will didn't help, Rika was busy either teaching classes or going to school, and Michael was almost constantly gone. I was the only one who had absolutely nothing else to do with his day.

Not that I minded. I liked what we did here and where we were taking our other real estate interests, but I wanted to get over to The Pope. This time, alone.

Handing the stack of paychecks to Caroline so she could dole them out, I waved good night and made my way out the front door.

Clouds loomed, rolling over the dark city like a flood of ocean waves, and it was unusually warm. Hot, even. I could smell the tar on the streets.

My phone rang, and I dug it out of my jeans pocket as I unlocked my car door and opened it.

"Hello?"

Tossing my duffel bag into the car, I took the phone with my other hand and switched ears.

The line was silent.

"Hello?" I asked again.

And then the voice said, "Have you fucked her yet?"

I raised my chin, my spine straightening. Heat flooded my veins.

Damon.

I didn't know what it was about his voice that rattled me. It always had, in a way, but I hadn't realized it until now. After going so long without hearing it.

Glacial. That's what it was. He sounded like the point of a blade digging into your skin.

"She's pretty when she sleeps," he told me. "So many nights I watched her next to me, wishing I could sleep like that."

My hand ached, and I realized my fist was strained around the doorframe. I unclenched my fingers.

"It's almost Devil's Night. A few days," he pointed out as if I didn't know. "Any plans this year?"

My mouth stayed closed. I raised my gaze, slowly turning my head left and right, looking for any sign of him.

Have I fucked her yet? I assumed he meant Banks. Which meant he knew she worked for me now.

"You know I'm not stupid." He wasn't asking a question, emphasis on the word "know." "You above everyone know that. Do you really think you'll find me at The Pope? You think that whole place isn't wired and I wouldn't see you coming? That Banks would've let you in there if she thought for one second I was there? She will always be mine."

Cars drove past as the hot wind whipped down the alleyway where I'd parked. Part of me hoped he was right. She might lead me to him.

"You've been so bored, haven't you?" he taunted. "So bored, because having me around gave you an excuse to be the deviant you already were. To turn inside yourself and have a real good look at that monster. You're not noble behind closed doors, Kai."

"Where are you?" I asked.

"Around."

I twisted up my lips at his coy response.

"Rika's alone too much," he went on. "With Michael gone all the time, you really shouldn't have positioned yourself so far away from her across the river."

I barely registered the change in subject, closing my eyes.

"She slept in the most tantalizing white silk panties last night." His tone was almost confiding, and I felt my hand tighten around the phone. "It was nearly unbearable, watching a body like that go to waste in that cold bed alone. God, I wanted to fuck her. Dark room, half-asleep . . . she might not have even known the difference."

He was lying. Fucking with me. There was no way he got in that apartment. Michael might have been gone at times, but he'd taken significant precautions. Increased security, changed all the passcodes, hired additional personnel . . . He even tracked her phone and car. I should feel guilty about that, since she was my friend, too, but we knew she'd put up a fight, and it was pointless. Michael was right. It was necessary.

I was honestly surprised he hadn't tagged her jewelry, too, since Damon wouldn't take her in her own car and would know to ditch the phone.

"But I have to bide my time," Damon said wistfully. "I've waited so long. I won't rush it."

Rush what?

"So much trouble you've gone to for nothing, buying The Pope," he continued. "You won't find me."

"I wouldn't say it was all for nothing." I fixed my eyes across the road at the hotel. "Your little ruffian is far more pleasurable than I thought she'd be."

Which was an entirely true statement. Let him infer whatever he would.

"I think I understand now why you like her so much. Why, without the skimpy clothes, makeup, and hair, you find her so alluring." I inhaled, liking this side of the playing a hell of a lot more. The side where I was on the offense. "She's so repressed. It's captivating to see her let go and lose herself. To realize she likes being seen as a woman." And then I dragged out slowly, "And that she likes doing things a woman does."

I could feel his silence like it was his hands shoving against me. Only I wasn't backing down.

"So quiet all of a sudden?" I teased.

"Nik is mine," he stated, his voice clipped. "You will never be to her what I am to her."

Nik? Was that her first name?

"And I will kill you in front of her," he added.

"Well, come on, then. Why wait until Devil's Night? Let's get this over with." I slammed the car door, walking toward the street and the sprinkle of rain that floated on the air. I had no idea if he was in The Pope or not, but I faced the building as if I was talking right at him. "Or you can run again. Either or."

"But that's not what you want," he said, the sly mischief back in his voice. "I told you, I'm not dumb. I know what you're after. And it isn't a showdown, it isn't revenge, and it isn't even Banks."

I leveled my eyes on a window above, willing him to appear.

"Go ahead," he challenged. "Ask me. Ask me what only you and I know that you don't want Will, Michael, and Rika to find out about."

My chest heaved with silent breaths.

"Ask me where I buried the body when I cleaned up your shit six years ago."

I closed my eyes, my heart dropping into my stomach.

He hadn't forgotten. He would never forget. Did I really think he would?

Going to prison for three years because I assaulted a police officer wasn't the worst thing I'd ever done. I hadn't even begun to pay for my crimes.

"Don't tell me," I choked out, completely deflated as I stared ahead, but I tried to be stronger. "Because if you do, I'll bury you with her. And I know you'd hate that."

I hung up, standing in front of the alley and still facing the hotel as that nightmare of a night played back in my head.

How we were having fun and everything got away from me. How I was confused and angry and couldn't seem to stop myself, and how the rage consumed me. How I wanted to hurt her, even though I didn't really know her, but I hated her.

How I loved Damon once, and how I knew Gabriel Torrance was wrong. I would do anything for his son. I *have* done anything for his son.

I killed for him, and last year he turned around and nearly killed me.

I looked up, back at the hotel, wondering if he was right. Had I wasted my time? Maybe I should've been following his precious little girlfriend instead.

Two things were certain, though.

He was here, in the city, and he still wanted Rika. Anticipating him hadn't been a mistake.

I'd call Gabriel tomorrow and relinquish my claim on the hotel. I hadn't signed a contract, so there was no deal.

I moved to turn around, the light sprinkles turning heavier as they fell on my head, but then I stopped. Looking into the alleyway across the street, I spotted Banks climbing out of an SUV alone. She looked around her, not seeing me, and raced to the same back door we'd entered just days ago.

What was she doing?

The thunder cracked overhead, splitting across the sky, and I dived across the street, racing as a car's headlights shone through the mist.

Reaching the back of the building, I dug out my keys and looked down, realizing I'd given Banks the hotel set. But I still had the code memorized. Punching in the seven digits on the keypad, I stuffed my keys back in my pocket and opened the door, quickly slipping inside.

I didn't tell her to do anything at the hotel today. She wasn't here for me, I knew that much.

Taking out my phone, I turned on the flashlight and made my way out of the kitchen and through the dining room and the lobby. Stepping into the open space, I turned my head right and left, searching for her. Where did she go?

But then I heard a dull hum, a noise buried as if in the walls or under the floor. Following the sound, I turned my gaze left and spotted the numbers above one of the elevators lighting up.

As it ascended higher and higher.

They were working?

Reaching out to press the *up* arrow, I paused and then pulled back. What floor was she stopping on?

I watched the numbers light up—eight, then nine and ten . . . And then they kept going—eleven, twelve . . .

And it stopped. The light didn't go any higher.

Twelfth floor.

I quickly punched the top button, jamming it several times as my blood started to boil.

You've got to be fucking kidding me. The elevator *did* go to the twelfth floor.

I waited for it to descend again, keeping my cell phone handy in case I needed light.

How the hell did she get the elevators working?

As soon as the doors opened, I stepped inside, punched the twelve and then the button for the doors to close.

She knew he was here the whole time. She'd been seeing him, watching us fumble about and listening to our conversations. I mean, I knew she wasn't on our side. She never made any secret about where her loyalties lay. So, why did I want to throttle her more than him right now?

I clenched my goddamn jaw so hard, my teeth ached. If she liked ruthless men so much, I'd show her how ruthless I could be.

I slammed my hand into the 12 again, so angry I barely noticed that it wasn't lighting up.

Or that the elevator wasn't moving yet.

What the fuck? Wasn't it just running a minute ago? Why wasn't it working now?

I hit the button a few more times, looking around for any lights to show that the elevator registered where I wanted to move, but nothing.

The fluorescent lighting was dim inside the elevator, and I looked around for any other buttons to push or anything else that looked unusual. Anything to indicate how to get where I wanted to go.

The elevator went to the twelfth floor. A twelfth floor existed. I knew that now.

I pushed the 11 just to see if it would work.

And it did. The 11 suddenly lit up, and I felt the cables shift around me and gravity weigh me down as I began to ascend. The doors opened on eleven, and I glanced up long enough to see the dark hallway in front of me before I hit the 13 and quickly closed the doors again. I rose higher once more, stopping on thirteen as the doors opened, allowing me entrance to the floor.

I closed the elevator doors again. How was she getting the elevator to stop on twelve?

Maybe there was another stairwell access on one of these floors? They had to have one that reached twelve. What if there was a fire or the elevators broke?

I reached out and tried the only other thing that came to me. I pressed the 11 and the 13 together.

To my surprise, they both lit up.

But I still didn't feel the elevator move.

Instead, a short whirring came from behind me, and I jerked around, seeing a silver panel rise to reveal a hidden keypad in the elevator wall.

My heart skipped a beat. So, that was it. That was how she was getting to the twelfth floor.

And she knew it the last time we were here.

Walking over to the keypad, I noticed clear buttons with black numbers on them, along with a small screen that was lit up green.

I punched in the only code I knew. The one for the outside doors to get in the building.

Nothing happened.

I tried again, pressing the # symbol afterward.

Still nothing.

It was a different code. One I hadn't gotten.

But something Banks said once made me pause.

"*. . . and when it was investigated, there's not even a possibility for the elevator to stop there. The floor is walled in.*"

But that wasn't true. She'd stopped on this floor.

Keeping my back to the doors of the elevator, I leaned in close to the back wall, laying my head on the steel. I ran my hand up the edge, noticing a gap where the wall met the panel.

A gap.

This wasn't a wall. It was a door, and this elevator opened from the front *and* the back.

Jesus.

Suddenly the door shifted in front of me and started to open. I jerked back as the silver wall—and secret entrance—peeled back and Banks stood in front of me, her eyes snapping up when she noticed me.

I glanced past her briefly, taking in the massive, dark expanse behind her. There were no room doors with numbers, no hallway, no shitty carpeting . . .

It was a penthouse.

I turned my glare back on her. "You knew all along."

She looked at me, her body still and rigid.

I stepped into the penthouse, forcing her to take a step back. "Take me to him."

"He's not here."

But I advanced on her, moving forward into her space with a warning look.

"He's not here!" she growled.

"You're a fucking liar!"

"I suspected he might be, so I came to check it out. Again," she added as I walked past her and took a long look around.

The rooms were dark, the living room curling around the corner and giving way to a library and parlor, with a few hallways leading off to various places, probably bedrooms. There were couches and lamps, tables and rugs, the whole place set up like a home with a better view.

As I turned the corner around the elevator, I noticed the balcony through the two sets of French doors we'd been trying to get to the other day.

This apartment looked like it took up an entire floor. Which meant it might have several balconies wrapping around all sides of the building.

"How did you get the elevator working without the electricity on?" I asked.

She stuffed her hands in her pockets. "The elevators have a different circuit breaker."

"And you knew that when we were here last time?"

She averted her eyes.

Obviously.

The lingering scent of cloves drifted into my nostrils, and I recognized it right away.

Damon mostly smoked Davidoffs, but once in a while he'd indulge in Djarum Blacks. The odor lingered, and I would never forget it.

"You had to know I would never give him up to you." Banks' voice was solemn. "I know what you and your friends are capable of."

I whipped around, unable to keep the snarl off my face.

"What I'm capable of?" I asked her. "So, he's the victim?"

I approached her, done with her one-track mind and everything being either black or white with her. "I was his friend. I always stood by his side, and he's done nothing but try to hurt us. He's a threat."

I spun back around and charged farther into the penthouse, making my way down one of the short hallways.

I darted into bedrooms, taking in a little dust, some ruffled bedsheets, and a dank smell, probably from the place being closed up for however long.

Stepping into one room, a balcony visible through the double doors, I immediately spotted an ashtray on a dresser and walked over to inspect it.

I picked up one of Damon's black cigarette butts in a sea of white ones and brought it to my nose. The earthy and spicy scent had the same overpowering sweetness I remembered.

I dropped it back in the ashtray, noticing all the white Davidoffs, too. Both of his brands.

Gazing around the bedroom, I took in the mussed sheets with the pillows at the foot of the bed, the bottles of Corona in the trash, and the floor littered with the foil wrappings from inside his cigarette boxes that Damon had a serial killer obsession with folding into tiny parcels until they couldn't be folded anymore.

"He may not be here now, but he was," I said, turning around to face her.

She held my gaze, remaining silent.

"Where is he now?" I asked, walking toward her.

"I don't know."

I cocked my head, repeating my question. "Where is he?"

"I don't know."

Another step toward her. "*Where* is he?"

"I don't know."

I backed her into the wall, heat filling my glare. "He's very possessive of you, isn't he?"

She folded her full lips between her teeth, and there were so many things I didn't yet understand—why Damon was so attached to her, why she was so loyal to him, and I didn't have the slightest idea who the fuck she really was, but one thing I knew for sure. I could mess with Gabriel, I could dangle Rika like a worm on a hook, but this girl, right here, was the one person to drive Damon insane.

She was his weakness.

"Perhaps I don't need to look for him, after all," I told her. "I have you, and he'll come to me, won't he? With the right motivation."

Her eyes snapped up to mine, and I caught a flinch of worry before she hid it.

But that one flinch was everything. It was a crack—one of the only ones I'd seen—in her hard, cold exterior.

And for a moment I forgot all about Damon Torrance.

"Ask me not to hurt him," I said, my voice cracking unexpectedly.

But she just stared at me, her gaze faltering only slightly.

I inched closer, feeling her body's heat. "Did it ever occur to you that all you would have to do is ask?"

I needed Damon so I could get the location of the goddamn body out of him before he decided to use it against me, but I didn't have to hurt him. That was up to him. And maybe her.

She searched my eyes, the endless abyss of her green ones starting to glisten. Her chin trembled, and she shook her head slowly, at war with herself.

"You can't, can you? You won't ask me for anything."

She dropped her eyes, her chest caving.

"Do you love him?" I asked.

"Yes."

Her head was still down as she whispered, but I heard the quick reply well enough.

"Yes," she repeated, nodding. "I love him so much. More than I'll ever love anyone." Her teary eyes rose and met mine again. "I can control him. If I can find him. Just give me a chance."

But I barely heard the last part.

Yes.

I love him so much.

More than I'll ever love anyone.

She did open her heart, it seemed, but it was only for him.

I straightened, a frost setting in.

"Are you crying?" I asked. "For him?"

She wouldn't say the words, she wouldn't beg me, but it was in her eyes. She was just as much his now as she was back then.

"Fine," I said, leaning in and taunting her. "Cry for him, then, and beg me. Beg me to leave him alone, and I will."

Her jaw flexed, and the blush of anger crossed her face.

"You have a chance to save his life, Banks. All you have to do is beg me. Come on. I want to see it. How far will you go for him?" I bared my teeth, seething. "Beg!"

She cried out, her gloved hand coming across my face.

My head snapped to the side, and the burn of the slap spread to my lips.

My heart fucking leapt.

Again.

"Fuck, you're pathetic." I smiled cockily as I turned to face her again. "His little lapdog, aren't you? If you're good, does he allow you the privilege of licking his cock clean after he's fucked a real woman?"

"Ugh!" She growled, slapping me across the same cheek again.

My neck ached with the sudden blow this time, and I sucked in a breath, absorbing the pain. She was strong.

I dipped my tongue to the corner of my lips, tasting the metallic cut where my teeth had torn the skin.

"You'll never be more than what you are now." I dived in, slamming my hands on the wall behind her, bringing us nose to nose. "Something for men to use. That's all you are. And in fifty years you'll end up alone, never knowing what this feels like."

I ran my thumb over the drop of blood at the corner of my mouth and wiped it on her cheek.

She snarled, knocking my hand away, but I was fucking high, and I didn't know if I was pissed off, turned on, or desperate for this confrontation, but I dived in and lost control. My body did the thinking.

I grabbed the back of her neck in one hand and her ass in the other and plastered her body to mine.

"What *this* feels like," I growled over her lips, pressing my dick—hard and already desperate for her—into her groin.

She whimpered and her body instantly stiffened like she was frightened, but she grabbed my shoulders anyway, her fingers digging into my skin through my shirt.

"And what *this* feels like," I whispered, slipping my hand down the back of her jeans and squeezing a handful of her smooth, soft ass in my hand.

She gasped, squeezing her eyes shut, but I didn't miss the way she moved her leg to the outside of mine, opening up her thighs a little more for me and rolling her hips.

I didn't know if she meant to do it, or maybe she was just like me. Just letting it take us over.

"I'm not begging you for shit," she said, a tear spilling down her cheek.

"Fuck Damon." I slammed her back into the wall, lifting her up and grinding my dick between her legs. "This is you and me."

She panted as she locked her legs around my body. The small streak of blood on her cheek started to glow with her sweat, and I didn't stop touching her or let up, because if I gave her a second to think, she'd stop this.

"I liked you," I whispered. "I still remember how good those stolen moments with you felt."

Out of all the women, my mind always found her.

And I couldn't wait for more. I snatched up her lips, silencing all of our words and worries and baggage and shit, and kissed her, dipping my tongue inside and tasting her like she was my fucking meal.

Cold girl—hard girl—why was I obsessed? Why was I jealous that she'd probably given how many other men in that house a piece of her but would barely spare me a one-word sentence?

Fuck her. She wanted me. I didn't care about the bullshit that came out of her mouth. We weren't teenagers anymore, and I wasn't the good guy. She was going to do for me what she did for Damon or David or whoever the fuck else came in and out of the Torrances', and she was going to know that I was just as ruthless. She underestimated me, but she wouldn't forget this. That I owned a piece of her just like they did.

I ripped open her jacket and yanked it down her arms. "Take off your shirt."

I dropped her to her feet, her hat sliding off her head and letting her hair fall free as I pulled my pullover and T-shirt over my head and let them fall to the floor.

She paused, holding up her arms and covering her still-clothed body. "I—"

But I grabbed her and kissed her again, cutting her off. She moaned into my mouth, and I ripped open her flannel, sending buttons flying, and I pulled away, pausing just a moment when I saw the bindings covering her chest.

What the hell?

I'd have to ask her about that when my head cleared later.

I looked down at the desk, seeing a letter opener, and I grabbed it, slipping the cool brass blade down the inside of the wrap and yanking hard, slicing open the material and seeing her beautiful breasts spring free. I breathed hard, briefly taking in the marks on her skin from being wrapped so tight before I pushed her shirt down her arms and came to her, plastering her chest to mine.

"And what this feels like," I breathed in her ear, light-headed at the feeling of her hardened nipples pressed into my chest.

I wrapped my arms around her, going mad with the way her back felt as soft as water and with the way her hair caressed my arms, leaving chills.

She clutched me, panting and nervous. "I'm his. I belong to him."

I nodded, forcing her back toward the bed. "Say it again."

I dived into her neck, biting the skin there.

"I belong to him." She moaned, letting her head fall back. "I'll never be yours. I hate you."

"But you want me."

And I pushed her back, sending her falling to the bed.

Holding her eyes, I unfastened my belt, ripped open my fly, and pushed the rest of my clothes down my legs and off my body.

She sucked in air faster and faster, her eyes widening and locked on my cock as it stood up rock hard and ready, just as it had been since she'd started hitting me.

I needed that now. Passion. And it didn't matter that it was anger. As long as the feelings were strong.

Tears filled her eyes, and I watched her breasts, just big enough to fill my hand, and couldn't wait to own every damn inch of her.

"Do you want me to stop?" I challenged her, stepping up to the bed and looking down on her. "Here's your chance. Ask me to stop, and I will."

She was silent, but then her jaw locked, her eyes grew angry, and she snarled. "Yeah, I knew you were all talk. Go ahead and stop, then, pussy."

I broke into a smile.

Reaching down, I gripped the top of her jeans and panties and yanked them down her legs, the oversize clothes sliding off without any trouble. She cried out, squeezing her eyes shut, but I knew it was just her pride talking.

Banks had been around rougher guys than me, but I'd make damn sure she didn't forget this. The little Torrance slut was all mine for however long she kept her legs spread.

I came down on her, groaning at every inch of her skin hot against mine.

I lifted up her knee and nibbled her lips as I settled myself between her legs. God, I could feel the wet warmth at her center. My body started to shake.

I covered her mouth, feeling her whimpers and moans vibrate under my lips.

Working my hand down between us, I positioned myself and started to push.

She gasped, her muscles suddenly tensing. "I'm scared."

"Don't be. Damon doesn't have to know you loved getting fucked by me more than him."

And I growled, thrusting hard and deep and sinking into her tight body, my brain barely registering a thin barrier giving way.

She cried out, tossing her head back with her face twisted up in pain. "Ah! Oh, God!"

What the fuck? I stilled.

Her body shook, her nails dug into my shoulders, and she was breathing a mile a minute. It was pain, not pleasure.

I stopped breathing.

No, no, no . . . What? No.

I lay there, staring down at her as my cock throbbed inside her. A virgin?

I could feel the confusion etched on my face.

She was a fucking virgin?

She gasped again and again, trying to catch her breath. It slowly calmed as the shock ebbed away, and we both just lay there, her expression starting to relax.

She opened her eyes, looking up into my pained face.

Oh, God. What did I do?

Her lips slowly curved into a half smile. "Yeah, you didn't see that coming, did you?"

CHAPTER 15

BANKS

Present

What the hell's going on?" He looked down at me in agony, all the meanness and cockiness from earlier now gone.

I knew what he was confused about, but I didn't answer. I blinked through the tears in my eyes.

It had hurt. Just like Damon said it would.

I wanted to pull away from him, but then he'd know I couldn't take what was happening. I couldn't help but squirm under him, though, and try to shift the pain.

It burned, and I was uncomfortable. My throat swelled with the tears I was trying to hold in.

Of course, I knew it would only hurt that once, but once was all I would ever suffer, so help me. I clenched my jaw to keep my chin from trembling. I didn't want to give away the shame I felt. I would never fucking do this again. It didn't feel good.

"Get off me." I grunted. I was cold, I ached, and he felt like an intrusion. Like something that shouldn't be inside me.

"It's okay," he whispered under his breath, gently pushing my hair out of my eyes. "It's okay."

"You got what you wanted, so get off me now."

I was breaking, and the tears broke free, running down my temples, into my hair. I was ruined. Damon was going to hate me now.

But Kai just shook his head slowly, still looking down at me, befuddled. "I didn't know. I ... I thought ..." His fingers fell down the side of my face and then down my arm. "What the fuck is happening?"

His forehead dropped to mine, and I was about to shove him off, but I hesitated. Why the hell did he care? Wasn't this what he wanted? Whether it was my first time or my hundredth, he'd used me like the toy I was to him. What did it matter?

"Who are you to him?" he asked, lifting his head up to look down at me.

"It doesn't matter. I'll still choose him. He never hurt me like this. Not like you did."

He winced, and I could tell I'd cut him. Kai worried he was bad, and he tried to be sinister, but not so deep down, he was good, and it was who he was. He would never change.

He didn't like hurting me.

He shifted his body, pulling out of me, and I flinched at the renewed soreness between my legs as I tried to close them.

But he didn't move off me. He stayed nestled between my thighs.

"Look at me," he told me.

Slowly, I raised my eyes again, and he touched my face.

"I would've been gentler your first time," he said.

"I don't care." I shook my head. "I don't care about any of it."

Shoving my palms into his chest, I pushed him off me and shot off the bed, bolting.

But he caught me from behind. Wrapping an arm around my waist, he hauled me back, and I gasped, both of us falling back on the bed. I lay on top of him, my back molded to his chest.

My scream was cut off by his mouth as he threaded his fingers through the back of my hair and twisted my head, holding my mouth to his.

I thrashed and jerked, elbowing him as I tried to twist away, but he didn't let me go. His mouth, strong and demanding, moved to my jaw, my cheek, and my ear, sucking and biting, and I growled, throwing my left hand over my body and slapping him.

"Hurt me. Do what you want with me," he gasped in my ear. "I deserve it."

He brought his legs up between mine, bending them at the knee and spreading my own.

His hand slipped between my legs, and I cried out, suddenly afraid, but he stopped and just rested there, unmoving as he held me in his palm.

"Kai!" I yelled, fighting him.

His lips stopped on my cheek, breathing hard and hot. "Not tonight."

What?

"I'm not Kai," he said, "and you're not Banks."

There was something pleading in his voice that gave me pause.

"Thunder Bay doesn't exist, and we're not in The Pope," he continued. "It's six years ago when I was happy and excited, and you were curious about everything, and my words were all it took to touch you."

My entire body stilled, and tears suddenly blurred my vision as he whispered to me.

"You're the girl I didn't know, and we could be anyone in that confessional. Everything else fell away. Everything. We could hide and fuck with the world in that little room. It was just us."

I closed my eyes, exhaustion seizing me.

All those years ago. That wasn't really me, was it?

I relaxed into him, unable to find the will to fight.

I almost remembered being her. Back when I still hoped there were possibilities. When I thought there was some way I could have him and have the fun things that normal girls had. When I let myself crave those stolen kisses and his eyes on me, imagining him wanting things a man wanted from a woman and wanting them from me.

My lungs burned, and I sucked in a breath, realizing I'd forgotten to breathe. God, all that need flooded back, washing over me and heating up my skin. I'd starved myself dry, and I suddenly felt like nothing but bones so weak I could break. I was so hungry.

I turned my head, meeting his gaze an inch from mine. His fingers relaxed in my hair, while I stared into his dark pools, my mind too foggy to think.

"Hold my eyes," he said softly. "Just keep looking at me."

I did. I just dived and surrendered and fell.

The confessional.

We were back in the confessional. We were younger, and it was no one but us. Tucked away, safe.

I was safe.

His hand between my legs started to move, rubbing back and forth so gentle and slow. "No one sees us," he breathed out. "There's no one but you and me. We're invisible. We don't exist."

I nodded weakly, but my lids started to droop with the sensation of his caresses. *Oh, God.*

"Keep your eyes on me, baby," he told me.

I blinked several times, refocusing as his hand drifted up, running over my stomach. His touch sent shivers down my arms, and I moaned, struggling to hold his eyes as his hand came to my breast. He cupped it, kneading so softly and taunting me.

I caught him glancing at my chest, his mouth open and his gaze thick with hunger like he wanted what was in his hand in his mouth instead.

Licking my lips, I felt him move to my other breast, fondling the nipple until that one, too, had tightened into a pebble. Butterflies swarmed in my belly, and I started to feel the pulse in my clit throb, wanting his hand back there now.

His fingers dug lightly into my skin, running back down my torso and stomach, sending shocks out of every pore on my body as he grabbed me a little harder between the thighs this time.

I closed my eyes and arched my back, feeling his erection pulse under me. "Kai . . ."

Every touch, every breath, heightened the weightlessness taking over my body. I was floating, the room was spinning, and I didn't want to get off the ride.

Turning my head, I parted my lips, searching for his.

His teeth caught my bottom lip, dragging it out tauntingly.

"This is what it should've been," he told me. "It wouldn't have hurt so much if I'd gotten you ready first. I'm sorry. I should've gone slowly."

Opening my eyes, I looked up at him. Instinct told me to bolt. Tuck back into my shell and stay in the darkness.

But I wasn't Banks tonight. He wasn't Kai, and we weren't here. None of this was happening.

"So, go slow with me, then," I whispered.

He only hesitated a moment before sliding out from under me and laying me down on the bed. I immediately raised my arms to cover myself, a golf ball in my throat and my heart palpitating.

I wanted him, but I was still shy. No one had ever seen me naked.

Life had gotten a hell of lot more complicated in the last ten minutes.

He wasn't looking anywhere but in my eyes as he came to hover over me.

"I want you." He gently pulled my arms down.

His stare bored into me as he ran his hand up the center of my torso, gliding between my breasts to my neck. He dived down, covering my nipple with his mouth, and I threw my head back, moaning. "Kai," I said again.

I placed my hands on his arms as he held himself up with one hand and used the other to grope the breast he was kissing. His hot mouth sucked on the tight, hard skin, drawing the nipple out and then going in for more before he began moving around all over.

I shuddered. "That feels so good."

He quickly switched over to the other one, leaving his hand where it was and keeping me warm.

He trailed down my stomach, and I shivered, fisting my fingers in his hair.

"Open your legs," he said huskily.

I lifted up my head, and my eyes instantly fell between his legs, seeing him hard and thick.

Without looking up, he descended lower and lifted up my leg by the back of the knee. "Gotta get you ready, babe."

He dipped his head between my legs, burying his mouth, and I tried to push him off. "No, don't do that—"

But with the subtle flick of his tongue, my eyelids suddenly felt so heavy.

He swirled around just above the hood, rubbing me with his mouth as his hand circled my thigh, holding it up, and his body settled in between my thighs.

Licking and nibbling, his assault was soft at first, sending my stomach reeling and fireworks shooting down my legs. I felt like I was on a swing twenty stories up, leaning back with my hair flying in the air.

I wanted more. Deeper.

Then he started sucking. Everything. In, out, and around, kissing my skin down there and still kneading my breast with one hand. I lifted up my head, watching him.

"You're so fucking tight down here," he panted, gently biting me. "But you're going to stretch. I promise."

I bit my lip as he looked up at me.

"Do you like this?" he asked, licking me up and down slowly.

My cheeks heated with a blush, and a small smile crossed his face.

"Or this?" He watched me as he swirled his tongue around my clit over and over again.

I lost my breath, my eyelids fluttering.

He grinned, taunting me. "Or maybe this?"

And then he covered my clit with his lips and sucked strong, pulling and tugging, the heat of his mouth torture as I arched off the bed and groaned. "Ah," I moaned breathlessly.

"So beautiful," he whispered. "Are you ready, kid?"

My stomach quivered with anticipation, and I wasn't even annoyed he called me "kid" again. For this one time, it sounded endearing.

I nodded, slipping my hand into his hair. I wasn't sure what I was ready for other than just more. I just wanted more.

Coming up, he kissed me, working my mouth open and dipping his tongue inside. I groaned, my body taking over as I grabbed his hips and parted my legs, lifting up my knees and letting him in.

My nipples brushed his chest, and I pushed up, kissing him back with full force. His smell, his skin, his taste . . . in this moment, I was new.

Kneeling over me, he reached down between us and positioned himself at my opening. The tip pushed inside, and the tight burn immediately made me freeze up again.

"It hurts." Every muscle tightened up, and I was afraid to move.

"Look at me," he said.

I raised my shaky eyes, staring at the flat spot on his bottom lip.

"Bend your knees more," he told me.

I did, my fingers curling into his hips.

"Now, relax your thighs," he instructed. "Spread 'em wide and let them fall to the bed, okay? Open for me. Just open."

I laid down my thighs, knees bent and spread for him.

He pushed a little more, and I sucked in a breath, but I didn't try to stop him. He paused himself and leaned down, whispering over my lips. "You're torturing me. I just want to sink into you so bad."

"It's not in yet?"

He shook with a laugh. "Not all the way. Does it still hurt?"

I was about to say yes. It was definitely uncomfortable, but . . . I guess it didn't really hurt.

I shook my head.

Looking into my eyes, he slowly sank deeper, and I started to feel stretched and full and kind of strange.

"How about now?"

"I . . . I don't . . ." I stammered, adjusting to him. "I don't know."

He thrust all the way in, bottoming out, and hit me so deep, my eyes rolled back. Oh, shit.

"Kai . . ."

"Banks, Jesus Christ." He kissed me. "I love the way you feel."

I gripped his hips as he nibbled my mouth and neck and ear, and before I knew it, nothing was uncomfortable anymore.

"Put one hand on my shoulder," he said, leaning back up to look down at me. "I want you to feel me move."

I did as he told, and slowly, he pulled out. I briefly registered something wet, but he rolled his hips, sinking back inside me.

"Oh, God." I groaned.

It didn't hurt at all anymore.

Holding on to him, I watched his body move as the room filled with the sounds of our pants and moans. He slid in and out, pumping faster as his eyes moved from my gaze to my lips to my body underneath him.

"What do I feel like?" he asked.

I pulled him into me as he thrust again, craving the fucking more and more.

"Like fingers in my hair," I breathed out. "It's smooth and hard—I want to take more. And the pressure . . . ugh, right there."

I grunted, squeezing my eyes shut. I was coming.

I'd made myself come before, but it was different like this. Like it was a muscle locking up tighter and tighter and something swirling like a cyclone, getting higher, and I craved the release.

Pushing up, I grabbed his neck and kissed him hard and hungry. Sweat dampened his hair as I whispered in his ear, "Make me come, Kai." I smiled. "Make me come, and I'll let you watch me and what I do when I'm in the shower thinking about you. You like to watch, right?"

He growled, grabbing my wrists and locking them above my head with one hand. I laughed, surprised and nervous and so turned on.

"And here I thought I was being nice, going easy on you." He squeezed my ass in his other hand, pressing me into his cock.

I moaned. "Yeah."

He pumped faster and rougher, going mad on top of me, until all I could do was hang on. Until all I felt like was a toy built for him to get off, and in the moment, I didn't have one damn problem with that.

I loved that he saw me like this. Loved that he wanted this from me.

He thrust again and again, and my knees came higher, heat covered my body, and bursts of pleasure exploded low inside me, sweeping down my legs. I cried out, my body locking up as I held on to him, riding out the orgasm.

He grunted and pumped and finally thrust so deep, sinking into me and holding himself there as he threw his head back.

"God, baby. Fuck!"

He collapsed on top of me, our bodies and sweat melting together in heat and euphoria. *Jesus.*

I knew what I'd been missing all this time, but . . . I didn't think I'd be unable to resist it.

I didn't know if I was ever going to be able to.

Slowly, my breathing calmed, but I didn't pull away from him or the brush of his lips on my neck. Reality would seep in soon enough, and I'd enjoy the last few moments.

We just lay there. I loved his warmth and being close.

I loved feeling this.

"Why are you waxed?" he suddenly asked.

Waxed?

Oh. Down there, he meant.

His nose brushed my cheek as he leaned back, flushed, his eyes tired as he looked at me.

"I'm not complaining," he assured me with a half smile. "It was just unexpected. Especially for a . . . for a virgin who's not expecting any action down there."

I rolled my eyes, letting his playful jab roll off me for once.

But then my amusement fell away as I thought about how to answer him. As if it were any of his business anyway.

I'd been waxing myself for years. It was hard at first, but over the years, the pain of the task became easier to bear, and hey, I only had to do it every couple of months.

I tried shaving it when it first started to appear in my preteen years, but it grew back too fast and the hair came in too coarse. Not long after, I started doing my legs and underarms, too. Dressing as a boy, covering my hair, flattening my breasts . . . everything I could do to not be a woman.

"I wasn't supposed to change," I said quietly. "I wasn't supposed to grow up."

CHAPTER 16

BANKS

Six Years Ago

Y ou were right," Kai replied.

I nodded absently, not believing my eyes. We both watched the dancing woman flutter around the floor, almost like a butterfly but also like a child. So innocent and ethereal. She was beautiful.

So beautiful and . . . familiar.

Who—

Her hair whipped around her, and I caught sight of her face, an aching sensation instantly covering my heart. I lost every ounce of air in my lungs.

Oh, my God. No.

The music. "Night Mist." I'd heard this before.

I shrank back behind the curtains.

It couldn't be her.

"I thought it was just a story," Kai said in a low voice, still watching her dip her head and move her arms and feet with weightless grace. She flew. She always floated and flew, like gravity wasn't part of her reality. Still so exquisite.

"Do you know who she is?" he asked.

My eyes darted up to see him looking at me, his eyebrows etched in concern.

I nodded once. My stomach rolled, and I was too horrified to come up with a lie. "It's Natalya Torrance. Damon's mother."

"His mother?" Confusion spread across his face as he turned to her again. "But . . ."

But nothing. She disappeared three years ago when Damon had finally suffered enough. He had hurt himself, made me hurt him, and retreated into the horror show of his own head until one night she came for him one too many times.

I watched Natalya, her long, silky black hair floating around her in waves. I didn't know her well, but we'd lived in the same house for a couple years—before she escaped Damon's rage that night and fled.

She'd been gone ever since.

She was still beautiful, though. Of course, she would be. She'd only be about thirty-four years old by now. Gabriel first saw her in a ballet in St. Petersburg when she was thirteen. He immediately coveted her. By the time she was sixteen she was his wife and had already given birth to Damon. She was closer in age to her son than she was to her husband.

I doubted she took the effort to know much about me, though. I was a nonentity to her. She knew who I was and what I was to Gabriel, but she never seemed to care, and I might as well have been a speck of dust under her bathroom sink for all she seemed to notice me. She lived in a world all her own.

"Yeah, you're right." Kai studied her, finally recognizing her. "She left a few years ago, though. What's she doing here?"

I shook my head to myself. God, I had no idea. And I didn't know what would happen if Damon saw her here. She wasn't supposed to be anywhere near him.

This was her husband's hotel, though—she and Gabriel were still married, as far as I knew—but Damon had ordered her away. He'd said he would kill her if he ever saw her again.

I needed to get him out of here before he did.

"Should we tell him?" Kai asked.

"No," I shot out quickly, taking his hand. "No, he won't want to see her."

Or he shouldn't see her. I just needed to get to him and find some reason to get him out of the hotel. My father could deal with her without Damon ever finding out.

I pulled Kai out of the drapes and moved along the wall, quickly and quietly walking toward the doors.

"Oh," I heard her say.

And I stopped, closing my eyes. *Shit*.

"I didn't know anyone was in here," she said. "What are you kids doing?"

I released Kai's hand and slowly turned my head toward her. She stood there, in the middle of the dance floor, paused as if in the middle of a twirl, with her arms slightly outstretched.

"You're not supposed to be in Thunder Bay or Meridian City," I told her, stepping forward.

She regarded me for a moment, probably trying to recognize me through the makeup, but then the light came on.

"You," she said.

She remembered me.

But before I could advance on her, she turned toward the door, the light in her eyes brightening like a child. "Is my son here?" she asked. "It's been so long."

"You stay away from him." I charged a few steps closer. "I mean it."

Her gaze rested on me again, her smile coy as she fingered her tutu. "Do you like it?" She looked at me, hopeful, as if I hadn't said anything. "I still fit into my old costumes. I'm still pretty, aren't I?"

Pretty? What? She was absolutely mad.

"What's going on?" Kai came up next to me, but she barely spared him a glance before turning her eyes back to the doors.

She was going to search Damon out.

"He's a man now," she said wistfully. "Young and strong."

I shook my head, pushing at Kai behind me to move for the doors. "She's bad. We need to leave."

I spun around, grabbing Kai's hand, and reached for the handle.

"Tell him Mama loves him," she called out. "I'm the only one who loves him."

I whipped around, releasing Kai. "That's not love," I growled at her.

A sob lodged in my throat; I felt so helpless despite my anger. She wouldn't hurt him again. She couldn't. He wouldn't allow it.

But she ignored me, looking calm and even a bit excited.

"I hear he's quite the animal now," she taunted. "No girl in that town is safe. That's Mommy's big boy."

"Jesus Christ," I heard Kai mumble at my side. "What the hell did she do to him?"

"Has he touched you?" she asked me.

I ground my teeth together.

"He will, you know?" She took a step closer. "He's a ravager. Just like his daddy."

My head shook just slightly. That would never happen. My brother would never hurt me like that.

"I wanted him to take you." Her words left her lips softly and crawled inside me as she held my eyes. "Sleeping in his room like you do, he won't be able to resist the scent of his precious girl." She reached out, brushing her knuckles gently across my jaw. "His little treasure."

"Hey, hey." Kai pushed her hand down and pulled me back.

And then she finally turned her gaze on him. "I remember you. My son's friend," she said. "Does that mean he's here, then?"

My breath caught in my throat. *Damon.*

But the doors behind us suddenly opened, and I jerked my head, looking over my shoulder. My brother stormed through, the muscles in his face tight and his eyes furious as they locked on me.

"I knew that was you upstairs," he said, seething. "What the hell is going on? How did you get here?"

I quickly turned my body to face him, hoping to block his view of her.

But it was no use.

Her voice rang out behind me. "Damon."

And I closed my eyes, tightening my hands. *Damon.*

*P*lease, Nik," he begged, his lips trembling.

Tears streamed down my face as I stood above my brother as he sat on the edge of the bed. She was gone now. She'd gotten what she wanted from him.

But her perfume was still all over him. He always went to the shower immediately after. Why wasn't he now?

"I'm rotting." His whisper left him like a last breath as he bowed his head and stared at the floor.

I stared at the fresh cuts on his thigh—somewhere most people wouldn't be able to spot them. He'd done that a couple days ago. After the last time.

She was coming to his room more frequently now. He was growing so fast the past year, getting taller and bigger, his cheekbones and jaw losing their softness and becoming more like a man's. His shoulders had gotten broader, and basketball training over the summer had filled out his muscles.

When I found out what was happening years ago when I moved in, my brother refused to tell anyone. He refused to let me tell anyone. Eventually, I'd held out hope that she'd lose interest in him as he grew into adulthood.

She didn't. I realized she wasn't a pedophile in the strictest sense of the word. It wasn't about his body or his youth. It was about him, and she was just psychotic.

And jealous. He was in high school now. Lots of other girls—younger girls—to steal his attention away from her. She didn't like that.

I stepped up to him and reached out a shaky hand, touching it on his bare shoulder. He was still naked, the black bedsheet drawn across his lap, covering himself.

Bending down, I tried to catch his eye, pleading with him. "I would rather hurt myself. Please. Don't make me do it again. Please."

He dropped his head, meeting my forehead and breathing shallow, as if he were trying to hold back sobs. "Something's gotta give," he whispered. "Something has to. Do you want it to be me? Huh?" He grabbed my chin, holding it tightly. "Semja. I need you. Do it."

Semja.

Family.

I didn't speak Russian well—I hadn't grown up with it like Damon—but I'd learned enough to understand.

I shook my head as much as it could move in his grip. It was getting worse. When would it stop? He always needed more. Harder, stronger, more pain . . . "Please," I cried softly.

He growled and grabbed his belt off the bed, throwing his arm out to ready the first whip across his back.

"No!" I snatched it out of his hand. When he did it himself, he did it too hard. The guys at practice would ask questions.

I stood up, dropped the belt to the floor, and sobbed as I grabbed a fistful of his hair. No one would ask questions about cuts and bruises on his face. Damon was always in fights, so it was a likely story to hide behind.

Taking my fear and agony, I twisted it into anger and growled, slamming as hard as I could across his cheek.

And dived in. Again and then again and again. I had to get it over with. Just do it. I sobbed louder, tears pouring down my face.

Something's gotta give, he said.

He was right. The alcohol wasn't enough. Neither were the cigarettes,

*the girls he used and treated like shit at school, or the pain. Eventually,
he grew used to it all and needed more.*

*Something's gotta give. How much pain could he take before he
broke? How long until nothing was enough to appease him?*

I rushed up to Damon. "Just go," I told him, grabbing his arm.
"Let's go. Come on."

I pulled at him, ignoring the confused look on Kai's face, but
my brother was rooted like a tree.

His eyes were steel on her, hard and sharp.

"Baby," she cooed, coming up to him. "You're so beautiful. I
missed you so much."

I shook my head, pulling at him to get his attention. But he was
frozen.

"I know you lost your temper, and it's okay," she told him
sweetly, ever the delicate flower on the outside. "I'm okay. I love
you no matter what. And I promise it will be better this time. I'll
take care of you."

"Damon," I barked, trying to break the spell.

But his eyes were locked, following her as she crept forward,
closer and closer.

"I've missed you," she carried on. "I need you. I'm so lonely. I'm
so lost, baby, I—"

Just then, he darted out and caught her by the neck, his large
hand wrapping around her slender, pale throat.

"Damon . . ." I looked between him and her, not knowing what
to do.

She gasped but remained still as he pulled her up to her toes and
in close. His jaw was tight, and liquid heat raced through my veins
as I watched them stare at each other.

"That's my strong boy," she whispered. "You've grown so strong."

"Damon," I pleaded with him. "Look at me."

He simply stood there, gripping her neck, entranced.

"I've waited for you to come for me," she panted. "To take control. You're the man now. Whatever my son needs."

I closed my eyes.

"She's insane," Kai uttered under his breath at my side.

"Damon!" I yelled. "Look. At. Me!"

He held her, but she completely held his attention. "Take her," she urged him. "Wash her clean. Just like Mama used to wash you."

I broke down, the agony of years ago flooding back as I stared at my brother through my tears.

"You're the man," she repeated. "Everything is yours. Everything."

I shook my head. *Damon.*

"If you love her, she can hurt you," Natalya told him. "If you hurt her instead, she'll never escape you. You'll always own her. She's yours. You don't ask, and you don't care. Take what's yours. Take her." Her voice dropped so low I could barely hear. "Take her."

And all of a sudden, he finally turned, meeting my eyes.

No.

Tears spilled as I silently begged him. We'd been all alone in the world. We were only safe when we were together. I would never hurt him. He had to know that!

She wanted him to ruin us. To destroy anything left that was good in him, because Damon was the future of the family, and if nothing else, monsters were strong.

Damon might end up being so much worse than my father ever was.

"Take her," Natalya egged him on, running a hand up his chest. "She'll feed you. Take her. Show her what you are."

Stay with me. I held his eyes. *I know who you are. You protect me, you take me shopping on my birthday and let me pick out whatever I want, and you wake me up with my favorite fucking milkshakes when you come home in the middle of the night. I know who you are.*

"Lick her all up," Natalya breathed out. "Take her home and claim her."

The hint of fear in his eyes left, and he suddenly just stared at me like he was a machine. Like he wasn't really there.

Like it wasn't Damon anymore.

I sucked in a small gasp, paralyzed.

And then Kai was there. He stepped up, pushing me away, and gripped Damon by the wrist. "Let go," he demanded. "Let her the fuck go, Damon."

"We're all yours," she whispered to her son as if Kai wasn't there. "I'll take care of you, baby. I'll make sure her sweet little pussy is yours."

"Shut up!" Kai shouted at her. "You sick bitch!" And then he turned to Damon, who still held my eyes. "Look at me, man. Don't look at her!"

He wouldn't. No. He would never come at me like that. Not ever.

"Take her," Natalya urged again.

And I cried. "Damon!" Wake up.

"Don't look at her!" Kai bellowed, pushing at him.

"She's a part of you," his mother whispered like the taunt of a ghost. "She'll make you strong. Take her."

"Shut up!" Kai turned around and whipped his hand across her face, losing it.

And a breath caught in my throat as I watched her body whip around and land chest down on a round dining room table. Glasses clattered as they toppled over, the vase crashed to its side, and plates and silverware slid off the end as she jostled it.

But then I heard gasping and turned away from Natalya, looking at my brother. He hunched over, leaning on the back of a chair, and started dry-heaving with his head bowed as he spat and coughed.

I rushed over, still sobbing. "It's okay." I wrapped my arms around him from the side. "It's okay. It's okay. I'm here. Listen to my voice."

He lurched, nothing coming up but spit as he struggled to inhale any air. I squeezed him tighter.

So many kids who suffer abuse don't like to be touched, but when Damon was spiraling out, he couldn't get close enough to me. Like he just wanted to crawl inside my head, where he knew it was safe.

"She has no control over you." I hugged him close, whispering into his damp neck. "We're free. It's just us."

"It's still inside me," he choked out. "It hurts."

I squeezed my eyes shut, crying harder. "Hold on to me. Just hold on to me."

I knew what he wanted. What he needed. And I couldn't deny him. Not tonight.

I opened my mouth and bit down on the skin between his neck and his shoulder. Wrapping my arms around him, I felt him grunt as I dug my teeth harder into his skin. His arms snaked around me, and he held on tight, keeping me close. If Kai looked, it would just look like we were hugging.

But he was still focused on Natalya, whom I couldn't see behind my brother's back.

It's still inside me. It. I didn't know if he meant her or the terror and fright or something else. I just knew I felt so helpless.

Tears trickled down my face, tickling my skin and hanging over my soaked eyelashes.

"Harder," he whispered.

I bit harder, tasting his salty skin and surrounded by the familiar scent of his cigarettes. He wouldn't hurt me. He needed me.

He loved me.

I tasted copper, and I knew I'd broken the skin. He let out a breath and pulled back.

"Thank you," he said, and looked down at me, his usual eerie calm settling in over his body. "Are you okay?"

I nodded. "You?"

He gave a weary nod, turning around and adjusting his hoodie to make sure my teeth marks were covered up.

And I finally looked at Kai.

He stared at the ground where Natalya lay, and I couldn't make out the expression on his face as I moved around to his side. It seemed to change by the second.

Was he afraid? He'd done nothing wrong. If he hadn't shut her up, she . . .

I couldn't even think about it right now. My brother had completely locked up, and I couldn't wrap my head around what was happening to him. Would it happen again?

I was glad Kai hit her.

Damon walked up to his side, both of them glaring down at Natalya. She lay on the floor, having fallen back against a chair leg, but she looked like she might be hurt. Her eyes were closed, but her head bobbed lightly as she held her side.

"Are you okay?" Kai turned to Damon. "Man, I'm sorry. I didn't know—"

"Shut the fuck up," Damon bit out. "She was talking nonsense. Forget it. You understand?"

My brother glared at his friend, a threat lacing his words.

Kai didn't answer, just closed his mouth and stared at Damon. He knew it was a lie.

Blood seeped through Natalya's fingers, and I searched the table, finally seeing the stem of a wineglass broken and lying on its side. One of the sharp edges was doused in blood. She'd been cut.

"She's hurt," Kai went on. "We need an ambulance. I think she hit her head, too."

"I'll take care of it. You've done enough." He glanced over his shoulder at me. "You put her in danger. She shouldn't even be here."

"I didn't see you making a move to do anything."

"Enough." I stepped forward.

We had bigger problems. Natalya's sanity had clearly deteriorated even more since she'd disappeared three years ago. All that stuff she'd said, and right in front of Kai . . . There was no telling how out of control she could become. Gabriel didn't like to be embarrassed. What were we going to do with her?

"Leave," Damon told Kai. "I'll call my father."

Kai regarded him, looking uncertain. "No, it's my fault she got hurt. I want to make sure she gets to a doctor."

"And when she tells someone at the hospital that you hit her?" Damon retorted. "Yeah, I'm sure that'll do wonders for your college applications." He shook his head. "Just get out of here. My family will make sure she's fine and kept quiet. Don't worry. No one wants a scene."

Kai hesitated, probably worried about making sure she was taken care of, but the Torrances obviously had some serious family history, and he had to understand Damon wanted his father to see to Natalya. No hospitals. No cops. We all had a stake in keeping her quiet.

Kai took my hand. "Come on."

But Damon grabbed me and yanked me over to him. "Mine," he said to his friend.

"Like hell." Kai scowled at him. "I saw it on your face, man. You're a mess. You would've hurt her."

Damon just shook his head at him, not bothering to defend himself. That was something I admired about my brother and wished I could control in myself. People will think what they want to think, not because they believe they are right, but because it's in their nature to maintain that they are. By defending yourself, you feed the appetite for drama. By not, you've ended the conversation. You. Not them.

But I couldn't help but also wonder if Kai was maybe right. What would've happened if he hadn't interceded?

Damon turned to me, jerking his chin. "Go with him, then. Go."

What?

"It's okay," he told me. "Leave if you want."

"Damon—"

"You want to, I know you do. I don't need you. I never did."

My chest caved. Why was he doing this? Why did he always do this?

"Come on." Kai took my hand.

But I pulled away. "Just go." I bowed my head, unable to look at him. "Go back to the party."

"Banks."

"I'll never leave him," I bit out at Kai.

Not ever. I stepped over to my brother and took his hand, willing Kai to just go.

Twice tonight I'd chosen Damon. He didn't know we were family, and he might understand more if he did, but that information still wouldn't change anything. Damon came first. Always.

My brother squeezed my hand, a subtle gesture telling me he forgave me.

"Chicks, man," he said to Kai, a touch of humor in his voice.

Silence stretched between them, and I could feel Kai's eyes on me. He was a good guy, but he wouldn't take being jerked around a third time. I stared at Natalya, each second Kai stood there stretching out like an eternity.

"Yeah," he replied. "Crazy night, huh?" And then I saw him back away out of the corner of my eye. "See you Monday at school."

And then he left, my heart aching more every moment he didn't turn back around and come back through the doors for me. Later, when I was alone and lost in my head, I'd wonder what would've happened if I'd followed him. If I'd taken his hand and hid away with him the rest of the night.

Damon pulled me in, kissing my forehead. "Good girl. You never let me down."

Natalya moaned, her eyelids fluttering open. Blood saturated her hand, and although it looked like a nasty cut—or several nasty cuts—the flow wasn't too bad. We needed to get her to a doctor, though. She'd need stitches or something.

Damon handed me his phone and then squatted down, staring at her. "Call David," he told me. "Tell him to get his ass here to pick you up, and go wait for him in the lobby."

"Why can't you take me home? Let's just go—"

"I'll be home later," he said, his eyes still on her. "I need to clean up here."

CHAPTER 17

BANKS

Present

I speed-walked down the busy street, swerving around pedestrians with one hand in my coat pocket and the other holding a large envelope with yet another contract for Kai to sign. He was supposed to be at the dojo, but when I got back from my errands this morning, he'd texted, telling me to meet him at his club instead. He knew I didn't have a car, dammit.

And I wasn't ready to face him.

Last night, in that hotel, buried on a secret floor and in a room with no phones, no television, and no one but us, it was unimaginable. Like a dream that I was pulled away from, and I kept closing my eyes to chase sleep again just so I could go back there. Was that only a few hours ago?

He'd tried to pry a little more information out of me last night, but he didn't push too hard. When my guard went up, I knew he didn't want to ruin what had just happened. He was good about reading my signals, I'd give him that.

He'd wanted to take me home, but I was gone before he could fight me again. I dived into the rainy night, everything that had felt so good suddenly ebbing away, and I didn't know how to get it back. Guilt and shame, the feeling of Damon's eyes on me, judging me, why couldn't I get over it?

So, I fucked a guy. Who cares? I liked it. Sue me.

But it was daytime now, and the consequences might be slow, but they were coming. My skills didn't extend far enough to juggle my desire for one and the demands of another.

Jogging up the steps of Hunter-Bailey, I swung open one of the double doors and walked inside, the citrus furniture polish immediately surrounding me. Wood shone everywhere, and the grandfather clock in the lobby ticked by to my left.

I stepped up to the small desk. "I need to see Kai Mori, please."

The young man, with black hair and in a simple suit with a thin tie, nodded as if expecting me.

"He'll still be in the lounge." He walked around his station toward the next set of double doors. "Just take a right as you enter the dining room."

Hmm. Women weren't typically allowed in the club. I was surprised he was letting me in so easily. I guessed Kai had taken care of that.

He cast open the doors, stepping aside so I could enter, and I immediately veered to the left, briefly noticing all of the staff in the dining room setting the tables for lunch.

Entering the lounge, I looked around for a moment, taking in the den-like feel of the large room. Brown leather couches gleamed in the lamplight, while forest-green drapes dressed floor-to-ceiling windows around the room. Gold sconces, deer, elk, and even a lion head were hung high above, and plaid throw pillows were tossed on chairs and sofas. A bar lay at the back, shelves of books lined the walls, and a tapestry depicting some kind of war hung over the fireplace.

Christ. This room was decorated with the theme "If the Nazis had won . . ."

I scanned the room, quickly spotting Kai over by the windows. His coat was off, his sleeves were rolled up, and my mouth suddenly went dry at the sight of him. It almost hurt to look as he sat there, hunched over a table of papers.

Those hands were all about me last night. And that beautiful, stern expression that looked almost angry and kind of made me want to smile was lost in pleasure the last time I saw it.

So controlled and so cold, but he could be so rough, too.

Michael and Will sat on either side of him, one on his phone and the other slouched in his chair with his rocks glass pressed to his forehead and his eyes closed. I made my way over, ignoring glances from the dozen or so other gentlemen in the room.

Kai glanced up as I approached. "You're late."

His tone was curt, but his mouth wasn't, curled at the corners as if he was just thinking about why I barely got any sleep last night.

"I had to go to Thunder Bay this morning," I told him.

"Why?"

"Gabriel wants to know why you haven't signed the contract."

He stopped what he was doing and looked at me again. Michael turned away from his phone.

"What did you tell him?" Kai asked.

I tossed the envelope with a fresh contract inside on the table in front of him. Some of his papers fluttered about in protest. "That you're delaying," I said. "The same thing I've been telling him."

"What—"

But he stopped whatever he was going to say, picking up his phone, which was buzzing.

Annoyance on his face, he answered. "Yeah."

He listened while someone on the other end talked, his eyebrows digging in farther.

"A&J Plumbing?" he said, sounding confused. "I didn't call any—"

I leaned over the table and held out my hand.

He stopped, looking at me. I grabbed the phone.

"I left the keys for him in an envelope under the desk," I told the kid at the dojo who I knew was on the other end, "and I turned off the alarm system at the house for him. Tell him to start upstairs in the bathrooms. I need a full estimate as soon as possible."

"Uh, yes, ma'am," he stammered, and I hung up.

I'd made the call to arrange for plumbers, electricians, and contractors on my way back from Thunder Bay. I figured I'd be at the dojo, though, so I thought I was meeting him there.

I handed Kai's phone back to him.

"Is that for my house?" he questioned. "What did I tell you?"

I straightened, sticking my hands in my pockets. "Vanessa arrives in three days," I told him.

His scowl slowly fell away, and I saw Will out of the corner of my eye put his drink down and lift his head up.

Kai said nothing.

"Part of the update from Gabriel this morning," I explained, feeling the same knot build in my stomach that I had when Gabriel told me. "Surreal, isn't it? What you've gotten yourself into?"

All three of them just sat there, and I didn't know if they were stunned or mad or what, but they definitely weren't happy.

"I'm sure you fancy yourself the architect of some grand scheme," I continued, "but the agreement you made moves forward regardless of whether or not you're ready. Your bride will soon be on her way here. I've arranged a suite at the Mandarin for her while we do repairs at the house."

Kai picked up the envelope, his jaw flexing as he ripped it open, pulled out the paperwork, and began flipping through pages.

"He didn't make the revisions," he said, scanning it.

"Nor will he, I daresay. Take it or leave it."

Kai was cornered, and he knew it. But really, what was the problem? He knew how to get on the twelfth floor now. He didn't need the hotel, and he didn't want any connection to the Torrance family. Why not just back out? Why had he agreed in the first place?

"If I don't sign, it's open season on Damon," he warned.

"Michael, me, Will, Rika . . . we'll handle it, and we'll do it any way we like."

I nodded, understanding. If he didn't sign, Damon would have no promise that he'd be welcome back in the city. If he came home, they might go after him.

"But if I don't sign," he said, his voice lower, "you'll leave."

I'd leave? Was that what was binding him to this stupid agreement?

I saw the lump move in his throat.

He didn't want me to go.

And I wasn't sure how much I wanted to anymore, but that contract couldn't make me stay if I really wanted to leave. He had to know that. I was only here at Gabriel's behest.

"I can leave anytime I want," I reminded him.

"You would go back to him, wouldn't you?"

I dropped my eyes, not wanting to have this discussion and especially not wanting to have it in front of his friends.

His voice was eerily calm. "Do you want me to sign it?"

"Yes," I gritted out. "I want Damon home."

He watched me, his eyes hard, but he didn't make any other move. The guys listened silently.

"I woke up last night, wanting you again," he said.

My heart pumped harder, the heat of embarrassment rising to my cheeks.

Leaning back in his cushioned chair, he drew in a deep breath. "I fucked up, guys," he said, this time to his friends.

Michael looked over at him. "We want what we want, right?"

Kai shook his head at me.

So, Damon wasn't the only goal here. Somewhere along the way, it had become about me, too. Gabriel made me work for Kai, so I did. But no contract, no Banks.

"You wear his clothes," Kai said to me. "You barely eat. He

controls your freedom, your food, your friendships . . . What do you want, kid? If you were him, if you were a man, what would you do? What would you take?"

I shot off, rounding Will's chair, and came up next to Kai. Leaning down, I snatched the contract and one of his fountain pens from the table, flipping to the final page. I quickly scrawled *Kai Mori* in his damn near exact handwriting as I'd seen on other documents at the dojo.

Throwing the pen down, I flipped the contract back into place, slid it into the torn envelope, and handed it to him.

Let's end this. I was calling his bluff. *Call off this idiotic agreement and let me go, or give the papers to Gabriel and let my brother come home.*

"Now you have a slave until your wedding," I challenged him. "What will *you* do with me? Order my clothes off right here and bend me over the table, big boy?"

He took the envelope, a bitter grin on his lips. "Nah. That's nice and sweet. Something I'll do to the new little wife," he taunted. "My toys get a little more wear and tear."

I heard Will snort to my left and then he blew out a breath. "Damn."

Michael ran a hand over his face, looking exasperated, and Kai just stared at me. He stood, picking up his jacket from the chair and rolling back down his sleeves.

"Get to the dojo," he ordered me. "It's going to be a long day."

Hours later, and I was sweltering. He was working my ass off.

After I'd dealt with the plumber and two contractors who both told me a year was a reasonable estimate for that piece-of-shit hovel Kai lived in, I'd made it back to the dojo to spend the rest of the fucking day dealing with grunt crap. A washing machine exploded, some dumbass Storm player friend of Michael's dropped his cell phone in the toilet, a chick on her fourth aikido class this week puked in the lobby, and why the fuck was I dealing with this bullshit?

Kai was pissed, and I kept talking myself out of walking out today. No one could keep me here, and I wasn't bound to a stupid contract. I told myself it was for my brother. Sit tight and just breathe until it was time.

I told myself I wouldn't let Kai win. He was trying to push me, and my pride was at stake.

And I told myself I had a duty. I'd made a commitment to Gabriel's house, and I would not bend.

But the truth was, I had nowhere else to go. I'd gotten a paycheck today. A real check, made out to cash for more of a wage than I made in a month with my father. If I left now without another plan, I was going to be alone. Gabriel wouldn't take me back if I broke the deal, and I'd be out of the loop, unable to be Damon's eyes and ears any longer.

I had every reason to stay.

But my temper wasn't made any better when Rika and Alex walked in while I was mopping up chunks off the floor, their rivers of hair, hundred-dollar perfume, and cute short shorts in sixty-degree weather amplifying all the shit I was feeling.

Especially my jealousy.

Every inch of Kai that touched me last night had touched her once.

I'd always resented her. From the moment I'd first heard about her, Michael, and Kai in the steam room at Hunter-Bailey. But things were different now. My attachment to Kai was growing, and every moment he and I were in the same room and he wasn't touching me made me long for him more.

I hated that they saw each other every goddamn day. I could barely contain my hatred as I stared at her back as she walked to the locker room.

I finished tossing the dirty towels into the washer, and I charged out of the laundry room, shoving the swinging door so hard it hit the wall.

It was time to go home. I needed a break and a nice, long walk away from here.

I headed into the office to tell Kai, but he wasn't there. I was about to leave and look for him, but the landline on the desk started ringing. I quickly picked it up.

"Sensou."

"Who is this?" a guy asked, sounding confused.

"Who's this?" I shot back.

"Oh. Banks," he said, finally placing my voice. "It's Michael. Where's Kai?"

I took the cordless and drifted into the hallway, looking lazily from left to right. "Walked off for a few minutes, I guess. Can I give him a message?"

"No. I don't trust you, remember?"

I laughed under my breath, strolling farther down the hallway. "That's wise of you, Michael. You're learning."

But I stopped, seeing Rika and Kai in the lobby. I remained hidden in the hall, watching them chat. The sternness that always hardened his eyes into the look of a perpetual student was gentler now. Relaxed.

It was hard to breathe.

He stood too close. Smiled too softly at her and touched her arm too long.

"But you trust Kai?" I asked Michael, still staring at them. "With all of your treasures?"

"What's that supposed to mean?"

I shook my head, watching as Kai made his way for one of the great rooms and Rika came my way, back down the hallway.

I turned, relaxing into the wall and looking down as she passed. She disappeared into one of the workout rooms.

I cleared my throat. "Nothing," I said. "I'm bored. Any message or not?"

He didn't say anything.

"Fine, I'll tell him you called."

"Wait."

I stopped, putting the receiver back to my ear. "Yes?"

I heard his sigh on the other end, but the guy clammed up again all of a sudden. I waited, hearing only silence.

"Hello?" I prodded.

"You think you're so smart, don't you?" he finally asked. "Okay, then. If you were me, in my situation, what would you do to strengthen your hold on all your irons in the fire? You said we were weak. Where? With what?"

I nearly laughed. Was he serious?

I strolled back down the hallway, suddenly intrigued. "Are you asking me for advice?"

"I'm asking you to put your money where your smart mouth is, brat," he bit out. "Pretend you run my crew now. What do you do?"

"What makes you think I'd help you?"

"Because I think you're dying for some real use of your skills."

Well, he was right there. Kai wasn't using me to my full potential, and I loved having a seat at the table. I'd kill to tell him exactly what I thought of him and his junior high operation.

I stopped at the entrance to the workout room and stood back, watching Rika throw blocks against her Wing Chun dummy. She maneuvered, hitting the posts fast but methodically, pausing every so often to correct her stance.

And it suddenly hit me.

Michael was stroking my pride.

Sensou meant "war" in Japanese. This place, the name, what they did here . . . it was part of a larger goal.

Rika might be soft, but she was training. Michael might be careless, but he was aware. Will might be weak, but he had Kai.

And Kai was getting ready.

These people were my enemies.

"If I were you," I replied calmly, "the first thing I'd do is fire me. I'm not your friend."

And I ended the call.

I wanted this over.

I was sick of the go-around and waiting, and while I knew my brother was partly to blame for all the shit he found himself in last year, he had every reason to resent these people. They didn't fight for him. So easily they gave him up, didn't they?

And I had every reason to hate *her*.

I moved to the doorway, leaning against the frame and watching her work.

Even if Damon came home, even if some miracle reconciled him with his friends and there was no longer any bad blood, Kai Mori would still never be anything more to me than he was right now. Not with her around. He'd fucked her because he'd wanted her, and even if that desire lessened over time, it would never disappear. Just look at her. The perfect package. Smart, rich, pretty. And they all just thought she was the sweetest thing, too.

I brought my hands up, absently cracking my knuckles, bending each finger back until I heard the *cracks* and *pops*.

Yeah, anger was better. I'd gotten so lost last night, sinking into how good everything felt, being held and touched and kissed . . . But it brought nothing but confusion.

Anger was a straight line. It had a target.

"Do you need something?"

I blinked, raising my eyes. Rika had her head turned, looking at me over her shoulder as she panted. I hadn't realized she'd noticed me.

Unable to hide my amusement, I slowly stepped in the room, moving toward her. Damon and I had both inherited our father's methodical nature, but Damon also had some patience. I didn't.

"Have you ever actually been in a fight?" I asked, gesturing to the dummy.

"Yes. Why?" She straightened her back, making herself a little taller.

I walked around the wooden Wing Chun, appraising her. "You spend a lot of time on your stance and your form," I told her. "Most people who fight are fighting to survive. There are no rules. No fair play. No time to maintain proper striking distance. All your plans will go out the window."

"Don't worry," she assured me. "I know how to pull hair, scratch, and kick if I need to."

"And bite," I added, watching her turn back to her dummy. "When Damon ties you up again, show him what a scrapper you are. It'll amuse him."

She whipped around, fury in her eyes.

And I couldn't stop the smile that peeked out. Yeah, I knew all about *Pithom*, Michael's family's yacht, last year and how he scared her. Not that I approved at the time, but God, I hoped he was going to do everything he could to make trouble for her now.

I dropped my voice. "I know you kept the guys from going after him last year. I know you insist on staying at the penthouse alone, without protection, when Michael's out of town." I inched forward, not blinking once. "I also know you like a man's hands on you, and they don't necessarily have to be your fiancé's, do they? So, when Damon comes for you, be sure to put up a good little fight for good measure, okay? That way Michael believes your lies when you tell him you didn't want every inch of it."

Her face twisted in fury, and she growled, swinging back her fist and knocking me across the jaw. I stumbled a step to the side, losing my breath and closing my eyes on reflex.

But the heat of adrenaline flooded my chest. *Yes.*

I quickly righted myself again, forcing myself to face her. The ache sank deep into the bone, and my skin burned. Touching the corner of my lip, I pulled my hand back, seeing blood on my fingertips.

"Thank you," I told her.

Using everything I had, I twisted and whipped the back of my hand across her face, sending her flying to the floor. She caught herself, landing on her hands and knees, and I could hear her sucking in air, the wind having been knocked out of her. She pounded her fists onto the floor once, growling in anger, and before I knew it, she twisted around, lunged for me, and shoved her hands into my chest, both of us tumbling back onto the mats.

"What the fuck is your problem?" she bellowed, crashing down on top of me.

But I swung us around, sending her to the ground with me straddling her instead. Grabbing the blond hair on the top of her head, I leaned in. "Just keeping your world in perspective, Erika Fane! Not everyone bows at your feet!"

I pounded my fist down into her face, but she shoved at me, making me lose my hold. I gripped her neck instead and slammed her twice more.

She snarled, knocking my hat off my head and yanking my hair, forcing my head down and my scalp to scream. I winced in pain.

Dammit!

I should've cut off my hair. Years ago. It was just the only part of me that was still Nik and not Banks, and I'd hung on to it for some reason.

I lost my hold on her, giving her just enough time to push me off. She released me, sitting up and throwing out her leg, kicking me in the stomach.

And I couldn't breathe. My throat closed, and I struggled to inhale. I coughed, hunching over. Did my stomach go through my goddamn spine?

"Are you done?" she shouted, and I noticed she had a trickle of blood coming out of her nose.

A momentary pang of satisfaction hit me through the pain. She'd made me bleed, after all. It was only fair.

"Not just yet." I launched for her, grabbing her neck again and curling my fingers so hard, my nails dug into her skin.

She gasped, her eyes going wide as she grabbed for my wrist. I knew I'd broken the skin.

Hands grabbed me from behind and pulled me away, off her.

"What the hell?" I heard Kai growl. I whipped my head around, briefly turning my glare on him.

He was still in his workout pants from before, but now sweat matted the ends of his hair and his chest glistened.

"No, screw that!" Rika shoved at Kai, seething. "Let's finish this!"

I laughed under my breath, seeing the four crimson half-moons tattooed into her skin over her jugular where a small scar she already had sat. I gazed down at my nails, seeing blood mixed with the dirt.

I lurched for her again, but Kai caught me, yanking me back.

"Enough!" He came between us, yelling. "Everyone is watching you two. What the hell is going on?"

Bystanders lingered outside the room, peeking in at the commotion. Turning back to Rika, I sucked at the cut in my cheek and spat the blood at her feet.

She launched for me again.

"Dammit!" Kai gripped me by the collar, pushing me back. He pointed his finger in my face, his teeth bared as he fixed me with a warning look.

Turning back to Rika, he tilted her head up, checking her bloody nose. "Are you okay?"

Is she okay? Your little princess threw the first punch, asshole.

"I'm fine." She jerked her head out of his hands, challenging me. "I can take anything you got!"

"I'm sure! In both ends, I hear!"

She came for me again, but Kai pushed her back, turning to me. "What the fuck is the matter with you?"

"I don't like her, and I don't work for her, so I'll do whatever I fucking want!" I gritted out.

"You'll do what I want," he whisper-yelled, getting in my face. "End of story."

Looking around me, he spoke to the audience gathered. "Carry on, everyone. It's over." And to Rika, "Leave us alone, please."

She didn't move for a moment, still glaring at me and red from the exertion, and her ponytail hung on by a thread. But she finally walked past us, leaving the room.

I heard the voices slowly fade as everyone went about their business and left.

"What do you have against Rika?" Kai questioned. "You haven't spoken to her once or barely spared her a glance. What is it?"

Taking my cuff, I wiped the blood off my mouth, not answering him.

"Are you jealous?"

I cast him a "fuck you" look and went back to staring at the mirror behind him.

I could feel his eyes on me, eating away the small distance between us and wrapping around my body like a cage.

"What did you mean about 'in both ends'?"

"You know what I meant."

Their little threesome in the steam room. Kai took the front. Michael got the back. How many times had it happened after that?

"You heard about Rika and me?" His voice was low. "About the steam room?"

Who hadn't heard? They were seen, it was all over the club, and it was no secret how he felt about her. It was there every time he looked at her.

"I—"

"No." I cut him off. "I've had my fill of your stories, and I couldn't care less—"

"Shhh, shhh, shhh . . ." He pressed his finger to my lips, shaking his head at me. "Let's not do this here, okay? We need to talk about it, but somewhere we can really talk."

And his gaze turned dark, telling me there was another meaning to his words.

Really talk? Where?

Dropping his hand, he walked around me, leaving the room.

"What do you mean?" I barked after him.

"You'll find out," he threw over his shoulder and then disappeared.

CHAPTER 18

BANKS

Present

An hour later, and I'm still on edge. I was tired before the fight at the dojo, but now I was wired, awake, and pissed at myself. My cards were on the table now.

She knew I hated her, so there was no getting close to her if I needed to, and Kai was probably relishing my disgusting display of jealousy. What had Damon told me, time and again? It's always best to say as little as possible. The more of a mystery you are, the less leverage they have.

And I went and fucked it all up.

I walked down the quiet street, entering Halston Park, the shopping district of Meridian City. It was just after nine, and I looked up at the sky, finally able to see a few stars. The lights everywhere else in this town were too bright to see many anymore.

What did Alex want? She'd texted, saying that Kai wanted me to meet her at McGivern and Bourne. I'd never been there, but I knew it was an upscale department store.

Rounding a corner, I swept some hair out of my eye and tucked it back under my hat as I approached the building's glass doors.

I raised my hand to knock but stopped, seeing that it was dark inside. There were a few emergency lights shining way in the back, lighting hallways, but this store was closed. Why did she tell me to come here?

Screw it. I dropped my hand and turned to leave.

"Oh, don't you dare!" a woman's voice shouted.

I spun around, seeing Alex coming out of the doors. She wore a billowing, sexy white blouse that hung off her shoulder, with black leggings and brown leather boots up to her knees. It occurred to me I'd almost only ever seen her in workout clothes. Aside from Michael's party.

She skipped over and grabbed my hand, pulling me along.

I dug my heels in. "What is this? Isn't this place closed?"

"Not for us," she singsonged. "Come on."

She swung the door back open, forcing me inside.

"What's going on?" I whined.

"Kai's orders," Alex answered. "Shut up and follow me."

A security guard in a dark gray uniform came over, locking the door behind us. "Have fun, ladies."

"Thanks, Pip," Alex chirped.

"Phillipe," he corrected.

"Whatevs."

I narrowed my eyes on her. "You know him?"

"Nah, we just met. He fell fast, though."

I rolled my eyes. What was going on? Clearly, the store was closed. Except for us. Why?

My combat boots squeaked across the marble floors, and I glanced up again, momentarily forgetting to resist her as the air in my lungs expelled.

Whoa. At least five floors were stacked on top of us. We stood at the bottom of the atrium, and I turned my head around and back and forth, seeing how the flights above us circled the perimeter of the open space, all the way to the skylight at the top of the building. Every floor could look over the edge and see us down here.

A massive chandelier hung high, and everything sparkled white and gold as the scent of leather and perfumes wafted over me.

We passed display cases of jewelry, perfume counters, and purses, while pictures hung everywhere, displaying beautiful people on yachts and in luxury snow cabins brandishing their ten-thousand-dollar watches or suede boots that you could easily pick up here, and then you, too, would be magically transported to a yacht in the Mediterranean or a cabin in Aspen or a polo club in Scotland.

I used to dream that my mom and I would go shopping someplace like this when I was little.

Someday, when we were rich and all the problems were gone, we'd have pretty things, I'd be popular, and my *real* life would have started.

It still seemed like part of me was dreaming of that. Always waiting. Biding my time.

"Have you ever been in here before?" Alex asked, leading me into an elevator.

"No."

"It's nice, isn't it?" She pressed the button for the fourth floor and the elevator doors closed; we immediately began to ascend. "Did you ever see that old movie from the eighties? *Mannequin*?"

I crossed my arms over my chest, shaking my head.

"Well, this window dresser works nights in a department store like this, and it always looked like so much fun to be him, you know? Having the whole place to yourself to try on clothes, explore, and play with everything."

The elevator stopped, the doors opened, and she walked out, not waiting for me to follow her.

"Look, it's after nine." I trailed behind as she strolled through a maze of racks. "I still have a couple things to take care of tonight. What am I doing here?"

She delicately picked up a piece of silk something—lingerie?—and matching underwear. "Trying on clothes, exploring, and playing with everything," she replied frankly, inspecting the garments.

She held the top up to me, and I reared back, seeing spaghetti straps, lace, buttons, and a shitload of missing fabric that should've been covering the stomach. *Jesus.* That wasn't clothes. It was the scraps left over from the clothes.

She pursed her lips, appraising me. "Hmm . . . dark brown hair. Olive skin. The slate gray, yes. That'll do really nicely."

"Do nicely for what?" I tensed. "I'm not wearing that."

"Oh, for fuck's sake." She dropped her arms, sighing. "Would you please have a drink? Lots of drinks?"

I turned around to leave. This was the last thing I needed today.

But a body suddenly blocked my path, and I sucked in a breath, backing up again.

Will Grayson stared down at me, smiling.

"What are you doing here?" I burst out. He wasn't staggering, and his eyes weren't hooded as usual. "Sober for once?"

He laughed and walked around me, starting to sift through the panties on the table. He picked up a black G-string and threw it at Alex before turning back and looking for more he liked.

That better be for her.

"Look, I gotta go." I spun back around and walked toward the elevators.

"Doors are locked," he called.

"Don't worry." I glanced over my shoulder at him. "That won't stop me."

He tossed another garment to Alex, speaking to her. "Go pick out a few more things."

She nodded and walked off, and he made his way to me. I stopped and turned.

"Look." He sighed, gazing at me like I was a child. "You seem like you don't have a lot of friends, and wow, that's a real shocker, but Alex seems to like you, and I like her, so I try to be a friend."

"That must cost you a pretty penny."

He cocked an eyebrow, not appreciating my remark. "She arranged for the place to be open after closing hours so you wouldn't get skittish on account of all the . . . oh, what's the word?" He tapped his chin, pretending to think. "People?"

Whatever.

Yeah, I don't like people, but it's a conscious choice, not a hang-up.

I could deal with them. If I wanted to. Which I didn't.

"Kai wants you to buy clothes," he continued. "They don't have to be sexy or girly or even as stylish as those awesome hand-me-down guys' jeans you're wearing with the indents of Damon's packs of cigarettes on the back pocket. But they have to be nice, they do have to fit, and they do have to be *yours*. I'm here to make sure you do that."

"I would rather eat my hand than let Kai Mori pay for my shit," I gritted out.

"He's not paying. Graymor Cristane is." He walked into me, forcing me to back up. "You're an employee, and you represent us. We have an expense account for clothes. It's not personal. It's business. And you always look like shit, so here we are." He threw out his arms, gesturing to the massive, dimly lit, empty department store we now stood in at nine thirty at night.

That they'd completely arranged with my comfort in mind.

"Now, sit down," he ordered. "I need to go get a bra to match your new underwear."

A little more than an hour later, we were in Will's car, driving through the city with the back chock-full of bags. I couldn't believe what had happened. Or how fast it had happened. Alex was like a tornado, and she and Will talked too fast to let me think or argue. They started picking out stuff I hated, and before I knew it, I was tossing out garments I didn't like and keeping ones I thought I *might* be able to wear. And after a few more minutes, I participated and shopped and shit.

I sat there, still a little stunned.

I'd probably just get rid of most of it. Put it in the Goodwill donation box and make tomorrow someone's Christmas morning, right?

Or hey, I was sure my mom would love the stuff. Why not?

I didn't like anyone paying for my things. It made me obligated.

But it was kind of fun indulging in the fantasy that this was all mine. That for a few minutes, I had bags and bags of little treasures and pretty new things that had never belonged to anyone else and any woman in town would envy me for.

I'd even enjoyed the feel of the slate gray lingerie when Alex shoved me in a dressing room to try it on. I thought about what Kai's face would look like if he saw me.

"Well, thanks." I glanced over at Alex in the seat next to me as Will drove. "And thanks for the ride home."

She gave me a sincere smile. "You're welcome. And you could've worn one of your new outfits, you know." Her eyes fell down to the same dingy attire I'd worn into the store.

I shrugged. "I'm going to sleep soon. The day is over. No sense in taking a chance at getting something dirty."

I turned my eyes on Will, watching him take a drag off his cigarette, while Alex started typing on her phone. They had a weird relationship. They were friends who slept with each other, but they also slept with other people.

But who was I to talk? I didn't have a single healthy relationship in my life. At least they enjoyed each other.

My phone vibrated in my pocket, and I dug into my jacket, fishing it out.

"Hello?" I answered.

"Hey, trouble."

That smooth, deep tone poured like syrup into my ear. Only one person could make those two words sound like a threat.

My chest rose and fell faster and faster, and my heart raced.

God, I hadn't heard his voice in so long, and I shot my eyes over to Alex and then to Will, making sure I hadn't drawn attention to myself. Will watched the road, while Alex had turned her gaze out her window.

"Hey, um . . ." I breathed hard, licking my parched lips as I kept my voice low. "I can't really talk right now. Can I call you back?"

"Did you have fun tonight?" he asked.

Tonight? How did . . .

God, Kai was right. Damon was watching me, too? Or he was having someone watch me. Did he know about last night?

"They will hurt you," he told me. "And he will toss you out like trash, because that's what sluts are. Trash."

My chin trembled.

"If I was going to let my kid sister pass her pussy off to my friends," he said, "I'd have at least given you to Will for first dibs. He was the most loyal."

I stared at Will as he drove, completely oblivious to whom I was talking to.

"I gotta go," I told my brother.

"He's going to die," he spat out.

He. Kai?

"Not because he betrayed me, but because you did," he explained. "This will be all your fault."

My heart pounded so hard it hurt. There wasn't a doubt in my mind that Damon would do it. He had nothing to lose.

And he was single-minded in his idea of what was right and what was wrong. Betrayal was unforgivable.

I cleared my throat, keeping my words vague, since Alex and Will were sitting here. "I'll take care of it."

"I'm already doing that. It's Wednesday night. He's usually at the cathedral around this time, isn't he?"

I closed my eyes. "Don't," I whispered.

But he'd already hung up.

"Hello?"

The other end of the line was dead.

Goddammit. Kai worked late on Wednesday nights. Then he showered and ate and drove to Thunder Bay to the Cathedral of St. Raphael. Sometimes he went in the confessional, sometimes he strolled and looked at the art. Sometimes he was in there less than ten minutes, sometimes more than an hour.

He went every Wednesday, though. Every. Single. Wednesday.

He was supposed to be an expert in self-defense, right? Wasn't "varying your routine" a preventative measure, goddammit?

I stuck the phone in my pocket. "Can you take me to St. Raphael's?" I called out to Will.

"In Thunder Bay?" He glanced over his shoulder at me. "Why?"

"I just need to get there."

"What about your clothes?"

"I don't give a shit about the clothes," I bit out. "Just let me take your car, then? Please!"

"All right, all right." He sighed and jerked the wheel left, turning and speeding down the narrow cobbled street toward the highway. "I'll take you."

I pulled on my seat belt. "Go fast."

CHAPTER 19

KAI

Present

Kai?"

I turned around, following the voice.

The cathedral was all but empty, except for me and a couple janitors lurking somewhere, but the doors were still unlocked. I wasn't expecting anyone. Keeping my arms folded over my chest, I walked down the Stations of the Cross to peer around the massive marble columns.

Banks stood at the back of the church, near one of the holy water fonts, slowly turning her head back and forth, looking for me.

How did she know I'd be here?

No, of course. She'd done her research, hadn't she?

I let my eyes fall down her form. Wasn't she just shopping? I saw all the charges come in on the card, but she still wore her same grungy clothes with the newsboy cap covering her hair as before. Although, some dark strands fell around her face.

It was funny. She seemed to do everything she could to distract from the fact that she was a woman, but she didn't realize that the clothes she wore only amplified her face. Without her curves or smooth skin, you had no choice but to rest your eyes on the one part of her you could see.

Unfortunately, after last night, I'd seen everything else, and I knew what she hid now. Arousal wound its way through my body.

I stepped out from behind the column, walking toward her between the pews. Her head immediately snapped to me.

"Are you here alone?" she questioned, her eyes flitting about again.

I fought not to smile. What was she up to? She seemed nervous.

"Not anymore," I said, playing with her.

"Well, I just . . ." She continued to look up and around, glancing at the balcony and down the aisle toward the altar. "Um, I knew you'd be here, that's all. Thought it would be, um . . ."

"Um . . . ?"

"Uh." She swallowed, still looking around, for what, I didn't know. "Uh, I thought it would be a good opportunity to discuss the wedding. This is a nice space for it. Should I reserve it?"

I laughed under my breath. "Sure. Why not?"

Whatever. I wasn't getting fucking married, and even though I no longer needed access to the hotel, I really loved having access to her. I liked her.

A lot.

Plus, she was my only link to Damon. I wasn't ready to give her up yet, and she'd be gone the second I told Gabriel there was no deal.

"Did you already have your 'confession'?" she asked.

"No. I haven't done that since . . ." I lowered my voice. "Since the last time with you."

"Really? But you come here every week."

"Do I?" I teased.

Now, how would you know that?

But both of us knew she'd been my own personal satellite, circling me from a distance for God-knows-how-long before I showed up at Gabriel's that day.

I moved toward her, down the aisle, and let my eyes roam the vast hall. Dark wood gleamed everywhere, from the ornate arches a hundred feet above us to the confessionals in the back to the dozens of rows of pews around us. I hadn't been here for a mass in years, but the smell of incense and sickly sweet flowers still lingered from Lent six months ago.

"Did you know that out of Michael, Will, and Damon, Damon was the first one I met?" I told her. "We didn't all become friends really until high school, but I knew Damon long before that. We were both confirmed here when we were ten." I looked up and around again before meeting her eyes. "Together. Classes every Wednesday."

Her eyes shifted. "And you come here because . . ."

"Because I might not know where he is, but I know where he's been. He's as likely to come back here as anywhere."

She thinned her eyes, looking confused. "Why would he have any reason to return here? To the cathedral?"

She really didn't know? Huh.

Well, I suppose Michael and Will didn't know, either, so it wasn't odd for Damon to keep things to himself. Some things anyway.

Things that made him vulnerable.

Well, I wasn't going to be the one to educate her. I came here every Wednesday, the same day of the week we had our classes when we were ten, for several reasons, the most important being I knew this church was significant to Damon.

In this one instance, though, I liked being one step ahead of her, and since she still wasn't on my side, I wasn't going to give up my information.

"You look really pretty," I said, noticing some faint mauve lipstick that closely matched the regular dark pink of her lips.

"You're not answering my question. What aren't you telling me?"

"Everything that you can use to get ahead of me."

She looked away, annoyed. But she knew she'd do the same in my position. We weren't partners—not yet.

"Fine," she bit out, backing away. "Fair enough. I'm sorry I bothered you."

Spinning around, she headed for the back doors, but I called out, stopping her.

"I saw the charges on the company card," I informed her. "Why aren't you wearing your new clothes?"

"Oh, I am."

She twisted back around, reached inside her jacket, and lifted up her shirt, displaying a dark gray lace piece of lingerie accentuating the fuck out of her stomach, perfect breasts, and beautiful skin. The bottom hugged her waist just above her belly button, and every curve—the mound of her breasts to the swoop running down to her hip—was like someone squeezing my lungs.

"Shit." I locked eyes on her and lunged.

She yelped, darting into a row of pews and leaping three rows down before I could get to her. I laughed.

Whipping around, she held my eyes, fire flowing between us, and I placed my hands on the back of the pew in front of me as she stood rigid and waited.

"You have good taste," I teased. "I'm surprised."

"Will picked it out."

My smirk fell. "Did he see you in it?"

She nodded, looking all too pleased to admit that. "He even got my underwear size correct. Although I don't think there's really enough fabric there to call a G-string 'underwear.'"

That motherfucker! I leapt over the pew, and she ran down the row, back into the aisle. I followed, chasing her and watching as the hat fell off her head and her hair came tumbling down, swaying as she tried to escape.

I caught the back of her jacket, pulling her into me and then pushing her into the wall of the confessional, pressing my body to hers. God, I could feel her now. The binding on her breasts was gone, and she was soft everywhere.

Threading my fingers through the back of her hair, I lightly pulled, forcing her chin up and her eyes on me.

"You're such a brat, you know that?" I said. "I might spank you if I didn't think you'd ask for seconds just to piss me off."

"I'll never behave for you."

"Is that so?"

She leaned in, whispering over my mouth. "You're not scary without your mask, Kai Mori."

I tightened my fist in her hair, and she grunted, arching up on her toes to relieve the pressure.

I wasn't scary? Meaning I didn't intimidate her in the least.

Dammit, she was a handful. Constantly pushing me, her fucking pride not willing to acquiesce an inch.

I bared my teeth, speaking low as I pulled her closer. "You got quite a mouth on you on top of the trouble you're already in for fighting today."

I heard her swallow as she stiffened. "I don't want to talk about her."

"I think you need to." I pulled my head back up, looking down at her. Anger deepened the crease between her eyes, and I could tell she wasn't playing anymore.

I grabbed her by the jacket again and pulled her around the confessional.

"What are you—"

"We need to go someplace we can really talk," I told her, forcing her through the door.

My foot hit the kneeler, but there was also a wooden chair, and I pulled the door closed, sitting down in it and bringing her into my lap.

"Just let me go."

"No."

"No?" she burst out.

The room was pitch black, and I could barely even make out her shadow, let alone any colors. A small bit of light breached the wicker screen and a little more through the cracks in the door, but other than that, we were hidden from the world.

Again.

"I won't touch you," I promised. "I'll take my hands off right now, because"—I rested my forehead on her shoulder—"what started between us here six years ago started off honest. If nothing else, just let there always be that. Just listen."

The last time we were here together, she heard everything. Everything I didn't want people to know. And I wanted one person who knew me. I didn't want that tainted between us simply because I was afraid of what she would think. I needed her to understand.

She breathed hard, but she was still, making no move to leave.

Loosening my grip, I kept my hands resting on her waist. "My father used to tell me stories about Japanese warriors," I told her, keeping my voice low, "who, if they were defeated in battle, would commit what's called the *seppuku*. Ritual suicide." The images from the books I'd seen flashed in my head—men and women kneeling with a sword clutched in their hands. "Using a short blade, they'd impale themselves and slice open their stomachs. This would regain them their honor."

She listened, and I leaned back, bringing her with me.

"They'd rather kill themselves than live the rest of their lives with the shame," I explained. "And not just them, but it regained their family's honor, too."

She remained still, but I felt her relax just a little.

"Getting arrested changed everything for me," I continued. "My future, my family, my hope . . . Even after I got out, I could still see it in my parents' eyes. The sadness in my mother's and the disappointment in my father's." My eyes stung, and I felt her relax against my chest as she listened.

"What could I do, short of sticking a fucking sword in my gut, that would make my father see me the same way again?"

I wrapped my arms around her waist, hearing the cathedral creak around us as the wind blew outside.

"I couldn't be with a woman, Banks. I couldn't touch them. I couldn't drink or smile or hardly eat. I couldn't do anything that would bring me pleasure, because I wasn't worthy."

I hesitated, not wanting to hurt her, but she needed honesty.

"We put Rika through such hell last fall," I admitted. "We blamed her and targeted her, put her in danger and scared her. We terrorized her, Banks."

I dropped my voice to a whisper. "She saw me the worst I'd ever behaved, and she still talked to me. Still listened. Still wrapped her arms around me and fuck it . . ." I choked out, tears welling. "We just, the three of us, needed that moment. Each for different reasons, but she made me feel like I wasn't alone anymore. She made me feel wanted and strong. And it brought me a little peace for the first time in a long time."

I could feel her body shaking in my arms, and her breathing quivered. She cried softly. "But you . . ." I buried my nose in her neck, smelling something heady and fragrant. "You make me feel driven. You make me hungry and on fire and wanting to slow down time instead of wanting to rush through it. It's you I look for when I walk in the doors in the morning. Not her. You."

She exhaled a heavy breath and twisted her head around, finding my mouth. We kissed, her lips melting into mine and our tongues finding each other, taunting and teasing, biting and taking. I groaned, my dick swelling inside my pants, growing painful.

"You can touch me now," she whispered between kisses.

And I didn't need her to say it twice.

I ran my hands around her waist, feeling the lace and skin and squeezing her, because my adrenaline was running so hot I was losing control. She was so sweet.

I cupped one of her breasts, holding her to me and savoring the feel of her.

"I like the top." I kissed and nibbled her neck "I love it."

"I'll pay you for the clothes."

I peeled off her jacket, letting it fall to the floor before lifting her shirt over her head. "Yes, you will."

My suggestive joke didn't seem to piss her off, because she kissed me again, her tongue brushing against mine.

"For starters, you can behave yourself," I told her, kneading both breasts in the gray lace again.

"I'm a street punk, Mori," she taunted, leaving little kisses across my cheek that were driving me crazy. "I fight dirty."

"Not anymore. It's your turn now."

"My turn for what?"

I pushed her up from my lap and twisted her around, bringing her in again to stand between my legs.

Looking up at her faint outline in the dark, I held her hips as her hands rested on my shoulders.

"To confess," I told her. "Time to wipe the slate clean."

She made no move and remained silent, probably thinking about what she should do. What should she tell me? What shouldn't she tell me?

"Go ahead," I prompted her.

"I . . ." Her fingers slipped around the back of my neck, and she let out a nervous laugh. "Uh . . . bless me, Father, for I have sinned. It's been . . ."

She trailed off as I unbuttoned her jeans and let them fall down her legs.

"Six years since my last confession."

She stepped out of the pants, to the outside of my legs, and sat down, straddling my lap.

I closed my eyes for a moment, running my hands down to her

ass. I was back there again. In the Bell Tower, long before everything went to shit, and I was happy.

"I . . ." She pressed her groin into mine, leaning in. "I don't know where to start. I'm nervous."

"That many sins, huh?"

I heard her laugh, and I smiled.

"Okay, let me help you." I squeezed her in my hands. "Did you think about me a lot during the last six years?"

"Yes," she whispered.

I dug in my fingers, feeling her smooth skin and the lace of the panties.

"Were some of the thoughts good?" I questioned.

She leaned her chest into mine, her lips brushing my own. "Yeah."

Electric heat swirled low, and I could feel damn near every little bit of her between her legs. My cock was straining against my pants.

"Did you touch yourself, thinking about me?"

She started panting, slowly rolling her hips against the hardness. I felt her nod.

And I took my hand away from her ass and brought it back down with a sharp *whack*.

She yelped, jerking back. "Hey!"

She rubbed the area I smacked, but I took her hand, bringing it back to my shoulder.

"That's pretty naughty," I told her. "So, what did you use . . . a vibrator, a pillow . . . ?"

She breathed nervously now. "Um, my . . . my, my hand."

I spanked her again and then kissed her hard, cutting off her cry. I rubbed the spot I hit, feeling her body slowly relax again.

"Did you like last night?" I asked.

"Yeah."

Another whack.

She lurched forward, gasping. "Kai . . ."

"Do you like me?"

She panted in my ear and clutched my shoulders tight. "Yeah."

Whack.

"You like me a lot?"

"Yes!" she cried.

Whack. She grunted, running her hands all over me and her lips across my jaw.

"You getting hungry, little one?"

"Yeah."

Whack.

And she moaned this time, starting to dry hump my cock.

"Have you ever lied to me?" I asked, my tone deep.

She paused, and I smacked her twice this time, knowing that was definitely my answer.

"Ah!" She pressed herself into me.

"I can play dirty, too." Lifting her off me, I spun her around and yanked her panties down her legs. I shrugged out of my jacket and unfastened my belt, pulling out my cock and feeling relief at giving it some room.

I pulled her back down on me.

"This is called reverse cowgirl, little one," I growled in her ear. "Hang on."

I pushed her forward, her hands shooting out to grasp the little ledge under the priest's screen, and I held her leg at the curve where it met her hip and used my other hand to guide my cock. Finding her wet, I nudged her opening and, at the same time, thrust my hips, pulled her back into me, and slid inside in one shot.

She sucked in a breath, and my head fell back as I groaned.

So hot and tight.

Whimpering, she tightened her muscles around me, holding me inside her. "Oh, my God," she gasped under her breath.

Grabbing a fistful of her hair, I pulled her head back and pulled out, thrusting deep again.

"More, faster," she moaned.

And I started fucking her. Faster and harder, pounding into her as she gripped the ledge in front of her and used it as leverage, backing up into me.

This was what I wanted. What I always wanted, since the first time I'd seen her. Someone who knew me and wanted to dive with me.

All the years feeling helpless, someone telling me when to eat, sleep, walk, and speak. I came out of that place feeling less than human. Feeling less than a dog. I was stripped away, afraid of the consequences if I got angry or violent or mean, so I held everything in, because I was never going to go back there. I was never going to be that man again, because I'd killed a part of myself and killed my parents when I went away.

And I was still in prison when I got out, living like a machine so I wouldn't make any mistakes, and I wanted to fucking feel something. I wanted to push and pull and fight and fuck and own this whole goddamn world again.

I wanted to take.

I squeezed my eyes shut, reveling in how beautiful she felt. Releasing her hair, I ran my hands over her ass, wishing there was enough light to see if it was still red from the spanking.

I grabbed her hips and just held on as she took over, pushing back into me, sliding up and down my cock.

"Hey, Kai!" someone shouted. "Yo, where are you?"

Will.

Fuck.

Banks gasped, and I clamped a hand over her mouth, standing us both up with my dick still inside her.

"Shhh," I warned in her ear. Pinning her against the wall, I spread her legs wider, pulled off my shirt, and held her tight, continuing my thrusts.

But then Alex's voice came, too. "Banks!"

What the hell? I clamped my hand tighter the more Banks started to moan.

"Is he here? Did she find him?" I heard Alex ask.

"I don't know. His car is still out front," Will added. "Kai!"

Banks pulled away from my hand. "They dropped me off," she whispered. "They're probably checking to make sure I found you. We should stop."

"No." I kissed her neck, feeling my orgasm coming as I groped her breast.

"Ah," she whimpered. "Go harder. Please."

I kissed her lips and cheek, her ear and neck, everywhere I could reach as I held her hard against me.

"Yeah, yeah . . . oh, God."

I put my hand over her mouth again, but we were so close, I didn't really give a shit if Will and Alex heard us. Only that Banks would be embarrassed when she came to her senses.

"You weren't built for them," I said in her ear as I reached around and rubbed her clit. "Not Damon or Gabriel or anyone else. You were made for me, and I want you in my bed tonight."

"I'm not sleeping in that shithole."

I smacked her on the ass, and her breath caught before she reached around and grabbed the back of my neck, kissing me with a laugh.

I didn't know if Alex and Will had left or not, but I didn't hear anything anymore, so they either split or heard the noises pouring out of the confessional and then split of their own accord.

I rubbed her faster and faster, thrusting as deep as I could. "Come on, baby. Come on."

"Kai," she whimpered.

And then her body tightened up, freezing in place and just holding on as I pounded, bringing her ass back into me harder and harder.

She cried out, coming and breathing hard as she went limp, letting it wrack through her body.

God, I wished I knew what was in her head at that moment.

A few more seconds, and I reached my climax and thrust, spilling inside of her and my fingers clenching the sweat-soaked skin of her hips.

She held fast to the little counter, desperate for air in the now stuffy confessional as little moans escaped her.

Pleasure swept through my entire body, and I felt dizzy as I rested my forehead on her back.

She was incredible.

But holy shit, my mom would kill me if she knew what I'd just done and where. I didn't really care, though. This was me, and this was what we did.

A buzzing sound came from somewhere, and I paused, wondering if it was my phone or hers and if we should just let it go.

But slowly, she pulled away and dipped down to retrieve her jeans.

She dug the phone out, and I saw a green light flash, knowing it was hers that had been buzzing.

She swiped the screen and tapped a few times, then read.

"What is it?" I asked, seeing her just stand there frozen.

She dropped her hand to her side, not looking at me.

"Vanessa arrived early," she said quietly. "She's here in Thunder Bay."

CHAPTER 20

BANKS

Present

The faint *ding-dong* of the doorbell carried up to Damon's room, and I closed the lid to Kore II's tank, walking to the window. The limo my father sent for Kai sat out front.

My stomach knotted. It was time to meet Vanessa, and I didn't want him in this house with her. I didn't want her anywhere near him. Why did he come?

I swung open the bedroom door and descended the stairs, hearing my heartbeat in my ears. I could tell him I wanted to stay with him, and this would be over. I could tell him I wanted to be with him, and he would take me, and we could both leave here.

But I couldn't guarantee him my loyalty. I knew I couldn't.

Closing the door at the bottom of the stairs, I rounded the banister and headed down the next set of stairs, already hearing Hanson open the door and greet the guests.

"Good evening, Mr. Mori," he said. "Mr. Grayson. Miss Fane. Please . . ."

Will and Rika, too? I was kind of grateful, actually. They didn't want to see Kai do something stupid, so if they stepped in, I wouldn't have to. I wouldn't have to choose.

Kai came into view, and my steps slowed as I locked eyes with him. It took everything not to smile.

I loved how he looked up at me and just stared. I loved how his right eye pierced a little more than the left. And I loved how just the sight of him made my stomach flip.

His gaze fell down my body, softening as he took in my new clothes. Nothing over-the-top, but the new jeans fit at least, and I really liked the white V-neck T-shirt and cute military jacket. I'd even donned a tiny bit of the mascara Alex forced down my throat last night at McGivern & Bourne.

"Kai, how are you?" Gabriel approached, holding out his hand.

But his tone was false, and Kai's body was tight. They weren't fooling each other.

I descended the rest of the stairs and stepped up next to my father, not really sure if that was where I was supposed to be. If it wasn't, I might be in for another confession later.

My ass was still a little raw from last night.

Gabriel cast me a quick look and then turned back to Kai. "You got her out of those rags," he said. "Well done. We kind of miss her around here, actually."

My father nudged my chin with his fingers, and Kai's eyes narrowed on him.

"Will," Gabriel greeted, shaking Will's hand. "Good to see you again."

Will nodded, probably the one who knew my father the best out of the three of them, since he and Damon had been pretty close.

"And Erika Fane." Gabriel stepped forward, invading her space and holding out his hand. "Gabriel Torrance. I believe you know my son."

Her eyes shifted, looking uneasy, but she took his hand, shook it, and pulled away quickly. I couldn't believe Michael let her come without him. He was kind of blind, but I hadn't pegged him for ignorant.

"Crist is a lucky man," he told her. And then he moved aside, gesturing for them to enter. "Let's step into the den."

Gabriel turned, leading the way down the hall, and I followed, walking at his side. But a grip caught the back of my jacket, and I sucked in a sudden breath as Kai hauled me backward.

To his side.

We kept walking, and he didn't look or speak to me further.

"Where is she?" Kai asked Gabriel. "Vanessa."

The quivering in my stomach from having him close changed to another fucking knot at the mention of her, and I fisted my fingers.

"Around," Gabriel taunted and walked into the study.

He stepped over to his desk, and everyone filed in, leaving Hanson to close the door. Will immediately found the leather sofa and planted his ass down while Rika moved to the side of the room.

Kai took the seat opposite Gabriel on the other side of the desk.

Gabriel tipped his chin at me. "Go check on dinner."

"She doesn't work for you anymore," Kai interjected.

"Actually, she does. Technically speaking, of course."

No contract. No agreement.

But Kai didn't take the bait, relaxing in his seat. "I'll meet the bride first, thanks."

My father laughed under his breath. "Hanson." He picked up the cigar sitting in his ashtray. "Fetch my niece."

The man nodded, quietly slipping out of the room.

I looked out the patio doors, seeing a group of young women sitting at the tables several yards away. I couldn't make out their faces, but Vanessa's white-blond hair was easy enough to pick out as she sat with her back to me.

What if he was attracted to her?

"So, when's the wedding?" Gabriel asked, and I blinked, seeing him look at Rika.

For a moment, I thought he was asking Kai.

Rika replied, "No specific date yet."

"And where's Michael?"

Her eyes flashed to Kai before she answered. "Away at a game for the day."

My father smiled, the thoughts in his head barely keeping themselves contained as his eyes raked over her body.

Kai rose and wandered to the bookcases, placing himself in front of her. My father was eye-fucking her, and Kai knew it. His forehead was creased, troubled, but he remained quiet, not speaking or looking at me. What was he thinking about?

And finally, a light knock pierced the silence.

Everyone turned or looked up as the door opened and Vanessa Nikova entered.

I don't know what I expected. Maybe for her to be awkward and look anywhere but at him, or maybe for Kai to be surprised and instantly attracted, losing all semblance of thought at the sight of her.

But they locked eyes and just stared at each other for a minute as she slowly closed the door.

That was worse.

I darted my eyes to him, watching him take her in as if he was actually considering her.

She walked into the room, wearing a silver cocktail dress that made her seem ethereal with her blond hair and big blue eyes. She had much the same coloring as Rika, but Rika was different. She was alive, and Vanessa looked like a doll kept in a box. Not a fingerprint on her.

She wasn't so pristine on the inside, though.

She approached Kai, and I saw him straighten, bracing himself. Holding out her hand, she smiled, her perfectly manicured eyebrows softening for him.

"Hello," she said sweetly.

I did half an eye roll before catching myself. Two-headed snake.

"Hello." He took her hand, shook it, and finally released it. A couple seconds too late in my opinion.

"Vanessa, this is Kai Mori." Gabriel made the official introductions. "And his friends William Grayson III and Erika Fane."

Vanessa turned, her heels clacking as she stepped over to Will and shook his hand. Turning to Rika, though, she paused, clearly assessing her as the other reached a hand out with a tight smile.

"Rika is soon to be married to Michael Crist," Gabriel explained. "Another friend of Kai's. Unfortunately, he couldn't be here today."

Vanessa eased, the crack in her façade sealing up again as she shook Rika's hand. "Nice to meet you."

The room fell silent as we all just stood there, and I could hear the dogs barking in the distance, probably hungry. Gabriel fed some and starved others, and while the experienced ones knew that barking only made it worse, he constantly had new blood coming in and learning the torture all over again.

"Well," Vanessa finally spoke up, trying to make light. "We'll have no trouble bonding like this."

Gabriel laughed, Kai offered a smile, and I scowled.

Why was he smiling?

Why was he even still here? What was his game now? He wouldn't actually marry her, for crying out loud, so why attempt to bond?

"I need some fresh air," she told Kai. "How about you?"

His head turned like he was about to look at me, but then he nodded, stopping himself. "Sounds great."

She smiled brighter, showing teeth, and led the way out the patio doors. "And don't follow us," she joked to Hanson, who had moved to chaperone. "We need privacy."

I shot the back of her head a glare as they disappeared outside.

The grounds were extensive. They could be gone for an hour. Long enough for her to charm him any which way she wanted.

"Go check on dinner."

I looked over, meeting Gabriel's eyes. And now I was going to serve dinner to the man I was sleeping with and his bride. Fantastic.

Charging out of the room, I slammed the door closed, knowing full well my father knew I was angry. He wouldn't care. He knew I'd do my duty anyway, no matter how much I pissed and moaned.

A dog yelped outside, and I didn't know if it had been attacked by another dog or disciplined by a trainer, but then another one howled the most gut-wrenching sound, like it was begging. For what, I didn't know, but I walked into the kitchen feeling like I wanted to join him. Howl and scream and fight until I either escaped or someone put me out of my misery.

"Hey!" Marina exclaimed, seeing me enter as she washed her hands at the sink. Her delighted eyes took in my clothes. "You look great. When did this happen?"

I assumed she meant my "makeover," but I wasn't in the mood. Seeing the steaks for dinner on the cutting board, I sauntered up and picked up a large chopping knife lying on the block.

And I started slicing.

"Those are the steaks—"

Marina stopped, watching me cut strips, slicing through the prime meat with the sharp knife like it was butter, and then chop the slices into chunks.

"Those are the steaks for dinner!" she said, rushing up to the island. "Banks, what are you doing?"

I looked at her, feeling my heart race, and shot her a closed-mouth smile. She reared back, narrowing her eyes.

She probably couldn't remember the last time I'd smiled at her.

Finishing my task, I took a large bowl out of the cabinet, tossed in all the chunks of meat, and grabbed the dish, taking it out the back door.

This wouldn't end well for me, but God, it felt good. And I couldn't stop myself.

W"here are the steaks?" Gabriel asked, glaring down at the left-over corn chowder from the guys' lunch today and the plates of baked piroshki—a hand pie with meat filling that Marina was preparing for lunch tomorrow.

"I fed them to the dogs," I said.

Will snorted, and I heard a scoff, most likely from Vanessa, but I continued to stare at the wall ahead of me, ready to suffer whatever consequences were coming.

I could feel Kai's amusement. He sat across the table, and I was almost sure he was staring at me, too.

Gabriel exhaled hard. "A couple weeks with you and she's back to being as bold as brass," he said to Kai. "Just like when she was a teenager."

The table was silent, except for Will, who'd started eating.

"She knows how to be disciplined, though," he added.

"Oh?" Kai prodded.

I blinked long and hard. That wasn't anyone's business. *Not here, not now.*

But Gabriel continued. "Ask her to take off her gloves."

Fucker.

I instantly locked my hands behind my back, out of sight, as everyone turned their eyes on me.

Gabriel couldn't discipline me right now, so he did what he had to do to retain his pride. He humiliated me. Kai hadn't seen me without the gloves. Not since I was seventeen, before I was "disciplined."

"Another time, maybe," Gabriel said, sounding pleased with himself. "She'll soon be your problem anyway."

"Oh?"

This time it was from Vanessa.

"Part of the contract," Gabriel explained, taking a slurp of his soup. "Kai gets you, the hotel, and Banks. Until the wedding, anyway."

She remained silent, and since she sat below me, I couldn't see her face, but there was enough hesitation to know what she was thinking.

Or what she suspected.

"She's a good worker," Kai chimed in, picking up a hand pie and sniffing it.

"Well, good," Vanessa sighed, playing stupid. "Why don't you go unpack my suitcases, Banks? Let us eat."

"I arranged a suite in the city for you."

"I've changed my mind." She waved me off. "I'll stay here."

I glanced up, finding Rika's eyes, neither of us looking at all pleased with being here.

Fine. Whatever. Not that I was here that often anymore anyway, but I'd rather she was in a hotel where I was even less likely to run into her.

I twisted on my heel and walked toward the door.

"And don't give my clothes to the dogs," she called out.

I wouldn't dream of it.

I pulled the door closed behind me and headed upstairs to one of the guest rooms. I honestly didn't mind the task if it got me out of that room.

I found her Louis Vuitton luggage next to the bed in a room around the corner from my father's and went through her things as slowly as I could, hoping Kai, Rika, and Will would be gone by the time I was done. Unfortunately, she hadn't brought as much as I thought she would.

Of course, she'd be going into the city to shop, so she only packed a few bags. I hung up most of her clothes, placing sweaters, workout gear, and underthings in the drawers and arranging all of her products—moisturizers, cleansers, makeup—neatly on the en suite counter out of consideration for the staff who'd have to tidy the room, instead of for Vanessa.

I tucked the bags under the bed, straightened the comforter, and gave the room a once-over, making sure drawers and closets were closed before heading back into the hall.

It had been more than an hour. Maybe they'd left by now.

But when I headed for the window on the upstairs landing, I noticed the door to the third floor was cracked.

I'd closed that.

Opening it up, I looked up to the top of the stairs, seeing light coming through the open door at the top.

I climbed the stairs softly, on guard. No one went up there except Damon and me.

"Of course he would have snakes," I heard Rika say and heard her footsteps across my brother's floor.

What the hell was she doing in his room?

"What's the matter with you?" Kai asked.

"I could ask you the same thing." She sounded worried. "Have you completely lost your mind?"

I tensed on instinct. Why had they snuck off together? Was Will in there with them? I stopped at the top and hung back, listening through the cracked door.

"This is stupid," she pleaded with him, "and what I've respected about you is that you don't do stupid."

"I have a criminal record that says differently."

She let out a scoff, and I heard more footsteps.

"A long time ago you told me something important," she went on. "'Whenever you want to make an impression and you think you've gone far enough, go one step further. Always leave them wondering if you're just a little bit crazy and people will never fuck with you again.'"

"And?"

"And you've gone more than one step further."

I heard some shaky breathing, and I wasn't sure who it was from, but Rika's tone sounded upset. Concerned as a friend would be.

"I like who I am now, and for better or for worse, you're partly responsible," she told him. "But this? This mistake could ruin you. This isn't the life we want for you."

I heard more steps, and since I couldn't see them through the crack, I gathered they were near the tanks on the other side of the room.

"There's a plan here," he told her, speaking softer. "You have to trust me."

There was silence, but I almost wanted to hear more. She was concerned for him, and she sounded as confused as I was. What was this plan? I wanted her to press him further. He might tell her things he wouldn't tell me.

But the conversation was over.

I pushed open the door, seeing Kai turn and Rika look up as I stood there.

His eyes flashed to my gloves, and I crossed my arms over my chest. "No one's supposed to be in here."

Kai approached. "But you are," he said, tossing me one of my hats he must have found in here.

I caught it, remaining silent.

"Why are you allowed? When did you move in with this family? You weren't sleeping with Damon, because you were a virgin with me, so what was he doing with you, huh? Who exactly are you?"

I half smiled. "Your favorite enemy," I replied.

But just then, he darted out and grabbed my hands. I clenched my teeth together as he pulled off one glove and then the other, dropping them to the floor.

Goddammit.

He held them tightly, staring at the backs of my hands. Only one had the cigar burn on it.

I wore two gloves, though, to keep up the pretense.

I could hear his angry breathing getting faster. But he didn't ask questions. I guess he was smart enough to figure out how Gabriel disciplined me.

Thankfully, it only took once for me to learn, though.

Rika shifted her head just a little, trying to be discreet as she got a look. The circular scar was about the size of a quarter, the flesh bumpy and pink. It wasn't an old scar, but it had faded a lot over the past few years. I glanced at the small mark on her neck, knowing she got it from the same car accident that killed her father years ago.

"You don't know what you're doing to me," Kai choked out, sounding solemn.

I turned my head away and kept my mouth shut.

Rika started to walk out, giving us privacy, but I stopped her.

"No, stay," I told her. "He'll need his friends."

He stared down at me, getting in my face. "Do you want me to marry her?" he asked. "And this will be us? You, my little sidepiece whom I sneak off to fuck in the middle of the night. Huh? You'd like that?"

"You think I'd put up with that?" I retorted.

My face was starting to crack and my chin trembled, but I tightened every muscle I could muster, keeping the tears at bay.

"Look at me," he whispered as Rika stood close but looked away. "Look at me."

I didn't.

"I like you," he told me. "I want you in my house. I want to see you in my bed. I don't want to not see you every day. Be with me tonight."

But I couldn't. I couldn't be with him for anything more than stolen moments.

For one simple reason.

"Do you hate Damon?" I asked him.

He squared his shoulders, and I could tell a wall was going up. "He's not a factor with us. He has no place in my life."

"Well, he does in mine," I stated. "I love him."

Before he could say anything else, I spun around and left, jogging quickly down the stairs.

Enough, goddammit. Just leave. Everything was fucked up because of him, and I wanted it back to when it was simple. When I was single-minded in the fact that I was loyal to one person, and that, alone, was my purpose.

When I didn't want to say yes.

When I wasn't falling in love.

I reached the bottom of the stairs and shot through the door, bumping straight into David.

"Hey," he said. "I was just looking for you."

I blinked away the tears in my eyes and looked away. "What?"

But then creaks and footfalls fell behind me, and Kai and Rika both stepped out of the stairwell, too.

I groaned.

David backed up, looking questioningly between the three of us, but he carried on. "Okay, great," he said, nodding. "Everyone in one place. Perfect." And then he looked down at me. "Gabriel needs you for a few moments. Bring them into the guesthouse."

And he turned to leave.

The guesthouse—I grabbed his arm, narrowing my eyes. No. That's where Gabriel took problems to deal with them away from prying eyes.

But David just laughed under his breath and leaned in to whisper. "It's okay. Everyone will leave in one piece. I promise."

Traipsing past the terrace and the flickering lights of Vanessa's welcome celebration getting underway, I led Kai, Will, and Rika around the pond to the guest quarters. It was more like a starter house, the size much bigger than any apartment my mother and I ever lived in. Kai and Will had been there before. It was where Damon always took his friends on the rare occasion he invited anyone over.

This way, no one ran into his mother. Or saw me. It was fully furnished and decorated, with three bedrooms, two bathrooms, a full kitchen, and a great room. What did Gabriel need them out here for that he couldn't take care of in his office?

Beautiful glass panes surrounded the front of the house, and I spotted a few men inside the cottage. My pulse quickened. What was going on?

I fought not to spin around and get them out of here. This didn't feel right.

But David said they'd be safe. He wouldn't lie to me.

Before I could make up my mind, though, the glass doors opened wide.

"Kai!" my father boomed from inside as Ilia held the door open for us. "Come on in!"

Kai walked around me, my feet still rooted to their spot. Rika and Will followed, and I finally moved, sticking my hands in my pockets, my fingers sliding into place on the grips of the blades I hid there.

"How do you like it?" Gabriel held out his hands at the massive room. "Just refurbished. I thought I'd make it your and Vanessa's home when you visit. It'll be nice to have some family around again."

Ilia closed the door behind me, and we all stepped farther into the room. Three men loitered behind my father, spread out casually, but they were moving. Albeit slowly, as to not attract attention.

But they had mine. They were positioning themselves around us. Ilia stayed at my side, while Lev and David were absent, probably on an errand somewhere.

"What do you want?" Kai stopped behind a cushioned chair, looking at Gabriel. "We're heading out."

My father moved behind a desk and picked up a black fountain pen, holding it out to Kai. "Just the small matter of a signature."

I let out a breath. He wasn't in danger, after all. This was just about the stupid contract that Kai would never sign. I was guessing he didn't hand in the one with the signature I forged yesterday morning in anger.

"Send it to the dojo," he told my father. "If there are no more changes to be made, I'll sign."

"You'll sign now. Vanessa is here, and the wedding is being planned." He looked at Kai, all patience and pleasantries now gone. "Now."

Kai took a step. "How do I know you didn't slip in a contingency that I haven't seen? I'm going to take my time to read it again before I agree to anything."

My father dropped his hand and shot a glance over to Ilia, nodding to him.

What—

"Sorry, kid," Ilia mumbled.

Huh?

And then he grabbed me.

"Hey!" I cried out.

But he hauled me across the room, and I twisted my head around, trying to see what was happening. Everything went down so fast. My father's men each grabbed one of our guests, and Kai sliced his attacker across the face with the heel of his hand, sending the other man collapsing to his knees.

He immediately looked at me as I was forced over behind the desk with my father, and then someone whipped a steel bar across his shoulder blades, and Kai went down, grunting. He stumbled, shaking as he tried to see Will and Rika, who were each being restrained by their arms.

"What the hell is going on?" he bellowed.

I twisted in Ilia's arms.

"No contract, no agreement," Gabriel gritted out. "No hotel, and Banks is ours."

"I don't give a shit about the hotel!" Kai shouted as he was hauled off his knees by the one who'd hit him. He shoved the man off and turned, glaring at my father. "And she doesn't have to stay anywhere she doesn't want to. She's not your property!"

His eyes burned, looking both furious and ready.

Gabriel turned to me. "You want to go with him? Go."

No. Don't do this. I pleaded with my eyes.

"Go," he told me again, the challenge thick in his tone. "See how long he wants you. See what happens when you try to crawl back here, because you know how I reward disloyalty. Go."

I squeezed my eyes closed for a moment, feeling all their gazes on me. This was unbearable. If I left with him, I left with nothing. Completely dependent on Kai.

I wanted him, but my father was right. Would I really exchange the devil I knew for the devil I didn't? I couldn't rely on what might or might not be between Kai and me. He was the next five minutes, and my family was the rest of my life.

"You want him?" Gabriel prodded again. "Go."

He pushed, and I trembled, trying to hold in the tears. *Please.* Kai was waiting for me, and this was torture.

I could hear Kai's breath shake as he held out his hand. "Come on, baby," he begged. "Just reach out."

My fingers hummed, wanting his touch. Wanting to take his hand.

But I curled them into fists and met his eyes, slowly shaking my head.

And Kai just stared at me, his expression frozen, but his chest slowly caving. The heat of shame spread over my face. I hated hurting him.

But we both knew this was over before it even began.

"Don't look so surprised," Gabriel told him, self-satisfaction in his voice. "She loves him. She'll always choose him."

The hint of hurt in Kai's eyes turned hard, and he straightened up, smoothing a hand down his shirt and jacket as he glared at me.

My father turned to me, amused. "I don't think he wants you anymore."

I swallowed the lump in my throat.

"If you don't come, it's war," Kai threatened me, his tone as dead as a machine. "And I will make this hurt. Dare me."

I heard my father chuckle, but I knew Kai wasn't bluffing. And this might not even be about Damon anymore. He was angry with me now.

And then, all of a sudden, it happened. Kai shot out, grabbed the pen, and scribbled his signature across the line.

"Kai, no!" Rika cried out.

"No," I gasped under my breath. Every bit of air left my lungs as I stared in horror at the signed contract.

Oh, my God.

He flipped the pen, letting it fall onto the desk, and shoved the contract at Gabriel, his expression defiant. Then he reached over the desk, grabbed me by the collar with both hands and hauled me over, my legs and feet sending papers, a tray of files, and a lamp crashing to the floor.

"Kai," I breathed out, clutching his hands as tears welled in my eyes. What had he done?

He stood me up in front of him, both of us facing Gabriel as

Kai wrapped his arm around my neck. "Now you're mine," he threatened in my ear. "At least until the wedding."

"Attaboy." Gabriel smiled as he picked up the contract and flipped all the pages back into place.

"Kai, what did you do?" Rika rushed forward.

But Kai didn't say anything.

"I'll inform your bride of the good news," Gabriel told him.

Kai clutched my collar in one hand, pushing me to the side as he backed away.

"We'll be in touch," he assured Gabriel.

And he squeezed my hand, dragging me out of the cottage as Rika and Will both jogged to catch up.

"Kai, listen to me!" Rika tried to get his attention.

But Kai just kept walking, leading us around the house and into the driveway. I stumbled, my muscles burning to keep up.

We stopped in front of their cars.

"Kai!" Rika growled. "You can't do this!"

"You're not thinking straight, man," Will chimed in. "We need to get that contract back."

"That contract is the least of my worries," Kai spat out, reaching the cars. "I needed leverage, and now I have it."

"No, screw that!" Rika yelled. "You can't—"

"Damon has something on me!" Kai said, cutting her off.

What?

He spun around, looking at all of us. "Something bad, okay?"

Everyone froze, just staring at him.

What? He had something on him. Why wouldn't I know that?

"What does he have on you?" Rika stepped up to him.

"Does it matter?"

"What does he have on you?" she shouted again.

Kai stared off, fury in his eyes, but hesitant. What didn't he want to say?

"His mother," he finally said. "She's dead because of me."

My mouth fell open slightly, and I stared at him in shock. Rika and Will were quiet.

She was dead? I mean, I suspected she might be by now. No one had seen or heard from her since that night six years ago, but I thought it might've been Damon or Gabriel who'd finally done her in.

Not that I really cared. As long as that bitch was gone, I was happy.

Kai's jaw flexed. "Devil's Night, six years ago at The Pope," he explained. "She was . . . *hurting* Damon. And she was trying to hurt Banks. I lost it, and I attacked her. She got hurt in the fall."

That night came flooding back. The terror, the disgusting, vile words she spoke, Damon's pain, and . . . Kai losing his temper, hitting her, and the blood. He'd protected us, and if she was dead, then good fucking riddance.

"You're just telling us this now?" Rika blurted out. "After all this time?"

"I didn't know I killed her. Not until last year on the yacht," he said. "You, Michael, and Will were in the water, and Damon and I were fighting. He fucking taunted me with it. A little tidbit he'd saved just in case." He sucked in a breath. "After I left the hotel that night, she didn't survive. He got rid of the body to protect me. Now he's using it to threaten me. That's why I need to find him. I'm not risking going back to prison."

"And if he's lying?" Will argued. "How do you know he's telling the truth?"

"Would you take that chance?" Kai bit out. "Because she hasn't been seen since. Either he produces his very-much-alive mother or her body, so I can move on with my fucking life and not have this hanging over my head. And if I don't get one or the other, I'm going to shut him up forever."

"So, that's why you've been so concerned with finding him?" Rika asked.

And then Will added, "You should've told us sooner, man. Like last year."

But Kai ignored their protests, pushing me to Will. "Just take her," he ordered, whipping off his jacket and wiping his nose with his thumb. Blood stained his fingertip. I didn't see him get hit, but he must've. "Bring her to Darcy Street and then leave," he told him. "I need to calm down before I deal with her."

And he didn't look at me as he climbed into his car and shifted into gear, taking off as fast as he could.

Rika and Will stood with me in the driveway, watching him speed off, and Will jostled me. "I guess you're in for it now."

CHAPTER 21

BANKS

Present

Kai!" Rika growled into her phone. "Pick up!" And then she ended the call, sounding exasperated. "Dammit."

That was the third time she'd called him since we left Thunder Bay. Will drove, and Rika sat in the passenger seat next to him, while I gripped the blades hidden in my pockets as I sat in the back seat.

Leverage. He'd said I was leverage. Was she really dead? He couldn't know for sure, but I guessed that's what he was trying to figure out. Nothing like having a potential murder hanging over your head.

Would Damon really throw him to the wolves?

"We need to talk to him," Rika told Will as he lit a cigarette.

But I watched him shake his head. "We need to leave him alone. Kai knows what he's doing."

"He didn't plan that turn of events, asshole! It's all about her." She jerked her head toward me. "And he's in it now. I need to get ahold of Michael."

She checked her phone again, and I turned my eyes out the window, seeing the city lights shine on the black water of the river as we crossed the bridge.

I wasn't bound to that contract. Indentured servitude wasn't a thing anymore. I could run, and I would. I'd been useful; my father got what he wanted. I'd be welcomed back now.

And my brother certainly wouldn't expect me to honor the agreement.

"You need to talk to him."

I heard Rika's words, but it wasn't until I caught her watching me out of the corner of my eye that I realized she was speaking to me.

"Excuse me?"

"You need to talk to him," she told me. "You backed him into this corner. Take some responsibility."

I laughed under my breath, looking away again. *Jesus.* None of this was my fault, and I wasn't taking the blame. Men and their idiocy, and I was sick of being collateral damage.

"You heard what he said," I shot back. "I'm leverage. That's all he wants with me."

"Do you really believe that?" She eyed me. "He could've just taken you if that's what he wanted. He signed that contract because he was angry. With you," she pointed out. "He'll listen to you. I've known him a long time, and once he calms down—"

"I knew him long before you came along," I snarled. "I don't need you to educate me on who he is."

She pressed her lips together, shutting up.

"And I've known him a hell of a lot longer than both of you," Will shot off. "Kai's acting out of character, but he works shit out better when he's left quiet, okay? If he talks to anyone, it'll be Michael." And then he nodded to Rika. "Try him again."

She sighed and picked up her phone, dialing her fiancé once more.

"And you," Will called out.

I looked up, seeing him eye me in the rearview mirror.

"Shit's gonna hit the fan regardless of that contract. You know that, right?"

Yes. Yes, I knew that. Even if Kai put away his anger and Natalya was alive and well, Damon was still coming.

And there was a very good chance he wouldn't win.

Will blew out a stream of smoke, flicking the ash out the window as we turned onto Darcy Street. "If you ask Kai not to hurt Damon," he told me, "then he won't. All you have to do is ask."

I clutched the door handle, ready to bolt as soon as the doors unlocked.

But I slowly relaxed my fingers, thinking about his words.

Maybe Will had a point. Kai could be intimidating and scary and just as mean as I could be at times, but he wasn't cruel. He could be reasonable.

I dropped my hand from the door as the car slowed at the top of the incline.

"Here we are," Will said, putting the car in park.

I looked out the window again, seeing Kai's black brick house with ripped shades hanging over the windows and the flickering porch light, looking like something out of one of those movies, the "you go in but you don't come out" types. What did he use this place for? He didn't live here.

Where did he sleep? Where did he cook his meals and shower and screw women other than me?

"He's waiting inside."

I met Will's eyes in the mirror again. "How do you know?"

"He just texted," he informed me, holding up his phone. "Here's your chance."

We'd left him less than an hour ago. He wasn't going to be calm yet.

"Just talk to him," Rika said, turning to me. "Please."

The last thing I wanted to do was anything for her. Tension crawled over my skin, and I pushed open the door, suddenly wanting to be out of there more than away from here.

Fine. I'd ask him. Not because they wanted me to, but because it might work. Damon could come home, I could keep him away from them, and they could all go on with their lives here in the city while my brother and I continued with ours.

I slammed the door and immediately began walking up the steps to the house.

But my gaze flickered farther up the hill to the house perched on top, seeing a single light on the second floor. And I slowed.

It looked like a lightning bug hovering over a black lake at night. There was nothing up here. No other houses or businesses, and the light from the city couldn't even pierce the thin forest surrounding the area. We were high and isolated, just that house and Kai's. Did he know who lived there?

Chills spread down my arms. It was beautiful, kind of turn-of-the-century gothic with pointed gables and a black gate.

"Are you okay?" Will called, and I looked to see him leaning out the window.

I turned back around, shooting him a middle finger over my shoulder as I headed for the house again.

Once I was on the porch, I twisted the doorknob, finding it unlocked.

There were no lights on inside, except for the moonlight streaming through unshaded windows. I entered the foyer and heard Will pull away right before I closed the door.

A loud click sounded, and every hair on my body stood on end as I shot my gaze left and right. Where the hell was he?

The house looked the same as it had last time. Still barely any furniture and anything that was here was covered in sheets. No lamps, and when I reached out and flipped the switch on the wall, the old light fixture hanging above did nothing.

Dust clotted the floors, but when I stepped farther in, I noticed some particles floating in the air. Like someone *had* been here and disturbed it.

I looked around, hyperaware. "Kai?"

The wind outside kicked up, and I heard screeching from above. Like a branch scraping against a windowpane.

"Kai!" I called again, louder this time. "Where are you?"

My hip vibrated, and I realized it was my phone. Digging it out, I swiped the screen and looked at the message.

Close.

I whipped around, back and forth, shooting my eyes everywhere, trying to see where he was. I walked into the living room and then the dining room, scanning corners and behind doors.

"What the hell?" I growled.

I couldn't see anything. No shadow, no form, and I couldn't hear anything, either. The house was completely silent.

"I'm not playing your games!" I yelled up the stairs.

My phone buzzed again.

You already are.

I shook my head. What did he think he was doing? A little sick fun?

Of course, I remembered Kai's version of fun. Devil's Night six years ago. The hotel, the chase, the ballroom, the drapes . . . the fear.

I didn't mind how it excited me that night, but I wasn't in the mood now.

"I'm leaving," I shouted to the empty air.

And turning around, I twisted the doorknob again.

But it wouldn't turn. What? I jiggled the handle, pulling at it, the door pounding against the frame as I yanked.

A green light blinked to my left, and I looked at the wall, spotting a keypad. My stomach sank. He had an alarm system and automated locks.

I yanked on the door again, it still not opening.

I spun around. "I want out!" I told him. "Or I'm kicking out a window!"

Another text popped up.

> You said I wasn't scary. Are you scared yet?

I looked up to the *second* floor. "I'm annoyed."

> Liar.

Asshole.

I heard a creak from above me, and I shot my eyes up again. The wind was howling through the trees outside, and I was very alone right now.

With him somewhere in this house.

If you ask him not to hurt Damon, he won't.

I wet my dry lips and forced out my words. "I need to talk to you."

> Find me.

"Where are you?" I called, staying rooted right where I was.

I waited several seconds, but no response came. No voice. No text. Was Kai even here? I mean, I didn't know for sure that it was him texting, right? Someone could have stuffed his body in a furnace, taken his phone, and was now doing the creepy *Saw* thing where they ask you if you want to play a game, but really, you have no choice, so you play before you're chopped up by a meat slicer in a slaughterhouse.

And there went my imagination.

I squeezed my phone in my hand. "Where are you?" I yelled again.

Upstairs, came the text finally.

Jerk.

Fine. Fuck you, then. I stepped up the stairs. "If I have to find you, you're going to bleed," I said.

But then a text rolled in.

Getting warmer now.

I looked left to right, keeping alert as I slowly climbed the stairs. "Why are you doing this?"

But only a one-word response came as I took another step.

Warmer.

A cool sweat broke out across my forehead. The floorboards under my shoes creaked as I reached the top of the stairs, looking right and seeing the bedroom door wide open. I could see the bottom of the bed and sheer white curtains blowing in the wind coming through the open window. I didn't think that was open the last time I was here. I couldn't remember.

Instead, I turned right, heading for the other bedroom.

Cold.

I stopped, breathing hard. So, he was in the master bedroom. I couldn't swallow.

Get a grip. He's fucking with you.

Turning around, I headed back for the master.

My phone vibrated, and I looked down.

Can I tell you something else?

"What?" I growled low.

And the next text rolled in.

You'll never leave this house.

My mouth fell open, I stopped breathing, and I couldn't piece together one fucking coherent thought. Kai . . .

I spun around to bolt, but there he was. He stepped out of the bathroom, dressed in jeans, a black hoodie, and his silver skull mask.

I halted, rearing back as I gasped. "Wha . . ."

Everything was black. He was merely a shape. The dark clothes, the shroud of night, the black of his eyes . . . only the whites were visible, letting me know there was a man in there.

"Kai . . ." I held out my hands. Fuck, why couldn't I think?!

A silvery tingle hit me low, and I clenched my thighs, suddenly feeling like I had to go to the bathroom.

He slowly stalked toward me, putting one foot in front of another, and I scrambled with shaking hands, snatching my blade out of my pocket.

"Back the fuck off!" I choked out, holding the blade in front of me.

But he just kept walking, each step in perfect time, until I was against the wall, right outside the master bedroom.

He didn't stop, and I darted out, growling. "I'm not scared of you."

He cocked his head, his mask seeming to say *Oh, yes, you are.*

The space between us got smaller and smaller, and I lashed out, trying to scare him. He grabbed my hand, though, and I cried out as he tore the blade from my fingers, flinging it off over the railing. I heard it clatter to the ground, somewhere downstairs.

Pinning my wrists to the wall at my sides, he pressed his body into mine and held me to the wall.

I sucked in air, short and fast, because my chest couldn't expand with him on me like that.

And he just stayed there.

His head tilted down at me.

Watching me.

I couldn't even hear him breathe. The only indication he was alive was the rise and fall of his chest against mine.

"What do you want with me?" I breathed out, sobs lodged in my throat.

Why wasn't he saying anything?

The house moaned around us as the wind kicked up again and whirred through the little cracks in the walls.

And I was just there. Alone, no one for miles, and a mask hovering over me and feeling like a knife at my throat.

Fuck, I was scared. Oh, God, oh, God . . .

Sweat broke out over my back, and heat spread down my legs where his body touched mine. Our thighs layered, one of his between both of mine, my chest becoming sensitive and aware of the heat of his body. His groin was pressed against mine and the pressure increased between us, even though we weren't moving.

Fuck . . .

And I still couldn't breathe. I couldn't breathe because I was throbbing everywhere. My body was pulsing and heating, and I wanted to scream, bite, and . . .

Give in.

Why didn't I want to run?

I let my head fall forward, into his chest, exhausted and hungry and wanting to dig my claws into something.

"I'm scared," I whispered. "I'm scared of you even with your mask off."

Because of everything you make me feel.

He didn't move. Just held me there, his grip on my wrists loosening a little.

I looked up, speaking low as my lips brushed his mask. "I . . ." I didn't know what to say.

Am I really just leverage in this cat-and-mouse game between you and Damon? Just a tool?

I mean, Rika was right, wasn't she? He could've just taken me if that's all it was about. He wanted me to choose him in that guesthouse.

He wanted *me*.

And I wanted him to know I had to make an impossible choice. But in my head, tucked away where I kept my secrets, it would always be him. Ten years . . . twenty years down the road I would watch him from a distance and see him build his life and be happy if he was happy.

I wanted him to know I loved our foreplay.

I wanted him to know I loved him.

"I wish I could keep you," I said. "People like me don't get what they want, though. They earn what they need to survive, and even if there weren't so many secrets between us, I don't fit in your world, Kai."

"My world?" he said, looking down at me. "Wanna see my world?"

And he stepped away from me, walking into the master bedroom.

Huh? What did that mean?

I took a deep breath, feeling like I was going to fall without him there to hold me up, but I forced myself to straighten and follow him.

I suddenly heard a scraping sound matched with a dull thunder, and I snapped my head up, walking into the bedroom and seeing Kai pull out an entire panel of the wall.

What the hell?

The fireplace—or fake fireplace, I guessed—was attached to a section of flooring that swerved outward, opening the wall from floor to ceiling.

There was a secret passageway.

Without looking back at me, he disappeared through the hole and left the entrance open.

Where was he going?

This house was starting to make a little more sense. I knew there had to be a reason he bought it.

Carefully stepping up to the opening, I peeked in, my eyes falling on the only thing in there. A staircase. It led down, with lighting strung along the wall, and I tuned my ear, listening for noises. But I heard nothing. Not even the sound of his steps.

"Kai?" I called. "Where are you?"

But my words just fell into the void. How deep did this go?

I tucked my hair behind my ear and tightened my jacket against the chilly draft as I walked in. And descended. I left the door open, though, just in case.

The steps were sandstone, and the walls were lined with wiring connecting the lighting installed in small intervals. I continued down the spiral staircase, hugging the wall for support and feeling the air getting crisper the farther I went. Circle after circle after circle; I had to blink several times to keep from getting dizzy.

What was all this for?

After what seemed like forever, I finally reached the bottom, and I looked ahead, seeing a tunnel. Moonlight streamed in from above, and I knew I shouldn't be scared, but I was a little. If Kai was hiding this, what else was he hiding? *Just go, Banks. The less you know, the more you fear, so go learn more.*

I walked along, keeping my eyes and ears alert as I stepped over the steel-grate flooring and looked down to see a stream of water. Looking up, I saw another grate and the black sky with stars above. It was a sewer for rain runoff. The rock walls and tunnel had been constructed several decades ago, most likely. There were arches to my right, and I could tell the tunnel used to veer off to provide access to other areas of the city, but the passageways had been bricked off. There was only one way to go. Straight.

"Kai?" I called again, looking ahead. "Kai, are you down there?"

Of course he didn't answer. Maybe he couldn't hear me anymore.

I sped up my steps and headed down the tunnel, coming to another stairwell. I looked up, unable to see the top. It just kept going.

I swallowed, my throat so dry. I hadn't had anything to eat or drink for hours.

Well, up was good, at least. The top must come out at ground level.

I jogged up, repeatedly glancing behind me to make sure no creepy things were on my tail. My muscles began to burn, and I slowed a little, not used to such a steep incline. Where did this go?

Reaching the top, I spotted a door opening into a room, just like the one I'd come through.

I reached out and pushed the wall open a little more to get a better look, the partition easily sliding away. What the hell was this?

I stepped into a massive room with vaulted ceilings and furnishings. Hardwood floors gleamed in the light coming from the burning fireplace, and a long Persian rug lay under the black leather couches and fancy wooden tables. Art adorned the walls, a silver lamp sat on a desk strewn with papers, and I heard music coming from somewhere outside the study.

My pulse raced.

I followed the sound through the room and stepped into a large foyer, my head falling back and my eyes taking in the empty space above me as I turned in a circle.

"Oh, my God." I trembled.

Another room, a living room, I think, sat across the hall, a wide staircase rose behind me, and two other hallways stretched on either side of the stairs, leading to the back of the . . .

House.

This was a house.

His house.

Everything I expected Kai's house to be and more.

I could smell the fresh paint as I took in the ornate frames that adorned the pictures on the walls, and the beautiful tables, chairs, and sofas spread out throughout the study and living room. A crystal chandelier hung above me, tinkling with the slight breeze coming in from the tunnel.

It was a house designed by a man who cared about detail, reflecting both his Japanese and Italian heritages. Sleek, balanced, and uncluttered, but also ornate, rich in detail, and lush like a European manor.

I walked up the black staircase, following the music as my body flooded with adrenaline. Did his friends know about this place?

It was large and spacious, but also dark and cozy. Like a hidden chamber shrouded from the outside world.

Like he'd created his own personal confessional right here.

Or . . . his own Bell Tower, grave, The Pope . . .

Upstairs, I trailed down hallways, following the soft voice singing a song I finally recognized to be some version of "Paint It, Black," and I passed a bedroom with the door open and stopped.

The black four-poster bed was perfectly made, white sheets, comforter, and pillows, and I stepped in, seeing a framed picture on the wall. A black night with a red sun, rain, cranes flying . . .

And there was that Japanese symbol in the center again. The same one from Sensou's sign.

War. That's what it meant. Just like the name of the place.

I heard the shower shut off, and I walked toward the doorway, turning a corner toward the en suite.

Kai stood at the large round mirror with a towel wrapped around his waist, combing his hands through his hair. Droplets of water glistened on his back, and steam filled the room.

"Kai."

He paused, fixing his eyes on me through the mirror.

"What is this?" I asked, slowly entering.

"The house on the hill."

"And this is your house?" I clarified. "Your real house?"

I knew it was—his scent was everywhere—but I wasn't sure what I knew and didn't know anymore, and I needed to hear him say it.

He nodded, smirking. "You didn't actually think I lived in that dump, did you?"

I snorted, but I was so damn ready to cry, too. I was so exhausted. "Kai, Jesus—"

I started to protest, wanting to question him about what the hell was going on and why he hid this place, but he turned, shaking his head.

"Just give me ten minutes, okay?" he said, looking just as weary as I was. "Just give me ten minutes with you, and then we can get serious."

Walking over to me, he peeled off my jacket and set it down on a bench near the tub.

Which was running with water. Bubbles rose higher as the fountain faucet poured water into the deep, white basin, and it was my instinct to fight him, but he spoke up, cutting me off.

"I'll explain everything in ten minutes."

My eyelids drooped, and I didn't know what time it was, but it had to be late. I let him undress me.

Everything came off, and he didn't try to grope or kiss me, although I wouldn't have really minded if I wasn't so tired.

"Get in the tub," he told me.

I stepped in, immediately feeling delicious chills spread up my legs as the heat of the water soaked my skin.

Slowly, I sat down, submerging myself up to my chest, and brought my knees up, hugging them. Kai pulled off his towel, and I thought he was getting in, but he grabbed some lounge pants and slipped them on.

Something under my skin jolted at the sight of his nakedness, and I bit my lip. He looked up, and I looked away, but I could feel his stupid smile at catching me staring.

Moving my clothes to the counter, he sat down on the bench and grabbed a bath sponge, dipping it into the water.

Then he pushed all of my hair over my shoulder and began soaping my back.

I twisted my head, reaching for the sponge. "I can do it."

But he pulled it away, saying gently, "I know you can."

I didn't like people doing things for me. It was uncomfortable being taken care of. I wasn't used to it.

Dipping the sponge in again, he squeezed the water over my back, letting it cascade down my skin, and I closed my eyes, surrendering.

"Oh," I breathed out.

My head fell to the side as he rubbed the hot sponge over my shoulder and up my neck, and it felt like a blanket I never wanted to leave. We didn't speak, and he didn't order me about, simply tipping my head back and pouring water over my hair before he washed it, and I kept my eyes closed the entire time. His fingers on my scalp, the hot water over my head, and the smell of him and his body wash made me dizzy and high, and I'd never felt so good.

I almost felt happy.

After he rinsed my hair, he washed my body, slipping the sponge between my legs, and I grew more alert, opening my eyes.

"Use your hands," I told him. "They feel better."

I saw his lips turn up in a smile, and he put the sponge down, soaping up his hands.

Slipping them between my legs, he hovered close as he washed me.

I was about to close my eyes again, but I heard a phone beep.

He turned his head, trying to see the screen where it lay on the counter. Then he let out a sigh and pulled his hands away, drying them off.

"What is it?" I sat up, hugging my knees again.

He stared at the phone, swiping the screen and reading. He frowned and tucked the cell into his pocket, standing up.

"Michael," he told me, leaning down and kissing my forehead. "He's at the gate. I need to go deal with him. I have clothes in the bedroom, so find whatever you want to sleep in, and I'll grab some food on my way back up, okay?"

I nodded, reluctantly letting him go. He walked out, and I watched him until he disappeared down the hallway.

So, obviously his friends knew where he lived, then.

Although, I wondered if they'd ever been up here. In my research there was never any indication that Kai had this hideaway. I never saw him or his friends come to this house.

It was beautiful, though. And of course, I was right all along. There was no way he lived in that hovel.

I finished washing and pulled the plug on the water, rising to my feet. Picking up a towel off the nearby rack, I dried myself, wiping away all the suds, and wrapped the soft, thick fabric around my body.

After I brushed out my hair—and got nosy, smelling his cologne—I went into the bedroom and pulled one of his T-shirts out of a drawer. I'd always worn my brother's stuff, because that's what he gave me to wear, but I smiled, putting on Kai's shirt. I wanted to feel his clothes on me and his smell around me.

Glancing at the empty doorway, I quickly slipped it on and then took the towel back into the bathroom, tossed it in the hamper, and folded my clothes lying on the counter.

"No!" I heard a shout and stopped, turning my head.

"How could you take her anywhere near that piece of shit?" another voice bellowed.

Michael. I was surprised I could hear him all the way up here.

I dropped the clothes and crept lightly back through the bedroom and back down the hall, coming to the top of the stairs.

Looking over, I saw that the foyer was empty, but I was in just a shirt. I wasn't going down there if people were here. I walked to the top step and stopped, hearing shuffling coming from the study.

"I don't need to clear anything through you. She makes her choices!" Kai growled back.

She? Meaning me?

"Rika is mine!" Michael's voice lowered, but the fury was just as strong. "*My* partner, if you have any concept of what the hell that even means. We make decisions together!"

"You know, I'm right here!" I heard Rika yell. "Talk to me!"

Oh, they were talking about Rika.

And I guessed Michael had found out about the dinner tonight. Kai wasn't supposed to let Rika go to Gabriel's, I guessed?

I spotted Will hanging back near the wall, his arms crossed as he just watched.

Kai continued. "You were the one who said she was one of us. She can carry her weight. She's an equal, so—"

"She's not equal!" Michael shouted.

And everyone fell silent.

Dammit, I wished I could see their faces.

"She will never be equal!" he went on. "She will always mean more than you."

My heart pumped wildly, and I could only picture Kai's face as those words hung in the air. Was he hurt Michael would say that?

But if it were me, wouldn't I expect to mean more to the man I was going to marry than his friends?

Judging from the silence coming from the room, everyone was realizing the dynamics of their little crew were getting a very clear dose of reality.

"I love you guys," Michael said, "but are you fucking dense? You're my friends. *She* is *everything*. Maybe someday you'll know what the fuck I'm talking about."

And the next thing I knew, he stalked out into the foyer toward the door, holding Rika's hand as she cast a mournful look back at the guys. I reared back, out of sight.

I could tell she was sorry they got yelled at, but what do you do? Michael had been scared for her.

And he certainly wasn't the only man who didn't want his woman around my father.

They left, and Kai and Will filtered into the foyer, looking the worse for wear.

"What does this mean?" Will asked him, looking at his friend.

But Kai just stared at the door Michael had left through. "It means we need new Horsemen."

CHAPTER 22

BANKS

Present

Hello, hello?" A cheery voice pierced my sleep.

I squeezed my eyes shut tighter, finally noticing the light shining through my lids. What the hell? I was deadweight.

I yawned, rolling over and stretching my arms into the air as I registered a door closing and the rustling of bags.

"Did I wake you?"

"Duh," I grumbled, recognizing Alex's voice.

Seriously, what was it with this chick? Every time I turned around she was breaching my safe space. I wished she didn't like me so much.

I blinked my eyes open, yawning again. "What time is it?"

Not waiting for an answer, I turned left and right, searching the bedside tables in Kai's room for a clock. I must've fallen asleep before he even got upstairs last night. He and Will had to talk, so I lay down, in his shirt, to wait.

"There's no clocks in here," I thought out loud, sitting up.

"Yeah." She sauntered over and plopped down on the bed next to me, on the mussed side where Kai must've slept.

I frowned, kind of disappointed we slept in the same bed for the first time and I was passed out.

"This house is another dimension where time doesn't exist, apparently." She did spirit fingers at me, oohing like a ghost.

Holding her phone up, she checked the screen. "It's two thirty."

"In the afternoon?"

She nodded, fitting an arm under her head. "You must've been tired."

"And Kai just left me here?" I threw off the covers.

"Of course not. He worked from home today," she explained, "so he's been here the whole time, but now he's busy with the caterers, and I just got here, so he asked me to wake you."

I looked at her. "Caterers?"

"For the party?" she pointed out, jogging my memory. "The pajama party Will wanted to have for Devil's Night?"

Oh, yeah. I'd vaguely heard about that. I hadn't realized Kai was hosting, though.

I stood up, smelling coffee and bread. I noticed a tray sitting near the door. "But Devil's Night isn't for a couple more days," I told her.

"Yes, but they're men now. No parties on work nights."

She smiled sweetly, and I looked around for my clothes. Oh, right. I'd left them in the bathroom.

"I have so much to do." I dived into the en suite, but my clothes weren't on the counter where I'd folded and left them. They weren't anywhere. *Shit!*

If Kai signed the contract, then maybe Damon got word and would be home anytime. I needed to talk to him. Had he told Kai the truth about Natalya?

"You have nothing to do," she called, her voice getting closer, "nothing to worry about, and nothing to think about. Kai's handling your boss, there's no word about Damon's return yet, and Kai has absolutely nothing for you to do today. So, eat."

I walked back into the bedroom as she set the tray of food on the bed.

"I can't eat," I told her. "I can't stay here. I . . ."

I trailed off, heading over to the chest of drawers. Yanking open a couple of them, I checked for some kind of clothes, finally locating a pair of lounge pants in the third drawer down.

"You can do anything you want," she told me, her tone stern. "And I'd say we're all due for some fun, wouldn't you?"

I half smiled, unable to help myself. *What is this thing you speak of? Fun? Never heard of it.*

"If you leave," Alex said, "Kai's just going to follow you. And then all of us will follow him. And I think trouble knows where we are and has always known, and one night will make no difference."

I paused. Yeah, Kai *would* follow me. I had no doubt that was true. If, by some miracle, I found Damon, I needed him alone.

"Now . . ." She smiled while walking over to the boutique bags sitting on the chair, a light in her eyes as if she'd won the argument. "Knowing your shyness, I took the liberty of picking out special pj's for you for the party tonight."

Hours later—and a couple drinks coerced into me by Alex—I guessed I was ready to head down to the party, which was already in full swing. Kai had left the house after I ate the late lunch Alex had brought me, so I hadn't seen him at all since last night.

I wondered if he was worried. Or in a bad mood over the fight with Michael last night. Or if he was angry with me. He might see it as my fault, feeling forced to sign that contract, and even though I knew it wasn't, I also knew we kept digging ourselves in deeper. And *that* was definitely, in part, my fault.

If he knew Damon was my brother, he might understand why my feelings were so strong for him and not expect me to make choices he knew I couldn't make.

I should tell him. One less secret, right? But there was no guarantee he'd give up the vendetta, and what was more, he hadn't used me as leverage yet, but he could. I didn't want him knowing *exactly* what he had in his grasp.

But I definitely needed to talk to Kai. What was he going to do about the contract? What if Vanessa showed up here?

And why had he kept this house off the radar? Why the secret entrance?

Ugh. Maybe I should wear those "pajamas" Alex got for me, after all. Perhaps his one-track mind would kick in and he might be more forthcoming?

Yeah, no. There was no way I was wearing a black halter top with panties clearly visible underneath a long sheer skirt. She even tried to get me into heels, for crying out loud.

I ripped everything off and dug in Kai's drawers until I found a pair of boxers. I slipped them on and donned a fresh white-collared shirt of his from the closet. I let her put a little makeup on me— some eyeliner, mascara, and lipstick—but my hair stayed messy. I told her I was going for the cute bed-head look, but really, I just wasn't ready to go full force. Not that I might not like dressing up and having my hair done, but one thing at a time. I needed to feel some semblance of familiarity. Too much was happening too fast.

But at least I was more covered than she was in her tiny red silk boxers with lace trim and pinstriped corset. I might try on something like that but definitely in private.

"Come on." She pulled my hand.

Stepping into the hallway, I was taken aback by how dark it was. I looked both ways, noticing how the lights from earlier were now turned down and, instead, lit candles glowed atop holders on small tables lining the hallway. Music drifted up from below, and I could hear the doorbell ringing.

Laughter and faint chatter mixed with the clacks of heels and tinkling of glasses.

We headed down toward the staircase, but as soon as we reached the top step and I saw all the people, some I recognized as old classmates of Damon's from Thunder Bay and others as Storm players from Michael's team, I locked up.

"I don't like . . ." I pulled my hand away from hers. "I'm not sure I belong here. I don't like this. I feel . . ."

I didn't know what to say. My body was covered, and I'd run around The Pope all those years ago in boxer shorts, too, but now . . .

Look at all those women. Dressed in lingerie. Sexy. Tan. Beautiful. I didn't want to dress like that, but I also didn't feel like I fit in like this, either. The only person I wanted to wear stuff like that for was Kai, and I couldn't do this. This was his scene, not mine.

I took a step back. It would be more fun to stay up here and explore the rest of the house anyway. There were dozens of rooms, and an attic, I was sure. Not to mention, if there was one secret passageway in the study, there were bound to be more. Anything would be more fun than this.

But hands caught my hips from the back, and Kai's whisper was suddenly in my ear.

"Where do you think you're going?"

I folded my arms over my chest. "I don't flaunt myself for the enjoyment of men."

His chest shook with a laugh behind me. "Well, good. Happy to hear it, because I'm the only man whose attention you should be trying to get, and baby, you got it years ago while wearing another man's clothes." He kissed my temple, his hot breath sending chills down my spine. "So, you can imagine how fucking beautiful you are to me right now wearing mine."

My heart fluttered, and all of a sudden I felt braver.

Without another word, he walked past me, down the stairs, to greet his guests. I stared at the muscles in his back, visible since he only wore pajama pants like a lot of the other guys, and felt myself heat up again.

But I no longer felt nervous. I started down the stairs with Alex.

The party wasn't actually as busy as I thought. He could've easily packed over a hundred people on the bottom floor, but there seemed to only be about seventy to eighty of their gang's close, personal friends. Basketball players, business associates, old high school friends . . .

And the place was set up like a slumber party, in keeping with Will's theme of pajamas.

Tables filled the dining room, covered with an assortment of snacks, and "Heavy in Your Arms" played over a sound system around the house.

Servers circulated with more hors d'oeuvres, including wine-glasses filled with milk and topped with a huge chocolate chip M&M'S cookie. I smiled, loving how it reminded me of being a kid. Not any of *my* memories of being a child, per se, but how a kid ought to grow up. Massive pillows were also flung in piles, while young women, some in sexy little nighties and some in men's paja-mas like me, lay down, snacked, and chatted.

There was even a beautiful tent in the corner of the living room made out of sheets and strung with white Christmas lights on the inside.

"This seems so unlike Kai." I looked around, noticing how the atmosphere had made people kind of playful. Some guy, well over six feet, was diving into the tent after his squealing girlfriend.

"It's not like him at all." She downed a shot of Patrón and sucked on a lime wedge. "I planned this."

"Why?"

She shrugged. "Will needed to have some fun with his friends.

Kai thought it was a good idea, so he opened up the house. Finally."

She handed me a shot, but I waved her off. I was still nervous, and I wanted to keep my head clear.

"If Kai had more skill," a man said, "he would figure out how to have you without signing a contract."

I whirled around, seeing Michael approach me. And he didn't look like he was teasing.

But Kai followed, shaking his head.

"Shut up," he grumbled.

Michael wore black pajama pants and no shirt, scanning me up and down. "You clean up nice." He smiled, lowering his voice to a whisper. "Even better than the last time I saw you in pajamas."

I stopped breathing, and he turned toward the party, both he and Kai watching everyone as I waited for the shoe to drop. The last time he saw me in pajamas was six years ago, and while Kai would assume he was talking about all of us at The Pope that night, Michael's hushed whisper was insinuating how he'd sneaked into Damon's bed and on top of me before that. How he'd discovered I was Damon's sister.

So, Michael knew who I was. So, what? He also knew it didn't change anything, and Michael didn't interfere when it wasn't necessary. Damon always liked that about him. While Will was nosy and Kai tried to rein Damon in, Michael rarely interfered with how Damon wanted to have a good time.

Kai was going to find out, but I hoped he wouldn't just yet.

"You two were about to come to blows last night," I pointed out, changing the subject. "What happened?"

Why was he suddenly attending a party at Kai's house, acting like everything was fine?

Michael swallowed his beer, bringing his glass down. "Nothing. We fight, and we move on. We're not girls."

Idiot.

"What the hell is she wearing?" Kai asked, looking out toward the foyer.

I followed his gaze, seeing Rika enter and hand her coat to the attendant. She wore sleep shorts with avocados all over them and a matching shirt that read *I Avo Crush on You.*

Michael started laughing under his breath, shaking his head. "I can't believe she still has those pajamas. My mom gave them to her when she was like fifteen, and I felt so bad for her. But she wore 'em anyway. That's what she must've gone back home for today, I guess."

He walked over to her, and she tried to hide her embarrassed smile as he scooped her up in his arms and laughed with her.

"So, we could wear just regular pajamas?" I eyed Alex, who avoided my glare.

"Like I said, you can do whatever you want."

Yeah.

I needed to get the hang of that.

*S*econd *door after the stairs.*

The candles were burning down, so Kai asked me to grab a handful more from the closet in the hallway. I knew some of the doors led off to the basement or were used as coat closets, so I found the one indicated and turned the knob.

It went deep. Shelves lined the back as well as the sides, and I stepped in, my finger hooked into the loop of the candleholder as I reached up to yank the chain for the bulb.

The chain clicked, but the light didn't go on. I looked around me, still able to see fairly well with the candle I'd carried in.

Okay. *Candles, candles, candles . . . Where are you?*

Bending over, I set my holder down and scanned the shelves, moving things out of the way and kind of wondering why I was searching for candles when there were flashlights and batteries right here in front of me. But rich people liked having parties by candlelight, so . . .

I looked over, finally spotting the candles on the other side.

But suddenly, the door slammed shut, and the room darkened more, leaving only the light from my small candle. I shot up, twisting around.

"So, I hear you kicked Rika's ass," Michael said, blocking the door and moving toward me. He was tall and imposing, and there was no way around him.

My heart pounded harder, but I shook it off.

It was just Michael.

"I didn't walk away unscathed," I said, turning back around and grabbing some tapers out of the box.

"And I heard you made a comment about taking it 'in both ends.'"

I laughed under my breath, facing him again. "And you're here to fight for her honor?"

"Rika can fight her own battles."

Clearly.

And clearly she had no choice but to do just that, because it would never occur to Michael to be jealous or possessive or angry. He would never be troubled with grand gestures, would he?

I shook my head. "God, do you have any pride?"

He pushed me back against the shelves, and I dropped the candles.

Leaning in, I could barely see anything but his broad chest in front of me as he hovered. I tried to control my breathing.

"How about this?" he asked, seething. "Rika is my earliest memory, and I've loved her forever. The sun rises with her. It always has. And everything we do, we do together. Everything." He bared his teeth. "No one judges us, and we'll roll right over anyone who tries. You got that? Look in the fucking mirror the next time you want to cast aspersions on her character. All you'll see is your own self-hate and jealousy. What you don't know about us is a lot."

I stared right back at him, neither of us faltering, but my pulse was racing a mile a minute now. Would I have minded if Rika had Will in that steam room?

No. I might not have shared her open mind, but I wouldn't have cared. He was right. It was jealousy.

And it was my problem. Not hers.

Light fell into the closet, and I looked over Michael's shoulder to see Kai standing there. He must've come looking for me.

Michael turned around, but he didn't move out from in front of me. I reached down and picked up the candles as Kai's eyes narrowed on the scene. I was sure it looked bad.

"What's going on?" I heard a female voice and looked up to see Rika standing next to Kai and looking in.

Oh, awesome. The whole party's here.

"I was just about to ask that myself," Kai said, still staring at Michael.

And Michael finally moved aside. "Just setting her straight."

Kai walked in, and Rika followed, closing the door.

"Are you okay?" he asked, approaching me.

"She's fine," Michael offered.

"I was asking her."

Kai glared at his friend, but Rika stepped forward, placing herself between them.

"You didn't need to say anything," she told Michael. "If the situation were reversed, I'd feel just as weird about it."

"I don't feel weird," I interjected. "How's the nose, by the way?"

She shook her head, giving me a half smile. Walking up, she said, "I'm not a threat to you, okay? I love Kai, but I'm not a threat to you."

"I don't care." I moved around them. "Let me out."

"I think you do care." Michael stepped into my path, but he didn't touch me. "Real bad, in fact. And I kind of understand. Wanna get even?"

I paused, looking up at him, confused. "What?"

Even? As in . . . ?

"What are you talking about?" Rika asked him.

He turned to her, casting a quick glance at Kai. "Kai got you. Why shouldn't I have her once?"

"You're out of your mind!" Kai pushed in, inching into Michael's space. "I don't share."

"Since when?" His friend straightened, both walls rigid as they dared each other. "Why don't you let her make the choice? See what she says."

Kai looked completely out of sorts. Like he wasn't sure if he should laugh or fight.

I stood there with my mouth hanging open just slightly and still trying to figure out if this was a joke.

Rika didn't look at all confused, though. She stared at Michael, looking worried.

"You're very beautiful," Michael said, turning back to me, his eyes softening. "Rika had Kai. Do you want to have me? And then everyone's even?"

I was dumbfounded. He wasn't serious.

"Michael." Rika stepped up. "I don't like this game."

"Am I playing?" he asked her.

And she tensed.

I met Kai's eyes, and his gaze bored into me. He might be waiting for what I had to say on the matter, but if I chose wrong, he was going to step in.

He wasn't sharing.

And I fought a smile, but I didn't want him to.

I watched Rika stare at Michael and him look back, and then his eyes faltered, weakening at the sight of her.

He was playing with me. She was his, and he was hers, and they knew who and what they wanted.

But I still didn't like Michael messing with me. I could play, too.

I pushed him back. "Screwing you puts me on an even keel with her?" I told him. "I don't set my sights that low. I want to be on an even keel with Kai."

His eyebrows dug in; he wasn't following me. I met Rika's eyes. And she broke out in a smile. "She is clever, isn't she?"

"What's going on?" Michael looked between Rika, Kai, and me. "What does that mean?"

Reaching out, Rika took my hand and gently pulled me over to her. "It means, if Kai got to have me, so does she." And then she looked at Michael. "What? Fair's fair, right?"

He frowned, turning to Kai, who stood there looking just as shocked.

My heart raced, and I wasn't sure if I was bluffing when I said it, or I just hadn't thought that far ahead yet when I ran at the mouth like I always did, but I knew one thing. I loved the feel of Kai's eyes on my back right now. I loved him watching me, and I knew everything was for him.

She put her hands on my hips, and I opened my mouth to protest. "I don't—"

"What does he do that you like?" she whispered, leaning in close.

"Um . . . teeth?" I stammered. "He bites my lips."

She panted, her mouth hovering over mine. "Yeah, I like it when Michael does that, too." And she did it, thrusting out and dragging my bottom lip between her teeth.

I whimpered, my breath shaking with my growing desire.

"Except Michael," she breathed in my ear, "bites me down here."

And she took my hand and made me touch myself. I smiled excitedly. "Shit."

She kissed me, and I placed my hands on her hips, kissing her back. What the fuck was I doing?

She closed her eyes, biting my lips again and flicking my top lip with her tongue, her hot, sweet breath warming me all over. I moaned, a nerve between my legs starting to throb.

"You should see them," she whispered, nibbling my ear. "They're about to lose their minds."

I shook with a quiet laugh and tilted my head back, letting her lips devour my neck. I loved him watching me. Loved him seeing me feel pleasure.

Bringing my head down again, I let my hair fall in my eyes as I leaned in close to her, pressing our bodies together.

And I took charge. I pushed her back, we fell into the shelves, and I held her face as I kissed her again, surprised when she moaned and ground on me.

"Touch me," she panted against my lips.

"Oh, shit," Michael gasped.

And I smiled, diving in for her mouth again and again as I slowly slipped my hands up her shirt. She took that as a cue and pulled the T over her head, leaving her topless. I bit my lip and met her eyes, holding them as my hand rose and cupped a breast.

She breathed out a groan.

"Banks," I heard Kai breathe out, but I didn't look at him.

Rika started unbuttoning my shirt, and every nerve under my skin craved to be touched. I couldn't get it off fast enough. I could feel Kai's tongue on my spine even though he wasn't touching me. I felt his teeth and his hands on my breasts.

The shirt fell to the floor, and we came together, pressing our bodies together as my nipples brushed hers. I ate up her lips again, wanting to see Kai's face so badly. But I didn't know if I should turn around. I didn't want to break the spell yet. What if he was angry?

We kissed and licked and panted and bit, and every inch of my skin cooled with sweat as she squeezed my right breast and ran her tongue up my throat. We grasped each other's hips, grinding on each other. God, I was wet.

"Take off her boxers, Rika," Kai suddenly said in a husky voice. Like he was out of breath.

Rika grinned, encouraged. She slipped her fingers inside my waistband and yanked it down. I smiled, stepping out of them.

I did the same to her, pushing down her sleep shorts, nearly all of our clothes piled on the floor as we continued to buck and grind.

And I finally turned my head, while she nibbled my ear. Michael stood behind us, but Kai had moved to the corner by the door to get a better look. He watched, his body painfully tense, and his cock a hard, thick ridge jutting against his pants.

We both looked at the boys as we held each other close, cheek to cheek, as Rika left feathery little kisses on the corner of my lips.

"We want to get fucked," she said to Michael.

I nodded, a smile dancing across my lips as I watched Kai's dark eyes and slipped my hands down the back of her panties, taunting him.

He stalked over, threaded his fingers through my hair, and pulled my head back, kissing me so hard and rough he stole my breath.

Before I knew it, Rika was swept away, and I heard a tear of fabric before Michael's raspy whisper, "God, Little Monster, I love you."

Kai bent me over, my panties were yanked down, and I put my hands on the shelves in front of me as his cock crowned me. I had time to suck in a quick breath, and then he was thrusting, sheathing himself in me in one move.

I cried out, feeling him bottom out, the sweet pain touching me so deep. I looked over, briefly seeing Rika's front pressed into the shelves as Michael held her knee out to the side, opening her for him as he thrust up and inside of her. His head was buried in her neck, and she reached around, holding the back of his neck as he went at her hard and fast.

Kai growled, fisting my hair and pulling my head back. "I think you enjoyed that too much," he said in my ear. "Did you?"

I whimpered, barely able to think as I closed my eyes. "Well, I'm not going to try to break her nose anymore, if that's what you mean."

He let out a little laugh. "Good."

And he pulled me up more, and I twisted my head, tasting his mouth as the room filled with moaning and panting. Then I pulled back, looking up into his eyes as he fucked me.

I wouldn't stop him. I wouldn't ever stop him. What was done was done, and I'd steal and covet all the moments we had left. I closed my eyes, savoring the feel of him for my memory.

He gripped my hips and breathed in my ear. "I like you, little one."

I smiled, hating that stupid nickname as much as when he called me "kid."

"I like you, too."

I love you.

Waking up the next morning, I looked and noticed Kai wasn't in bed next to me again. What time did he get up? He went to bed with me, but did he even sleep? He always seemed to be doing something, moving or thinking or running around. I wiped my eyes awake and yawned, counting the chimes of a grandfather clock somewhere in the house. It was a little after eight. Later than I usually got up, but we'd only gotten to bed six hours ago, too.

Rising, I walked to his dresser and opened the drawers, finding another pair of boxer shorts. I slipped them on and then trailed to the closet, opening the door and going wide-eyed as I was confronted with the massive space. I'd dived in here yesterday to grab a shirt for the party, but I hadn't had time to appreciate it.

I walked in. And kept walking. His smell flooded my head, and I almost felt dizzy.

The walk-in closet was exactly Kai, and I shook my head, feeling so stupid. I should've pushed harder. I knew exactly what kind of house he would have. Didn't I tell him? Beautiful décor, expensive furniture, all of his starched shirts lined up on wooden hangers with just the right amount of equal fucking space between each piece of clothing and the next, for crying out loud. A man who took pride in every single minute aspect of his life.

I ran my hands down the line of white shirts, feeling the soft, cool fabric between my fingers. Good God, I was surprised he let me touch him with my germs. I laughed to myself. He was like Christian Grey meets Howard Hughes meets Patrick Bateman. *If I find a chainsaw or an ax inside the house, I'm outta here.*

I pushed all the hangers down to the end, smashing the shirts together and wrecking his perfect little world, laughing to myself as I pulled a blue long-sleeve off a hanger. Slipping it on, I buttoned it up, locked my hands behind my back, and left the closet, whistling.

I had to get back to my place to get a change of clothes at some point. I'd been in Kai's clothes for two days now.

Leaving the bedroom, I walked down the hallway and descended the stairs, heading around the banister, toward the dining room. The caterers had cleaned up all their setup last night after most of the guests had left, but I caught sight of the sheet tent still sitting in the living room and pillows scattered about.

"He's not at The Pope. We searched the twelfth floor," I heard Kai say.

I slowed down, stopping right before the dining room.

"Are you sure he's not on another floor?" Michael asked.

"Yes. He's not fucking there."

Damon.

I peeked in, seeing Kai and his friends, including Will, Michael, and Rika, lounging around the table as they nibbled some breakfast. No one was really dressed yet, still wearing their sleepwear.

Rika held up a large yellow envelope, her other hand fanning over a pile of little boxes. Were those matches?

"We don't know this is from him," she told Kai.

"Who else would it be from?"

"Look at the postmark!" she burst out, sounding angry as she tossed the envelope at him across the table. "It's from Mexico City. He's not here."

"Look at the matchbooks!" he growled back. "He could've had anyone mail this from anywhere he wanted. And he addressed it to you. This is a message. He's not just threatening me anymore."

He grabbed the envelope and flung it back at her.

Matchbooks. I studied the pile of small boxes and books on the table that had obviously come in the envelope, seeing a silver box that I recognized right away as being from Realm, a nightclub the guys frequented here in Meridian City. Were they all from this area? Was that why Kai was worried?

Michael ran his hands through his hair and down over his face.

"So, what are you going to do?" she challenged Kai. "Lose your minds running around in circles while he laughs at us? Damon is playing games. He won't do anything."

"How do you know?"

"Because he had a dozen chances with me last year, and he stopped! Every time!" She rose from her seat, pushing it in. "He enjoys fucking with our heads. That's all. Just leave it alone."

"Why do you always say that?"

Rika hesitated, staring at him. "What?"

Kai lowered his voice to normal and approached, challenging her. "Every time we want to deal with him, you tell us to leave him alone," he bit out. "He has shit on me. He tried to kill Will. What the hell is the matter with you? Why are you protecting *him*?"

Her mouth fell open, and my heart sped up. She looked affronted at the accusation.

Her eyes shot to Michael and then Will, who all stared at her the same as Kai. Protecting him? Why would they think that?

No one said anything, and then she blinked, scoffing as she grabbed her plate and walked away from all of them, toward me and the doorway.

I stepped out from behind the wall, out of her way, and she charged past me without a glance.

Kai noticed me, and his expression softened. "Are you hungry?" he asked. "There's breakfast."

I looked at the spread on the buffet table, nodding. "Yeah, in a minute."

I turned and walked past the stairs, into the study, and saw Rika disappear with her plate out into the garden.

After last night, I didn't think we were friends, but I was curious. If my brother sent her a package to scare her, why wasn't she more concerned? It wasn't only Kai picking up on her signals, either. The way Michael and Will had looked at her . . .

I followed her outside, thankful for the clouds blocking out the bright morning sun. She settled herself on the ground, leaning up against a tree. Resting her head back, she placed her plate of food at her side but didn't eat.

I walked over to her.

"Hey," I said as I crouched down and lay on the ground.

She nodded, still looking preoccupied.

"Damon sent you matchbooks?" I asked, not hesitating. "Why?"

She shrugged. "I collect them," she answered. "My father used to bring some back from his travels, and I started hoarding them. Michael carried on the tradition, bringing me back ones he finds on trips out of town I don't join him on."

So, Damon knew she liked them. "And he sent you ones from Meridian City," I figured. He wanted her to know he'd been here. Or that he was here now.

She was quiet for a while, and I wanted to ask more—ask why she wasn't angry—but we weren't friends, and I knew she didn't trust me. After what happened last night, though, I hoped we could talk a little easier.

"You grew up with Damon?" she asked.

"For a while."

She opened her mouth to speak but then stopped, hesitating.

"Did you ever . . . see anything?" she asked, picking at her thumbs in her lap. "Things that might've happened to him?"

What?

She knew?

"Did Damon tell you something?" I questioned.

"No, of course not." She shook her head. "Michael's brother, Trevor, did, though, once. I had no reason to trust him, but I can't imagine why he'd make up a story like that. It made sense, given the way Damon is."

She finally looked up, and I was afraid of what she'd say. Damon didn't want anyone to know about anything that happened at home. I couldn't talk about this.

"He said Damon's mother . . ." she said, looking like she was struggling to get the words out, "that she started hurting him when he was twelve." And then she closed her eyes, lowering her voice. "Raping him."

So, she knew. Had she told Michael?

"God, it makes me sick just thinking about it." She sucked in a breath, looking away.

But then she just shrugged, waving me off. "Never mind. It's still no excuse. I just think if he wanted to act he would've a long time ago, and we should just leave well enough alone. Maybe he's suffered, and while I'll never forgive him, let him try to find what peace he can. He's sick, and no good comes from poking a sleeping bear."

I agreed with her. It was still no excuse. Plenty of people had it rough and behaved just fine.

In theory.

But when you're in the thick of abuse and still live with the torment in your head every day, it's a little different. No one handles it. They just fake it better. How else do you cope with the terrible shit you've been through?

"He never cried," I told her, my voice quiet. "I've never seen him cry."

She remained quiet, and I turned my eyes up to the sky.

"When she'd come in, he'd make me hide," I continued, my pulse echoing in my ears. "In the closet with his headphones on. And after it was done, he would let me out, and then he'd go take a shower. Sometimes he was in there for an hour. Sometimes three or four."

Tears sprang up, and I closed my eyes.

The creaks of the bed would breach the music in my ears sometimes. I could still hear it.

"He'd stay in the shower for however long it took to get himself straight again," I told her. "Sometimes the cuts were on his arms or his chest. Depending on the season and what his clothes would cover." Silent tears streamed down my temples. "When he was fifteen, he started slicing the bottom of his feet, so he would feel it every time he walked. I didn't understand how he could run on the basketball court with the pain. His socks were soaked in blood sometimes." I looked over at her, the blue of her eyes shimmering like a pool. "And there were other things he'd do. Ways he'd make me hurt him . . ." I paused and then continued. "Until the night it was time to hurt her."

Damon had beat his mother bloody one night, and we thought that was the last we'd ever see of her. That was the night he stopped hurting himself, because he learned how good it felt for him to hurt others. He didn't need to suffer anymore.

"Damon eats pain," I told her. "He will find some way to take it and twist it and fit it down his throat, so he can swallow it. He's made of it. You all can endure it until you overcome it, but Damon . . . he wants to be in hell."

It's where he shines.

I turned my eyes back up to the sky, sliding an arm under my head. "But still . . . he never cried."

CHAPTER 23

KAI

Present

A feathery touch caressed my face, and I stirred, realizing I'd been asleep. My head was like deadweight, and I couldn't lift it.

Blinking, I saw light pour into the room and Banks lying next to me. I grinned. I'd always hated sleeping with other people—like actual sleep, in the same bed.

She was so quiet, though. And I liked seeing her the moment I woke up.

Reaching out, I snaked an arm round her waist and pulled her in close.

But she was stiff, and something was off. I closed my fingers around her skin, but it wasn't skin I was feeling. It was clothing.

I opened my eyes fully and saw that she had her head turned toward me, watching me.

Her eyes looked sad.

"What is it, baby?" I pushed myself up on my elbows and turned toward her, keeping my arm around her. "What's going on? Why are you dressed?"

She was wearing the same outfit she came in a couple days ago.

Her whisper was small as she brushed the back of her hand across my cheek. "Don't forget how this feels."

I dug in my eyebrows. "What?"

Pushing myself up, I sat on my knees and noticed her phone in her hand. An unsettling feeling hit me. What did she mean?

I grabbed her phone, and she let me, quietly watching me as I read the screen.

Look out the window.

I didn't recognize the number, and she didn't have the contact saved. No name. A single text.

I looked at her, searching for an explanation, but she seemed paralyzed.

I slid off the bed. Walking to the bedroom window, the one facing the city in the distance, I looked out, my stomach immediately sinking.

A cloud of black smoke poured into the sky, and it was coming from this side of the river. From Whitehall. I could hear the faint siren of the fire trucks from here, and a helicopter even hovered close.

"What is that?" I asked, turning my eyes on her. "What's going on?"

She swallowed, sitting up with her head bowed. She wouldn't even look at me.

"What is that?" I yelled, grabbing her and hauling her up.

Her breathing quickened. "Sensou."

No. I released her and bolted out of the room, running down the stairs. But the front door opened before I got there, and I looked up to see Michael, Will, and Rika bursting through.

Will caught me, trying to keep me from running outside.

"It's too late. It's gone," he said, pushing me back and looking pained.

My hand shot to my hair, and I stared out the front door, seeing all the smoke blacken the sky.

God, no.

Rika cried softly in the foyer, and I thought of everything I had built in that place. All my father's weapons he'd donated when I opened it up. Gone. All the records and leases, everything was there! I did all of our business out of there.

And the clientele we'd built up? Gone. It would take months to rebuild.

I clenched my fucking teeth together, the pain of the loss damn near unbearable.

"There will be more fires," I heard Banks say.

My sadness morphed into anger, and I whipped around, seeing her walk slowly down the stairs.

Damon had texted her.

"And he'll bring them to Thunder Bay, too," she warned. "It's out of Gabriel's control."

How long had she let me sleep? Just long enough for the fire to wipe out everything?

I held up the phone, checking the time on the text.

Six minutes ago.

I pressed the phone icon on the message and brought it up to my ear, letting it ring.

But a voice recording came on, saying the line was out of service. He was using a burner. I ended the call and spun around, launching the phone out into the driveway and into the brush beyond the gate.

After a moment, Michael chimed in. "Fire trucks are already there. Get dressed."

But I approached Banks as she cautiously stepped to the bottom of the staircase.

"I didn't know," she said.

"Would you have stopped him if you did?"

Hurt flashed across her eyes, but her silence said everything.

A shadow fell over the room, blocking out the sunlight, and I turned to see Gabriel's guys, the same ones who'd collected her from Michael's party that night, standing right outside the door.

The shaved-head one—David, I thought—looked past me and tipped his chin at her. "Let's go."

"She's not going anywhere." I turned, putting me between them and her.

"Vanessa is gone," David said, stepping into the house. "Someone got to her. Scared her off. She wants no part of this."

"I don't give a shit," I growled back, gesturing to Banks. "*She's* not going anywhere."

"The wedding is off. No deal," he repeated, and I moved to advance on him, but he opened his jacket, putting his hands on his hips.

It was a casual action, but a gesture with purpose to make sure I saw the gun he had tucked in a holster under his arm. I moved for him.

But Michael shot out his hand, stopping me. "They have guns. We have nothing. Be patient."

Every fucking muscle tightened, and I balled my fists, squeezing them so hard they hurt.

"Don't worry." David smirked. "We won't force her to go if she wants to stay."

I turned, meeting her eyes, and when she faltered, I knew what her decision was. My blood boiled.

Fuck you.

Maybe she was actually choosing them or maybe she thought she could keep Damon away from us if she left, but I was done trying to be the man I thought I should be. The man I was in high school.

No begging. If she liked men who took, I could take.

She walked past me, and I turned, watching her leave with them.

She spun around, walking backward as she spoke to me with tears in her eyes.

"It was all so easy," she said quietly. "All you had to do was find out my name."

I faltered. What was she talking about? I knew her name.

They left, and the four of us stared after the black SUV as it sped out of the driveway.

The smoke from the fire had drifted up into the hills, and I could smell the burning wood and tar from the roof. There would be more fires, and this was just the start. Devil's Night didn't even start until midnight.

I turned to Rika, seeing her eyes dry but red. "Now do you see?" I told her. She had to stop expecting better of him. That was our place. Our business. My livelihood.

"So, Devil's Night is coming no matter what we do," Will chimed in.

I nodded. "And we have one piece of leverage," I said, turning to Michael. "Do we want to use it?"

But strangely, he smiled. "Actually," he said. "You have another card to play."

I do?

He leaned in, crossing his arms over his chest. "Her name . . . is Nikova," he told me. "Think real hard. It will come to you."

Nik.
   I thought maybe Nikki? Maybe Nicole?

Nope.

Nikova.

The female variant of Nikov. As in Gabriel Torrance, born Gabriel Nikov, whose family adopted the more "American" surname of Torrance for their business dealings when they immigrated.

Gabriel still used Nikov, though. From time to time.

And it seemed he wouldn't allow his illegitimate daughter to have his family name, so the mother, to spite him, gave it to her for her first name.

Clever, really. It probably pissed him off, but he couldn't stop her.

"What are you doing here, boy?"

I walked into Gabriel's office, Will and Michael at my side.

Two of Gabriel's guys stood off to the back, guarding the door we'd just entered through, but my eyes flashed up to Banks, who stood at her father's side dressed in Damon's clothes again.

So much made sense now.

But it didn't make anything better.

"I've come for my bride," I said, staring down at him in his chair. "Let's get this over with."

But he just sat there. He didn't bark or yell like I thought he would.

Instead, he just shook his head, looking weary and lost in thought. "Damon . . ." He trailed off, breathing hard. "I thought he would grow out of his impulses and learn that expending energy on small potatoes like you was a waste of time." He took a puff of his cigar. "He has far more patience than I gave him credit for, though, and he is singular in his desires regarding his friends."

"We're not his friends."

"He won't stop," he assured us, actually looking regretful about that. "And he scared Vanessa off, so the contract is null and void. You should be happy."

I leaned down and placed my palms on his desk, feeling Michael and Will close in behind me. I stared at him, waiting for him to meet my eyes.

But Banks was watching me. I didn't have to look at her to know that.

He finally put his feet down and looked up.

"I'm not relishing being let off the hook," I replied calmly, biting out every word. "I'm singular, as well, and I'm not running. A deal is a deal, and you're stuck with me."

"Well, I have no more nieces to give you."

I glanced at Banks and then back at him. "You have a daughter," I pointed out.

His eyes flashed to me, I heard Banks suck in a breath, and goddamn, I nearly smiled.

"And I don't care if she walks down the aisle in those grungy jeans she's wearing right now," I told him. "Get her ass to the church tonight, and you have my word that I won't hurt your son. But if she's not there . . ."

I reached into my breast pocket and pulled out a cell phone, holding it up.

His eyes narrowed. "What is that?"

"Is that . . . ?" Banks stared at it and then looked to me. "You didn't destroy it?"

I stood back up, tucking it back into my pocket. The cell phone was our yearbook in high school. It held pictures and video of all our deeds, good and bad, including the videos of the crimes that sent Damon, Will, and me to prison.

After Damon escaped last year, we intended to destroy it, but then we decided a little leverage wasn't a bad idea. After erasing the videos that incriminated us in any further crimes, we loaded a couple flash drives with the ones of him.

And saved them.

The phone was for effect.

Of course, I could use the videos to threaten him like he was threatening me, but I still needed to know where Natalya Torrance was. I needed it dealt with.

I turned and walked for the door, my friends following.

"She's a bastard," he called out. "One of my many. What makes you think marrying her gives you any power over me? You know I don't give a shit about her."

We stopped, and I turned my head over my shoulder, my eyes instantly locking on Banks.

She stood unmoving, staring at the desktop in front of her. Instinct told me to take her out of here right now. Take her home and make sure she never had to hear anything like that again.

But she'd made her choices.

"You may not," I replied, "but Damon does. He cares about her very much, doesn't he? You could be dead in five years, but I'll have your son—and sole heir—exactly where I want him." I met Banks' eyes. "If I have her."

He took something I loved today. Now I'd take what he loved.

CHAPTER 24

BANKS

Present

Kai left the room, followed by Will and Michael, and the office fell silent until we heard the dull thud of the front door slamming shut.

Then my father launched out of his chair, swung around, and grabbed me with one hand, squeezing my jaw.

I gasped as his fingers dug in.

"I wish I could kill you," he bit out, getting in my face. "I would snap your fucking neck in a second if I didn't know that piece-of-shit son of mine would lose his little temper and do something stupid."

He shoved me away, and I fell into David, who grabbed me before I fell and righted me.

"Make sure he gets her used," he told David.

My breath shook. "What?"

But he didn't answer me. He swung around the desk and charged out of the room, leaving me alone with the guys.

I pulled away from David and scurried off to the side, putting everyone in front of me. What the hell did he mean?

One of the young guys, McCandless, moved toward me slowly, a smile in his blue eyes.

But Ilia stepped up from the other side, putting a hand on his chest, stopping him.

A moment of relief hit me. I could take on one, but I couldn't take them all. David, Lev, and Ilia wouldn't hurt me.

But then Ilia's icy-blue eyes turned toward me, and he moved, taking off his jacket. "I've wanted this for a long time," he said, tossing his jacket on my father's desk.

My stomach sank to my feet, and my mouth fell open. God, I was going to throw up.

Combing a hand through his blond hair, he reached out and grabbed me, pulling me into his body.

I growled, twisting away, shoving him, and bolting. I ran for the door, but the two guards were there, and Ilia grabbed my jacket from behind, hauling me back and throwing me to the ground.

"Ah!" I cried out, pain shooting up my back, but I quickly flipped over and scrambled away.

The patio doors were there. It was only late afternoon, but it was getting dark. I could lose them in the forest.

Something caught my ankle, though, and pulled me back. I dug my nails into the hardwood floor, trying to get my knees under me to push off, but his weight crushed me down, and I was panting for air as my lungs constricted.

My jacket, secured only with buttons, was ripped off me from behind, and my hair hung in my face, my hat having fallen off at some point.

I looked around for David and Lev, not able to get my head up very far, but I couldn't see them. Where were they? They wouldn't let this happen, would they?

I squeezed my eyes shut, shaking with a silent sob I refused to let out.

I heard a shuffle behind me, more grunts, and it sounded like a table was falling over, but I couldn't see.

And then his hand was in my jeans. They were being yanked against my hips, and everything inside kicked in. I thrashed, kicking and trying to twist around as I bared my teeth. As soon as I could face him, I was going to bite. Everything I'd told Rika to do.

He gripped my hair tight at my scalp, pushing my head into the floor as he pulled down my jeans. I clenched my jaws together, my face twisted and every muscle tight.

No.

No!

"Aren't you going to scream?" he taunted in my ear. "Cry?"

No.

I felt him working his own jeans behind me, and then he leaned in again, slipping a hand down between my legs. "You can be mine," he whispered. "Such a sweet little whore."

And I jerked up, twisting my neck more than it should've gone, and bit his cheek.

"Ugh!" he growled and turned away, loosening his grip long enough for me to shoot over and grab anything I could reach.

I latched onto the leg of a small round end table and pulled, catching a crystal bowl that tumbled off. Taking it, I swung around and smashed it into the side of Ilia's head, shards of glass falling everywhere as the dish crumbled in my hand.

Pressing the pieces left into his skin, I barely even noticed the sharp pain in my own hand as the chunks dug through my glove.

He cried out, tumbling to the side. I quickly kicked off my boots and jeans, still around my knees, and scrambled away from him. I slammed my hand down on Gabriel's desk, pushing myself up, and saw the gold letter opener lying there.

"Come here, you bitch."

Grabbing the sharp object and gripping it tight, I whipped around, not sure how close he was. It caught the side of his face, slicing a crimson line from ear to mouth.

He grabbed hold of his cheek, falling to his knees again. I fisted my hand, feeling the pain of the glass, and hit him as hard as I could again and again and again until I couldn't breathe anymore.

He fell to his back, spent, and I stared at him, my fingers still gripping the knife tightly. I fought not to go and sink the blade into his chest.

I wanted them all—everyone—to know they couldn't hurt me. I didn't allow it.

Raising my eyes, I glared at Lev and David, who stood on the other side of the room with Gabriel's guards. David had one in a choke hold, and Lev had the other pinned to the wall. That was what the scuffle was about that I'd heard.

They were protecting me, after all.

I dropped the letter opener on the floor and picked up the napkin sitting on top of Gabriel's dinner dishes on his desk. Blood trickled down from my nose, around my lips, and dripped from my chin, and I wiped it away, tasting the metallic saltiness filter through my teeth.

I wrapped the napkin around my cut hand and stalked over to the man at David's feet, squeezing my fist in his hair. "Get him and get out of here," I said in a low tone, pushing him toward Ilia.

I'd be dead in a day if I called the police.

But justice would come. I'd make sure of it.

Lev released his guard, and the two of them stumbled out of the office, taking Ilia with them.

I sniffled, tasting more blood drip down my throat as I walked for the guys. I was still in my underwear and a T-shirt, and there was blood in my hair, making a few strands stick to my face. That was all Lev and David saw as they watched me warily, as if they no longer knew me.

Shit, I wasn't even sure I did.

But strangely, I didn't mind. This was who I was supposed to be.

"Get Marina," I told David, walking past him and out of the office. "I need a dress."

I stood outside the cathedral doors, in the entryway, holding my arms out to give Marina room to work. My body was tugged in a dozen different directions as she pinned, sewed, and tightened the gown she'd given me when I was sixteen but never wore. It was the only dress we could find so quickly.

I stared at the closed doors in front of me. *I hate him.* But why wasn't I more nervous? Why wasn't I scared?

All I felt was anger. And drive. I didn't care what happened to me right now. Let him do his worst.

"Can I put mascara on you?" Alex asked.

"Why not?" I mumbled. I rubbed my lips together, feeling the red lipstick she'd already dabbed on them. I wanted to look nice, but not for him. Something inside me was different. I wasn't thinking about all the things I wanted to be anymore.

I just needed to be louder about it.

She worked on my eyes, adding some liner, and yanked the plug of the flat iron out of the wall, having finished curling chunks of my hair into loose waves.

"I have flowers for you," Marina thrust a bouquet in my hands.

But I just cocked an eyebrow, staring down at the white roses. And then I tossed them off to the side, letting them land on a velvet bench. It was nice of her to go to the trouble, but she knew better.

I couldn't hear anything happening inside the church, other than the echo of the odd kneeler being pushed up or down in the pews. Alex quickly dabbed more powder on my nose, probably still a little red from the attack before.

My body was still knotted from it. I hadn't seen my father, Ilia, or the two guards since I threw on my clothes and bolted from the house before he found out what went down. I wasn't scared for myself so much as for David and Lev, who went against orders and protected me. We all dived into a car and drove away, Marina meeting us here shortly after, having snatched the gown on her way out.

I was actually grateful. To have the dress and Alex fixing my face. I felt armed. I wanted to be bold, not invisible. Not look how I always looked, fucking apologetic and like I was always trying to make up for existing. I was here, and fuck 'em.

I waved Alex away and grabbed my dress, lifting it up to walk toward the doors.

"What are you wearing?" Alex burst out.

I turned to see her looking at my feet.

I glanced down to try to see what the problem was.

My combat boots, some of the black scuffed off the toe, sat on my feet loose with the shoestrings untied, as usual.

"They match," I told her and turned back around.

But I heard her heavy sigh behind me.

Dropping the dress, I pulled open the doors, not waiting for a cue. I hated formalities, and if Kai wanted to suffer so badly, why not just go to city hall?

People lingered around the front of the nearly empty church, a few random parishioners in the pews toward the back. Everyone, one by one, stopped to stare.

I hoped my black dress made a statement. The bodice was charcoal and tight, leaving my shoulders and arms completely bare, while the white tulle was full around the bottom with a sheer black overlay.

Kai stood at the front of the church, facing Michael to the side, but his head was turned toward me. The dress was dreamy and beautiful, and I hoped like hell I looked good in it.

Without waiting for any music to start, I walked, fixing my eyes on the altar as I marched down the aisle. The room was silent, and I absorbed the heat of a dozen pairs of eyes on me.

My father sat in the front, but I knew he was going to be here. Hanson had found me a while ago to sign the marriage license.

Michael stood at the front, next to Kai, while Will and Rika were off to my left.

I could sense other bodies here, too, but I assumed they belonged to my father's side. Once he calmed down and stopped blaming himself for not getting rid of me sooner, he must've realized that while I went into this marriage with nothing, I'd come out with my rightful half.

Or all of it if Kai should happen to get hit by an untimely bus.

A priest with white hair and glasses came out from behind a podium, noticing me, and moved quickly down the small set of stairs to stand at center. He looked nervously to Kai, probably realizing how abnormal this "ceremony" was.

Kai uncrossed his arms and let his eyes fall down my form, a skeptical look on his face. Walking over to me, he nodded, and we both stepped up to the priest.

"You wore a dress," he said under his breath. "Color me surprised."

Ass.

But I gave the tall man in front of us a sweet smile, taking in his fancy white robe with gold embroidery.

"I've never worn one," I replied quietly. "A gown, I mean. And since I'm only getting married once . . ."

"Oh, you'll have plenty of opportunities to wear gowns, married to me," he assured me. "I plan on making this marriage as torturous as possible for you."

But I shot back, tipping my chin up. "Go for it while you can. I'll be a widow soon, I'm sure."

I heard his quiet laugh at my side, but he dropped the banter as the priest looked beyond us to our pathetic guest list.

"Be attentive to our prayers, O Lord," he rang out, opening his arms to everyone, "and in your kindness, pour out your grace on these, your servants, Kai and Nikova, who, coming together before your altar, they may be confirmed in love for one anoth—"

"Skip to the vows," Kai gritted out.

The priest halted his script, looking flustered. I almost snorted. Poor guy. It was weird, though, hearing my name like that. No one used it, except my mom and Damon, and they called me Nik.

My father didn't like "Nikova," though, so I got used to using "Banks." That's who I was now.

The priest cleared his throat, taking a deep breath. "Kai and Nikova, have you come here to enter into marriage without coercion, freely and wholeheartedly?"

"I have," Kai answered.

I hesitated but finally nodded, feeling the weight of my father in the room. "I have."

"And are you prepared, as you follow the path of marriage, to love and honor each other for as long as you both shall live?"

"Yes," Kai hissed, sounding in a hurry. "I am."

My heart jumped. God, was this really happening? "Yes," I replied.

I couldn't detect Will behind me, and Michael was as still as stone, but I could hear Rika's constant fidgeting on my left.

"Are you prepared to accept children lovingly from God and to bring them up according to the law of Christ and his church?"

What? I shot my eyes to Kai, who simply stared at the priest with his eyebrow arched.

No fucking way. We might be here under false pretenses, but this was horseshit. I wasn't even going to pretend to agree to that.

"Keep going," Kai told him, and I realized he wasn't having it, either.

I breathed a sigh of relief.

The priest looked down at his book, seeming flustered before stuttering on. "Since . . . since it is your intention to enter the covenant of Holy Matrimony," he said, finding his voice again, "join your right hands, and declare your consent before God and his church."

Kai turned toward me, and all I could do was lock my jaw so no bad words slipped out. I faced him, and he took my hands, but I refused to close my fingers around his. Even despite the tingling that was shooting up my arms.

"Kai Genato Mori," the priest began, "do you take Nikova for your lawful wife, to have and to hold, from this day forward, for better, for worse, for richer, for poorer, in sickness and in health, until death do you part?"

Until death . . .

He stared at me, his gaze faltering, and I saw a glimpse of the man sitting at his father's table, telling me the story about steak.

And then he smirked. "Until death," he specified. "I do."

My lungs emptied, and I squeezed his hands only because I needed mine to stop shaking.

"Nikova Sarah Banks." The older man turned to me. "Do you take Kai for your lawful husband, to have and to hold, from this day forward, for better, for worse, for richer, for poorer, in sickness and in health, until death do you part?"

I couldn't believe this was happening.

Kai squeezed my hands back, signaling it was my turn to talk, and I pulled out of his grasp, shooting him a glare.

"Until death do us part," I mumbled. "Which shouldn't be long from now, so yes, I do."

Kai smiled, laughing quietly at me.

Fuck you, it wasn't a joke.

"May the Lord in his kindness strengthen the consent . . ."

The priest carried on with his blessing, and the rest passed in a blur as we exchanged rings, and the priest offered kind words to those in attendance.

The breath I'd been holding expelled, and I dropped my eyes. *Shit.*

We were married.

I glanced at Kai, both of us facing the priest again, and anger boiled under my skin. *I'm going to be the worst fucking wife you ever have.*

"Your kiss is your promise to each other," the cleric said to Kai. "Go in peace to glorify your union, and you may now kiss your bride."

Kai turned toward me, and my heart jumped into my throat, but . . .

But he didn't stop turning.

He spun all the way around and charged off, back down the aisle from where I came, leaving me standing there like an idiot. I blinked long and hard, embarrassment warming my cheeks. *Prick.*

One by one, Michael, Will, and Rika fell in behind him, every one of his witnesses storming down the aisle and leaving the church. He didn't look back, but I knew every other eye in the place was on me. The priest didn't even know what to do. He just fucking stood there.

So, Kai was going to be the worst husband, too, from the looks of it. Slow clap for him. That was vile, and I was actually impressed.

CHAPTER 25

KAI

Present

I reached into the large bowl, snatching up a wad of soba noodles and refilling my dish.

"Fucking hell," I bit out through my teeth, thinking about the mess I'd gotten myself into. How the hell did everything spiral out of control? What was I even after anymore? What was the end goal?

I wanted to find Damon. That was it. Determine if there was more danger to Rika, Michael, or Will, and find out what he did with the body, so I could handle it and either turn myself in or come to terms with the sick bitch getting exactly what she deserved. And if so, then making sure she was well hidden and dealing with it if she wasn't.

I didn't even know what to do in a situation like that. The idea of seeing it all again, even talking about it . . . I closed my eyes. I didn't get rid of bodies. *Jesus.*

A moment. My life was a series of huge mistakes made in sheer moments when I lost control.

Except today. When I looked at her and said those lies, vows I didn't intend on keeping—but in that moment, I did. How perfect my world would've been if I could've swallowed my pride and told her I loved her and she let me hold her. No matter what, everything would've been okay if I could've seen her smile on her wedding day.

Lifting the chopsticks, I closed my mouth around some noodles and vegetables, looking at my phone and noting no other texts rolling in as I chewed. Will had waited for Banks to come out of the church so he could bring her here. She would've argued and fought, but the threat of the cell phone loomed, and she would've eventually agreed.

It had been over an hour, though. If she wasn't here soon, I *would* go get her.

But just then I heard a click, and I looked up from the dining room table and watched her open the door, slowly stepping into her new home.

She looked around, and I relaxed back in my chair as she closed the door and squared her shoulders. I smiled to myself. What was I going to do with her?

Her head finally turned, and she locked eyes with me. I swallowed my food.

"Come in," I told her, pushing the bowl back.

Hesitantly, she stepped toward me, entering the dining room. "Which bedroom is mine?"

"Mine."

Her stubborn shoulders fell a little. "I'm tired, Kai."

"You're also my wife." I picked up my glass, taking a drink of water. "Your precious big brother must be crawling the walls right now."

She shook her head, looking disgusted by me. "I'm not your pawn, so trust me when I say marrying me won't make me any less difficult."

Oh, I hope not.

I stared at her, taking in the gown she wore today and nothing else. She'd come completely empty-handed, unless she had her little knives tucked in a garter under that dress. Did she think she wasn't staying long enough to move in?

I'd have to have her clothes brought here. Or she could wear mine.

"I'm not worried," I said. "You'll bend."

She scoffed, and I took a clean bowl and a fork, loading some of the yakisoba into the dish. "Come and eat." I set the food and utensil on the table, nodding at the chair across from me.

She just glared at me.

"Eat, and I will show you which room is yours?" I bargained.

But she didn't sit down. Instead, she walked over to the buffet table and grabbed two more bowls. Coming back over to the table, she took the fork and loaded up both bowls with noodles, piling them high, and taking nearly everything that was left.

I usually made enough for leftovers to last three days.

"What are you doing?" I asked her.

"My men are outside. They followed us here." She stuck forks in both bowls and picked them up. "They need to eat, too."

What—who?

"*Your* men?" I challenged. "Those pricks who work for Gabriel? Tell them to leave."

I shot out of my chair and stalked toward the window, pulling back the curtain. And sure enough, that same black SUV sat in my driveway. I could see the bald one in the driver's seat.

"You tell them," she shot back. "They put themselves on the line for me tonight, and that's how you reward loyalty?"

"Put themselves on the line? What do you mean? What happened?"

She looked away, shaking it off. "Nothing. Just . . ." She paused, searching for words. Then she looked straight at me. "They won't leave. They work for me, and they can't go back there. That's it."

She turned and walked for the front door, stacking one bowl on top of the other to open the door.

"They work for you?" I raised my voice. "How do you plan on paying them?"

"Easy," she said, her eyes shooting around her to the house and everything around us. "Half of what's yours is now mine."

And she walked out the door, slamming it behind her.

I just stood there, strangling the air in front of me. Son of a—fucking—God—what the fuck?

Dammit, she's such a little shit! What the hell did I want with two guys hanging around my house all the time? They were going to be in my way, and I don't like people in my space and messing my stuff up. I was just getting used to having her around, dammit!

I swung back my leg to kick the buffet table, but I caught myself, stopping. It was, like, expensive, and an antique and shit, so . . .

Pulling the curtain back again, I kept an eagle eye out, making sure she didn't try to run off with them or something. The passenger-side window rolled down, and I spotted the younger one with the black Mohawk in the seat.

She slipped the bowls in through the window, and the kid sniffed it, looking pleased. She spoke to them for a few minutes, sparing a few glances back at me, and I finally let the curtain go, leaving her to it.

I didn't like how they looked at her. Like they had more of a right to her attention.

But I guess, who wouldn't want her attention? Nikova Banks was a beautiful woman.

Seeing her in that dress today in the church was as close as I'd come to losing complete control. I was at war with myself the entire ceremony. She hid so much under her clothes, but that dress certainly brought it all out. The smooth skin and incredible curves . . .

Her hair, her makeup . . . I didn't know why she'd gotten herself done up—I didn't for one moment think it was for me.

The front door opened, and she entered the dining room, seeming a little calmer.

We held each other's eyes, and I felt a pang of need for her. For a chance to salvage what this day had turned into and treat her well.

But I didn't deserve her. No matter what she'd done or how her choices had hurt me, I'd taken her hand today with as much force as I'd taken her innocence in that room in The Pope. She needed to be left alone.

I gestured to the table for her to sit and eat.

She sat down and placed her bowl in front of her, picking up the fork. But she stopped, noticing my bowl with a set of chopsticks lying across the top.

Finding a spare pair on the table, she put her fork down and picked up the sticks. Of course, she probably had no interest in using them. I'd just given her a fork, and it was her stubborn nature that you didn't tell Banks what she could and couldn't do. It was the problem of me *assuming* she'd want a fork.

She tried to fit them in her fingers, but they kept slipping.

I walked over to her right side and reached out. "Like this."

I took them in my fingers, ignoring her scowl as I fit both between my forefinger and middle finger, using the latter to steady and the former to control movement. I bobbed my pointer finger up and down, showing her that was the one that moved. Opening it wide, I picked up a piece of cabbage and closed it, securing it between the sticks.

"I can do it," she said, snatching them back.

And she did. Within a few more tries she had the hold right and was able to pick up her food and get it into her mouth, albeit shakily. The platinum band on her finger gleamed in the soft light of the chandelier. I felt a pang of guilt now that I'd calmed down. She should have a diamond on her hand.

"They're called *hashi*," I told her, gesturing to the chopsticks. "In Japanese."

Rising, I picked up a small ceramic chopstick rest and set it in front of her. "And this is called *hashioki*. When you're not eating, you rest the ends of your chopsticks on here. Or"—I pointed out, gesturing to my bowl—"you can lay them across your dish. But not in the food and never crossed."

"Why?"

"Because it's . . . rude," I told her. There was another reason having to do with deceased people and offerings and traditions, but I had a feeling that would only incite her rebellion.

I sat back down, letting her eat. My head was swimming. I'd be lucky if I got any sleep tonight.

I had to get the guys who were outside rooms in here and get them on payroll. As well as figure out what the hell they were going to be doing for me.

I had to get back down to Sensou and meet with the insurance adjuster. Figure out what the next step was. Would we reopen?

I needed to see my parents, too. I was surprised I wasn't getting calls tonight, in fact. If they hadn't heard yet, they would soon. Surprisingly, I wasn't really sorry. I just didn't like explaining myself. Probably because I couldn't.

And tomorrow was Devil's Night. We still hadn't found where Damon was hiding out, so he might be on us before we were on him. Or maybe nothing would happen. Maybe Rika was right, and he was fucking with us.

I still needed to deal with him, though. I couldn't keep going, having things hanging over my head. Maybe we'd just bring everyone here for the night. Put the place on lockdown.

She finished her bowl and looked into the larger one, seeing if there was any left. I smiled, liking that she clearly enjoyed my cooking. Steaks and all.

She tipped the bowl over, using the chopsticks to shove any lingering noodles into her smaller bowl, and I closed my eyes, laughing quietly.

She'd just broken about three rules of etiquette. My father would piss a brick if he saw it.

But I watched her face and lost myself in those red lips; she really was incredible.

"It's a pretty dress," I told her. "Where'd you get it?"

She finished chewing quietly, not looking at me. "Marina," she said. "Gabriel's cook. She made it for me when I was sixteen."

The reminder that Gabriel was her father hit me again, and I had so many questions still.

"My father was having a party," she explained, "and Marina thought he might let me come if . . . if I was pretty enough."

Pretty enough?

"Did you go?"

She shook her head. "I got all dressed up. Hair and a little lipstick. But Damon wouldn't allow it. He made me stay upstairs."

She gave a little laugh, like she was trying to brush off his possessiveness, but . . .

Territorial is fine when it's in the bedroom. It's not fine when it keeps someone you're supposed to love from living a life.

All the pieces began to fit together. Devil's Night six years ago. How he wouldn't let her even speak to me. How he had those guys take her away. How she always seemed to lurk like a mouse—in the confessional, at the cemetery—afraid of the cat coming out to snatch her up.

How they latched on to each other at The Pope. How she was the only woman I'd ever seen him hang on to like a life preserver.

Given what I knew of their parents, it was no wonder they made their family just the two of them. It was the only place they were safe and loved.

"Come here," I said, dropping my voice to a whisper.

She narrowed her eyes.

She had every reason to hate me after what I'd pulled today. After Gabriel and I tossed her back and forth like a possession. Had she ever been anywhere but Meridian City or Thunder Bay? Did she at least finish school? Did she have a single friend who wasn't a guy in Gabriel's crew?

I leaned in, suddenly wanting everything. I wanted to show her the world.

"Fuck him and your father," I said gently. "Fuck me and the shit that comes out of my mouth."

Her eyebrows dug in deeper; she looked confused.

Snaking an arm around her, I pulled her onto my lap, and she immediately tried to push me away.

"I wanted this," I told her, looking in her eyes.

She paused.

"For no other reason than I wanted you." I threaded my fingers through hers, brushing against the band on her finger. I'd get her an engagement ring next week. Even though we were never engaged. Maybe she'd like to pick it out, actually. "Damon knew what a treasure you were, and he loves you. But he won't keep me from you." I tipped up her chin to meet my eyes. "This isn't about him or the hotel or your father. I want you."

"And if I don't want you?"

My gaze faltered, but I decided to be direct. "Don't you?"

I hadn't misread signals. She liked me.

"I won't hurt him," I said, knowing what her worries were. "But I do need to protect myself, so I need to see him. Do you understand?"

"You promise?"

She looked so vulnerable. I couldn't ask her to choose.

I nodded. "Promise." I squeezed her, one hand on her waist, the other on her thigh. "I'm going to fix this, but I can't account for him. If he pushes me too far, I'll be forced to act. You know that."

I saw her swallow as she stared at her lap.

"I want you," I told her again. "And I don't care what your name is, and I don't care who your parents are or how much money you have or don't have. I just want you, upstairs, and dressed in nothing but my sheets."

A beautiful, small smile pulled at her lips. "I won't be Banks tonight?"

I shook my head. "And I'm not Kai."

"Just for tonight?"

I nodded, loving our little game. "Just for tonight."

She stood up and slowly pulled all of her hair over her shoulder. "The dress is a corset." She turned her back to me. "Will you help me unlace it before I go upstairs?"

My heart pumped harder.

I ran my hand down the crisscrossed lacing and pulled out the string tucked into the dress. Untying it, I pulled the long, black lace out of a few loops and then worked my fingers up her spine, loosening the laces. My body was wracked with pleasure. I loved undressing her.

The dress slowly began to fall down, more of her slender back coming into view, and I reached my hand inside, feeling her nakedness.

There was nothing. No bra, no panties, no slip, nothing but her, completely pure and beautiful and innocent underneath the dress.

The gown fell to the floor, and my cock throbbed and swelled. Her ass, her shoulders, her legs—golden skin that she sure as hell didn't inherit from her father's side glowing in the dim light.

She turned around, her eyes falling on my pants and the bulge growing there.

She started breathing faster, her gaze turning heated. "Fuck the sheets," she whispered.

And she slid down, spread her legs, and straddled me. I groaned, unfastening and yanking open my jeans. I took out my cock and rubbed the tip up and down her length, finding her so wet already.

She lowered herself, hugging me close and moaning as I filled her.

Fuck. I grabbed her tits, covering the nipples with my mouth, one by one, as she held the back of the chair and began moving in and out, rolling her hips faster and faster. She rode me, her moans and whimpers getting louder, and I leaned back, taking her ass in both hands, and just fucking watched her.

God, I was lucky.

"So, do you still like me?" she asked, playing.

I laughed a little. *I more than like you.*

"I think I'll keep you," I told her instead. "And no one keeps me from you. Got it?"

I kissed her chin, trailing kisses along her jaw. "Not your father, not your brother, not your men." I squeezed her ass again, pulling her in deep. "I want your smart-ass mouth." I kissed her lips. "I want every memory you're going to make from now on." I kissed her forehead. "And I want this." I gripped her, yanking her into me as I bit her neck. "In the car, on this table at breakfast tomorrow, everywhere . . ."

Her body grew tense, and she wrapped her arms around me, bouncing faster and faster. "So, you *do* like me, then?"

I smiled at her joke. *Little shit.*

"Yeah," I told her. "I like you a lot."

A lot.

unbuttoned the collar of one shirt and pulled it off the hanger, slipping my arms into it. It was just after six in the morning, and I could smell the rain in the air as soon I woke up. I buttoned my shirt and walked to the bedside table, grabbing my phone and pausing when I saw the leather gloves she always wore lying next to the lamp.

I shifted my gaze to her, seeing her hands, one resting on the pillow and the other over her stomach. A smile pulled at my lips. She took them off.

The scar looked almost like a red ink stamp across the back of her hand, and I squeezed my phone, anger building. Gabriel was going to pay for that. And for a lot more.

Her lips were slightly parted, and I noticed a chocolate-colored strand of hair that had fallen on her lip. Leaning down, I softly pulled it off before giving her a kiss, lingering just long enough for her scent to cast a trail of heat from my heart to my groin.

I groaned, reluctantly pulling back up. *Not now.* She needed sleep, and I wanted her to wake up to breakfast. She said she liked eggs.

No.

She just said she *ate* a lot of eggs. Maybe she didn't like them all that much. They were cheap, low in fat, and sustaining. Perfect for a person of low income.

I looked down at my ring, finally feeling it sink in that she was mine now. Until she ran away again, anyway.

And she had a life to live if I had anything to say about it. No eggs. I was going to enjoy indulging her.

Opening my phone, I left the room, quietly closing the door behind me as I checked the weather for today. I should never have gone to sleep last night. I had no idea what today had in store, but I should've been ready earlier. The body's need to waste one-third of its life span unconscious was an error of evolution. Look how much I could've gotten done.

Cloudy all day, high of sixty-eight. Evening thunderstorms. Great. I needed to get the house closed up, some supplies and food, and I had a flood of phone calls from friends back home wondering if we were going to be in town tonight and employees wondering if they should find new jobs. No and yes.

That fucking prick. I'd promised I wouldn't hurt him, but after what he did, I might not be able to stop myself.

My phone rang as I walked down the staircase, and I checked the screen, seeing a number I didn't recognize.

I slowed, staring at it.

Damon. I hadn't heard from him since the day on the street in front of The Pope. He must've been getting a new burner phone every time he made his little calls.

I smiled to myself, fingering my wedding ring with my thumb. He wasn't going to be in a good mood.

Answering the phone, I brought it to my ear.

"Where is she?" he said, not waiting for a greeting.

"Sleeping."

"I will get her back," he told me.

I took a deep breath and walked to the front door, looking out the little window on the side. Banks' *men* were still out there.

Impressive.

"So, come on, then," I told him. "Come to the house and take her back."

His chuckle filled my ear. "Oh, I will," he said. "But I'm smarter than you. I'll get my leverage first."

What leverage?

I didn't want him here. I didn't want him near her. But I was ready to shut him up. He wouldn't be getting her back.

"I'm the only one who's taken care of her," he argued. "The only one who's loved her. You can't ask her to give me up. You know why? Because it's an impossible choice and you don't want to know that she just might not choose you."

I shook my head, opening the front door. I wouldn't ask her to make that choice anymore. I would just keep fighting, because I loved—

I suddenly felt like the wind had been knocked out of me.

Because I loved her.

"You see me in her, don't you?" he taunted, lowering his voice. "Do you really want to be faced with her every day? Could you really love her, knowing who she is and that I'll always divide her attention?"

I ground my teeth together and stalked out into the driveway, pounding on the hood of the SUV twice. The guys inside jumped up, pulling their feet off the dash. I headed back for the house, knowing they would follow.

"Where are you?" I asked Damon.

"I wish I could tell you," he nearly fucking chirped. "I really do, because it's just too good. If only you'd done just a little more research, man."

"Damon—"

"It's really a miracle for me that you haven't yet realized."

"Damon!"

"Can't talk," he said. "But I'll see you soon."

"Tonight?"

And I heard a click.

"Damon!" I yelled into the phone. What did he mean "soon"?

"Yes." I heard a voice behind me.

I turned around, looking at the dead call on my phone screen. I could call him back, but the phone would be off, no doubt. Plus, it was a waste of time.

I saw David and the kid, Lev, step into the foyer, the younger one yawning.

Walking over to the table in the hallway, I dug out a set of keys from a small chest on top.

I tossed the set to him. "The third floor is yours," I said. "Banks will organize your tasks in this house and outside of it, and I'll put you on payroll. She's sleeping now." I stepped up to them, weighting my instructions heavily, so they knew I was serious. "Don't leave her alone here or let her leave, and when she wakes up, tell her I've gone to run an errand, and I'll be back soon."

"You." I looked to Lev. "Go to Delcour. Bring Will and Rika here and keep them here. Tell them to pack an overnight bag."

"They won't come with me," he argued.

"I'm texting them now to let them know you're on your way. Go."

He sighed and took the car keys from David, heading out the front door, and I got on my phone, shooting a text to Michael to meet me at The Pope and then another one to Will and Rika.

"Check every window and door," I ordered David, grabbing my car keys and walking out. "Once everyone arrives, it's lockdown. You got that?"

He nodded. "Got it."

CHAPTER 26

KAI

Present

I moved absently through the ballroom, replaying everything in my head. That Devil's Night all those years ago. Banks and me. The woman dancing.

How long had Natalya Torrance been there? How often did the Torrances use their secret floor? She had left Damon three years earlier. Had she been there the whole time?

There was something I was missing.

The morning light streamed through the windows, revealing the dust floating in the air, and I looked around, noticing the floor littered with flyers. There were stands for sheet music still sitting on the stage, and a few round tables around the dance floor.

I inhaled a deep breath, rubbing my eyes. She wanted to be close to him.

But then that raised another question. The Pope wasn't very old. Where did the family stay when they were in town *before* The Pope was built? That was what picked at the back of my mind, and why I hadn't paid any attention to it. It didn't seem important, but it was weird.

And when something feels off, it is.

"Hey, what's going on?" Michael called out.

I turned my head, seeing him come into the ballroom. I'd

dragged him out of bed and told him to meet me here. I should've told Will, but I'd rather someone stayed close to Rika when Lev went over to pick them up.

I shook my head. "I know to listen to my instincts, and I ignored them."

"Why? What's wrong?"

I turned toward him. "This place was built in the early nineties," I told him, "but this was a family hotel, and the rumor circulated that the family had a secret floor in every hotel they owned."

"So?" He sighed, looking tired.

"So, Damon's family is one of the oldest in Thunder Bay," I pointed out. "The Nikovs have been in this area since the thirties. Wouldn't it have made sense to start their businesses close like we've been doing to monitor them more easily before expanding abroad?"

They built hotels long before the nineties. Why wait to build one close to home until then?

"You're right." He stared off, looking lost in thought. "Why wouldn't they have had a hotel in Meridian City first?"

Not to mention the fact that there had been no move to build another one or reopen this one. He didn't want somewhere local where he could have business meetings, put up clients, host parties . . . ? It made no sense.

It was probably nothing. So, he didn't open a hotel close to home. It was odd, but so was the family.

I looked at Michael, shaking my head in exhaustion. My brain was fried.

But he was frozen. He stared ahead, focusing on nothing as the wheels turned in his head.

And then he breathed out, "Shit," and dived into his pocket, pulling out his cell phone. "No, no, no . . ."

I advanced. What the hell?

He breathed hard, dialing a number and putting the phone to his ear. "Rika . . ."

"What's wrong?" I barked.

But he just pointed at me, already walking for the door. "Get in the car!"

"What?"

He bolted, and I had to run to catch up to him. We ran out the back, and I didn't argue or try to stop him. Michael never lost his head, and if he did, there was a reason. He jumped in his Rover, and I left my car next to it, hopping in his passenger side.

Before I even had the door closed, though, he punched the car into reverse and slammed on the gas, making my body vault forward. I shot out a hand to catch myself.

He sped down the alleyway and swung the car around, shifting into drive, and then took off down the city street and toward the bridge.

"Robson!" he yelled to whoever finally picked up the other line. "Who owned Delcour before us?"

Delcour? What—

He listened to the other man talk, worry etching his face. "I know it changed hands a lot," he shouted. "But it was built in the thirties. Who built it?"

No, no, no . . . He didn't think—

Delcour, the Crist family apartment building, was a jewel in the black city. It was artfully designed, boasted the best views, and the architecture was mysterious and alluring.

And it easily could've been a hotel back in the day. It even had a ballroom.

Good God.

Michael raced, swerving around vehicles, and pulled the phone away from his ear, pushing more buttons. "Baby, come on, come on," he pleaded, putting the phone to his ear again. "Come on. Answer the phone."

"Delcour?" I shot out, turning to him. "Are you fucking kidding me?"

How?

"All this time," he choked out, squeezing the steering wheel so hard his knuckles were white. "The Torrances sold Delcour in the eighties and built the new hotel in Whitehall to profit off the stadium."

"Delcour is the original Pope?"

He pulled his phone away, redialing. "Rika, goddammit!"

We crossed the bridge and sped through the warehouse district, turning onto Parker Avenue.

"You knew?" I pressed. "You knew they owned the building? It was their hotel at one point?"

"No, I didn't know!" he growled. "We weren't even born yet, for Christ's sake! I just knew it was built in the thirties and that we didn't always own it."

But Michael's father's lawyer had just confirmed. The Torrances were the original owners. And if there was a hidden floor at The Pope, then . . .

"Rika, answer the fucking phone!"

He threw his cell against the windshield, and it tumbled across the dash and onto the floor.

"Just get there," I gritted out.

White lace panties. You've got to be kidding me. He might've been in the building, but he couldn't have gotten into their apartment, could he? Would he really have been there and been able to resist making contact with Will? Alex?

Michael hit the gas, horns honking around us, and pulled up in front of Delcour, screeching to a halt.

Throwing open our doors, we ran out of the car and into the building, the doorman scrambling to hold the door open.

"Did you see Rika?" Michael shouted to the man behind the desk as we ran to the elevator.

His eyes snapped up, going wide-eyed as he tried to find his words. "Uh, no, sir."

We got in the elevator, Michael pressed the button, and the doors closed.

"Do you know if the building has a hidden floor or hidden apartment or anything?" I questioned.

He shook his head, sweat covering his brow. "I don't know shit. I don't pay attention to anything my family does. You know that."

Which included buying this building or learning anything beyond what he needed to know to get his fucking ass to his penthouse, I gathered. He was so self-absorbed. Did he ever trouble himself to learn or listen to anything anyone said? Get curious, maybe? If it were me, and I had free rein to the place, I would've explored every corner of this building.

Not Michael, though.

Basketball, Rika, food, sex, and sleep were the only things catching his attention.

The elevator shot past twenty-one floors and slowed to a stop at the top of the building. The doors opened, and Michael and I shot out, rounding the corner and racing into his apartment.

Lev and Will stood in the center of the living room, and Michael made right for them. "Do you have her? Where is she?"

"Hey, what's up?"

Rika's voice came from above, and my head snapped up; she was coming down the stairs with a brown leather overnight bag.

Michael bolted up the stairs, skipping two at a time, and grabbed her. He wrapped his arms around her and lifted her up, hugging her.

I exhaled, dropping my head. He hadn't taken her. Maybe he wasn't here, after all.

"Baby," Michael gasped. "Why the fuck didn't you answer your phone?"

She hugged him back, looking confused. "I . . . It's in my handbag, I think," she stammered. "I was upstairs packing. What's wrong?"

But he just shook his head. It was no time to explain.

"Sir," another voice said, and I looked back to see Patterson, one of the building's managers, step into the penthouse. "Is something wrong? Jackson downstairs said there might be a problem."

"I'm not sure," Michael answered. "Have you seen anyone suspicious coming and going from the building?"

"No, sir." He approached, looking concerned. "I would've taken measures if I had, I assure you."

"Yes, I know."

But I piped up, addressing Michael. "When did the Torrances sell off this place?"

He took Rika's hand and grabbed her bag, walking down the stairs. "Nineteen eighty-eight, Robson said."

I nodded. "So, computerized controllers on elevators didn't start until later last century," I thought out loud. "Knowing he was selling off the building, Gabriel wouldn't have upgraded the system to include codes for the hidden floor. Which means they had a much simpler way to access the twelfth floor than the newer hotel across the river."

No keypad. Definitely no fingerprint recognition or key cards.

They had to have a separate elevator, but . . .

Delcour's elevators had been remodeled. They'd been pulled out, the shafts renovated; the hidden floor would've been found. Unless . . .

"Are there any other elevators?" I asked Patterson. "Anything? Not in common use. Even out of service? Or another stairwell?"

He shook his head, proving it a dead end, but then he stopped, appearing to think of something.

"Well, there's a stairwell on the first floor leading up, but it's been walled in. It doesn't go anywhere anymore."

My shoulders fell.

"And there's a service elevator in the basement," he added.

I shot my head up.

"But it's boarded up," he told us. "I don't think it's been used in . . . thirty years?"

Well, that'd be about right.

I took a step toward him. "Show us."

He led the way into the elevator again, and we descended past the lobby, past the parking garage, underneath the street, and down one more level. As far as it would go.

Michael kept hold of Rika but shot me a weary glance. I didn't think he'd ever been down here, and the idea that Damon was in the building, especially on nights when Michael had games or was out of town, was almost crippling.

Stepping into the basement, two levels belowground, Patterson led us down a hallway and around a corner. Water raced through the pipes above us, and I could hear the soft rumble of the furnace coming from somewhere.

We headed down a hallway and entered a small open area, and there it was. The old service elevator.

Patterson stopped suddenly, though, looking confused. "The boards have been pulled out," he said.

I followed his gaze, seeing all the two-by-fours with rusted nails jutting out of them scattered out to the side. How long had it been since he'd been down here?

The old elevator didn't look very wide, and it was crusted with grime and cobwebs, but there was an old-fashioned dial above the doors. No numbers, but a light glowed behind the stained glass, showing that it was receiving power.

"You've got to be kidding me," Michael mumbled, sounding at a loss for what else to say.

I pushed the button, the elevator doors immediately opened with a *ding*, and everyone just stood there a moment.

But I took the first step.

The floor shifted on the cables just a bit, but it seemed stable enough, and I held the door open, gesturing for everyone to get in.

The inside was small. Carpet covered the floor, and the walls were dark cherrywood on the bottom and mirrored on the top.

There was only one button inside. Once everyone crowded in, I told Lev to go back to my house and let Banks know I'd be home soon, and then Michael told Patterson to send security down here after us. Then I closed the doors and sent us up.

The cables creaked, and I could feel the vibrations of their movement under my feet.

"A year," Michael said. "He's been coming and going, watching all of us, for a fucking year. From right here."

"It actually wasn't that hard to figure out," Will added, speaking for the first time.

I glanced over at him. I hadn't talked to him a lot lately, and I wondered how he was holding up. Was he okay with all of this? He had a lot of shit in his head over Damon, I was sure.

I'd talk to him later.

The elevator crawled up the building, stopping on its own on what I assumed would be the hidden floor. I wasn't sure if it was the twelfth floor in this building, same as The Pope, or if it was a different floor this time.

The doors opened, and all of us looked ahead, out into the vast room ahead of us.

Long and wide, it was like a large sitting room with doors off to the side and the back, probably leading to bedrooms and a kitchen. *Jesus.* It was huge.

It was designed like a luxury suite with a common area, but the extent of it wasn't completely visible yet. A fireplace sat off to the right, while windows covered the east wall with velvet drapes and the light from the cloudy sky outside filtering through.

"Unbelievable," Rika said as we all walked in and spread out, taking in the large room. "All this time this was here, and we didn't know."

Yeah. And he'd been here. The cigarette scent was pungent.

Portraits covered the walls, and there were several sitting areas with cushioned chairs and tables. I drifted up to a table, seeing a bottle of Dewar's half-gone, and an empty glass. I lifted the glass, sniffing it.

Michael searched the rooms while Rika stayed with me and Will looked out on the terrace. But Damon wasn't here. Maybe he saw us coming somehow or maybe he had jumped over to The Pope.

"Why wouldn't he have just left the country and stayed gone?" Rika stuck her hands in her jacket, her blond hair falling over her shoulders.

But it was Will who answered. "Because everything he wants is in Meridian City."

"But all the times I was gone," Michael said, drawing closer, "she was so vulnerable. He could've done anything."

"But he didn't, so just calm down," Rika countered.

"He fucking watched us!" Michael scowled at her. "He lurked like some sick fuck right under our noses!"

Rika averted her gaze while Will ran a hand through his hair. Michael was right. It was definitely creepy as fuck, but . . .

"Rika's right," I added. "Why didn't he do anything? I worked late alone at the dojo countless nights while he was probably right across the street at The Pope. Will was right here. Rika was alone here. Why didn't he act?"

Everyone was silent as the thought hung in the air. What was he waiting for? Why did he just sit here, doing nothing? He'd had a year and multiple opportunities.

"Because just that," Will finally offered. "Michael, Rika, and I are here at Delcour. You and Banks are in Whitehall." He paused, dropping his eyes. "The rest of the world has nothing that Damon wants. He wanted to be here. Close." His eyes flashed to mine. "To us."

I shook my head. *Bullshit.*

But it rang true. Why he stayed. Why he waited until now. "Devil's Night. All of us. His friends. It's his favorite time," I mumbled.

"How do we find him?" Michael asked.

I shook my head, thinking. But then a text rolled in, and I took out my phone, swiping the screen.

Games are better with more players, don't you think?

Another number I didn't recognize. Why did he keep this up? *Come on. Let's do this.*

Another text popped up.

The Pope. 9 PM. Don't come alone. I won't.

"No need. He's not hiding." I answered, walking to the elevator. "Get in your street clothes and meet me at my house within the hour."

I had to get home. He needed leverage, and he'd go after her.

I entered the elevator, leaving them behind, and remembered one last thing, calling out, "And don't forget your masks."

"Why?" Will shot out.

"Because it's Devil's Night." I pushed the button, the doors starting to close. "And I'm not getting caught this time."

CHAPTER 27

BANKS

Present

Making my way down the stairs and into the kitchen, I gazed around the dim, empty room, a little fuddled at what my next move was. If I were home, I'd be grabbing a fistful of whatever Marina had on the table that morning, or if I were at my apartment, I'd be boiling up an egg and fixing a piece of toast, in a rush to get wherever Gabriel had ordered me to go.

I didn't have anywhere to go.

I didn't have a job anymore.

I was only at the mercy of my brother, and all was quiet so far this morning. Except for the fact that I had no idea where the hell Kai had gone. David had knocked on my door earlier to check on me, to hand off the bags of new clothes he'd picked up from my apartment, and to let me know Kai had run out and would be back in a while.

I was actually pretty grateful for the clothes. All I had here was my wedding dress, and while I would've happily worn something of Kai's, I really liked the more form-fitting jeans and black short-sleeved blouse I'd picked out of the bags. It felt good to try something new.

Turning on the light, I walked around the marble island to the refrigerator, glancing at the trees outside the wall of windows to my right. The wind was in high gear, the leaves whipping under the towering thunderhead above, and I remembered a storm was coming our way today.

Another round of chills spread across my arms.

Opening the fridge door, I sifted through an array of food I barely recognized and a lot of other things I'd never tried. Tofu and meat wrapped up, green- and orange-colored juices, and some interesting mushroom dish with sauce that actually smelled pretty good. There were also eggs and milk, as well as two shelves of fruits and vegetables. No cheese or cookies or soda. Should've known he'd be a clean eater.

I grabbed the eggs.

Turning around, I set the carton on the counter and pulled a pot off the rack.

"You're smiling."

I looked up, seeing David walk into the kitchen.

Was I smiling? I let the corners of my mouth fall. "Well, I don't mean to."

He chuckled. Pulling off his jacket, he hung it on the chair on the other side of the island as Lev walked in behind him.

He yawned, his black hair hanging in his eyes as he tossed some keys down on the counter. My mind trailed. For a moment, he looked like Damon. When Damon came in late, with that dreamy weariness in his eyes, because he was so drunk he was actually at peace for once, all he wanted was sleep.

"Kai will be back soon," he told me.

"Is everything okay?"

He shrugged. "I guess we'll find out."

Ooooookay.

I proceeded to pour three juices and then looked up at them. "You guys hungry?"

"You cooking?" David reared back, looking shocked.

"I know how to make eggs, but . . ." I turned, opening the

fridge, a little overwhelmed. "He has enough food here to cater a wedding."

Their eyes lit up, and they shot out of their chairs, circling the island.

"Well, we just had a wedding," David said, bending over and scanning the shelves "So, fuck it. Let's make a feast."

"That'll make a mess," I pointed out. "Kai doesn't like messes."

He snorted, pulling out meat wrapped in brown paper packages. "His *wife* can do whatever she wants in *her* house, right?"

I grinned. "I guess we'll find out."

I bit into the beignet, my teeth sinking through the air pockets of the soft pastry. "That's actually pretty good," I told Lev, licking some powdered sugar off my lip.

He scarfed his down, nodding. "My grandma raised me. She used to make them all the time. It's not Marina's cooking, but I can live off it if I have to."

I laughed to myself but then stopped. "Marina," I thought out loud.

Her prick of an employer, and all the other pricks on Gabriel's payroll coming in and out of the house. I shouldn't have left her behind.

Lev walked back to the stove, flour smudged on his face, as David ate the steak he'd cooked up and shoveled more eggs onto his plate.

"Banks."

I jerked my head toward the entryway and saw Kai standing there. He didn't spare the guys a look.

"Come here," he told me and then turned and walked out of the room.

I wiped my hands on the dish towel and brushed off the dusting of flour on my shirt. I followed him, momentarily fiddling with the new ring on my finger, but I forced myself to stop. Dropping my hands, I stopped in front of where he stood in the foyer.

"We'll clean the kitchen up," I assured him.

"I'm not worried about that." He shook his head, his eyes softening. "I'm glad you're having fun."

The front door opened, and Will stepped inside, carrying a bag and followed by Michael and Rika.

Kai turned back to me. "Have your guys finish eating, and then I need them outside."

"What's going on?"

He paused for a moment, holding my eyes with concern in his. Taking my arm, he led me back to the wall.

"Did you know that Delcour also belonged to your father at one point?" he said in a low voice.

Delcour? "What?" I didn't know what to say. "It did? No, I didn't know. I didn't manage his businesses. Not his legitimate businesses, anyway. I think I would've heard something, though."

"He owned it before you were born," he informed me. "It used to be a hotel. His family built it, in fact."

A hotel. So . . .

"So, the secret floor . . ."

"Is there, as well." He nodded, knowing what I was asking. "Looks like Damon was dividing his time between the two properties."

You've got to be kidding me. That meant that when I was there, dropping off the contract at Michael's party that night, my brother might've been in the building. I had no doubt he was in the city, but God . . .

Why had he never told me about Delcour?

"I'm ready to be done with this," Michael said, dropping a duffel bag at the foot of the stairs. "He's got us running around like assholes."

"Exactly." Will walked out of the kitchen with a beer. "We

shouldn't even go to The Pope. Let him come to us. Let's just leave the fucking door wide open. Why not?"

The muscles in Kai's jaw flexed, and I knew he was frustrated.

"Please, don't call the police." I dropped my voice, leaning into him. "Gabriel won't . . ."

"Won't what?"

I didn't want to tell them what my father's next move would be. It might only give Kai ideas. "He won't let Damon embarrass him with another arrest again," I told him, keeping it vague. "I can get him under control. If I can talk to him—"

"He's not coming near you."

"He's my brother—"

"It's not happening!" Kai barked. "I will deal with him."

"Will's right." Rika stepped forward. "Throw him for a loop and make him come to us. All this time he's been here, he's yet to be a lethal threat anyway."

But Kai just laughed, sounding more condescending than amused. "And sharks will circle things they're trying to decide whether or not they'll eat, too." He looked down at her. "Sometimes they leave. Sometimes they bite. He may want to have a few words with us," he gestured to Michael and Will, "but he'd love to get his hands on you two." And he looked between Rika and me. "I'm not taking the chance that tonight is the night he decides to do that."

"Exactly," Michael replied.

"We're meeting him later." Kai pinned me with a stare that was more of a warning. "You, Rika, and Alex will stay here with Lev and David."

"No!" Rika bellowed.

"Absolutely not!" I shouted. "I have just as much right to see him. If anyone can calm him down, it's me. We're not staying here and making cupcakes while the men go off hunting! If you think—"

Kai grabbed me, wrapping his arms around my torso, under my

arms, and lifting me up. "I love you," he whispered against my lips as he backed us away from the others. "And he can send me to prison again for a very long time. I'm not letting that happen now that I've found you. Please."

His dark eyes, clouded with fear, were only for me. No one else would see.

He loved me?

I stared at him, wondering what was happening in his head. Why me? We didn't fit. Was this really my home now? My bed upstairs? My clothes? My husband? Would I have our kids and know anything about being a mom?

God, the future looked so different now. These were things I thought would never be my life.

Instead of the direct line in front of me—a tunnel—my future seemed more like turning in a circle to find a road and instead finding only meadows and hills and mountains. So much to explore. No set path. I could walk and never step in the same spot twice.

But, for some reason, that didn't really scare me. I wanted to dream again.

"Please, don't hurt him," I told him.

"I'll try not to."

He set me down and kissed my forehead before turning away.

But I pulled him back, whispering, "I love you, too."

A smile flashed across his lips. Taking the back of my neck, he pulled me in again, kissing me on the lips longingly and then twice more, slowly.

Holding my eyes, he took a step back and turned to his friends. "Let's get this place locked up like a tomb."

CHAPTER 28

KAI

Present

"This is fucking amazing, in all honesty."

Michael strolled around the twelfth-floor room, taking in the little clues Damon had left behind—clothes, cigarette butts, a few dead cell phones—and the amount of space so expertly hidden in the building. You really wondered how something so incredible could go unnoticed. I suppose we don't see what we're not looking for.

"It's a huge city," he continued, sifting through papers on a desk. "Damon's always been a night owl. He could lie low during the day and then sneak out of his little hideaways at night to roam the city while we slept."

"It's not in his nature to be alone, though," Will added, still hanging back in the doorway.

He wouldn't come in. I didn't ask why.

"Nice fucking view." Michael sighed, looking out the windows.

I glanced at the bed, the sheets still a mess, and the pillows still where Banks and I had left them. It didn't look like he'd been here since we were.

"All right, come on." I stuffed my hands into my black hoodie and walked for the doorway. "He's not here. We'll wait for him in the lobby."

Hesitantly, Michael followed me out, and all of us stepped back into the elevator. It was after nine, and Damon hadn't said where in The Pope to meet, but we'd checked the floor anyway, just in case. Plus, the guys wanted to see it.

We trailed into the lobby, and I turned in a circle, scanning the space. Rain was starting to fall out on the street, and lightning flashed through the windows, followed by a roll of thunder.

Something felt off.

We hadn't seen him in a year. He'd been gearing up for an entrance. He wasn't just going to stroll into the hotel and say "Hey."

My phone rang, and I let out a sigh. I pulled it out of my pocket and didn't even bother to look at the screen.

"Where are you?" I asked.

"Right where I need to be."

"What does that mean?"

He didn't say anything for a moment. Then he asked, "Do you think she loves you? More than me?"

"Where the hell are you?" I squeezed the phone in my hand, feeling the guys draw close as they heard me. "We're here. Waiting."

"She's a part of me," he went on. "And I'm a part of her."

"You share blood." I walked to the front doors, looking out the glass. "That doesn't make a family."

"And that's where you're wrong," he said, a bite to his tone. "Blood is the tie that binds. The knot in your soul that says no matter where you go or what you do, there's someone in this godforsaken, shithole hell of a world you're forever connected to."

"Where are—"

"It can be a curse," he continued. "A burden. But it can also be your heartbeat. Your center, your purpose, your belonging . . ." He let out a breath, slowing down. "I've fucked up, I've lied, I've nearly torn myself apart in front of her, but she understands that that's what family is about. Family is what life gives you to help you endure. Their place is by your side. No matter how much it hurts, they're the people who are *always* by your side. It's duty."

Not when it was abuse. She was my family now, and he would never hurt her again.

"And unfortunately, Kai . . ." Damon sounded almost amused. "Nothing could tear me away from her side, either."

"Where are you at?" I demanded.

But he just responded, "She's mine." And then I heard a click.

"Damon!" Empty air sat on the other end of the phone. "Damon!"

"What the fuck is going on?" Michael stared at me.

But I didn't know. Why did he call? Why not say that shit to me in person?

Why was he jerking us around? Again?

And then it hit me.

Leverage.

"He's not coming," I said.

"What?" Michael inched closer.

And I turned my eyes on him. "The girls. He knew we'd leave them at the house."

CHAPTER 29

BANKS

Present

U gh," Alex growled, pulling her hand out of the pumpkin and whipping the orange slop off her hand and onto the newspaper.

"You said you wanted to bake pumpkin seeds," Rika pointed out.

"Yeah, well, I didn't know this was where they came from."

I forced a half smile, trying unsuccessfully to get my mind off Kai and my brother. Placing a tea light inside my jack-o'-lantern, I picked up the lighter and reached back inside, lighting the wick.

Carving pumpkins was a pathetic way to keep myself busy when all I wanted to do was jump in a car and go search out Kai and Damon, but if I left, Rika would follow, and then, of course, Alex, and I couldn't be responsible for them. I'd bide my time until Kai called. If he didn't within another hour, though, I was going, and I didn't care who jumped in the car with me. I loved them both, and they wanted to hurt each other. How in the hell was I going to get us all out of this?

Lev and David strolled in, picking at the snacks on the counters as they watched us finish up. I carried my pumpkin to the kitchen windowsill over the sink and placed it facing out toward the garden.

The colorful trees blew in the wind, and I heard needles of raindrops hitting the window.

A crack of lightning flashed through the windows, and I

jumped, my heart skipping a beat. Thunder followed, its hollow drum pounding overhead.

Turning around, I jerked my chin to the guys. "Storm's coming. There's candles, flashlights, and batteries in the hall closet. Go grab some, would you?"

"'Kay." David stood from where he leaned on the counter, his and Lev's smiles both on Alex before they turned around.

She offered a flirtatious look in return.

"Those are some mighty healthy-looking boys," she teased, following them with her eyes as they left the kitchen. "Are they a team?"

I popped my head up, and Rika just shook her head, smiling as she carved her pumpkin.

"When I'm bored I think about sex."

"And when she thinks about sex," Rika chimed in, "somebody's getting laid."

Alex plopped the top back on her lit pumpkin. "It feels good, doesn't it? Should we be ashamed of doing things we enjoy? No."

I watched her wink at me and then saunter out of the kitchen, hopefully not in search of the guys.

Rika continued working on the eyes, and I wrapped up my newspaper, pumpkin seeds and all. If Alex wanted to bake them, then she could have at it. I'd gotten about as domestic as I was going to get today.

"I liked your dress," Rika said, not looking at me. "It was perfect."

My dress?

Oh, the wedding. The dress was still sitting in a pile on the dining room floor, now that I thought of it.

"Do you think you'll be happy?" She leaned down, carefully slicing with her small serrated knife to form an eye.

"I'm not unhappy," I told her. "I know that."

She nodded, still concentrating on her work. "Kai's a good man. He's family."

I knew. And I knew what she was telling me. I'd better make him happy, too. Things might be complicated, and it might be a very long time before they loosened the reins enough to widen their circle to fit me, but I admired her loyalty.

I walked up, pushing a tea light and lighter over to her for whenever she was ready. "So, how's your wedding planning going?"

A wide smile spread across her face. "I'm having ideas," she replied coyly. "Wanna help me shop?"

"Shop?" I couldn't contain the abhorrence on my face. "For dresses?"

She looked at me, leaning in. "For a train."

"A train? As in . . ."

"All abooooard," she singsonged.

Huh?

But before I had a chance to question her further, all the lights in the kitchen died, and the whole room went dim.

"Whoa." Rika straightened on her stool.

I charged across the kitchen, quickly flipping the switches on the wall.

But the lights were out. "Flashlights and candles!" I yelled down the hallway. "Move your asses!"

"I can't believe they went out already." Rika rubbed her arms as if she had a chill. "It's not even that bad out yet."

"All right, here." David and Lev came rushing back, setting the supplies down on the island.

I handed Rika a utility lighter. "Light the candles in the holders in the dining room?"

She took it and hopped off her stool, leaving the room. Alex stepped back in, and I handed her some candlesticks. "Can you spread out a few upstairs in the hallways? Lev, go with her."

David handed me a flashlight, and I took some candles and a lighter to put in the living room while he jogged upstairs.

I went into the den first and dumped out a small tray of paper clips from Kai's desk. Placing the candle on it, I lit it and left, doing a double take to make sure the secret entrance to the tunnel was closed.

Walking into the living room, I broke out in chills, feeling a draft. I looked up, seeing the curtains blowing and the rain falling through the open window.

"What the hell?" I dumped the candles on the couch and ran over to the window, grabbing it and trying to pull it down again. "How the hell is this open?"

Rain splattered the windowsill, droplets bouncing against my shirt as I put all my weight into yanking the window back down.

"Why is this open?" Rika rushed up to me, grabbing the window. Both of us pulled, finally getting it to slide back down.

"I have no idea." I breathed hard and dusted off my hands. "Thank you, though. It's getting bad out there."

"Yeah." She peered out the window, her long blond hair hanging over her shoulders. "Kind of wish we were home. Devil's Night is even better in the rain."

I rubbed my arms, shivering. *I wouldn't know.* But I could guess what everyone was getting up to back home tonight. I didn't have the wistful look in my eyes like Rika did, though.

I could imagine she'd grown up quite differently from me. In safety, security, and a bit sheltered. I grew up with Damon, on the other hand, and I'd seen enough destructive behavior that Devil's Night seemed tame. I didn't find it liberating or fun. While she'd wanted to break away and find some trouble, I craved the calm and quiet.

Something hit the floor above our heads, and we both instantly looked up to the ceiling. Boards creaked as if someone was walking across the second floor, and we followed the sound with our eyes.

"Alex," Rika said.

I nodded, although Kai's—and my—bedroom was right above us. She had no reason to be in there.

I picked up my flashlight from the couch and started to walk out of the room. "Come on."

We jogged up the stairs, the hair on my arms standing on end. We hadn't left that window open. I looked around, shining my flashlight left and right, on high alert.

"Alex?" I called out, heading down the hallway to our bedroom. "Alex, are you okay?"

I swung open the bedroom door, caution keeping me from going in as I shone the flashlight all around. There were no candles lit in here, and I searched the corners, the bed, and behind the door.

Everything was exactly how I'd left it.

I was about to head into the en suite, but then I heard a creak coming from behind me. Rika and I both turned our heads.

"Alex?" I called out.

Walking over, I opened the door and shone the flashlight inside the spare room.

"What the fuck?" Lev exclaimed. He pushed off the bed, standing up and refastening his jeans. Alex rose from where she knelt on the floor and shrugged at me with a sheepish smile.

I shook my head, barking at Lev, "Get with David and go to the basement. Check the fuse box."

He cleared his throat, trying to hide his grin as he brushed past me out of the room.

I turned to Alex. "They're all yours once they're done for the night. Hold your horses."

She opened her mouth to speak, but something pounded the ceiling above us, and we all shot our eyes up.

I gasped, my breath stuck in my throat. That wasn't any of us.

"What is that?" Rika asked.

I grabbed her arm, pulling her into the hallway and then jerking my chin at Alex. "Let's go!"

They followed me, all of us running back down the hallway and the stairs. "Lev!" I called. "David!"

Swinging around the banister, I ran toward the kitchen and yanked open the door to the basement.

"Lev!" I squeezed the flashlight in my hand, shining it down the dark stairwell. "David!"

Jesus, where were they?

The ceiling creaked again, and then again, in small intervals, as if someone was walking above us.

"Banks," Rika gritted out like a warning.

I know. I know. Something was wrong.

I started to back away from the basement door, looking from left to right. "Your phone . . . where is it?"

"In the sitting room."

We all twisted around, and I kept the flashlight on as we dashed across the foyer. I double-checked the locks on the front door to make sure they were still secure.

Entering the sitting room, Rika went straight for the couch and dug in her handbag, pulling out her cell.

Then something dropped on the floor above us, a *thud* vibrating through the house.

"What the hell?" Alex stood over by the window, flashing her light around.

Rika turned and met my eyes, ready to dial, but then her gaze flashed behind me. "Banks."

I followed her gaze, twisting around. Kai stood in the doorway wearing his mask.

I let out a breath. "Kai." I rushed over to him, wrapping my arms around him and hugging him close. "What the hell? You scared us."

He was safe. The knots in my stomach started to unwind.

"Did you come in through the secret entrance?" I asked, feeling his arms come around me and hold me tight. "Where are Michael and Will?"

"Banks," Rika called.

I pulled back, turning my head toward her. "What?"

She looked between her phone and me, and I heard it vibrating in her hand. "Kai's calling me."

What?

Her gaze flashed to the man in front of me, and her chest caved. She started shaking her head, backing up. "That's not Kai."

I dropped my arms from around the man's waist, a lump swelling in my throat as I looked back up to the mask.

Black eyes met mine—a familiar coldness staring back at me. *Damon?* I backed away, his eyes still on me. "Oh, my God."

"Put the phone down," he told Rika. "Now."

But I knew she wouldn't listen to him. Turning my eyes on her, I shook my head, pleading with my eyes. It would only provoke him. I could handle this if I could keep him calm.

Her fist tightened around the phone, and I could tell she was struggling with what to do. But ultimately, she stuffed the phone in her back pocket and grabbed a bottle of Johnnie Walker by the neck from on top of the liquor cabinet, readying herself.

"So, how are my snakes?" Damon asked, pulling off his mask— or a replica of Kai's—and smoothing a hand through his hair.

I looked at my brother's face for the first time in a year. His black hair was longer around the ears and his face looked a little thinner, but his angular jaw was still tight, the muscles flexing now and again. It was his only tell that he was holding in more anger than he was letting on.

I took a slow step back, just in case.

"You're scared of me?" He tossed the mask down on the chair.

"Where are David and Lev?" I asked.

"Tied up in the basement."

I shook my head. "You can't take all of us," I warned, seeing Alex shift out of the corner of my left eye.

He just laughed under his breath. "Don't worry. There's one of me for each of you."

Then he tipped his chin up, whistling a call. I stopped breathing as I watched two more men, both dressed like Damon in hoodies and jeans, round the corner into the room, also wearing copies of Kai's mask.

Three men stood before us, and every muscle in my body tensed. "Who—"

But Damon cut me off. "Now," he ordered.

And they charged for us.

"Damon, no!" I shouted, whipping around with my hands in front of me, ready to take them.

But they pushed right past me, both of them heading straight for Alex. One took her from behind, fisting her hair with his hand gripping her neck, while the other pressed into her front, securing her hands behind her back as she growled and tried to thrash.

Rika pushed off, heading right for them.

"I could snap her neck in a second," the one behind Alex threatened, staring at Rika and jerking Alex's head in both his hands.

I didn't recognize their voices.

Rika stopped, her hands balled into fists, one of them still holding the bottle. Her eyes turned to Damon. "You fucking coward!"

"No, I'm smart." He smirked. "They wouldn't last five seconds trying to take you on."

"Hey, fuck you," the one pressed to Alex's front said.

I turned to Damon. "What do you want?"

"You," he said.

"Bullshit!" I growled. "You always had me! Why wait until now to show your face?"

But before he could answer, Rika came forward. "You tried to kill us," she charged. "Will . . . You tied a cinder block around his ankle, tied his hands behind his back, and threw him into the ocean." Her voice cracked. "Do you know what you put him through? You're a fucking horror."

"I know."

My eyes shot up again; I was taken aback by his response. He sounded almost sincere.

"I have so many things wrong with me," he said, a trace of solemnity in his voice. His gaze trailed around the room, avoiding ours. "I loved going to school. I went every day. Even when I was sick. Remember, Banks?"

I narrowed my eyes. Of course I remembered. Damon was the last person in the world you'd expect to have great attendance. The only time he skipped was when his friends did.

"School was the only place I knew I'd be safe," he continued. "And later on, when I got older, there was music and booze and girls . . . It was like a party every day. Sometimes it was even enough to get me out of my head, so I hardly even noticed what was happen—" He dropped his voice, forcing the last words out. "Happening to me."

Tears burned the back of my eyes.

"I had my friends, my team, and you," he said, raising his eyes to me. "All to myself. The only girl I ever trusted. No one was going to take you away from me. I don't like change." And then he glanced at Rika. "You were change."

He started walking toward her.

"Damon, no," I barked.

He stopped and turned his head toward me. "Then come with me."

"Where?"

"Home, of course," he told me, and then looked at Rika. "I want Rika to show me the St. Killian's renovations. Maybe take a walk in the catacombs."

He stared at her, his threatening eyes insinuating more than he was saying. She shook her head nervously.

"I'm not going anywhere with you," she gasped out.

"But it's Devil's Night," he teased, inching toward her. "Come on. Kai, Will, and Michael will follow, no doubt. We'll have fun. Just like old times."

She scoffed, looking more daring. "Is that what you waited a year for? Devil's Night?" She glared at him. "God, you really do need this, don't you? The old times, that rush, your friends who hate you now . . . ?"

He shot out, diving into her space and caging her in with his arms planted on the wall on both sides of her head.

"Damon!" I shouted.

"Don't worry, babe," he answered me. "She's not scared of me. Are you, Rika?"

She gripped the bottle in her hand, staring defiantly up at him.

"You hate me because of the things I do, but you love Michael for all those same reasons."

"Michael didn't try to kill his friends," she said.

"Oh, you've always hated me," he retorted. "I remember you at fourteen, running out of a room as quick as you came in when you saw me at Michael's house. People dictate rules based on how they want to be treated, but I'll tell you something. When someone else misbehaves, it's black-and-white, isn't it? We judge, and we condemn, but when we do it, it's a gray area all of a sudden. Other people are subject to your convictions, but not you, right? Not Michael?"

Her jaw flexed as she glared at him.

"People are hypocrites, Banks," he told me, still staring at her. "They do the same things they'll hate another guy for doing. The only moral compass I trust anymore is my own."

He grabbed her by the jaw, holding her firm. "And I've come to the conclusion," he bit out, "that a man deserves whatever a man can take."

She shook her head, her face twisted in anger. "I hate you."

He dived in close, whispering, "I love that you hate me."

And then he leaned into her right ear, and she reared back but then stilled as if listening. I couldn't see his mouth, but his jaw appeared to be moving. And she wasn't pushing him away. Was he whispering to her?

I watched her eyes, pinched together in fury, sharpen, and then, all of a sudden, her chest caved as her body froze. Her gaze fell, and she just stood there like she couldn't move.

Damon straightened back up and looked down at her, releasing her. "Fuck the world, Rika. You're welcome."

She pushed him away, breathing hard. But he just laughed.

I stepped up. "What did you say?"

But just then, lights shone through the windows, and I blinked, knowing a car had pulled up.

"Oh, look who's home," Damon taunted, looking toward the windows.

Rika took her chance. She swung the bottle across his head, the dull *clank* knocking him to the side as he brought his hands up to shield himself and fell into the wall like a rag doll.

Without hesitation, she threw the bottle at one of the guys holding Alex, making him duck for cover long enough for me to rush over. The other one spun around, and I punched him in the jaw, following with a kick to the groin. He stumbled, falling to a knee, and Rika grabbed Alex.

"Run!" Rika yelled.

"This way!" I led them across the foyer and into the den. "Through here, hurry!"

Pushing into the bookshelf with my entire body, I slowly got it to give way and crack open into the tunnel. Rika must've caught on to what I was doing, because she followed my lead and leaned into the shelf, Alex taking a cue from her.

Once we got it open enough, I pushed them through. They dived inside the secret passageway, but I didn't. I gripped the edge of the "door" and pulled it closed again.

"Banks, what are you doing?" Rika cried out. "Banks!"

"Just go!" I shouted. I needed to get to my brother before Kai did.

I raced back through the foyer, hearing someone pounding on the door while I heard the locks twist. Instinct told me to open the front door for them, but then I spotted blood on the floor, trailing down toward the kitchen.

They'd hurt him. Or kill him. I ran—down the hallway, behind the stairs, and into the dark kitchen.

The glass doors stood open on the other side of the island, and rain whipped in the wind caught in the funnel of the enclosed garden. Trees bent to nearly the breaking point, and one of the doors banged against the wall.

Where are you?

All of a sudden, I was grabbed from behind and hauled back, an arm wrapping around my shoulders.

I gasped.

"You don't love him, do you?" Damon asked, something wet touching my temple. "Because I'm about to make you a widow."

A widow? I opened my mouth to speak, but then my hand brushed his other one hanging at my side, my fingers grazing the cold steel barrel. A cry stretched my throat.

I turned my head, seeing blood matting his hair and dripping down the left side of his face. "Damon, what do you want?" I whispered.

And then I heard the front door whip open, echoing through the house, and I closed my eyes. "Please," I begged. "Please, don't. Please, just leave. Run."

"I raised you better than that," he bit out, spinning me around and gripping my shirt at the collar. "It was supposed to be us, Nik. Just us."

"If you just wanted me, we would've been gone when you got out of prison last year," I said, hearing Kai and the guys charge through the house. "What do you really want?"

Anger burned through his eyes. He glared at me, but I caught something else flash for a split second, too. As if he was ashamed of the real answer.

He dropped his voice, replying, "I just want it to be how it used to be." His eyes fell, but then he raised them again, the ice back in his stare. "And if I can't have that, then I'll make damn sure no one will ever be rid of me."

He pushed me backward, and I stumbled, turning around. Gripping my shoulder, he forced me through the open doors and into the courtyard.

Fuck, what do I do? My instinct told me to fight. Turn around, attack, and then run. But that wouldn't stop him or Kai from getting hurt.

What the hell would I do if it came down to one or the other?

"Get your fucking hands off her!" I heard Kai shout.

Damon whipped me around, putting me in front of him with an arm around my shoulders again. The icy rain drenched our clothes, and I blinked through the downpour, seeing Kai, Michael, and Will race into the courtyard.

Kai's eyes fell to my brother's hand, and I knew he saw the weapon.

"You won't hurt her," he told him. "I know you won't."

"I've been hurting her for eleven years." Damon tightened his fist on the back of my shirt. "There's not much I wouldn't do."

Kai remained still, his anger faltering. He wasn't sure if my brother was bluffing, but he wasn't certain he wasn't. Not enough, anyway.

"Where are Lev and David?" Kai asked me.

"He tied them up in the basement."

"And Rika and Alex?" Michael burst out.

"I sent them through the passageway."

Kai turned to Michael. "The house down the hill. Go!"

Michael bolted back through the house, and I let out a breath I didn't realize I'd been holding. I still didn't know where the other two masked helpers of Damon's were. Hopefully they'd bolted.

"Hey, man." Damon's tone turned gentler. "Missed you."

I assumed he was talking to Will, who, for once in his life, didn't look happy. A slight snarl curled his lips, and his glower was fixed on Damon like nothing had been forgotten or forgiven.

Kai took a step forward, calling out over the rain, "Why go through all this?"

"Because this is my home," Damon replied. Then he pulled me back into his chest. "And so is this."

"She's not your pet," Kai argued. "Or your property. She never was."

"I gave her everything."

"You treated her like a dog!" Kai bellowed, his worried eyes flashing to me. "You hurt her."

I swallowed the massive lump in my throat. I knew Damon treated me badly, even though I hated facing that fact. I'd just made excuses for it. *He's not well. He's alone. He needs someone he can trust.*

I loved him. What was I supposed to do? I could make him better. Right?

But if the sacrifices only come from one side, it's time to face the truth. He was hurting me.

"She tenses when I touch her," Kai told him. "It's subtle, and it's only for a moment, but it takes her off guard, like she's not used to it."

Did I do that?

"She's got a great imagination, but I think she's even better at taking care of business," he went on, holding my eyes now. "She's going to be in charge of things someday, and even though I don't know what exactly, it's going to be great."

Tears welled in my eyes.

"And I even like her in men's clothes," he said, softening his voice. "As long as they're mine."

Then he raised his eyes, telling Damon, "Just let her go, man. She's not going to hurt you. She loves you. And you love her."

I could feel my brother's shallow breaths behind me as he backed us up a step, still resisting. "The only ones who can hurt you are the ones you love."

I closed my eyes.

"Choose," he said.

I opened my eyes, and he spun me around, looking between me and them. "He can survive without you. You know that."

He meant Kai didn't need me. Damon did. That's what he wanted me to believe, but it wasn't entirely true.

"So can you," I replied. "You just hate seeing us survive without you."

His gaze narrowed, and I knew I had him. But before he could say anything, Damon was pushed on the ground, and I was shoved away.

I watched as Will jumped on top of him, knocking the gun out of his hand and swinging his fists like he'd been waiting a year for this. I guessed he had, after all.

"You fucking prick!" he shouted, grunting as he punched. "You're nothing! Nothing without us!"

The next thing I knew, Kai grabbed my arm and pulled me back, and I spotted Michael, Rika, and Alex running through the kitchen and back outside to us.

"His friends ran off," Rika told me, and then turned her eyes on the action.

I spun around, seeing Will still completely losing it.

"How could you go so far?" he burst out. "I'm going to fucking kill you."

He gripped my brother's throat in one hand, holding him in place, and hit him with the other.

Damon wasn't fighting back. He just squeezed his eyes shut, blood streaming out of his nose and down his face as Will attacked him again and again.

"When you have nothing, you have nothing to lose." His voice shook as he grunted. "Fuck it all, and fuck you."

Then, all of a sudden, he hooked Will in a headlock and pulled him down, restraining him. Then he flipped over, taking Will to the bottom as the latter just kept hitting him, throwing punches, thrashing, and growling from the bottom. Damon just sat there, his forehead bowed into Will's chest, breathing hard and taking the hits.

"Stop them," I begged Kai. "Please."

But he just stood there, letting Will get his revenge.

Blood matted Damon's hair, trickling down his face with the rain. He gripped Will's shirt and buried his head, trying to shield himself but not trying to stop it.

He knew he deserved this.

Will threw him off, stood up, and swung back his leg, kicking Damon in the head. I turned away.

I knew what he was doing, just letting Will punch him. If he was in pain on the outside, he wouldn't feel it on the inside.

I bowed my head, staring at the raindrops hitting the blades of grass as the fight went on and the sounds of grunts and hits filled the courtyard.

Too long.

And then I heard nothing. Slowly raising my eyes, I saw Will sitting on the ground next to Damon, his hands behind him, propping himself up and breathing hard.

Damon lay on his back, his knees bent up but unmoving.

Slowly, he started to turn over and, with shaking limbs, got himself up on his knees and sat there on his heels, looking like he barely had enough strength to hold his head up. Water cascaded down his face, making his black hair hang over his eyes, and I knew I couldn't ever not love him. Bleeding, broken, lost, and alone, he was back up, wasn't he? He would always be able to take whatever anyone did to him. *Twist it. Turn it. Swallow it.*

Kai approached, and I followed. He knelt down, staring at my brother.

"We didn't choose Rika over you," he told him calmly. "Or Banks." He leaned in, his tone firm. "*You* left *us.*"

Will watched Damon out of the corner of his eye, anger still raging through his eyes, but they glistened, too.

Kai stood up. "Where is the body?"

Rika and Michael inched closer, and I watched Damon take a deep breath. "Gone," he said.

Kai bent down and grabbed the top of his head by the hair. "Where?"

Damon raised his eyes, almost amused. "You didn't kill her."

I stepped toward him, and Kai let him go, straightening.

"What?" I asked.

"She was fine when you and Kai left the hotel."

"How do I know you're telling the truth?" Kai demanded.

"Because she was breathing when you left, wasn't she?"

"Well, where is she, then?" I asked. She'd need money at some point. It was too long for no one to have seen or heard from her.

"I need proof she's okay," Kai told him. "I still hurt her."

"No, she was hurting us." Damon pushed himself to his feet, struggling to square his shoulders. "And you stopped her. End of story."

"So, she was fine when I left the hotel?" Kai challenged him. "Was she fine when *you* left the hotel?"

Damon held Kai's eyes, giving nothing away as the silence stretched between them, and I knew . . . I just knew . . .

She was dead.

That night wasn't over when Kai and I left The Pope.

"Kai!" Alex shouted. "Oh, my God, hurry!"

We all spun around, spotting her inside the house, across the kitchen, and looking down the hallway.

She turned her worried eyes back to us. "Where's the fire extinguisher?"

We all shot off. Running back into the house, I raced through the kitchen, feeling Kai's hand take mine. We left Damon outside, and I knew that he'd run. A big part of me hoped he would.

Alex stood in the foyer, looking toward the sitting room, and Michael, Rika, Kai, and I rushed up to her, seeing the black drape crawling with flames. A small tree had crashed through the window, glass and rain covering the floor.

"The candles," Kai breathed. "Shit!"

I glanced at the floor, and sure enough, the fallen tree had knocked the candles onto the floor, causing the drapes to catch fire.

Kai pointed at Will. "Closet!" And all of them, including Michael, ran back down the hallway, swinging open the closet door and diving inside for the extinguishers.

I raced into the sitting room, seeing the flames spread up the curtain, and then I noticed the *shinai* hanging on the wall next to the window.

"Rika!" I called, running over and grabbing one off the wall.

The heat of the flames stung my eyes, and rain hit my arm as I reached up again, pulling another sword off the wall. I choked on the tears stuck in my throat.

He'd already lost the dojo. I couldn't let this happen again.

Rika worked with me, pulling everything off the wall and tossing it to one of the couches.

"No!" I heard Kai yell. "Banks, stay back!"

He ran in and grabbed my arm, yanking me behind him. "Put out the rest of the candles!"

The flames spread across the valance, and I rushed over to blow out the other tapers just in case the wind blew any more onto the floor.

Michael and Will ran in, Michael darting his horrified eyes toward us.

"Rika!" he shouted.

And I twisted around. A piece of the fabric hanging above, consumed in flames, spilled down, hanging by threads. She followed his gaze, looking up, and he shot off, hurrying for her. Suddenly, the gold rod broke, spilling down from the wall, and everything went in slow motion. The drapes, ablaze, came crashing down, and everyone reached out for her, but just then, she was grabbed by the shirt, hauled backward, away from the flames, and sent tumbling to the hardwood floor at the center of the room. She crashed onto her back, wincing out of fear or pain, I wasn't sure.

And I looked up and saw Damon. I hadn't even seen him enter.

Rika blinked a few times, the wind knocked out of her as Michael dived down and pulled her up.

"Jesus Christ," he gasped, holding her face. "You okay?"

She seemed stunned, just trying to catch her breath. Then she looked over, and so did I, Damon standing there with his jaw clenched.

Everyone was momentarily frozen, piecing together what the hell had just happened, but Kai turned back to the flames and pointed the nozzle at the window. He and Will sprayed the extinguishers up, down, and over, the bright, hot flames quickly turning to smoke, Will coughing as the fire was put out.

I exhaled, trying to catch my breath.

They set the tanks down, and all of us just stood there, tired, confused, or angry. I looked over to Alex. She had a hand on her chest, breathing hard, while Michael stood in front of Rika, both of them not saying anything.

Will fell down on the couch, resting his head in his hands, and Kai . . . Kai turned his eyes on Damon, finally.

"You think we won't call the police?" he threatened. "You should've run."

"I'm not running," Damon said, staring at the wall. "Call them."

I swallowed, pain stretching my throat. I knew Kai was looking at me. What could I say? *Please, don't.*

My father wouldn't let Damon go back to prison. He'd send him somewhere where he couldn't embarrass him again, and he'd keep him there, out of sight, for however long it took for Damon to get ahold of himself.

If I were Kai, I'd know Damon deserved to suffer. I'd know what I needed to do for the safety of my friends and family.

But I wasn't Kai.

I closed my eyes, my chin trembling. I was too close to the situation. My heart couldn't bear to see him suffer anymore.

"Rika?" Kai said, coming up to me and threading his fingers through mine. "Michael? Will? You guys do what you need to do. I can't deal with this now."

He pressed his lips into my temple. I couldn't ask any of them to just let him go, but I was grateful Kai stood with me.

No one spoke, and I opened my eyes to see Rika look away from Damon. There was anger in her eyes, but also conflict.

And confusion. He had just saved her from getting hurt or worse.

And what had he whispered to her before the guys showed up?

"Don't get confused," Damon told her. "I'm not a good guy. Call the police."

Michael turned, looking ready to hit him, but Rika pulled him back. "Get the fuck out," she growled to Damon. And then she turned away, breathing so hard her anger looked ready to spill over.

Damon cast me a look, and there was so much I wanted to say.

But we both knew he had to get out of here before she changed her mind.

He walked out, and I heard the front door swing open, the sound of the rain pouring in.

What if I never saw him again? Damon was all I'd had for so long. Everything was new now. My home, my days, even my clothes . . . I exhaled, pain twisting my stomach.

I ran out of the room and out the front door. "Damon!"

Tears streamed down my face, and I could barely see him through the blur in my eyes. But I saw his dark form stop and slowly turn around. Blood had dried around his eye, but the rain had washed most of it away.

"Did you ever love me?" I asked.

He slowly approached me, staring hard. "Love is pain, Nik," he told me. "It's never felt good."

"Not even my love?"

He dropped his eyes, shaking his head. "I don't want to hurt you. Anymore," he added. "That's all I know."

He backed up slowly, finally turning around and walking down the long, dark driveway until he disappeared into the night.

I just stared after him, into the empty darkness. *It's never too late.*

CHAPTER 30

BANKS

Present

The October wind howled outside, making the otherwise quiet house creak under the pressure. It had to be about three in the morning, but I wasn't making any move to check my phone. Kai and I sat on the bed, me in between his legs and resting back into his chest as he sat propped up against the headboard. I fiddled with his fingers, threading mine in and out of his. Today was Halloween.

"Do you feel it?" I asked quietly.

"What?"

I took a deep breath, filling my lungs and closing my eyes. "It's like everything is starting."

An enormous weight had lifted off my shoulders when Damon walked out hours ago. I wondered where he went and if he was safe. I worried that he doubted how much I loved him.

But I didn't realize how much I'd dreaded him, too.

At least part of me.

Not until he left the house, giving no indication he would come for us again, and the pain in my stomach I'd grown so used to over the years, that I barely noticed anymore, slowly started to fade away. He'd always held on so tightly. Too tightly.

But now it felt like my lungs could hold an ocean. I didn't have to do anything I didn't want to do anymore, and the best part? I could do anything I wanted to do now. Go to school, try on some heels, come home at dawn, travel, volunteer, go to a bar . . .

Have friends.

"If you want an annulment, I'll give you one," Kai said, his lips brushing my hair. "We can start over. Fresh. Maybe have a date. And a proper wedding after I ask you and if you say yes." He dropped his voice to a whisper. "I'll kiss you like I should've."

I gave a half smile. I could tell he felt guilty about our "wedding."

"No." I raised my hand, looking at my ring. "It's part of our story, and I don't want to change it. I like our story."

His arm slid around my waist, tight and possessive.

"So, what's next, then?" he asked. "What do you want to do with your life now?"

"Everything."

He breathed out a laugh. I definitely felt uncertain. And guilty. He'd already bought me clothes, but I wouldn't let him support me. I'd have to figure out something soon. I wouldn't be happy unless I contributed to our life.

And this house.

I meant *our* house, I guessed.

Which reminded me . . .

"Why did you keep this house a secret?" I turned my head, looking up at him.

His eyes smiled back down at me. "For the same reason I liked the confessional."

I pinched my eyebrows together, not sure I understood.

"I like my privacy, and I like my space," he explained, "and this is the one place where I can be left quiet, hear myself think, and not be distracted. I have perspective here." He pressed his lips to my temple. "I knew it wouldn't be a secret forever, but I wanted to enjoy renovating it and living in it before my friends started coming and going."

"Well, I think you're going to be distracted with me here," I pointed out. "I'm not that quiet."

His chest shook with a laugh behind me. "I don't mind your distractions."

I hoped not, because Alex left the lingerie she bought for me for the party the other night, and I planned on closing the gate, locking the doors, and being hugely distracting really soon.

"Are there any other secret passages?" I asked.

"Yes."

Tingles spread across my body. "Do they lead to fun things?"

"Yes."

I smiled, my imagination running wild. I was still nervous about where my life would lead now, but I was excited, too.

I laid my head back on his shoulder, looking up into his eyes. "Will your parents hate me?"

He shook his head. "No," he answered. "My father will hate me for about fifteen minutes, and then he'll evolve to being just disappointed again." He kissed my nose. "Just be who you already are. Loyal, honest, no-nonsense, blunt, and stubborn. He respects what he sees inside."

"And your mom?"

"All my mom will care about is that you love me." He smiled down at me. "And that we were married by a priest, of course."

I narrowed my eyes. *That's right.* It had occurred to me as odd that he'd arranged a church and a priest for a marriage he seemingly didn't want. In researching him, I had never gotten the impression that he was particularly religious anymore, other than showing up for the rare family christening and such. He'd done it for his mom's sake?

"She was why you—"

He nodded, his eyes softening as he held my gaze. "It was always for life, kid."

Always for life. I couldn't help but smile. I should've known. Kai didn't make mistakes.

I kissed him, his warm mouth sending tingles spreading through my lips and down my neck. We just held each other, taking our time for once, the kisses getting deeper and more demanding.

Leaving my mouth, he kissed my forehead and then my hair again.

"Sun will be up in a couple hours." He glanced toward the window near the bed. "So much for sleep."

Climbing out from behind me, he pushed off the bed, and I watched him step over to his dresser. Pulling out a pair of lounge pants, he turned to me. "Shower with me?"

I lay down, resting my head on my hand. Man, that was tempting. I didn't want to leave his side.

But something was still nagging at me. "You go ahead," I told him, grabbing my phone. "I need to check some messages."

He fixed me with a look that said he definitely wouldn't be long. I watched him walk into the bathroom and waited until I heard the shower run and the glass door shut.

Sitting up, I hurriedly scrolled through my contacts, finding who I was looking for.

Dialing, I waited as the line rang. It was the middle of the night. It might take a few tries before he woke up.

But to my surprise, the ringing stopped and a groggy voice growled at me over the line.

"Jesus, what?" Will barked.

I hopped off the bed and walked for the bedroom door. "Can you meet me? I need your help."

Pulling Kai's old Jeep off the highway, I headed down a gravel road, the thin forest to my left the only thing between me and my father's house. I spotted red taillights ahead and made out Will's SUV idling off to the right. He must've sped here. I was sure he was aggravated as hell with me, getting him out of bed before dawn.

I drove past him and glanced in my rearview mirror, seeing him pull off the shoulder and follow me deeper down the road.

Finding the worn path Damon used to drive on when he'd come home too late and the gates were locked, I took the left and dipped down a small incline, rocking back and forth as I drove into the brush, coming in from the back of the property. It was the only way to get there without anyone noticing.

Possibly.

There were still motion sensors and cameras and there was always a guard walking the perimeter, but I knew from experience that by this time of the night he was probably holed up in the kitchen, eating leftovers and watching TV.

Once I saw the lights up ahead, I knew I was coming up on the back of the garages. Stopping, I parked and shut off the car. There were nine dogs, last I'd seen. Hopefully we could get them all to fit.

I climbed out of the car, taking the keys with me.

"Don't you have a husband to slowly drain the life out of?" I heard Will complain as soon as I slammed the door. "What am I doing here?"

I held my finger over my lips. "Shhh," I told him. "I can't do this on my own. Just stop whining."

"Is there any reason you just didn't bring Kai?"

"Yes!" I whisper-yelled. "He would never have let me come back here."

I could've brought David and Lev, but they'd be shot on sight if they returned here.

And I wouldn't dare bring Rika. I'd have all of them angry with me for risking putting her in any danger. Michael wouldn't leave her alone anyway, not after what happened last night.

Besides, Will was . . . nice. He might bitch and moan, but he'd do anything to help someone out, I was pretty sure. I mean, he picked out my underwear. That must mean we'd bonded enough to ask favors of each other, right?

Turning around, I led the way toward the house, creeping quickly through the wet leaves and zipping up my new leather jacket against the cold breeze. Halloween in Thunder Bay was just as much of a big deal as Devil's Night, so the next several hours would be quite a handful for the town's police force. I doubted my father would send them after me anyway, no matter how stretched their manpower was later on tonight.

He'd definitely know I'd been here, though.

Jogging around the first garage, I snuck up to the big shop and pulled my keys out of my pocket. Gabriel knew I wasn't stupid, but he also probably figured I wasn't a threat. Not yet, anyway. I doubted he'd changed the locks in the two days since I'd been here.

Flipping up the keypad, I punched in the code, and when the alarm deactivated, I inserted my silver key into the door, twisting the lock.

"What are we doing?" Will asked quietly.

But I ignored him, slipping inside and pulling him after me. I immediately heard chains rattle and shuffling coming from several of the kennels. Glancing around, I saw that there was no one here yet and noticed a couple emergency lights on, giving me enough to see my way.

Grabbing a handful of leashes off the wall, I tossed three to Will. "We need to hurry."

"Wha—"

I opened the first kennel.

"They're going to fucking bark!" he blurted out.

"They will if you don't do exactly what I say."

If they started going nuts, the night guard would be out here in seconds. We needed to be stealthy.

I approached the dog—an older pit bull—that had been here since he was a pup. He stood without barking. He, at least, knew me and was well-trained by now, but the others might get skittish, so that's why I needed to be the one to grab them. Will could load them into the cars.

I gave him a rub behind his ear as I hooked his leash and gently pulled, leading him out of the cage.

"And if he just gets more dogs?" Will asked as I handed Brutus to him.

"Then we'll be back, I guess."

Hurrying, I pulled open all the gates to the cages and walked in, leashing the dogs and walking them out. The two Great Pyrenees came easily, but one was gaunt, her ribs showing through her coat, while the rottweiler, the two shepherds, and the two huskies all shuffled away, resisting. Reaching into the baggie in my pocket, I pulled out chunks of meat I'd brought with me, quickly offering it to them.

Will had the pit bull, and I handed off the two Pyrenees.

"Go put them in the back seat of your truck." I told him. "And hurry!"

Heading into the last cage, I saw the beagle lying down, just watching us. I moved for him and noticed he was shaking. My throat felt like it had needles in it.

I didn't have time to assess the damage, although I did see some scabs, so I didn't even try to motivate him. Scooping him up into my arms, I repositioned my hold on the other leashes and left the building, walking briskly.

Will and I made short work of loading all the dogs into the cars, and I debated tying them up but decided against it. They'd been trained to be aggressive, but I didn't want to risk one falling or jumping out of the bed and strangling itself. If they fought, I'd deal with it then.

Will jumped in his car, yelling at me through his open door. "Let's go!"

I dug out my keys, but then I stopped.

And looked back toward the house.

I didn't have everything.

Will started his engine, and I whipped around, waving my hand. "Stop, wait!"

A couple of low barks drifted from the cars as he shot his head out the window. "What are you doing?"

"Stay here," I told him.

"Banks!" he whispered after me. "What the hell?"

I ran up to the house and tried the door handle to the kitchen. It slowly gave way. My stomach churned. The guard had unlocked it to come and go, which meant he was around. Softly opening the door, I peered inside and saw the small TV on the granite counter in the far corner was turned on. There was also a plate of crumbs in front of it. He was probably in the bathroom.

Taking my chance while I had it, I dashed through the kitchen, down the hallway, and up the stairs. Opening the door to the tower room, I crept quickly inside and jogged up the stairs.

Damon could be here.

But when I opened the door, the room was dim, the only light coming from the moon outside, and it appeared still empty. A pang of disappointment hit me. I wasn't looking for him, and this probably wasn't the best place for him to be, anyway, but if he wasn't here, where else would he go?

Walking over to the dresser, I dug in the cabinet for both of the faunariums and quickly loaded Volos and Kore II into separate containers. If Damon wasn't coming home, then there was no one to take care of them.

God, Kai was going to kill me.

Giving the room one last glance, I left and didn't bother locking the door at the bottom of the stairs.

Racing back down the stairs, I ran right into a dark figure coming up and halted. One of the men, Sergei, stopped and looked up at me abruptly.

"What the hell are you doing?" He glared at me.

But I didn't answer. Quickly swinging around him, I pounded down the rest of the stairs. He immediately continued up to the next floor, his pace more urgent. He was getting my father.

I walked into the kitchen, spotting Marina at the sink. She turned her head, her eyes wide with surprise. "Hey."

I walked to the back door, fumbling with the handle and the cages in my hands as I opened it.

"Let's go," I told her. "You're coming with me."

"What?"

I turned my head. "We don't have time to debate. I'm not leaving you here."

With my father or these men.

She wiped her hands on her apron, confusion etched all over her face. "I can't leave."

"You can," I insisted. "You can come with me. This minute. Do you want to?"

Her mouth opened but no words came out. Her eyes darted down, then up, and I'd never seen her look more conflicted as she searched the room around her like it would give her the answer she needed.

But then she blinked and took a deep breath, ripping off her apron. I smiled.

We ran out of the house, leaving the door wide open, and I looked to make sure Will's truck was still just past the tree line. He turned on his headlights.

"What the hell do you think you're doing?" A bellow nailed me right in the back.

I stopped, squeezing my eyes shut. *Fuck.*

I heard a car door slam shut and opened my eyes to see Will out of his truck and making his way quickly over.

I looked at Marina. "Get in the Jeep."

She nodded and walked ahead, not looking back.

I twisted around. My father stood in black pants and no shirt with about four men standing behind him. He was masking his snarl, but I could still make out a hint of it.

"Get a new cook," I told him, clutching the faunariums. "And don't get any more dogs. I'm extremely difficult to deal with."

He laughed bitterly. And then he inched toward me, his men staying back.

"You're not taking my shit," he growled low.

I tipped my chin up. "Consider it my severance package," I said. "And be thankful I don't take more as payment for keeping my mouth shut about everything that goes on here."

His gaze narrowed on me. He knew what he was capable of, and he knew I knew. But my father was a smart man, and he knew I wasn't alone anymore. Was it worth the trouble?

A sick smirk curled his lips. "I heard about the episode at Kai's house last night," he said, biting out every word. "Tell your brother I want to see him. And if you fail to keep his behavior in check from here on out, I will have him hog-tied and dragged to Blackchurch. Without hesitation."

I clenched my teeth together. Damon had come out of prison far more hateful and distanced from reality than he'd ever been growing up. The last threads of everything I loved about him were thinning. Blackchurch would make him an animal.

"He's got one more chance," my father threatened. And then he cocked his head at me. "But maybe that's just what he needs. A year, or five, to think about that temper of his."

Anger poured in and out of my lungs, and I glared at my father.

"And if that happens . . ." He stepped closer, dropping his voice. "It's open season on you and your new little crew. Now, get the fuck off my property."

I backed away, not hesitating and not taking my eyes off any of them. It was unlike him to let me off the hook and just leave, having gotten the better of him, but he had enough problems. He had Damon to worry about.

Running into Will, I shoved my elbow at him, and we both moved, climbing in our cars and speeding off.

I kept my eye on the rearview mirror the entire way home.

What the hell?"

I heard Kai bellow, and I winced.

Slamming the car door, I turned around to see him, David, and Lev barreling across the threshold of the house and across the gravel driveway toward us.

"You're dead." Kai pointed to Will.

"Come on, man. Damn." Will opened the back of the Jeep. "She's your chick. Not mine."

Four of the nine dogs jumped out of the back of Kai's Jeep, and I tried to shield the small faunariums behind me, but it was no use. Kai narrowed his eyes on the dogs and then he snapped his gaze to my right, to where Marina was rounding the front of the car.

"What is this?" he blurted at me. Then his eyes fell to the snakes, turning even more alarmed.

"We went to Gabriel's," I told him. "And I, um . . . I got some dogs?"

"You went to Gabriel's?" His tone sounded like I was in a lot of trouble. "You just snuck off after the conversation we just had about loyalty and honesty and . . ."

"And I needed to do this on my own," I cut him off. "Not like 'Hey, here's my man, and he's going to fight you if you hurt me, so back off!' I needed to face him on my own. I'm fine. See?"

He crossed his arms over his chest. His biceps flexed, stretching his black T-shirt, and my stomach flipped.

I cleared my throat. "I won't go back. I promise. I just needed to handle this."

The wrinkles between his eyes grew deeper. I knew he wasn't mad I'd faced my father. Kai didn't treat me like a fragile flower. I think he was angry I went without him, though, and I understood that. I'd be mad, too.

But I also knew he would've taken the lead and stepped in for me if he didn't like what Gabriel said to me or how he looked at me. I needed to do this alone.

I heard shuffles across the rocks and panting and turned my head to see Will come out from between the cars with the rest of the animals. Though they were doing a better job of pulling him.

"Nine dogs?" Kai bit out, fixing me with a glare. "They're not staying here."

"Of course not," I said, trying to sound innocent. "I'll call the shelter when they open in an hour."

"Or we *could* keep them," Will suggested. "I mean, look at this shit. He's shivering."

And he bent down to scoop up the beagle, the little guy squirming because he was so nervous.

Kai looked bemused. And then he gave me a warning look. "Baby, I like it quiet. You know that."

"Totally." I nodded, trying to keep the grin off my face. "I mean they've been in cages all their lives. I could keep them down at the other house for like a couple days, too? Maybe fatten 'em up? Before the shelter just throws them in more cages, right?"

"Yeah, they could do with a little spoiling," Will added. "Let's just keep them."

"Oh, my God," Kai grumbled, turning back toward the house and shaking his head. "Nine dogs . . ."

I folded my lips between my teeth to keep from laughing.

Quickly handing Marina the cages, I chased after Kai. "Oh, and I kind of brought Gabriel's cook," I said, stumbling up to him. "We could use her, right?"

"Yeah, fine, fuck, whatever." He entered the house and started pounding up the stairs. "Bring everybody. Doors are open. Why the hell not?"

I snorted behind him, his sarcasm not lost on me. He was coming apart, and I loved it. This was *our* life, after all, and we might trip over each other for a while yet, but we weren't people who were okay with failing, either. We'd figure it out.

"Oh, and one more thing." I ran, catching up to him and jumping up on the stair above him.

He stopped in his tracks, letting out another sigh. "I think I might cry."

I tried not to laugh. Poor guy had had enough for one morning.

I stared down at his lips and broad shoulders and perfect hair and leaned in, desire heating my skin.

Wrapping my arms around his neck and pressing my body to his, I caressed his lips with mine, feeling him shudder.

And I whispered, "I still need that shower."

Then I took his hand, catching the heated look in his eyes, and led him upstairs.

EPILOGUE

Overgrown grass covered the soft earth as he stepped quietly through the headstones. A sea of plots lay beyond, over the hill to the left and behind him, spanning out as far as he could see. It really was the most peaceful place he'd ever been.

People were quiet here. Solemn expressions were as expected as angry ones, and talking to yourself was perfectly acceptable in a cemetery. Although, he could scream right now and no one would notice. No one else was here.

He looked up at the full moon, seeing the glow of a ring circling it and casting its faint light over the land. The granite headstone he looked for appeared ahead, and he approached it, a growing heat coursing through his veins as he fisted his cold fingers.

Coming to a stop, he let his eyes fall on the marker and then to his shoes and the land they stood on. And what was underneath.

He closed his eyes, letting everything wash over him.

Everyone thought he was inhuman. Incapable of feeling. Resistant to emotion. Sick. Unwell. A machine.

No.

He felt everything. He never shunned an emotion. Not one. He knew that letting it run its course was the only way to get rid of it.

Shame.

Fear.

Anger.

Love.

Worry.

Sadness.

Betrayal.

Guilt.

He owned every single one.

It sank through his eyelids and into his lungs through the crisp air, filling him up as tears sprang to the backs of his eyes.

But he didn't cry.

It soon coursed down his arms and hummed through his fingertips, before sinking into his stomach, the tight knots hardening into bricks and then molding to him, becoming part of him. They were there. They were his.

And then everything turned softer, fluttering its way past his groin and down his long legs and through his feet, cementing him to the ground.

I am here. I am me.

This is me.

He opened his eyes and stared at the headstone. And he felt nothing anymore.

Pulling his cigarette case from his breast pocket, he took one out and tapped the end of it on the tin. He stuck it between his lips and reached into his pants pocket for his lighter. Lighting the end, he inhaled a puff and blew out the smoke, putting everything back into his pockets again.

He took another puff and then pulled the cigarette out of his mouth. "You can thank Little Sister for this," he told the headstone. "It was her idea."

Banks was as clever as he was. If only she'd been as loyal.

"It could've gone other ways," he said to the grave. "Cleaner ways."

He took another drag, the flavor mixed with the cold air tasting good on his tongue.

"Universities use industrial digesters to get rid of cadavers," he continued, feeling amused. "They look like huge pressure cookers. You mix seventy gallons of water with a little lye and cook it until it's the right temperature and consistency. A body can dissolve in a matter of hours." He took another puff, pinching the butt between his fingers. "And then you can just . . . pour the body down the drain. Gone. Nothing."

The wind picked up, rustling in the trees.

"But it doesn't dissolve everything, unfortunately. Some pieces of bone and teeth survive, so those have to be crushed," he went on. "Now, sulfuric acid, although more dangerous than lye, can completely dissolve human remains. The downside is it does take longer. About two days." He nodded, dropping the cigarette on the plot and grinding it out with his shoe. "And that's inconvenient."

He'd lied to Kai. His mother's body wasn't gone. It was less than three miles from their houses. Right here in Thunder Bay.

Maybe he should've gotten rid of it.

"I just couldn't do it, though." His eyes fell on the headstone, his breathing turning shallow and his voice growing quiet. "I want you to exist," he whispered. "I want to never forget that the world is a bad place, that you were real, and that every day you're rotting under my feet."

He flexed his jaw and tipped his chin up, trying to feel taller. Remembering the pleasure of dumping her in this grave and not taking any care to place her body or wrap her up from the elements.

Unzipping his fly, he took out her favorite part of him and glared at the stone as he pissed all over the ground.

He wouldn't be back again. He was done with her.

But there was another who still very much deserved what was coming to her and who still needed to be dealt with. She was next.

Finishing, he tucked himself back into his pants and fastened them up again, taking one last, long look.

"Hey," someone called out behind him. "Cemetery's closed. What are you doing here?"

A caretaker.

He exhaled a sigh, not turning around. "Just paying my respects to my mother."

The glow of a flashlight behind him shone on the headstone in front of him. "Your mother? But that's Edward McClanahan's grave."

"Oh, is it?" he said, holding back his smile.

He heard the man's footsteps grow closer. "If you come back in the morning, I can help you find your mother's plot. What's her name?"

But he just shook his head. "Nah, it's okay. I'll be quite busy after tonight." And he turned, meeting the man's hazel eyes under gray brows. "I'll leave. Happy Halloween."

And then he walked away, back the way he came.

"Yeah, you, too," the caretaker called after him.

Indeed.

BONUS SCENE:
CLUES TO KAI'S HIDEAWAY

This scene originally took place after Kai
and Banks inspected the hotel for the
first time with Michael and Will.

BANKS

Walking into Sensou that evening, I immediately stopped and pinned myself to the wall next to the door, letting the group of people leaving squeeze through the walkway first. People in black karate uniforms, or whatever they were called, and some in just plain workout clothes carried their duffels out, laughing and chatting, not one of them sparing a look in my direction. Granted, that wasn't unusual. I was good at not being seen.

When they left, I started again, making my way for the front desk.

"Yes, hello," a man in a blue cap with a clipboard spoke to the desk clerk ahead of me. "I have a delivery for Kai Mori."

The young woman reached for the clipboard. "He's in a private lesson. May I sign for it?"

"Uhhh," he mumbled, sounding uncertain. "It's a large delivery. He usually wants to check the merchandise before I take off."

Merchandise? I peered around the guy, trying to be discreet, to see his clipboard, but his hand kept moving, and I couldn't make out what was on the invoice.

I cleared my throat. "I have something for him, too." I gripped the handle of the steel case I held in my left hand and grabbed the clipboard with my right. "I'll take these back to him."

"Hey, wait a minute," the delivery guy burst out, pointing at me.

But I bolted down the hallway, turning my head and jerking it toward the chairs in the lobby. "Park it. I'll be back."

I didn't wait around to see if he or the clerk would follow me as I charged down the dim corridor. The two main rooms, for large classes, sat on the other side of the lobby and featured several visible floors above with mezzanines to look down on the great rooms, as well as smaller rooms off to the sides on the second, third, and fourth levels. Most of which, I gathered from my research, were used for storage and extra office space.

Slowing my steps, I raised the clipboard and studied the paper on it.

Marchella Dining Set $29,900
Villarosa Buffet Table $5,700
Sanctuary King Bed $8,400

What the hell? I scanned the sheet, my eyes falling on other pieces of furniture—side tables, chairs, dressers, appliances. The address at the top was for Sensou. Why was he having these things delivered here?

Using my spare thumb, I flipped the page. Another invoice, dated about six weeks ago, for the delivery of other furniture. Two more beds, a dozen chairs, a kitchen table, a desk, and some artwork. All delivered here as well.

But unless these things were hiding in a room upstairs, they weren't here. What was he doing with all this furniture?

I dropped the clipboard to my side and started walking again, not sure why any of this mattered. It probably didn't, but then again, any information people deemed hidable was valuable.

Who was the furniture for? Was he keeping a mistress? Maybe that's why he didn't invest a stitch of time or money in his house? He must sleep elsewhere.

I shook my head, a knot twisting in my stomach. I didn't want to know. But I did, too.

I walked down the hallway, passing the office, the men's and women's locker rooms, and a couple of smaller classrooms without doors. Coming up on the third one, I could hear the sound of sticks slapping against each other in quick time.

"What are you doing?" I heard Kai snip.

Stopping and hanging back, I peered into the room, instantly spotting him, his body tight and rigid, as he circled his student. His glare looked pissy, and I felt more amused than I wanted to. He was so uptight.

Of course, so was I.

And then his "student" came into view, and the amusement left. Rika walked in a slow circle, matching his predatory stride but keeping the same safe distance from him.

He was with her more than her fucking fiancé.

"*Oji waza*," she answered him, but I had no idea what that meant. She held out her arms, the *shinai* in her right hand as she challenged him. "What did I do wrong now?"

"Counterattack and then initiate," he commanded, wiping the sweat on his face with his forearm. "Don't stop. Let's see it."

He positioned his sword, and she did the same, the tips touching before he stomped his foot and let out a loud growl and advanced.

She snapped up her sword, stopping him before she whipped her nearly four-foot bamboo stick at him instead, taking large strides as she gripped the handle of the weapon with both hands.

Why weren't they wearing their gear? Kendo had special robes, armor, and helmets to protect the fighters.

Too fast, she bolted to his side and smacked the stick to the back of his neck. I watched as he hunched forward, absorbing the hit, giving her just enough time to sweep his legs, push him backward, and send him crashing to the mat on his back.

"Ah!" he growled, squeezing his eyes shut as he landed.

Rika's mouth fell open, and she dropped the sword, shooting her arms up into the air and smiling.

"Ugh," Kai groaned as he rubbed the back of his head.

"Oh, yeah," she boasted, dancing around and smiling. "Uh-huh. I told you we needed our gear on, but oh, no. You said I'd learn better if I got hurt." And then she darted out her head, putting her hands on her hips. "So did you learn?"

Snarling, Kai pushed himself to his feet and bent over, swinging his staff off the floor as she danced around, doing fist pumps.

"Don't laugh," he chided. "Humility, Rika, remember?"

Which made her laugh more, completely pleased with herself.

I watched as his face softened and he rolled his eyes, a small smile playing at the corners of his lips. He hooked an arm around her neck and kissed her forehead.

Not like a lover—more like a brother—but I still clenched my jaw and dug in my eyebrows at the sight. There was an intimacy there. A connection between them.

Did he love her?

Damon was right. They were all under her spell. I knew she wasn't responsible for getting them all sent to prison, like we all thought last year, but when my brother couldn't abide her presence, they chose her over him. I saw his side.

"Good job," Kai said. "And don't forget the screaming. It's important for intimidation."

"Ugh."

He walked with her toward the doorway, and I straightened, backing up against the wall of the hallway.

Rika stepped out first, stopping when she saw me. She only paused a moment, though, before casting him a glance and continuing down the hall, pushing through the women's locker room door.

Kai approached me, his eyes heavy on me. I handed him the case.

"The tools you requested," I said. "And the rope is in your trunk. Lev, Ilia, and David will be here in the morning for training, and you have an instructor set up, correct?"

He took the clipboard out of my hands, shooting me a look like I shouldn't have had it.

He started walking, looking at the invoice as he spoke to me. "And for you, as well."

"No, thanks," I answered flatly. "I'm a self-starter."

I could hear his quiet laugh as I walked behind him.

After the hotel this morning, he'd kept me busy all day, getting supplies to get onto the twelfth floor, going over the contracts with Gabriel, and hunting down old employees of The Pope for him to talk to. I didn't even try, though. Did he really think I would make this any easier for him? He could send me back to Thunder Bay. By all means . . .

"I also set up an appointment tomorrow for a landscaper," I continued, "and a few contractors to come out to your hovel to give an estimate on what it's going to take to get the place ready for Vanessa." I shoved my hands in my pockets, stealing looks at the taut muscles in his bare back that moved as he walked. "But really, it would be much easier if you just moved."

The comment was snide, but it was true. It would be cutting it close as it was, getting the furniture moved in and the wedding planned, much less having to contend with renovations, too.

"Cancel the appointments," he said without looking back.

"Fine." *You can deal with her when she gets here, then.*

Or maybe he wasn't planning on his new wife living with him at all. How about that? *Hmm.*

"I'll text you the dimensions of her bedroom, and you buy the décor you want," he instructed. "When I say so, you can start setting up her room. The rest of the house is off-limits to you. Got it?"

"Her room?" I inquired, unable to hide the amusement from my voice. "Don't you mean your room?"

He stopped at the front desk and set down the case, but I didn't miss the arched brow he shot me before turning to the delivery guy.

"Let me know when you need anything else, sir," the guy said, handing him keys.

Kai signed the invoice and swapped with him, handing him the clipboard while he took the keys.

Keys. So that's what was happening. Kai wasn't having furniture delivered here. He was having a truck of furniture delivered here. He didn't even want a driver seeing where it was going.

Now I was intrigued.

Acknowledgments

First, to the readers—so many of you have been there, sharing your excitement and showing your support, day in and day out, and I am so grateful for your continued trust. Thank you. I know my adventures aren't always easy, but I love them, and I'm glad so many others do, too.

To my family—my husband and daughter put up with my crazy schedule, my candy wrappers, and my spacing out every time I think of a conversation, plot twist, or scene that just jumped into my head at the dinner table. You both really do put up with a lot, so thank you for your patience.

To Jane Dystel, my agent at Dystel, Goderich & Bourret LLC—there is absolutely no way I could ever give you up, so you're stuck with me.

To the PenDragons—you're my happy place on Facebook. Thanks for being the support system I need and always being positive. Especially to the hardworking admins, Adrienne Ambrose, Tabitha Russell, Tiffany Rhyne, Katie Anderson, and Lydia Cothran.

To Vibeke Courtney—my indie editor who goes over every move I make with a fine-tooth comb. Thank you for teaching me how to write and laying it down straight.

To Kivrin Wilson—long live the quiet girls! We have the loudest minds.

To Milasy Mugnolo—who reads, always giving me that vote of confidence I need, and makes sure I have at least one person to talk to at a signing.

To Lisa Pantano Kane—you challenge me with the hard questions.

To Jodi Bibliophile—thanks for reading and supporting, and thank you for your witty sense of humor and for always making me smile.

To Lee Tenaglia—who makes such great art for the stories and whose Pinterest boards are my crack! Thank you. Really, you need to go into business. We should talk.

To all of the bloggers—there are too many to name, but I know who you are. I see the posts and the tags, and all the hard work you do. You spend your free time reading, reviewing, and promoting, and you do it for free. You are the life's blood of the book world, and who knows what we would do without you. Thank you for your tireless efforts. You do it out of passion, which makes it all the more incredible.

To Jay Crownover, who always comes up to me at a signing and makes me talk. Thank you for reading my books and being one of my biggest peer supporters.

To Tabatha Vargo and Komal Petersen, who were the first authors to message me after my first release to tell me how much they loved *Bully*. I'll never forget.

To T. Gephart, who takes the time to check on me and see if I need a shipment of "real" Aussie Tim Tams. (Always!)

And to B.B. Reid for reading, sharing the ladies with me, and being my sounding board. Can't wait to climb inside your head. Wink-wink.

It's validating to be recognized by your peers. Positivity is contagious, so thank you to my fellow authors for spreading the love.

To every author and aspiring author—thank you for the stories you've shared, many of which have made me a happy reader in search of a wonderful escape and a better writer, trying to live up to your standards. Write and create, and don't ever stop. Your voice is important, and as long as it comes from your heart, it is right and good.

Copyright © Penelope Douglas

Penelope Douglas is a *New York Times*, *USA Today*, and *Wall Street Journal* bestselling author. Their books have been translated into twenty languages and include the Fall Away series, the Hellbent series, the Devil's Night series, and the stand-alones *Misconduct*, *Punk 57*, *Birthday Girl*, *Credence*, and *Tryst Six Venom*.

VISIT PENELOPE DOUGLAS ONLINE

PenDouglas.com
🅕 PenelopeDouglasAuthor
🐦 PenDouglas
📷 Penelope.Douglas

LEARN MORE ABOUT THIS BOOK
AND OTHER TITLES FROM
NEW YORK TIMES BESTSELLING AUTHOR

PENELOPE DOUGLAS

SCAN ME

or visit
prh.com/penelopedouglas